Boxcar Red Leader

A novel of the Pacific Air War May 1942

By

Tom Burkhalter

Copyright Notice

Boxcar Red Leader: a Novel of the Pacific
Air War May 1942

Acknowledgements

Marianne Dyson was kind enough to read earlier drafts of this work and offer valuable criticism. Marianne's a pretty good writer, and her memoir, *A Passion for Space*, is well
worth reading.

Sherman Best read the first final draft of this book and offered invaluable critiques of some of the flying scenes, especially with regard to the B-26 Marauder, and praise for my work that is beyond price.

Brad Kurlancheek also read earlier versions of this work, but, as I was setting the final touches on the publication draft – the one in your hand – he helped me through one of those crises of confidence every writer knows all too well. Thanks, 'mano, I owe you one.

Last but not least, thanks to that bunch of bums in my writer's group, the CVKAWG!

In Memoriam

In April of 2016 we lost Sherman Best. Sherm flew B-26 Marauders in World War II, with the 322nd Bomb Group (Medium). Sherm, like most of the men of his generation, were called upon to do extraordinary things in their youth, things that shook the world and shaped history as we know it today. When they came home, though, the ones that did come home, they did something almost as extraordinary: They went back to their lives, and built families, homes, businesses, professions, in this country they had given so much to defend against the forces of fascism. That sounds remarkable, and yet, if you had had the privilege of meeting Sherman Best, you would have met a quiet, modest, kindly man; the kind of man who stood up when it counted. One cannot ask more than that of anyone.

Sherman Best with "Flak Bait" at the National Air & Space Museum. Photo courtesy of Linda Best Coviello.

I had the honor of talking with Sherm on several occasions regarding his experiences in World War II, and, in particular, on flying the B-26 Marauder.

Sherm told me that he wasn't initially thrilled to fly the B-26, as he had his heart set on flying the P-47 Thunderbolt. But his instructor in the B-26 assured him he would grow to love the B-26, and that is what happened.

The National Air & Space Museum is restoring a B-26 Marauder, "Flak Bait," an airplane that led a charmed life during the war, completing more combat missions than any other Allied airplane that survived the conflict. Like Sherm, "Flak Bait" belonged to the 322nd Bomb Group, and he flew 13 missions in her. Shortly before he died, Sherman Best, accompanied by his family, was able to visit the NASM's aircraft restoration center, where he sat one more time in the pilot's seat of a B-26.

We miss you, Sherm. Godspeed.

The Flight So Far

Jack and Charlie Davis fought in the Allied campaigns to save the Philippines and the islands of the Netherlands East Indies from invasion and conquest by the Japanese. At the end of the previous story, *A Snowball's Chance*, Jack is wounded and being air-evacuated to Australia. Charlie's B-17E, *Bronco Buster*, is shot to pieces on a reconnaissance mission to the island of Borneo.

By the end of April, 1942, the situation of the Allies in the Pacific is desperate. The Japanese have occupied the British colony of Malaysia and Dutch and Portuguese possessions all the way east to the island of Timor, only a few hundred miles from the Australian port of Darwin. Japanese bombers and fighters based on Timor begin to mount air raids on Darwin. To the north of Australia, the Japanese occupied the island of New Britain, with its important deep-water anchorage at Rabaul, and turn it into a major naval base. They have also occupied the town of Lae on the northwest coast of Papua New Guinea, only two hundred miles from the Australian outpost of Port Moresby, on the southern coast. The Zeros at Lae and the bombers at Rabaul are within range of the Australian base at Port Moresby.

Port Moresby is the only harbor capable of accommodating large sea-going vessels on the south coast of Papua. The strategic value of Port Moresby is enhanced by a nearby airfield, called Seven-Mile Aerodrome.

In the Philippines, American and Filipino resistance on the Bataan Peninsula has collapsed. A handful of American troops hold out on the island fortress of

Corregidor and the remaining harbor defenses of Manila Bay, under nearly continuous artillery and aerial bombardment. On the southernmost island of Mindanao, the Army Air Forces have one last remaining base, Del Monte Field, but it is surrounded by the Japanese Army by land and the Japanese Navy at sea. Japanese air raids make Del Monte all but untenable. Elsewhere in the Philippines the armed forces of the Japanese Empire are victorious. The efforts of the pilots and aircrew of the pursuit and bomber squadrons of the USAAF, as well as those of their British, Australian, and Dutch allies in the Southwest Pacific, have not succeeded against the Japanese other than locally and temporarily.

Allied codebreakers learn of a Japanese plan to invade Port Moresby. Possession of Port Moresby will allow the Japanese to interdict the eastern coast of Australia, rendering any attempt to send troops or supplies to Australia difficult and expensive at best. The Japanese invasion fleet, supported by a carrier task force, are at sea, headed for Port Moresby, as *Boxcar Red Leader* begins.

Chapter One

"May 6, 1942, on a beautiful tropical morning"

When the morning sun rose over the Coral Sea it illuminated a Lockheed Hudson of the Royal Australian Air Force as it flew out of a cloud bank. The light shone in through the windows on the right side of the airplane, straight into the eyes of a young man who was sound asleep. The light made him blink, which let in more light and brought him awake.

Captain Jack Davis opened one eye and shut it again immediately. Too late; the morning sun stabbed like a lance through his eye into his brain, setting off an unfortunate reaction. He turned his head to one side and cracked his eyes open, biting back the surge in his stomach and the sour bile threatening to spew outward.

After a moment he fought the spasm down and blinked. Despite the light spearing in from the windows the Hudson's cabin was still dim. Someone sat in the seat next to him, but the man's head was back, resting on the fuselage of the airplane, and his eyes were closed.

Jack took a deep, shuddering breath. Then the acid contents of his stomach threatened to rise once more. He unbuckled his seat belt, clamped his mouth resolutely shut, and made his way aft to the honey bucket. He got there barely in time to keep from spewing through his nostrils.

After three good heaves it was over. Jack knelt on the deck, cautiously assessing his stomach, and one more heave produced only a little burning, foul-smelling liquid. Then he was empty. Jack took a kerchief from his back pocket and wiped his mouth. Then he wobbled carefully from one handhold to another back to his seat and buckled himself in.

He took a deep breath, then another, and bit by bit training and instinct asserted themselves over the lingering nausea . Jack listened to the rush of air over the fuselage and the steady purring roar of two Wright Cyclone engines. The seat of his pants and his inner ear told him the airplane was flying straight and level. Jack blinked against the brilliant light from the ports along the fuselage. After a moment he became aware of four other people sitting in the uncomfortable canvas jump seats along the right side of the fuselage, silhouetted in the light of the sun. He blinked again.

There was a spectacularly foul taste in his dry mouth. He had *not* meant to drink that much with the RAAF mob last night, but he was pissed off about his orders, and so one beer led to another, and the more he drank the less he cared about being pissed off. He stayed even with the Aussies, which took some doing, and he wondered if there was something in their genetics that let them get away with drinking like that. Gauging the upheaval in his stomach and the nausea surging between his ears and behind his eyes there didn't seem to be a hell of a lot in his breeding to cushion the aftereffects of too damned much beer.

The kid sitting next to him stirred, opened his eyes, looked at him and nodded.

"Morning, Captain."

Jack croaked something in reply. The kid looked at him and asked, "Are you OK, sir? You look a little pale."

"I'm fine," Jack replied. He sat up in the seat. Pain shot through his head with the movement.

His right calf twinged where he'd been hit by shrapnel last February, in Java, trying to intercept a formation of Jap bombers. He almost bled to death before he could land his shot-up P-40 at the airfield near Perak. What was left of the Far Eastern Air Force in Java was in the middle of evacuating back to Australia, and he ended up at the 119th Army General Hospital at Berrimah near Darwin, where he'd already been treated for wounds sustained in the Philippines.

The Aussie doctors and nurses weren't impressed with him. There'd been unsubtle remarks about the intelligence of repeat customers. That was nothing compared to the oh-so-witty repartee of the RAAF types who came to visit. Ostensibly they wanted to hear about the fighting in Java, and swap stories about the devastating Jap air raid on Darwin back on February 19. Jack's squadron, the 17th Provisional Pursuit, did its unsuccessful best to stop the Japanese invasion of Den Pasar on February 19, so it seemed like a day unlikely to be remembered fondly by anyone except the Japs, who kept the airstrip on Den Pasar and blew hell out of Darwin. The conversation somehow seemed to return to Jack, a pursuit pilot in the US Army Air Forces, being a guest of His Majesty's Royal Australian Air Force.

His status wasn't unique. About the only thing the USAAF owned in Australia was a collection of increasingly shot-up, worn-out airplanes and their shot-up, worn-out pilots and crews.

Jack tried to work up some saliva without any luck. The wounds in his legs were through and through shrapnel wounds that barely left scars. In the adrenaline-induced focus of tangling with the Jap Zeros escorting the bombers he and Dave Malone tried to intercept near Surabaya, though, he didn't notice he was hurt or that he was bleeding. He followed Dave Malone into Perak, and, somehow, got his P-40 down in one piece. The Dutch doctors at Perak found enough blood donors to top him off and keep him alive. Between landing at Perak and waking up at Berrimah, though, his only memory was a vague one of watching his brother Charlie land a spectacularly battle-damaged B-17, while some colonel held him up so he could watch.

He blinked and took another deep breath. That was the second time he'd been shot up by the Japs, and he was tired of it.

The Australians provided expert medical care via the 119th Army General Hospital at Berrimah. The doctors kept him for a couple of weeks to be sure he didn't have any complications relative to the wounds in his legs or to the blood transfusion. Then they released him to the 49th Pursuit Group, where Jack found Walt Coss and Allison Strauss and some of the other survivors of Java flying for Colonel Squeeze Wurtsmith. They were assigned to Darwin to intercept bombing raids the Japs were mounting from the island of Timor. Jack flew a half-dozen intercepts with the 49th, acting as a flight leader, and collected another Zero. Then he came down with another tropical fever, not dengue, not malaria, but something that knocked him down and out for a week while the medics at Berrimah fretted over him yet again.

Then he got orders to return to the States for reassignment, flew one more mission with the 49th, and got on a RAAF Hudson bound for Brisbane and the first leg home. He cabled his fiancee, Irina Aradhana, and his mother, to give them the news. Then when the RAAF dropped him off at the USAAF depot at Garbutt Field in Townsville his orders were changed.

Captain Jack Davis was now headed to Seven-Mile Drome near Port Moresby in Papua New Guinea, wherever the hell that might be, for temporary duty with the 8th Fighter Group. And when he heard that he went out with the crew of the Hudson that brought him out from Darwin and tried to out-drink them. So here he was, in yet another RAAF Hudson, on the last leg of the trip north to Seven-Mile Drome and the 8th Fighter Group.

The kid lieutenant seated next to him was looking at him with concern. Jack was pretty sure from the kid's look that he was pale and probably smelled like piss and stale beer. Aside from the hangover, Jack wasn't sure whatever bug inflicted that last tropical fever on him was gone. He was lucky to be in a RAAF hospital staffed by Aussie doctors. An American doctor would've kept him on the ground for two more months, but the Aussies took a different view of things, what with the Japs right on their doorstep and not a hell of a lot to stand between the little yellow buggers and the Land of Oz. Despite all their ribbing about reverse Lend-Lease, the Aussies were damned grateful for any help they could get. Which his pals from the RAAF proved by taking him out on the town last night – or rather, last night and this morning.

Christ, those Aussies could put away their beer.

Jack moved again, trying for a more comfortable position, preferably one where his head didn't hurt. There was a clink when he shifted his feet. When he looked he saw a barracks bag tucked below his seat. It was his bag – it had his name on it, anyway -- but it bulged as if it held a couple of bottles of booze. Then he remembered Flight Lieutenant Barrows putting it into his hand before they put him in the taxi to the airfield.

"Something to remember us by," Barrows told him cheerfully. "You'll bloody well need it where you're going, cobber."

Whisky or rum or gin or all three, Jack was sure. Right now he thought he'd trade whatever was in the bag for a gallon of water.

Jack looked at the youngster sitting next to him. The kid didn't look old enough to shave, much less fly pursuits in combat.

"How much time you got?" he croaked, looking at the young lieutenant who had spoken to him.

"Time?" the kid asked in reply. He looked puzzled. "It's about 0800 hours, Captain, if that's what you're asking."

"Jehosophat. Hell, no. Time. Flying time. How many hours?"

"Oh! 203 hours, sir," the young lieutenant said.

"Two hundred hours? They send you here straight from flight school?"

"Pretty much."

Jack closed his eyes and leaned back against the seat, trying to work up some saliva, but his mouth was drier than ever. Holy howling jumping Jehosophat, another kid straight out from flight school. A hundred and forty cracked up P-40s on the route between Brisbane, Townsville and Darwin proved you couldn't stick kids fresh out of flight school into the cockpit of a P-40, or a P-39 Airacobra, for that matter, and expect them to be operational without an excessive accident rate. So just like Java the brass was going to stick green kids in the cockpit and hope they'd last against some of the best-trained, best-equipped pursuit pilots in the world.

"Any transition training?" Jack asked. He didn't open his eyes and his voice was still little more than a croak.

"Into what, sir?"

Jack opened his eyes and looked at the kid, who looked back at him without expression.

"Lieutenant, just where are they sending you?"

"8th Pursuit Group, sir. I understand they're in Port Moresby."

"Yeah, so I heard. Except it's the 8th Fighter Group now."

"Beg pardon?"

"Don't ask me. The Air Corps changed its name last year to Army Air Forces. I guess it's part of modernization. Otherwise your guess is as good as mine."

"Oh."

"Yeah. The 8th flies P-39s. You got any time in P-39s?"

"No, sir. I saw a couple at Townsville yesterday."

"You saw a couple?"

"Yes, sir."

"Get a chance to sit in one? Maybe go over the instruments and switches? Read the manual, even?"

"No, sir."

Jack blinked. He looked at the lieutenant's expressionless face.

"What was the last airplane you flew?" Jack asked.

"AT-6 in Advanced Flight Training."

Jack blinked again, trying to clear his head. God, he was thirsty. "How long have you been in Australia?"

"About a week."

"A week," Jack repeated. His stomach lurched. "A week. And you didn't get any transition training into P-39s?"

"No, sir. The personnel types couldn't seem to decide if I was going to the 19th Bomb Group or the 8th Pursuit. I mean, the 8th Fighter."

Jack licked his lips. "Do you have any water?"

"No, sir."

"Crap," Jack muttered. He unbuckled his seat belt and went forward. The radio operator sat before a bench mounted on the fuselage behind the flight deck. He was bent intently over his equipment, rotating a dial. He looked up when Jack tapped his shoulder.

"You got any water, Sergeant?" Jack asked.

The sergeant grinned. He reached under the bench and produced a canteen. "Here you go, Yank."

Jack smiled his thanks, unscrewed the cap, and drank. The water was metallic and a little stale and tasted of some chemical he couldn't place, but it was wet and even reasonably cool. Jack took a long deep drink and then another before replacing the cap and handing the canteen back to the radio operator.

"Where are we?" Jack asked the sergeant.

"About seventy miles south of Seven-Mile," the man replied.

"Thanks. Who's running this crate?"

"That would be Flight Lieutenant Harris, sir. 'Tiny,' we call him. You can't miss him. He's the little bloke in the big chair behind all the wheels and gauges and levers. On the left hand side of the airplane," the sergeant added helpfully.

Jack poked his head through the opening in the bulkhead that led to the flight deck and looked ahead through the cockpit windows. From the sweep of the horizon he figured they were cruising at an altitude of at least eight thousand feet, with maybe two-tenths cloud in a deck two thousand feet below them. Ahead of them he thought he could make out land. He understood there were mountains in New Guinea, so maybe that was what he saw. The land stretched away to the right. Above them the sky was clear and blue. The ocean below was a dark royal blue with waves and whitecaps visible.

The pilot, 'Tiny' Harris, was indeed a little bloke, or might have been considered little in at least one dimension. He didn't seem much on tall but he was built like a barrel, with arms like tree trunks and muscles that bulged against his uniform shirt. He wore a blue RAAF hat with the stiffener taken out of it and headphones over the left ear. Jack couldn't see his face until he turned suddenly and looked at him.

"Well, come on up, cobber. Never known a Yank to be shy."

"Thanks, skipper."

"No need for bloody formality. I'm Tiny Harris. I reckon you met that bloody fool that runs the radios for us."

"Briefly."

"He doesn't improve on long acquaintance. You hear that, Sparks?"

Tiny yelped suddenly and tore his earphones off. A moment later the sergeant peered over Jack's shoulder and said, "Sorry, skipper. Did you say something? Had a bit of an electrical surge there."

"Electrical surge my bleedin' arse. I'll put you up on charges, I will. See if I don't. Destruction of the King's equipment and whatever else occurs to me."

"Yes, sir. I'd be careful putting those earphones back on, skipper. The King's equipment is acting a bit dicey. Tropical conditions, you know. Heat and mold and all that sort of thing. Could cause a short circuit any time." The sergeant grinned and went back to his station.

"Nice spirited crew you got here, Tiny," Jack observed dryly.

"Pack of bloody dingoes," Tiny replied, pitching his voice to be heard over the engines. "Worse than a parcel of schoolgirls, for which I would trade them at any time. Got any schoolgirls on tap, Yank? And what's your name, anyway?"

"Davis, Jack Davis. And no, no schoolgirls, I'm afraid. "

"Pity. Come up to see the fun, have you?"

"Oh, we're having fun?"

"Too right. We're cruising along with two good engines bang on our heading with plenty of fuel. If our luck holds out we'll deliver you to Seven-Mile in ... Sam! ETA Seven-Mile, and be bloody quick about it."

Another man in RAAF uniform looked up from the tunnel to the nose of the airplane.

"Don't act the ruddy Pom," the man said severely. "We shall arrive at Seven-Mile in twenty-six minutes and twelve seconds. That's not including let-down time and assumes you can manage to keep us straight and level on the course I have given you."

"You call me a ruddy Pom again and I'll not bail you out of jail next time you go on the grog."

"In point of fact I did *not* call you a ruddy Pom. I simply asked that you not *act* the ruddy Pom. And I bailed you out last Sunday, which means you owe me."

"Oh. So you did. Well, carry on then." Tiny winked at Jack and said, "What are you going up to fly at Seven-Mile, Jack?"

"I've got orders to the 8th Fighter Group. P-39s."

"P-39s? P-39s! When are you Yanks going to start building Spitfires? Best bloody fighter in the world." Tiny patted the throttle quadrant. "You Yanks build good bombers, oh my word. But it's hard to beat a Spitfire."

Sam said, "Tiny flew a Hurricane once. Now he's bloody well got to fly a Spitfire."

"What's it like up at Seven-Mile?" Jack asked. "I've never been there."

Tiny looked up at Jack. He searched Jack's eyes before turning back to study his instruments. When he spoke again the cheerful bantering tone was gone.

"It's a fair cow," he said deliberately. "There's no denying that. The airstrip's as shoddy a job of work as you'll ever see. Too much bitumen in the paving mix, so it goes soft in the heat of the day. Then there's a ruddy bog at the east end which they try to fix with steel planking. That works every now and again. There's no repair shops and if you want a spanner or a spark plug you'd better have brought it with you, for there aren't any on hand. You'll live in bloody rotten canvas tents or grass huts. The Nips come over three or four times a week, day and night, and drop job lots of bombs. After that, often as not, their lovely little Zeros come down to play. Did I mention it was hot? Well, it is, and it's not to be wondered at, since you're only twelve degrees south of the equator. So it's hot and there's not much shade. There's a lot of dust and a lot of sun. There are flies, mosquitoes, snakes and ruddy huge centipedes. You're right by the sea and not far from the mountains so it rains like the devil every day. During the wet the equatorial front comes south and then the rain can set in for days and nights on end. Then if it's not raining it's humid, oh my word, is it humid, which is why canvas, leather, cloth and your bloody pink toes rot. Oh yes, there's malaria, dengue fever and dysentery."

"A tropical paradise."

"Too right. But that's just the day to day stuff. Bloody Buzz Wagner is in charge of the Yank pursuits at Seven-Mile. Only last week Buzz and his lads flew in to Port Moresby to relieve the RAAF's own No. 75 Squadron, which was down to its last three operational airplanes. No sooner does Buzz land than he says gas up, chaps, we're going to annoy the Nips up north at Lae. And he does. Loses a couple of blokes but he bags three of the little yellow beggars plus whatever damage the 8th did strafing."

Jack shook his head. "Jesus. Buzz Wagner. I heard he made colonel. I was with him in the Philippines."

"Wagner seems like the kind of chap to take his duty to, ah, prosecute the war quite seriously," Tiny commented.

"Yeah, you could say that."

Tiny nodded. "And now the whole Nip Navy is coming south to invade Port Moresby. We're supposed to remain overnight and see if we can help find the little yellow beggars tomorrow."

"Jehosophat. The Japs want New Guinea? First I've heard of it."

Jack looked ahead at the New Guinea coast. If the Japs were coming south in force it made at least some sense of why his orders to return to the States had been put on hold, and that he'd been ordered to temporary duty – TDY, in Army parlance – with the 8th. And Buzz Wagner was in charge up there. Wagner was now the youngest lieutenant colonel in the USAAF, and last December he was a first lieutenant and Jack's squadron commander in the Philippines.

"Yes, well, welcome to the ruddy war, what?" The Aussie pilot looked away for a moment to scan his engine instruments. Then he scanned the sky around them. Jack added his own eyes to the effort. When he looked back Tiny was watching him.

"You seem like you've been around a bit, cobber."

"Here and there. The Philippines. Java."

Tiny nodded. "Then you know what it is. Those lads back in the cabin seem a bit virginal to me, though. No offense."

"None taken," said Jack. "And they do indeed. You ever see Zeros this far south, Tiny?"

"Not yet," Tiny replied. "And I hope I never see a Zero if I'm flying this ruddy bus. But we are in range of the Nip Zeros at Lae. The chaps with 75 Squadron say they have at least a squadron of Zeros there and that's bloody Nip Navy pilots we're talking about. They may be little yellow bucktoothed cross-eyed beggars but it doesn't seem to make them poor pilots. Quite businesslike and determined from everything I hear."

Jack's mouth tightened. "You heard right," he said.

"Um. Yes, well, Lae is less than two hundred miles north of Port Moresby. That's only three hundred miles from our present position. I've heard of the little bastards prowling further than that from their nearest base."

"So have I," Jack agreed. "Thanks, Tiny. You mind if I come up when you get to Seven-Mile? I'd like to look the place over, get a feel for the layout."

"Always a pleasure to assist our gallant allies," the Australian said, smiling.

Jack smiled back and turned to make his way to his seat.

The lieutenants across the aisle were awake and looked up as he entered the after cabin. The other one, the kid he talked to earlier, glanced up at him and resumed looking out the window.

After he buckled in Jack looked the youngsters over. Great Jehosophat, the Aussie flight lieutenant was right. Even if these kids weren't literally virgins they sure as hell looked like virgins.

One of the lieutenants across the aisle was fat enough to strain his uniform a little. Of course that might be muscle. That kid looked like a frat-boy-

football-playin'-skirt-chasin'-beer-and-gin-drinkin'
type, sure enough. Fat and all, though, he could
probably sprint 100 yards in eleven seconds and
snag footballs out of the air with his teeth. From the
size of him, Jack had no idea how he'd squeeze into
the cockpit of a P-39.

Then there was the one that had that curly-
haired smiling innocent look going for him. Hell,
the kid's hair was even blond. Jack knew debutantes
back home who'd kill for hair that blond and curly.
Everything about that kid said "lamb". Jack
repressed a shudder. He knew where lambs were led
and he'd had enough of that.

He looked at the other two lieutenants, who
were sitting closer to the tail. They returned the look
without much interest.

"Samuels, sir," said the one closest to the tail.

"Breckinridge, suh," said the other one, with a
nod. He closed his eyes and went back to sleep.

Jack looked at the kid whospoke to him earlier.
"What's your name, lieutenant?"

The youngster held his hand out. "Ardana, sir,
James T."

Jack frowned. He shook the kid's hand.
"Ardana? You mean Aradhana?"

"No, sir. Ardana. Why?"

Jack shrugged. Aradhana was his fiancee's last
name, but he wasn't sure how well he wanted to
know Ardana, James T., who might not be around
after the first time he and his 203 hours of flying
time tangled with Zeros.

"No reason," Jack said.

The frat boy leaned over and stuck his hand out.
"Hiya, Captain, glad to meetcha, I'm Danny
Evans."

Davis looked at the hand and up the arm to the
smiling face. It was cool in the Hudson's cabin, but
Evans was sweating and the smile on his face didn't

go any higher than his upper lip. Reluctantly, Davis took the offered hand.

Knowing the guy's name was already more than he wanted to know about him.

"Evans," he said. "How much time you have?"

"Me? Couple hundred hours. All I'll need to whip the hell out of the damned Japs, I can tell you!"

"I guess so." Jack looked at the kid next to Evans, who smiled at Jack with that sunny freckled All-American face.

The kid said, "Bellmon, Captain, Gerald B. From Sioux City, Iowa. And I've got a hundred ninety eight hours."

That's already more than I wanted to know about you, too, Jack thought to himself as he shook hands with the kid.

"What you fellows going to fly?" Jack asked. *A-24s, B-25s, anything but P-39s*, he thought.

Evans said, "My orders say to report to the 8th Pursuit Group at Seven-Mile by first available transportation."

Jack looked at Bellmon. "Let me guess. You too?"

Bellmon grinned and nodded. He had great teeth to go along with that blond curly hair, shiny white teeth like a model in a magazine toothpaste ad.

Jack turned to Evans. "When did you guys get to Australia?"

"They stuck us on a god-damn cattle boat," said Evans indignantly. "The boat stank, the skipper was a Dago, the food was rotten and the crew stayed drunk most of the time. Took us two months to get to Australia."

Jack looked at Evans. "Lieutenant, when did you get to Australia?"

"Oh. Er, four weeks ago, sir. April 8."

"April 9, Danny," said Bellmon.

The two lieutenants started to wrangle about the date. Jack looked from one to the other, and then he looked at Ardana.

"So what did they tell you when you got here?" he asked Ardana, who shrugged.

"Well, Captain, things seem to be confused in Brisbane," Ardana replied. "The first personnel type I talked to didn't know anything. The second guy said I was headed for the 19th Bomb Group to fly B-17s. Then another guy said I had leave coming. Then it was the 49th Pursuit Group in Darwin, then the 8th Pursuit at Moresby, but I was to stand by. All that took about a week. Then they gave me priority orders to the 8th Pursuit and asked why I wasn't already in Townsville."

Jack nodded. "What do you want to fly, Ardana?"

"Captain, I'll go wherever they send me, but I want to be a pursuit pilot."

"Ace in a day, huh?"

"No, sir," Ardana said. "If it takes a week or two, that's fine with me. From the little I've seen so far I reckon it's going to be a long war."

Jack looked hard at Ardana, who returned the look. Then Jack nodded again. "Okay," he said. "That's good enough for now."

Jack leaned back in his seat and looked over at Evans and Bellmon. Samuels, he saw, had followed Breckinridge's example and gone back to sleep. All things considered it was a sensible choice.

"So how did you guys spend the last week?" he asked.

Evans actually turned a little pink. "Well," he said. "We got ten hours in P-39s."

Bellmon grimaced.

Jack looked at him. "What's the matter, Bellmon? You don't like the P-39?"

"It's kind of a dud airplane, sir. And the controls are awfully sensitive."

"You think so?"

"Well, I pulled back on the stick in my first takeoff and thought the airplane was going to do a loop before I got the landing gear up. Then I shoved the stick down and boy, did she want to dive! I got her straightened out but a couple of times I thought I was dead."

This melodramatic speech was delivered with a wide-eyed, earnest expression and accompanied by an emphatic nod.

Jack looked at Bellmon thoughtfully, then looked at Evans. "How about you, lieutenant?"

"Well, I didn't pull back quite as hard as Gerry did, but I was at 500 feet and about to stall just from that first little twitch on the stick."

"Weren't you told that the P-39 is very sensitive to changes in pitch?"

"Sure. Because of the engine being behind the pilot near the center of gravity instead of in the nose where it belongs."

"But you gave the stick a good yank anyway."

"Yeah," said Evans. "I got about ten hours in the airplane and I never did like takeoffs."

Jack looked at the big lieutenant again, and then looked at Bellmon. "How about you?"

"After that first time the guy I was working with told me to just think about it, so I did. I almost ran out of runway, thinking about it. Then I pulled back on the stick."

"I see," Jack said. "You're here, so I'm guessing you didn't crack up any airplanes."

"I only bounced it once or twice, landing," Bellmon said proudly. "All the guys flying P-39s there in Townsville said I did OK."

Jack sighed. "You know, it's not any of my business, at least right at the moment. But do you guys want to live?"

"Well, sure," said Bellmon.

Jack shook his head.

At that moment two things happened: the Hudson banked to the left and the twin .303 Browning machine guns in the turret five feet behind them fired a short burst

Jack was looking straight at Bellmon and Evans. Both of them froze, looking aft at the turret. Jack saw movement out of the corner of his eye. It was Ardana, turning in his seat to look aft through the window.

The turret guns didn't fire again, but the bomber stayed in its left bank. Jack watched Ardana for a second. The kid was concentrated on what he could see out the window, the eyes scanning intently.

Jack said, "Relax, Ardana. If that were a Zero on our tail you'd know it by now. Tiny isn't really throwing the airplane around or anything. Sure as hell not like he would if he were under attack."

Ardana nodded and turned to look at Jack. "How well do you know the pilot, Captain?"

"Tiny? Just met him. But he struck me as an experienced guy."

At that moment the radio operator came aft. "Sorry for the fright, Yanks, but it seems there's an air raid on at Port Moresby. The Skipper thinks it best to stooge about for a bit until the Nips go home." Atkins grinned. "Hope Billy didn't give you a fright when he fired his guns. Just test firing, you see, in case we meet the odd Nip."

"Thanks, Atkins," Jack said. The radio operator nodded and went back forward.

Jack looked back at Bellmon.

The Hudson rolled violently in the opposite direction and the turret guns hammered out a long burst, then another one as the Hudson dove and banked hard, pinning them to their seats.

Jimmy Ardana looked out the window as the turret guns fired again. Something glowing bright red flashed past the window and slammed into the

Hudson's wing. There was a small explosion and the airplane rocked slightly as more bright red balls flashed under the wing. The Hudson's dive angle steepened and the engines howled, running up to full throttle. Above their heads there was a rapid series of bangs and crashes and a scream cut short. Something that sounded like hail on a tin roof beat a tattoo on the skin of the fuselage and opened a series of holes overhead. The Hudson rolled in the opposite direction and shuddered violently. The body of the turret gunner slumped down in his straps.

Another burst chewed into the right side of the fuselage. Jimmy felt something whip past his nose and smash into the fuselage a few feet down.

Bullets chewed into Samuels and Breckinridge. Samuels' head exploded. Bits of skull and brain puffed outward as more bullets went through him back to front, sending meat and gobbets of blood in sprays. Breckinridge opened his mouth to scream but a bullet hit him in the neck. Two more hit him in the back, exiting out the sternum and the abdomen. Blood sprayed. Pink mist and the stink of a butcher shop and the sewer filled the fuselage.

All in the space of a heartbeat.

Beside him Captain Davis released his safety belt and lunged from his seat, straining against the g-force of the turn, reaching for the gun turret. When Davis unbuckled the belt holding the gunner's body in place it fell like a wet sack to the floor of the cabin with blood venting from what was left of the gunner's head.

Bullets hammered into the fuselage again. Jimmy heard Davis curse as he tried to climb into the turret as the airplane changed pitch, roll and yaw attitude in rapid succession.

Jimmy stared at the twitching bodies across the aisle. Breckinridge's mouth was still open, working as if trying to speak. Blood gouted freely from his neck. His eyes blinked and his hand reached up to his neck, twitched, and fell to his side. Then both bodies slumped towards the aisle as the Hudson's bank angle increased. Bright red blood flowed copiously from the bodies.

Bellmon had been liberally splattered with Samuels' blood and brain matter. As Jimmy watched he reached up and wiped the blood from his cheek, then stared at his red, dripping hand as the remaining blood ran off onto his already blood-stained uniform. Evans turned to look aft and his jaw dropped as he saw the blood gouting out of Samuels' neck.

Jack couldn't quite pull himself into the turret against the g-force of the turn. He could hear the engines pitching up as the RPMs increased.

Another burst of gunfire hammered into the fuselage, opening more holes. Wind screamed through them along with tiny rays of sunlight, shifting as the airplane turned.

Jack looked at Ardana.

The young lieutenant stared across the aisle at the ruined, bleeding bodies lolling freely against the straps holding them into their seats. One had no head and the other had half a neck, so it was obvious they were dead.

Jack reached out and kicked Ardana in the shin, hard.

The kid gasped and looked at him.

"Help me into the turret or we're all like them!" Jack yelled, pointing to the dead men.

Ardana looked at him, mouth working.

"Now!" Jack yelled. He turned away from Ardana, straining against the g-force of the Hudson's steep turn. There was another rattle of gunfire and then the roar of an engine and a shadow as another airplane passed over them.

Christ Almighty help me into this turret!

Jimmy watched Davis struggle to climb into the turret. He couldn't think. Things weren't making sense. He could barely hear the screaming engines, he hardly felt the g-force in the seat of his pants, weighing down his arms. Something replaced his heart with a huge drum that exploded with each beat. He tried to breathe but couldn't. It was like something had wrapped steel bands around his chest and the hammer-blow beats of his heart smashed against them.

WHAM!

The airplane staggered and reared up into a steep climb.

There was the merest hint, the merest nibble of a shudder in the airframe, coming from the tail.

Airspeed, someone said inside his mind.

The voice sounded familiar.

The bomber continued that shuddering climb.

Airspeed! The voice came again, then, more urgently, *airspeed, airspeed, airspeed!*

Airspeed, Jimmy thought. The bomber's in a climb. We're losing airspeed. We're going to stall and maybe spin.

You trying to kill us, Jimmy?

Jimmy blinked. He knew that voice. He'd known it all his life.

The tail of the Hudson came up and pushed over. In the moment the weight came off Jimmy unbuckled his seat belt, reached out and gave Davis a push.

Davis clambered up onto the gunner's little saddle, his head and shoulders disappearing in the turret. Jimmy looked around the fuselage as if seeing it for the first time and blinked again.

The dead men on the floor reeking of blood and open sewer, the abrupt maneuvers of the airplane, the holes and explosions, all the pieces abruptly came together in his mind.

They were under attack.

He was going to die. Maybe right here, maybe right now.

Oh shit.

Jack was sure, as the Hudson climbed toward a stall, that he was going to die. He gritted his teeth and all he felt was anger, not at dying, but at the thought of dying like this. He tried to get into the turret but now the angle of the Hudson's climb made it impossible. All he could do was lie there, straining.

Then the Hudson's nose pitched down. He held on to the saddle column for dear life and then, as the g-force came off at the top of the pitch-over, someone pushed him up into the turret. He got his feet into the stirrups and instinctively grasped the handles in front of him.

Suddenly he could see in all directions. The back of the turret was spattered with blood and bits of flesh and bone. The Plexiglas was starred and shattered, with the wind screaming in through the holes. The turret pointed aft at seven o'clock.

Jack had never been in a gun turret in his life but it seemed simple enough. There was a handle that came under his right hand. When he touched it the turret rotated. There was a button on top of the handle and there was a bloody god-damn Zero coming right up their tail! Jack looked into the gunsight but had no idea how it was set, so he waited until the Zero started to fire, waited a little more, and then touched the gun button. The guns hammered and yellow tracer licked out. The Zero rolled and banked away. Jack followed the enemy fighter's motion and when the guns pointed ahead of the Zero fired again. The Zero rolled inverted and dove away in a split-S.

He looked around. The Hudson was in a diving turn to the right and the ocean was coming up at a rapid rate. There was a coastline up ahead with green mountains rising in the distance, cloaked in brilliant white clouds. Two more Zeros dove on them from the west.

"Come on, you little bastards," Jack growled, turning the turret and elevating the guns.

"Sir! Sir!"

Jimmy looked away from the turret.

The radio operator stood in the passage, holding onto one of the overhead ribs, bracing himself against the turn. One sleeve of his uniform was torn and his hands were covered in blood.

"Sir, Tiny's hit bad and Sam is dead! Can you fly a Hudson?"

Jimmy blinked at the radio operator.

Then he realized that the Hudson was no longer maneuvering violently. It was in a standard rate diving turn to the left.

And that was predictable.

And they were under attack.

"Can you fly a Hudson?" asked the radio operator. His voice climbed in pitch.

Jimmy started forward. "It's just an airplane," he told the radioman as he pushed past him.

There were bullet holes in the bulkhead behind the pilot's seat. There were more in the cockpit Plexiglas. A pair of shoes extruded from the tunnel into the nose section and blood was splashed all over the right hand side of the instrument panel. There was blood all over Tiny and an ugly hole in his right shoulder. The man was pale and sweating. His eyelids were fluttering and his breath came in rapid gasps. He looked up at Jimmy. His eyes pleaded.

"C'mon, pal, let's get you out of there," Jimmy said. "Atkins, help me."

Jack looked up at the Zeros and darted a glance at the third fighter, who completed his split-S and was hanging on his prop, climbing up at them again. Two up, one down, and the Hudson in the middle. The two guys coming down were the immediate threat.

The diving Zeros split, one continuing on his original course, the other turning to one side to come in at another angle and catch them in a cross fire.

The Hudson was circling down in a nice predictable turn. They were meat on the table for the Zeros. What the hell had happened to Tiny?

Jack gripped the turret controls hard and started tracking the lead Zero. Maybe he was going down, but he'd take one of those little yellow bastards along.

Jimmy and the radioman pulled Tiny out of the pilot's seat. Tiny tried to push with his feet but wasn't a lot of help. Finally they got the wounded pilot clear. Atkins pulled him back into the radio compartment. Jimmy sat in the pilot's seat. Tiny's blood was all over the seat back and the seat itself. Almost immediately Jimmy's blouse and pants were wet with it.

Jimmy ignored the blood. He put his hands on the control wheel and his feet on the rudder pedals. Everything was different from the last airplane he had flown, and the column of engine levers and controls sprouting in all different sizes and colors to his right looked impossibly complicated.

"It's just an airplane," he whispered. Even to himself he sounded like a praying child.

Jimmy looked over his left shoulder and saw two Zeros diving on them. One of them split away to approach from a different angle. The engine on the left wing was smoking and running rough. He could see oil streaming from under the cowling.

Worry about that later, he thought, and looked around the cockpit.

The Hudson was still in a diving turn to the right and the water was awfully close below them. But as they came around in the turn he could see land not too far away, ten or fifteen miles at the most.

Five minutes max. If they could live through the next five minutes they'd be over land, at least. But they'd probably be lucky to live five more seconds.

"Here, sir," said Atkins. He reached past Jimmy and flipped a switch. "Autopilot's off, pilot's airplane."

Jimmy realized it was time to roll the dice. He looked at the throttles, which were all the way forward. He rolled out of the turn, headed toward land, and dove down for the water. The rush of air over the bullet-riddled fuselage and windscreen rose in pitch along with the screaming engines.

Jack had his eye on the two diving Zeros but he hadn't forgotten the Zero climbing up at them. When the Hudson came out of the turn and steepened its dive angle, heading for the surface of the sea, the climbing Zero leveled out and began to accelerate. That one was out of the fight for a few seconds. The two Zeros diving on them were still the greater threat.

He tracked the lead Zero, the one keeping a straight intercept course. The other guy, who had split off to take them from the side, gave up the idea, half-rolled and steepened his dive, coming down inverted.

Jehosophat, thought Jack, you had to hand it to those bastards; they were too damned good for comfort.

Jimmy looked over his shoulder again at the diving Zeros and then all around. That was when he saw the other Zeros and the airplane they were chasing, five or six miles ahead of them at two o'clock. The American airplane was a Martin Marauder, a B-26. Like him it was diving for the surface of the ocean but it had been hit worse than the Hudson. A bright streamer of fire and black oily smoke traced a line behind the bomber and both Zeros were working it over.

But that fight was miles away and he had his own problems because the rough-running left engine started to shake and smoke. Jimmy looked at the gauges over the throttle quadrant. The oil pressure gauge to the left engine was sinking and had almost reached zero. That engine was about to seize completely. Jimmy pulled the throttle all the way back to IDLE CUTOFF and put the propeller pitch to FEATHER. He felt the airplane start to skid into the dead engine and fed in opposite rudder to counteract.

Jimmy felt through his fingertips on the wheel and through the soles of his feet on the rudder pedal as well as the seat of his pants for what the airplane was doing. He'd never flown a multi-engine airplane in his life and he'd heard all sorts of horror stories about engine-out emergencies. He threw all of those stories out of his mind. You fly the airplane, his Uncle Kurt told him once. Fly the airplane, because when you're up here nothing else matters.

They were way too close to the ocean surface. Jimmy pulled back on the control wheel, gingerly at first, ready to come in with more rudder, and looked at the right engine gauges. The engine temperature looked high but with one engine out and three Zeros on their tail he wasn't about to throttle back. Gravity gave them airspeed in the dive but now that one good engine was the only thing keeping their airspeed up. Flying the airplane at the moment meant not stalling out and Jimmy had no idea how slow the Hudson would go before stalling and falling out of the air.

Jack saw the burning oil smoke come out of the Hudson's left engine as the power came off and the prop feathered. The rudder came in to compensate for the drag of the dead engine maybe a shade later than it should have. The airplane kept on course for the coast ahead. Then the Hudson leveled out, barely above the white-capped waves, and the Zeros diving on them leveled out as well. Jack knew what was going on in their cockpits. Hitting a fast-moving target just above the sea wasn't that easy. Your closing speed wasn't as great in an attack from astern, meaning you had longer to shoot at your target. On the other hand, if the target could shoot back, you'd be exposed to defensive fire that much longer. And there was always the ocean waiting for you to make a mistake and slam into the water at 300 mph.

The near Zero elected for a nice flat no-frills attack run from dead astern. His buddy was a little behind him. It looked like he was going for the same attack, three seconds after his leader.

Jack gritted his teeth as the guns in the wings and cowling of the near Zero began to flash. Yellow and red tracer reached out to him, zipping past the turret. The leader was a little off but Jack could see him correcting his aim. Jack centered the gunsight pipper just above the Zero's canopy and held the trigger down in a short burst. His own tracer hosed out, crossing the Zero's fire. The sparkle of bullet strikes danced briefly across the Zero's cowling but the Zero kept boring in.

The Hudson slewed and skidded to the left, spoiling Jack's aim as the first Zero banked away. The second Zero came in as the Hudson dipped its right wing and hit right rudder hard, forcing the left wing with the drag of the dead engine into a turn, then straightening abruptly before dipping to just above the water and pulling up slightly.

"Shit!" Jack snarled as his tracers flew wide of the second Zero, which banked away. But here came the third Zero and number one was completing a climbing turn, preparing to come down at them from an angle. Jack had his eye on that guy. His mind was running like one of those artillery computers he'd seen demonstrated as a cadet, gauging the approach of the third Zero and watching the turn of the first Zero. The first Zero was timing his attack with the third guy to catch them in a crossfire.

"Smart sonofabitch," Jack muttered. He settled the pipper on the third Zero, hosing him with short bursts a little further out, hoping for a lucky hit.

Jimmy heard the hammer of the guns aft and flinched when tracer flew by the cockpit of the Hudson. A Zero flew by to the right, barely clearing his wingtip. Even through the adrenaline and the frantic pumping of his heart he took in the clean lines of the enemy pursuit's silhouette and the elegance of the pilot's technique in the climbing turn away. The turret guns hammered again. The airframe shook a little as they fired, and shook again a hell of a lot harder as something hit the left wing and exploded with a hell of a bang. Jimmy sawed the rudder pedals back and forth and dipped the right wing, hitting the right rudder to bring the left wing around as he felt the asymmetrical forces acting on the airplane shade towards imbalance. He dove towards the water, keeping the airspeed up, gasping as he pulled back on the control yoke, so close to the waves he could have sworn he saw the feathered left propeller splash foam from the sea. He fought the urge to yank back on the controls and kept the Hudson skimming above the waves, low enough for spray to wet the windshield.

Ahead of him he could see the B-26 with its burning, smoking engine still flying, doing exactly what he was doing, right down on the water with the Zeros swarming it like coyotes circling and darting in on a wounded longhorn bull.

Oh hell, oh holy merciful Jesus, there were six more of the bastards coming down from the north! Four split off towards the B-26 and the other two turned in tightly, coming straight down on the Hudson.

Jimmy looked again. Then he laughed and cried and shouted out at the top of his lungs, because the airplanes coming straight for them were a pair of Air Corps P-39s.

Jack saw the high Zero tighten his turn in the gut-wrenching impossibly tight turn only a Zero could do and straighten out on a parallel course, accelerating when he came out of the turn. The Zero right behind them kept on course, firing as he came up from astern. Red tracer snapped overhead, something slammed into the right rudder and exploded. Jack centered the pipper and held the trigger down, longer bursts now, and strikes blossomed over the engine cowling of the Zero. Smoke poured out of the Jap fighter's engine and the pilot broke off his attack, climbing to the left. Jack tracked him, firing, but couldn't see that he scored any more hits. Then he saw the other two airplanes coming from ahead and hurriedly swiveled the turret around to meet the new threat, before realizing that the two newcomers were going head to head with the first Jap. The newcomers had a slimmer nose, shorter wings, they were P-39s! Tracer crossed between the P-39s and the Zero, then they flew past each other. The Zero kept going north after the Zero Jack had hit, which was also headed north, still smoking.

Jack looked up after the second Zero. It was climbing, doing that other Zero thing of damned near hanging on its prop and climbing straight up, something no American airplane could match. Then it nosed over, coming down at the two P-39s in a shallow dive, picking up speed as it came. The P-39s stayed together, opening fire on the Zero as it came in range. The Zero's machine guns and wing cannon opened up and one of the P-39s staggered, dropped a wing and fell a little behind before righting itself. By then the other P-39 and the Zero were flying down each other's throats. Jack didn't really see how they avoided collision. He thought he saw pieces fly off the Zero. The P-39 kept going, and then the second P-39 got a shot at the Zero in another head-on pass.

Only this time the Zero flew straight into the P-39, and both airplanes exploded in midair.

Jimmy was in trouble.

Something had hit the right rudder. The pedal jumped under his foot at the same time there was the hell of a bang from back aft somewhere, and then he'd lost a lot of control authority from the rudders. The P-39s flashed by and to the left he saw a Zero heading north, trailing smoke.

He looked at the engine gauges. The right engine had been left at emergency power too long and it was overheating. He looked over his shoulder but couldn't see anything of the fight between the P-39s and the Zeros. Ahead of him he could see P-39s and Zeros in a turning, swooping, swerving dance, intertwined with bright tracer. The damaged B-26 was still just above the water, running as fast as it could towards the shore now only a few miles ahead. As Jimmy watched, a P-39 spouted a long streamer of flame and skidded into a spin before coming apart. The two Zeros snapped out of turns and headed to the north, climbing steeply away from the P-39s that pursued them.

Very abruptly there was only the Hudson and the burning B-26 ahead of them, heading towards the land, flying above the surface of the sea.

Cowl flaps. Jimmy knew he should open the cowl flaps to help cool the engine. Jimmy looked at the engine controls. There were two of everything and he was relieved to see that the levers for operating the landing gear and the flaps were clearly marked. He couldn't spare a lot of attention from the controls to look for the cowl flap actuators as he nursed the Hudson up to one hundred feet on one engine and leveled out.

Jimmy had no idea if anyone was even alive in back of the airplane. The coast was a mile or two to the north and very clearly the best course of action was to set the Hudson down as soon as possible, preferably at their destination, Seven-Mile Drome. He hoped to hell the pilot of the B-26 knew where Seven-Mile was because the only idea Jimmy had for finding the field was to follow the damaged B-26.

He looked to the north and in the sky high above he saw little black puffs. Oh shit, those were shells bursting, fired from antiaircraft guns! Then he saw the little silver dots in among the black puffs, Jap bombers flying way high. Seven-Mile Drome was under attack. Would there even be a runway when he got there or would it just be a cratered surface? Maybe he should find a nice flat section of beach and set the Hudson down wheels up.

Someone laid a hand on his shoulder.

Jack swiveled the turret and scanned the sky around the Hudson. The surviving P-39s headed north in pursuit of the Zeros. Except for the B-26 ahead of them there was no one else around. Or so he thought until to the north and high he saw a formation of little silver glints. Abruptly flak burst around the little silver glints, which made them Jap bombers. Jesus, those bastards were high! How much warning would they need of an incoming Jap raid to stagger up to twenty something thousand feet in a P-39 with its crappy little single-stage supercharger that wasn't worth a shit above seventeen thousand feet? Jack took another look around to be sure the sky was still empty and climbed out of the turret.

Ardana's seat was empty. Jack ignored Bellmon and Evans, who were still staring at the ruined corpses of Samuels and Breckinridge. As Jack looked forward he saw the radio operator kneeling in the passage, putting a bandage on Tiny.

Jack went forward. Atkins never looked up. Tiny was unconscious, breathing harshly, gasping with pain. Atkins had a morphine syrette in his hand. He injected Tiny with it. Tiny gasped one more time and relaxed.

Jack realized that kid, Ardana, must be flying the airplane. He took two more steps and stood looking at the cockpit.

Jimmy Ardana sat in the pilot's seat. The back of his uniform blouse and his right sleeve were smeared in blood. The windscreen in front of the instrument panel was starred and holed and when he kept looking to the right Jack saw a pair of flying boots. There was more blood on that side of the cockpit. Jack figured it happened on that first pass. Sam and Tiny had been hit by bullets coming from above and left. Sam took most of them.

Ardana stared straight ahead. Jack saw his right foot jammed down hard on the right rudder pedal. He'd seen the fin on that side was pretty torn up after that Jap cannon shell hit it.

Very gently Jack put his hand on Ardana's shoulder.

"How you doing, kid?" he asked.

"Super," Ardana replied. His voice was a little high. "Do you know where the cowl flaps are on this thing? Right engine's overheating."

Jack looked at the engine control pedestal. A bunch of levers sprouted from the top of it and stuck out at odd angles – supercharger, throttle, propeller RPM, mixture, and above them two red covered knobs that must be the fire extinguisher. He worked his way down until he found the levers marked "COWL FLAPS" and opened the right-hand lever all the way.

"Thanks," Jimmy said. "You got any idea where the airstrip is?"

"Hell, no, other than seven miles from Port Moresby."

"I figured I'd follow that guy in," Jimmy said, nodding at the B-26 ahead of them. "That's if the Japs leave us an airfield to land on."

Jack looked up at the Jap bomber formation. It had wheeled and turned to the north, followed by erratic bursts of flak. The kid was right. The airstrip might be a collection of bomb craters by now. He ducked back to the radio compartment.

"Atkins. How's Tiny?"

"I've got him bandaged up, sir, and gave him morphine. He needs a doctor."

"Right. See if you can raise Seven-Mile, will you? Let them know we're landing right behind that B-26 that got shot up."

Atkins nodded and sat at his radio. Jack went back up front.

He looked off the left wing and saw a harbor and a town. He couldn't make out much except whitewashed houses with tin roofs. There were a couple of ships in the harbor. One of them was on fire. There were other fires in the town. The south side of the town seemed to be clustered around a little hill. The water was seventeen shades of blue, from a deep blue in deeper water dotted with whitecaps to the light turquoise shallows.

They flew down a shoreline running more or less east and west. The land was covered with deep green grassy-looking fields and forested with tall trees. The Hudson came opposite a little bay inlet with a hill behind it. Ahead of them the land ended in a cape to the south of another bay, this one long and narrow. The B-26 made a skidding left turn, then disappeared behind a ridge.

Jack held his breath a little as Ardana nursed the Hudson through a standard-rate turn. His eyes darted to the artificial horizon and the turn and bank indicator, both of which showed the kid maintaining good coordination in the turn. Then they were flying up the narrow bay with the B-26 once more ahead.

Atkins tapped his shoulder. "I can't raise Seven-Mile, sir," he said. "Sometimes you can't, after a raid."

"OK," Jack said. "Keep trying."

The radioman nodded and went back to his set.

"Where the hell is the airfield?" Ardana asked, straining forward in his seat.

Jack looked beyond the B-26. After a moment he saw what looked like a narrow dusty aisle amid the trees. There was a good-sized fire burning close to it and a haze of dust hung over the area from the Japanese bombing raid.

He felt his breath catch in his throat. It took him a second and even when it was over he could feel the shiver threatening to take over his hands. He wanted to sit down. No, he thought, what I really want to do is hide.

Then he looked at Ardana.

Jimmy felt his eyes widen as he realized that the dusty pencil line between the hills and among the scrubby-looking trees had to be Seven-Mile Drome.

The B-26 was heading straight for it, losing altitude, its right engine burning merrily. There was smoke from at least one fire coming from near the airstrip.

He darted a look at the control pedestal on the right. About halfway down were the levers for the flaps and landing gear. Then he looked at the airspeed indicator.

With one engine out, full flaps and gear down, what the hell airspeed did this airplane stall at? And how much of that so-called runway, which didn't look too long to begin with, would that poor bastard in the shot-up B-26 take? He darted a look at the engine gauges. Even with the cowl flaps open the right engine was overheating. It looked like the oil pressure was getting low, too.

The control yoke was slippery. Jimmy realized his hands were sweating, and his sweat mixed with Tiny's blood.

"It's just an airplane," he whispered to himself. "Just another airplane."

Ahead of them the B-26 lost altitude rapidly. It looked like the pilot was trying for the end of the runway. Then Jimmy realized the guy wasn't putting flaps or landing gear down. The B-26 was coming in gear up, which would block the runway.

"Just fly the airplane," Jimmy thought to himself.

Jack watched the B-26 stall and slam into the dirt airstrip in a cloud of dust and oily smoke, skidding in on its belly. He'd heard the B-26 was a hot ship with a landing speed that a few years ago would have been a respectable top speed for any airplane. The bomber slewed around, going up on its nose with its tail well off the ground and skidding around the nose and right engine. The wing broke off and for a heartbeat it looked as if the left wing would come right on over, with the whole airplane turning upside down, but the B-26 settled right side up.

That was when Jack saw the bomb craters in the runway. The B-26 blocked the end of the first thousand feet. Three bomb craters holed the runway more or less evenly the rest of the length of it. They could land on the end of the runway and pile into the wrecked B-26, or land over it and smash into one of the bomb craters.

Jack felt his mouth go dry.

Jimmy moved his hand from the flap lever to the landing gear control and brought it down. He pushed the control yoke forward a little and fed in the last of the flaps before bringing the throttle back.

The problem with flying single-engine in a twin-engine airplane was the asymmetrical thrust of the live engine and the drag of the dead engine. But if he killed the good engine there wouldn't be any problem at all. If he cut the power too soon, though, his airspeed would bleed off before he reached the airstrip, whereupon they would fall out of the sky like a big aluminum rock.

He'd once watched a fellow cadet back in flight school let his airspeed get too low on approach to landing. The result had been spectacular and fatal.

Jimmy looked at the engine gauges one more time and at that moment the right engine's oil pressure started to fall. That engine had seconds to live, and they were still a quarter-mile from the end of the airstrip, with a wrecked airplane blocking the runway. He hesitated a half-second and pushed the throttle on the dying engine all the way forward, splitting his attention between the oil pressure gauge and the rapid approach of the end of the runway. Jimmy leveled out as the engine roared back to full power, imparting a few seconds of acceleration as the last of the oil ran into it. Just as the oil pressure gauge fell to zero Jimmy chopped the throttle back to IDLE CUTOFF and feathered the propeller.

The Hudson cleared the trees at the end of the runway and Jimmy pulled back on the control yoke, ever so little, watching the airspeed bleed off and the altitude climb, before he put the nose back down. He didn't see the trees rushing by on either side; all he could see was the wrecked B-26 less than a thousand feet away, coming closer in slow motion like something in a nightmare.

Jack felt the sinking feeling in his stomach as the Hudson climbed higher. What the hell was the kid thinking? His best shot would have been to set the airplane down on the very end of the runway, stand on the brakes, and hope for the best, maybe ground loop the Hudson before crashing into the B-26. Now it just looked like he was going to land right on top of the wreck and add their own bones to it, and holy Hannah mother of God, he was nosing down, he was way too fast!

Chapter Two

"Seven-Mile Drome is lovely this time of year"

Major Charles Davis poked his head above the level of the slit trench where he and his crew took shelter during the air raid. Dust, smoke from burning oil and gasoline, and the ammonia stink of exploded bombs hung heavy in the air, but for a moment there was silence. Charlie, veteran of a dozen air raids, knew that a lot of that silence was the numbness of ear drums overtaxed by the nearby explosions of bombs. He looked down the slit trench at the other men occupying it.

Lt. Al Stern, his navigator, was just sitting up. Next to him was Charlie's current co-pilot, Lt. Mike Deering. In a tumble a few feet away were various arms, legs and bodies sorting themselves out. Charlie's hearing began to return. His gunners and the line crew cursed the Japs, the bombs and each other. Their voices were filled with fear and its aftermath but everyone seemed OK.

"Sound off!" Charlie said.

Al Stern waved. "Navigator OK," he replied.

"Bombardier OK," said Bob Frye.

Deering nodded. "Copilot OK."

On down the trench it went until it got to the mechanics and armorers who were servicing Charlie's B-17E, *Bronco Buster II*, when the air raid began. The crew chief, Sgt. Matt Galen, looked down the trench, obviously counting heads among his ground crew.

Galen turned to Charlie. "All present or accounted for, Major," he said.

Charlie nodded, his face a mask over his relief.

"Good. Let's see to the airplane, gentlemen," he said.

When Charlie stood up he heard the sound of engines.

"Jesus, Charlie, look at that," said Stern, raising his arm and pointing down the runway.

There were two twin-engined airplanes on approach. The first was a B-26 Marauder with one engine on fire. Behind the B-26 was an airplane with twin tails as well as twin engines. At first Charlie couldn't tell if it was a B-25 or a Hudson; then he saw that the wings sat lower on the fuselage than a B-25 should, and that made it an RAAF Hudson. There was a streamer of smoke behind the Hudson as well.

Charlie looked up and down the runway. There were three more or less evenly spaced bomb craters along its length. The bomb craters were still smoking. The guys in those airplanes were going to have a tough time getting in.

He watched the B-26 come straight in without dropping flaps or landing gear. "Oh crap," he breathed as the B-26 flared out. Charlie's hands and feet twitched on invisible controls

The B-26 slid on its belly. A rooster-tail of smoke and dust flew up behind it. The first sound reached them, the screeching, grinding moan of metal on tarmac. Then the wing with the burning engine separated from the fuselage, tumbling down the runway in a cloud of dust and smoke. The B-26 slid up on its side, right wing almost vertical, spinning counterclockwise before slamming into the ground, bouncing once before skidding to a halt.

Charlie looked up at the approaching Hudson. He could see now that the propellers on both engines were feathered. The pilot was coming in dead stick.

To Charlie, watching from the ground, it really did not look as if the Hudson could make it, between the B-26 wrecked on the runway and the bomb craters along its length.

The Hudson dove at the ground, pulled up steeply at the last moment, stalled in hard and bounced over the B-26. The pilot put the nose down again and pulled up more gently this time. The Hudson's main gear kissed the runway, tail just off the ground until the brakes came in with an audible squeal. The Hudson stopped, as near as Charlie could tell, right on the edge of a bomb crater.

Charlie found he had been holding his breath. He let it out with an audible exhale.

"You said it, skipper," Deering said. He shook his head. "I knew those Aussies were crazy but that was nuts even for them."

A couple of the beat-up rusted trucks the Australians used around the field tore past. Another followed quickly, and then a jeep pulled to a stop in front of the slit trench.

The corporal driving it got out and saluted. "Major, the colonel sent me to be sure you guys were OK."

"We're fine, Tony. How about you drive me down to the other end of the runway? Maybe we can help those guys."

"Sure thing, Major."

Charlie got in the passenger seat and Stern got into one of the benches in the back. The corporal put the jeep in gear with a clash and a groan and roared down the taxiway towards the stricken airplane.

Jimmy sat in the blood-soaked pilot's seat of the Hudson, looking over the starboard wing. The wing stuck out over a still-smoking bomb crater. He realized that although he held the control wheel with a very light grip, he had the balls of both feet jammed hard against the brakes on top of the rudder pedals.

Captain Davis picked himself up off the floor and looked at Jimmy.

"You OK, kid?" he asked.

Jimmy nodded and reached out to turn the master switch to OFF, shutting down the ship's electrical system.

Davis clapped him on the shoulder. "You'll be fine," the captain said. He turned to the rear.

Jimmy heard a few words exchanged, and remembered that Atkins, the RAAF radio operator, had the Hudson's pilot lying on the deck of the airplane, trying to keep Tiny from bleeding to death.

A couple of trucks rushed by, heading to the other end of the runway where the B-26 had crash-landed. Jimmy watched a jeep come towards the Hudson as well.

Abruptly he released the pressure on the brakes and took a deep breath. It was suddenly hot in the cockpit, hot and sweaty-humid. He smelled the familiar airplane smells of hot metal and oil and burned gasoline, overlaid with something more, the tang of blood, like a copper penny held on the tongue, and a faint but definite odor of shit.

Jimmy swung out of the pilot's seat, grimacing at the slick, sticky feeling of the blood congealing on his shirt and the seat of his pants. He looked down the fuselage as he stood and turned.

Davis was speaking in low tones and using emphatic gestures to the two surviving lieutenants in the aft cabin. Evans and Bellmon sat in their seats, so still and rigid Jimmy wondered if they'd been killed during the attack like the two men, sitting towards the rear of the airplane, whose shattered bodies still leaked blood and fluids onto the deck of the Hudson. Then Evans, the big beefy one, looked slowly up at Jimmy.

Evans' eyes were stunned. He blinked at Jimmy without recognition. His mouth worked but no sound came out.

Then Bellmon, the skinny one with the curly blonde hair, undid his seat belt and stood up. Evans looked away from Jimmy. In a moment he unbuckled his belt and stood, and Captain Davis pushed them out the rear entrance hatch.

Jimmy looked down. The Aussie pilot lay on the deck while Atkins, the radio operator, tried to stop the bleeding of the pilot's arm with a compression bandage.

Tiny's eyelids fluttered, and then the eyes opened and focused on Jimmy, standing there framed in the entrance to the cockpit.

"Looks like you got us down in one piece, cobber," he said. His voice was husky with pain and shock. "Thanks."

Jimmy knelt by the Australian. "Don't mention it," he said.

"Where's Sam?"

"Sam?" Jimmy asked, puzzled. He looked up at Atkins, who shook his head.

"Oh," said Tiny. "How about those blokes in the back?"

"Two guys dead," Jimmy replied. "And your gunner, too, I'm sorry to say."

"Timmy?" Tiny's eyes brimmed over with tears. "Mucking hell, it was his first trip."

Mine, too, Jimmy thought, but said nothing.

Outside the Hudson he heard the sound of truck engines and brakes. Then the airframe shook as someone came up the stairs in the rear door. Jimmy heard a rough Australian voice giving orders, and then the stairs shook again. He looked up and saw two Australians carrying a stretcher picking their way down the aisle of the airplane.

The one in the lead looked Ardana over. "You look a little banged up, Yank."

"I'm OK," Jimmy replied. He pointed at Tiny. "It's his blood."

Jimmy started to rise but Tiny took his hand. Even in pain and shock Tiny's grip was strong.

"Thanks again, mate," Tiny said. "Next time you're in Townsville look me up. The beer's on me."

"You bet," said Jimmy softly.

"Right-o, then, let's get you out of this," the lead stretcher-bearer said. The two men examined Tiny quickly and placed him on the stretcher, then rose and walked it carefully down the length of the Hudson's fuselage.

Jimmy sat with Atkins watching them until they maneuvered Tiny out of the airplane. Then Jimmy sighed and looked at Atkins.

"Is it always like this?" he asked the radio operator, who shrugged.

"Welcome to bleedin' Seven-Mile," Atkins said wearily. He started to put the unused bandages back in the first-aid kit.

Jack pushed Evans and Bellmon out of the Hudson ahead of him. A jeep shot past as he climbed out. A man with major's gold oak leaves sat in the passenger seat, looking at Jack as he went by. Before Jack could do more than recognize his brother Charlie, the jeep was backing up and Charlie jumped out, concern on his face as he took in the blood on Jack's jacket and trousers.

"Holy howling Jehosophat," Charlie said. "You look like hell. You OK, Jack?"

"Charlie," Jack said. "Yeah, yeah, I'm OK, but there's dead and wounded in the airplane."

Charlie turned to his jeep driver. "Go down to the RAAF dispensary. If those blokes aren't already on their way tell them we've got casualties on the airstrip."

The driver nodded and took off.

Then suddenly Jack found himself in a powerful hug from his brother, which he returned.

"Goddamned kid," Charlie said. "Last I heard of you they were flying you out of Java without a hell of a lot of blood left in you."

"Yeah, nice to see you too, Charlie," Jack replied. "Look, it wasn't that bad. And that was two months ago."

"Are you back on flight status?"

"Yeah."

"Hell fire and damnation. You're up here with the 8th, aren't you?"

Jack looked at him. His mouth twitched. "Clever as always, big brother."

Charlie looked past Jack to where the two blood-spattered lieutenants stood by the Hudson's hatch.

"Shit," Charlie said. His eyes narrowed as he took in the damage from machine gun bullets and cannon shells, and the shattered Plexiglas of the Hudson's blood-stained turret.

"What the hell happened?" Charlie asked. "Zeros?"

Jack nodded. "The RAAF pilot was wounded and four guys were killed, all in the first pass."

Charlie nodded towards Evans and Bellmon. "Are those guys OK?"

"Yeah, it's not their blood."

Charlie shook his head. "You said the pilot was wounded. Did you take over?"

"No, that was some kid who was with us. Jimmy something. I was up in the turret, shooting at Zeros." Jack looked at Evans and Bellmon. "Hey, you two! Evans, Bellmon! Get over here!"

The two lieutenants walked over to Jack. After a moment Bellmon noticed Charlie's gold oak leaves and came to attention, saluting. Evans straightened up and waved a hand in the general direction of his face.

Charlie flicked a glance at Evans but said nothing. He saluted with an offhand casual grace. "Rest, gentlemen. You've had a busy morning. In fact, you see that tree over there? Why don't you go sit under it until things get sorted out here?"

"Yes, sir," said Bellmon. He started to walk off. Evans stood there, looking somewhere between Charlie and Jack. Bellmon took him by the arm and led him off.

A couple of RAAF riggers in baggy shorts and the floppy Australian hats drove up in another rusty truck with a tow bar in the back. There was a sergeant next to the driver. The sergeant got out and looked from Jack to Charlie.

"Pardon me, Major. Where's Flight Lieutenant Harris?"

"Talk to Jack here," said Charlie. "He was on the airplane."

"Tiny got shot up pretty bad," Jack told the sergeant. "Didn't you guys get our radio call?"

"Radio station got hit in the raid." The sergeant turned to the driver. "Tony, take the truck back an' bring the ambulance."

"I sent my driver," said Charlie. "You'd probably like to get this airplane off the runway."

"We would. Thank you, major."

"Anytime."

The sergeant went into the Hudson. Two of the fitters from the truck grabbed a stretcher and followed him. There was a short filthy oath, probably as they came across the bodies in the aft cabin, and Jack heard them walking up the aisle of the Hudson.

A moment later the stretcher bearers carried Tiny from the airplane. They laid the stretcher gently under its wing and went back inside. Atkins came out, carrying a small bag, and sat beside Tiny's stretcher. The Australians carried the gunner's body out and laid it gently at the side of the runway. Their sergeant pulled the truck around to the rear of the Hudson.

Ardana came out. He stopped short and came to attention when he saw Charlie.

"Jeez, Charlie, tell him at ease, will ya?" said Jack.

Charlie smiled and waved at Ardana. "Like my kid brother said, at ease."

"You OK?" Jack asked Ardana.

"I'm all right," Ardana replied. The Australians carried one of the dead lieutenants out of the Hudson and carried the body over to place it by the dead gunner. Ardana watched them, eyes bleak.

"Charlie, this is Jimmy. What the hell is your last name again, kid?"

"Ardana," the lieutenant replied, shaking hands with Charlie.

"So you made that Hollywood stunt-pilot landing," Charlie said.

"Well, major…"

"He sure did," Jack said. "And a damned good one, too."

Charlie grinned. "Well, you walked away from it, so better than one or two of yours I've seen, Jack. And just what were you doing while Jimmy here was landing the airplane?"

"Standing behind him trying not to piss myself. Worked, too."

Charlie shook his head, still grinning. Ardana looked at Davis.

"What?" asked Davis. "You think I did piss myself?"

"He got up in the turret and kept the Zeroes off us," Ardana told Charlie.

"Oh? Do any good?"

Jack shrugged. "I winged one, I think."

Charlie turned to look at Ardana. "You up here for the 8th, lieutenant?"

"Yes, sir."

"How many hours you got?"

Ardana glanced at Jack before looking back at Charlie. "I guess about two hundred and four now, sir."

"It was two hundred and three until about a half-hour ago," Jack said.

"Really? You handled that Hudson pretty well. You find you don't like P-39s, lieutenant, come see me. I can always use a good copilot, and you could probably have your own airplane pretty quick."

"Uh, thank you, sir."

Charlie laughed. "Relax. Buzz Wagner would probably shoot me if I tried to shanghai one of his pilots."

"Buzz Wagner?" Ardana asked.

"I thought Fred Smith had the 8th," Jack said.

"Yeah, he's commanding the 8th. But he's down in Townsville and Buzz Wagner is Director of Fighter Operations here in Moresby." Charlie looked at Ardana. "Buzz – that is to say, Lt. Col. Boyd D. Wagner – will be your boss here."

"What the hell is a director of fighter operations?" Jack asked.

"Let Wagner explain it. Basically he runs fighter ops in the local area, just like the job title says."

A truck with a red cross painted on it drove up to the Hudson. A pair of medics jumped out of the open back. They went to Tiny, checked him over quickly, and lifted him into the ambulance. Atkins got in with them and the ambulance drove back the way it came.

The RAAF ground crew moved to hitch the tow bar to the Hudson's tail wheel.

"Shit!" Jack said. He darted into the airplane and grabbed his B2 bag. He looked at it. It was spattered with blood but untouched by bullets. He ducked back outside.

Charlie shook his head when he saw the bag in Jack's hand. "Is that what I think it is?"

"Snake bite medicine. I hear there are a hell of a lot of poisonous reptiles around here."

"You heard right. Look, Jack, I have about a half hour before I go out on a little look-see tour. When my driver gets back how about you come with me?"

"I should report in."

Charlie shrugged. "Buzz can spare you for a half-hour or so." Then he looked at Ardana

Jack saw where Charlie was looking. "Turn around," he said.

The back of Jimmy's shirt and the seat of his trousers were stiff with drying blood.

"Jehosophat," said Charlie. "You're a mess, kid. Look, you can't report in like that. I think I can get you a shower if a bomb didn't knock over our water barrel. Fresh clothes, hell, where's your bags?"

"In the Hudson, sir."

"OK. Why don't you get your bags out of the airplane and come with me and Jack?"

"Ah...yes, sir. But what about those two?" Ardana pointed at Evans and Bellmon, sitting under a tree.

"Mm. OK," Charlie said. He walked over to the RAAF sergeant and spoke to him for a few moments.

"Hey, you two!" Charlie called. He beckoned to the two lieutenants when they looked up.

"You guys go with the RAAF blokes," Charlie told them. "As soon as they get this ship parked and camouflaged they'll give you a ride up to the 8th Pursuit Group."

Evans glowered at Ardana.

"What about him?" Evans asked.

"Well, I'm going to take Mr. Ardana with me, lieutenant," Charlie said in a light tone. "That all right with you?"

Evans started to open his mouth, but before he could speak Bellmon said, "That's fine, sir."

"Good! Jimmy, here comes my driver. Grab your bags and let's go."

Ardana looked at the door of the Hudson and hesitated a half-second before going inside the airplane.

"Kind of a rough morning," Charlie observed.

"Yeah," said Jack.

Jimmy sat in the back of the truck with his bags scrunched in with him. Major and Captain Davis sat in back with him so they could talk.

He noticed that the driver didn't try to get out of second gear. The sun along the taxiway had dried its dusty surface to the point where they truck kicked up a lot of dust that hung in the hot, humid air.

Jimmy thought he'd been in heat during training in Texas. Coming from Montana he found the heat and humidity of a Texas summer around Kelly Field almost unbearable, but this was worse. Dust blew in and got up his nose and into his eyes. His shirt stuck to his back from the mix of drying blood, sweat, and dust. It felt like he was swimming in sweat and trying to breathe water.

Then there was the smell, or rather the blend of foul smells. He recognized rotten things, rotten meat, rotten vegetation; burning things, burning oil and rubber and gasoline being the first and sharpest, but burning meat under it, and the ammonia smell of explosives.

He looked southeast down the runway at the B-26. A group of ambulances and trucks clustered around it. A small bulldozer approached the bomber, followed by a truck with a crane and a sling. Jimmy guessed that was to move the B-26 off the runway.

Then he looked at the ground bordering the airstrip. There were wrecked airplanes and pieces of wrecked airplanes up and down the edge of the runway as far as he could see, looking as if they'd just been bulldozed out of the way. A wing stuck up out of a tangle of metal, light gray with a blood-red meatball on it. A Zero, maybe. Most of the rest of the wreckage looked to be types he was familiar with: B-26s, B-17s, B-25s, PBYs, Hudsons, P-40s. A couple of others looked to be civilian types he wasn't familiar with, maybe British. Jimmy's eyes widened. Hell, there was even something that looked like the nose section of an old Ford Tri-Motor.

Then they were in among the trees following a taxiway wide enough to accommodate a B-17. He started listening to the Davis brothers.

"Charlie, what's all this latrine intelligence about the Japs coming this way?" Jack asked.

Charlie shrugged "It's true. All sorts of Jap ships, carriers, cruisers, transports, coming down from Rabaul and their main base on Truk. Carriers stuffed full of Zeros and transports crawling with troops. Nobody has said anything about intentions but if you were Tojo and sent half your navy this way, what would you be after?"

"Darwin," said Jack. "The Aussies don't have shit there to stop the Japs and it's close to their bases on Java and Timor. Hell, the Japs are sending air raids from Timor to Darwin every few days."

"Maybe it's a good thing you aren't Tojo, then, 'cause it looks like all those ships are coming right here. Are you still a pretty good rifle shot?"

"Why?"

"Because if we can't stop those little yellow bastards this is probably where they're coming. Port Moresby is the only reasonable harbor on the south coast of New Guinea. From here they can mount an invasion of Australia, if that's what they want."

"Jehosophat. OK. So what's that got to do with my rifle marksmanship?"

Charlie scowled. "Are you jungle happy or something? If the Japs land, we'll lose Seven-Mile almost at once. And I probably won't be here to fly your ass out like I did last December. You'll end up like the Air Corps guys we left behind in the Phillipines, with a rifle in your hands, playing infantryman." Charlie looked at Jimmy and smiled.

"Not to spread defeatist rumors or anything, lieutenant," Charlie said, "But when was the last time you fired a rifle?"

"Basic training, sir," Jimmy replied.

"Did you qualify?"

"Yes, sir."

Jimmy didn't add that he had fired High Expert. He had been raised on a ranch in Montana and his father and grandfather taught him about firearms as soon as he was able to hold them securely.

The truck stopped in front of a crude rammed-earth revetment in among some trees. Men in what appeared to be the standard Seven-Mile uniform of shorts, hat and mosquito boots were refueling a B-17E parked in the revetment. On the nose of the bomber was the crude red silhouette of a cowboy riding a crow-hopping mustang.

"Bronco Buster II?" Jack asked. "What happened to the one I saw you land in Surabaya?"

"That's right, Colonel O'Donnell told me you were there when we came in." Charlie grimaced. "We brought her back to Surabaya from Balikpapan shot all to hell. Taxied up to the ramp and she fell apart right there, after I shut the engines down."

Charlie took a deep breath and let it out with a rush. "What none of us could believe was, aside from the gunners in the waist and the radio operator, who got a little singed when the bomb bay fuel tank caught fire, nobody got so much as a scratch."

"Lucky."

"You said it."

"What's in Balikpapan, anyway?"

"Probably half the reason the Japs went to war in the first place. Oil fields and oil refineries. Aviation fuel, even if the stuff has some aromatic crap in it that eats out the self-sealing lining in our fuel tanks."

"I don't remember we had any problem with that in our P-40s."

"You guys in the 17th Pursuit weren't there long enough." Charlie looked around. "Hey, Lefkowicz!"

One of the men looked up and trotted over.

"Yah, Skipper?"

"Did our shower survive the air raid?"

"Ah…don't know, sir. We were busy checking the ship."

Charlie nodded.

"This is Lt. Ardana," Charlie said, indicating Jimmy. "Take him with you and see if the barrel is still up there, and if it is let's get him out of those bloody clothes before he starts to stink."

The gunner grinned ever so faintly. "Yah, Skipper, can do."

"Just follow Lefty, there, Jimmy, and we'll get you taken care of."

"Thanks, major," Jimmy said. He grabbed his bags. Lefkowicz took one from him.

"This way, Lieutenant," he said.

The Fortress crews had a 55-gallon drum fed by a canvas rain scoop slung between some trees. The drum was equipped with a hose and a stopcock.

"Here you are, lieutenant," the gunner said. "Hope you've got some soap, 'cause we're fresh out."

Jimmy nodded. He opened his barracks bag and took out a smaller bag and opened it. Inside were four bars of soap wrapped in wax paper.

"What kind of soap is that, sir?" the gunner asked, peering curiously at the bars.

Jimmy thought about his grandmother, insisting on making her own lye soap and putting this in his bag before he left for flight school last year.

"Aw, my grandma makes this stuff," he told the gunner. "She doesn't believe in the store-bought kind. Says it won't take the stink off a man."

Lefkowicz chuckled. "Sounds like my grandma."

Jimmy handed Lefkowicz one of the cakes of soap. "Been carrying them for long enough I sort of forgot they were there," he said.

"Thanks, lieutenant," Lefkowicz said. He unwrapped the soap as Jimmy took underwear and a uniform blouse, trousers, underwear and socks out of his barracks bag.

"How come all you guys wear pistols?" Jimmy asked.

"Well, sir, the bomber crews carry them in case they get shot down. The ground crews carry them because of Jap paratroopers."

"Jap paratroopers? Are you kidding me?"

"No, sir. The Japs used paratroopers in Borneo. Never know when the little yellow bastards might try it again."

Jimmy nodded. Then he reached down into his bag and took out a yellow chamois sack, laying it with his clean uniform on a little table next to the planks that made the bed of the shower. He stripped quickly and got under the hose with one of the cakes of his grandmother's soap, spreading his bloody clothes on the planks at his feet.

The stream of water was warm and thin but it was better than nothing. Jimmy plied the lye soap vigorously, feeling the bite of it against his skin and his nostrils, trampling his clothes under foot to try and get some of the blood out of them. He didn't really have much hope of it, but he got the feeling that he might be glad to have those clothes someday, even if they were a little bloodstained. He got the soap out of his hair and eyes and the rest of his body, rinsed a moment or two longer, then closed the stopcock.

"That's better," Jimmy said. "Does it do any good to towel off?"

"In this heat? No, sir," the gunner replied. "Kind of like the shower, it's a moral victory and nothing else."

Jimmy chuckled. He patted himself dry but soon realized the sergeant was right. The sweat started in the heat as soon as he stepped out from under the shower. He put on his underwear and trousers, then pinned the insignia on his blouse. He got the soaked clothes from the shower and held them at arm's length, frowning at the pinkish fluid dripping off them.

"Reckon it's any use trying to get that out?" Jimmy asked the sergeant.

"You won't get anything else to wear for awhile, unless you inherit it, Lieutenant."

"Inherit?" Jimmy frowned. "Oh. Right. Never mind, then. Guess I'll find somewhere to soak them."

"May I make a suggestion, sir?"

"Please."

"Find some sort of basin or tub and put them in with a little water, so your clothes don't dry out. Then this afternoon it'll rain a foot or so an' fill up your basin. That's probably the best we can do for now."

"No post laundry, huh?"

"Kind of civilized for this shithole, sir, if you'll pardon my French."

Jimmy nodded and finished tying his shoes. He wadded the bloody clothes into a ball.

Then he dried his hands and opened the yellow chamois bag. Inside was a long-barreled .45 Colt Peacemaker and a holster rig. The holster was a combination cross-draw and shoulder holster, designed by his father and his Uncle Kurt as a present for Jimmy when he finished flight school. Jimmy's grandfather, Tom Ardana, gave him the pistol for his 18th birthday. When Jimmy put it on the holster hung above and to the inside of his left hip, with the barrel pointed down just enough to stay in place without the strap.

"Jesus," said the gunner. "Is that a .45?"

"You bet," Jimmy replied. He reached into the bag and pulled out a box of ammunition, opened it, and handed a gleaming brass cartridge to the gunner. Then he loaded the revolver, hammer to half-cock, loading gate open, a cartridge in five cylinders and an empty cylinder under the hammer.

Lefkowicz handed the cartridge to Jimmy. "Makes a .45 ACP round look kind of small," he observed.

Jimmy shrugged. "The .45 automatic is a good pistol," he said. "My Dad carries one, but grandpa always said there was nothing like the .45 Long Colt for peacemaking."

"Guess so," the gunner said. "If you're ready, sir, let's get back."

Jack and Charlie watched Lefkowicz lead Jimmy into the jungle down a little trail. They stood sweating in the heat for a moment as Charlie turned a critical eye on his crew and the airplane they were servicing.

"So where are you headed, Charlie?" Jack asked.

Charlie grimaced. "The Navy knows the Japs are coming south. What they'd like to know is where the little yellow bastards are. That's where we come in. As soon as we gas up we're going out to see what we can find."

"Do you come back here or go on down to Townsville?"

"Probably Townsville."

"So what's up north?"

Charlie looked at Jack. "You mean you don't know?"

"I just got here, remember?"

"Sorry. What's north is Simpson Harbor and a charming little town called Rabaul."

Jack nodded. "What's Simpson Harbor?"

"That's the reason the Japs took Rabaul at the north end of New Britain. It must be a good harbor. The Navy guys drool every time they talk about it."

"I'm guessing the Jap fleet isn't there."

Charlie shook his head. "Nope. But a lot of Japs were there two-three days ago that aren't there now. So that means they're going somewhere to do something we probably won't like."

"Guess so," Jack said.

"What about those kids you came in with?" Charlie asked.

"Replacements."

"Are they old enough to shave?"

Jack sighed. "I hope so. I'll probably end up holding their hands until they get their asses shot off."

Charlie shook his head. "Par for the course. You should see my new copilot. Didn't even go through multi-engine school before they sent him to us. Had about a hundred-eighty hours when he reported in."

"No wonder you asked about Ardana."

Charlie grinned. "Yeah. At least it looks like he can handle himself. What about the other two?"

"As far as I could see they just sat in their seats. I don't think they wet themselves, so that's something."

Charlie shrugged. "Don't be too hard on them. The first time can be kind of tough."

"Yeah." The two brothers exchanged a look.

"So they're going to stick those kids in P-39s? They get any time on them in Townsville?"

"Bellmon and Evans said they got about ten hours each."

"Jeez. Ten hours." Charlie shook his head and looked over at the refueling operation. He was silent for a moment. "Oh well. At least when we write Mom we can tell her we saw each other. She'll like that. When did you last hear from Mom, anyway?"

"Got a letter about two weeks ago, postmarked back in February. She's OK. Getting involved in war relief work."

"February? The last time I heard from home was last month. It was dated January. How do you rate?"

"I was in one place for a month."

"Which brings me to what I really wanted to talk to you about." Charlie put a hand on Jack's shoulder. "What the hell are you doing up here, Jack? I heard you had orders to go home."

"Where'd you hear that?"

"Us West Point guys, you know, we hear things. A classmate of mine is on the FEAF staff, works in General Brett's office."

"Well, as far as it goes, it's true. I had orders home, then that got changed, and here I am."

"What's that all about?"

"How would I know? Didn't you tell me once that the Army tells you to get ready to go to Alaska, and then they send you to the Panama Canal?"

"There is that. But hell, Jack, you've been wounded twice and you've got three kills..."

"Four."

"Four? When did that happen?"

"I flew for a while out of Darwin with the 49th."

"Jeeee-hosophat." Charlie took a deep breath and let it out. He looked at his airplane for a minute before turning back to his brother. "Hellfire, Jack, crazy pursuit pilots like you with *four* Japs and the DFC and a couple of Purple Hearts, they want you back in the States to ramrod some hot new outfit full of young maniacs like Ardana who don't know shit about the real war. They'll make you a major and give you a squadron and send your ass to Europe to fight Uncle Adolf."

"I guess they'll get around to that eventually, Charlie. My orders say this is temporary duty, not a permanent reassignment."

"You sound pretty calm about it."

"It's not like I can do much about either one." Jack shrugged. "I didn't want to be an element leader and I didn't want to be a flight leader, either, but I got pushed into the job both times. So I guess if the Army wants to make me a squadron commander they'll do that, too."

Charlie shook his head. "Lots of guys would jump at the chance of their own squadron."

"Career Army guys like you. I like the flying, Charlie, but I don't know if this is a career for me. Not after the war, anyway."

"What will you do if it happens like I think it will?"

"My own squadron? What d'you think? I'll step up to the plate and take a swing at it. But hell, Charlie, I haven't even been in the Air Corps for two years. You West Pointers get a lot of stuff about leadership and organization taught to you. All I know is what I've picked up by keeping my eyes open. The rest of it I'm going to have to pick up on the fly."

Charlie nodded. "Want some advice?"

"Sure."

"Find out who the good sergeants are, and ask their advice. You don't have to follow it, but don't be too damned proud to ask."

Jack nodded slowly. "Well, if I've learned one thing out here, I've learned to listen to people who know what's going on. Like sergeants who've been around."

"Good! Then you know more than a lot of guys, even from the Point. One other thing."

"What's that?"

You've got four kills. One more and you're an ace. Promise me for Mom's sake, and maybe for the sake of the beautiful Miss Aradhana, that while you're looking for that fifth kill you keep your head out of your ass and use your brain instead of your balls when you get in a fight, OK?"

"The beautiful Miss Aradhana, is it?"

Charlie leered. "You get killed, little brother, I might, just *might*, be tempted to offer the lady some consolation. In a gentlemanly, chivalrous way, of course."

Jack scoffed. "She wouldn't even look at you."

"She looked at you, and I'm a lot prettier than you are."

Jack laughed. "Now I know you're living in a Hollywood movie you're writing yourself. C'mon. While we're waiting for Ardana to shower and change, why don't you show me how you bomber ladies do a preflight?"

"You're on."

Jimmy and Lefkowicz came down the trail to the revetment as the rest of the Fort's crew finished their inspection of the airplane. Jack and Charlie were inside in the cockpit.

The RAAF truck with the tow attachment drove up and stopped in front of the bomber. Bellmon sat in the back of the truck, looking at the B-17. He waved when he saw Jimmy.

"Want a lift up to the 8th, Jimmy?" Bellmon asked.

"Sure."

Jack leaned out the window on the copilot's side of the bomber. "Ardana, tell whoever's officer of the day up there that I'll be along in twenty minutes or so."

"Yes, sir."

Lefkowicz helped Jimmy heave his bags into the bag of the truck and waved cheerfully as they drove off. Jimmy sat beside Bellmon and looked across the truck bed at Evans.

"Where'd you get the pistol, Jimmy?" Bellmon asked.

"Had it in my bag. Everybody else has one, so I thought what the hell."

Evans was running with sweat and breathing heavily. Big circles of sweat reached out from his armpits and down his back. His face was beaded with sweat, and he swiped at it irritably with a handkerchief.

"Get a nice shower?" Evans asked sourly.

Jimmy looked at him. "Got the blood off, anyway," he replied.

Evans started to say something else and stopped, looking away with a frown. "Hell of a place," he said as the truck crossed the end of the runway. "Look at all that wreckage. You'd think they'd clean it up."

Jimmy became aware again of the airplane remnants bulldozed into the bush on the side of the runway. He knew there had been some sort of airstrip here at Port Moresby since before the war, because air travel was one of the few ways you could get to the interior of the island of Papua New Guinea, and that was important to the Aussies because there was gold up there around some place called Wau. Jimmy remembered reading about that in National Geographic.

Jimmy looked down to the far end of the runway, which was clear. The B-26 had been pushed to one side. Crews filled in the bomb craters with rocks and dirt from a dump truck. Another truck came by with a load of what looked like long thin metal sections with holes punched in them, and Jimmy realized he was looking at PSP units – Pierced Steel Planking. They'd have the runway operational again pretty fast from the way they worked.

The truck wound slowly up the hill in second gear and stopped in front of a grass shack.

"What the hell?" growled Evans. "Where's the ops shack?"

Jimmy pointed to a crude hand-written sign over the entrance to the grass shack. It read "8th PURSUIT GROUP" on the top line and "OPERATIONS" on the bottom.

"This must be it," Jimmy said.

"You're kidding. This must be a joke."

Jimmy jumped out of the truck. Bellmon started throwing down bags as Evans climbed carefully down from the truck bed. One of the Aussies leaned out of the cab.

"All out?" he asked.

"I think we've got everything," Bellmon replied. "Thanks for the lift."

The Aussie smiled. "G'day, then."

The truck drove off down the hill.

Jimmy turned to look at the shack. The only hint of the modern was supplied by telephone wires and the clack of a typewriter coming from the dark interior. Otherwise it was just a grass shack with woven palm frond walls. The woven fronds didn't reach from the floor to the roof, but left a space, presumably for air to circulate.

"Well, here we are," said Evans sourly, wiping sweat from his face. "Welcome to paradise, New Guinea style."

A man in what seemed to be the local uniform of the day, cutoff trousers and shirt, stepped to the entrance. He wore captain's bars and pilot's wings on his shirt, with a .45 automatic in a shoulder holster. A long survival knife was hooked to the holster's strap. He lit a cigarette and then took notice of the three sweat-soaked lieutenants standing in front of the Ops shack.

"Who the hell are you guys?" the captain asked. He took a long drag on his cigarette.

Jimmy said, "I'm Ardana, sir, James T. We're looking for the operations officer."

"Why the fuck would you want to do that?"

"Ah, we're assigned to the 8th, sir. Replacements. Pilots."

Groves looked up at the sky and exhaled a cloud of cigarette smoke. "Oh, sweet bleeding Jesus. You guys are the replacements? Do you shave? Are you even old enough to know how to shave? Screw that. I don't know or care."

Captain Groves looked at Bellmon. "You. What's your name?"

"Bellmon, sir, Gerald B."

"Well, Bellmon, sir, Gerald B., how much time do you have in P-39s?"

"Nine and a half hours, sir."

Groves sighed and took another drag on his cigarette. "Nine and a half hours, sir. OK. How about the rest of you? Ardana, James T., you got any time in Airacobras? And what the hell is with that hogleg? Are you a cowboy or some such bullshit?"

"No, sir, I don't have any time in Airacobras, and I'm not a cowboy." Jimmy figured it wasn't time to point out that he'd been riding, roping and branding on the Ardana ranch since he turned thirteen. Groves wasn't talking about that kind of cowboy.

Evans took a step forward. "Evans, sir, Daniel H. I have ten hours in Airacobras."

"We're supposed to get five guys. Where's the other pilots?" he asked.

"Well, there were six of us on the plane," said Jimmy. "Two guys got killed."

Groves frowned. "Killed?"

"God damn, Captain, we were jumped by Jap Zeroes on the way in!" Evans said loudly. "Had dead guys lying all over us!"

"Is that right?" Groves replied. He looked at Bellmon, who nodded vigorously. "So you little lambs had it kind of rough on the way in?"

"Rough! We had bullets coming into the airplane and Jimmy here was throwing it around like ..."

"Stop," said Groves. He looked at Evans, who started to speak again. "Shut up, Lieutenant Evans."

Groves looked at Jimmy. "Ardana, right?" he asked.

"Yes, sir."

"You said six guys were on the airplane with you. That Hudson that leap-frogged over the B-26, that airplane?"

"Yes, sir."

"So there should be one more guy. Where is he?"

"Captain Davis went with his brother, Major Davis, who flies B-17s," Jimmy replied. "The captain asked me to tell the duty officer he'd be up as soon as Major Davis took off."

Groves looked hard at Jimmy for a moment. Then he nodded.

"What's that on your shirt?" he asked Evans.

"Blood."

"Oh? Yours?"

"No, sir."

"Lucky. Same with you, Bellmon?"

"Yes, sir."

"How come you're clean?" Groves asked Jimmy.

"Major Davis offered me a shower," Jimmy replied.

"No shit? Those guys from the 19th are pretty close with their creature comforts. What did you do to get on Charlie's good side?"

"I don't know, Captain."

"He landed the Hudson," Bellmon said. Evans scoffed and looked away.

"Is that right?" Groves asked Jimmy.

Jimmy nodded. "The guy flying the Hudson was shot up pretty bad, and Captain Davis took over the gun turret when the gunner was killed."

Groves nodded slowly. He took another drag on his cigarette.

"So you landed the Hudson?"

"Yes, sir."

A hint of a smile touched the captain's lips. "The Aussies are kind of nuts but I thought that landing was nuttier than usual," he said.

"Yes, sir."

"You do not impress me with your vocabulary, Ardana."

"Sorry, sir."

The hint of a smile faded from Groves' lips. He nodded. "It's OK," he said. Then he looked at Evans.

"Mr. Evans, I think you'll find in a very short while that being shot at by Jap Zeroes is not at all an unusual experience here at Seven-Mile. What do you intend to do if you're in a P-39 and a Zero is shooting at you?"

Evans looked at Groves. He didn't reply.

"Well?" Groves asked. "I'm waiting. Tojo won't. He'll just shoot your fat ass off, Evans."

Evans' mouth worked but he still didn't reply.

Groves walked up to Evans, who stood an inch taller and outweighed Groves by at least fifty pounds. The Captain stood three inches from Evans' nose, smoking his cigarette and locking eyes with the lieutenant.

"Christ Almighty," Groves said. "If you're that slow I don't know what can be done for you. I'll spell it out, though. You're going to have two choices. They're pretty simple choices, maybe simple enough even for you. You can fight, or you can die. Let's see how you handle it when it's your turn, schoolboy."

Groves held Evans' eyes for a moment longer. Then he turned abruptly and walked into the Operations shack.

Jimmy looked at Evans. "Shit, Evans, just keep your mouth shut for the rest of the day, will you?"

Evans reached out to shove Jimmy, who moved out of the way with a fluid, almost dancing motion. Jimmy's feet moved automatically, a little bit apart, right foot back, both hands clenching into fists and starting to come up to guard.

"Excuse me, gentlemen," said a new voice. It was dry and almost cynical in tone, the voice of a police officer, or an army sergeant, who is beyond any further surprise at the behavior of other humans. "Whenever you're ready, I'll take you in to the duty officer."

Jimmy stepped back and away from Evans but kept his eyes locked on Evans' chest.

"You and me, Ardana," Evans said. "Looks like you think you're some punkins with your fists but I'll squeeze you like a grape."

Bellmon looked from Evans to Ardana. Then he picked up his bags and walked up the two steps into the Operations shack. Ardana followed him. Evans stood in the dust outside the shack. The sergeant looked at him.

"You coming, sir?" the sergeant asked.

Inside the operations shack it was, if anything, hotter, but at least they were out of the blazing sun. Jimmy heard Evans stomping up the steps behind him.

Captain Groves sat on the edge of a desk made by laying a couple of planks across two cut-down 55-gallon drums. There was nothing on the desk except a hand-carved plaque reading "Officer of the Day." Groves flicked his eyes from Ardana to Evans but said nothing.

"If I could have your orders," the sergeant said. "And my name is Holmwood, by the way."

The lieutenants handed Sergeant Holmwood their orders. He handed them to a corporal who sat behind another oil-drum-and-plank desk. This desk had a small typewriter. The corporal took the orders and fitted a sheet of paper into his typewriter.

Groves lit another cigarette. "OK. Ardana, James T., you don't have any flight time in P-39s. Until we remedy that situation you're just a useless mouth to feed. Sergeant Holmwood, would you kindly take Mr. Ardana down to the flight line, find Chief Halloran, and ask the Chief to find an airplane for Mr. Ardana to sit in? And where shall we bunk these children?"

"What squadron, sir?"

"Better make it the 18th. Major Wolchek was under strength even before the raid yesterday."

"Yes, sir," said Holmwood. "In that case, let's put them in Tent 7."

"Has it been cleaned out?"

Jimmy saw a glance pass between Holmwood and Groves.

"Yes, sir," Holmwood replied.

"Good enough, then. You guys have any bags?"

"Yes, sir," Ardana replied. "They're outside."

"OK. Holmwood, have someone take their bags to Tent 7, will you?"

The sergeant nodded, turned to a private who was nearby. The private stood and walked out the door.

"Thank you, sergeant. Kids, your bags will be taken to Tent 7. Bellmon, Evans, why don't you head over there now?"

"Yes, sir," Bellmon said. He nudged Evans.

"Yes, sir," Evans said. The two of them turned and left.

Groves watched them go and sighed. "Two missions. Maybe. If they're lucky."

"Sir?" asked Ardana.

"Never mind. Sergeant Holmwood, take Ardana here and find Chief Halloran. He should be down on the flight line somewhere. Have him scare up an airplane for Ardana to sit in and have someone start teaching him the cockpit."

"Yes, sir," said the sergeant.

"Ardana, when you're done on the flight line someone can show you the way to the 18th Squadron's living area. Any questions?"

"No, sir."

"None? OK, take off."

"Come with me, then, Mr. Ardana," said Sergeant Holmwood.

Jimmy walked with Sergeant Holmwood down a dirt trail. Somewhere ahead of them there was the sound of an Allison engine starting.

"How much time do you have, sir, if I may ask?"

"People keep wanting to know that."

The sergeant looked at Jimmy for a moment before turning to look straight ahead again. Then he said, "A guy I know in intelligence told me that the average Jap pilot flying Zeroes has something like

800 hours of flying time. Before the war started about half of them, maybe, had some kind of combat experience in China."

Jimmy was silent for a moment as the raw adrenaline-fueled fear lacing his blood only two hours ago shuddered in his memory.

"I boxed in college," he said. "Experience and training count."

They walked a few more paces.

"Two hundred and four hours," Jimmy said.

"You might want to consider that the last half-hour counted the most," the sergeant said.

After a brisk ten-minute walk Jimmy saw the flight line. The P-39s were dispersed along a taxiway leading to the airstrip.

This was the first time Jimmy had even been close to a P-39. He'd seen them here and there during training, and from a distance on the flight line at Townsville, but had never even sat in one before or had a chance to read the pilot's manual.

"You and the two guys that came in with you will go to the 18th Squadron," Holmwood told Jimmy. "This is their dispersal area. If you'll look up there you'll see your quarters."

Holmwood waved his left hand back up the slope. Dispersed in and among the scrubby little trees were a collection of canvas tents and grass huts.

"Number 7 is the last tent on the left," Holmwood said as they continued towards the flight line. "Too bad none of the grass huts are empty. They attract spiders and snakes but the canvas tents get rotten and leaky pretty fast, or so the Aussies say."

Jimmy swatted at a mosquito. "What about snakes?"

"All kinds. Most of them poisonous. Oh, and then there's centipedes. They're poisonous too."

"Hell of a place to fight a war," Jimmy muttered.

"France was pretty, but we fought one hell of a war there, too, lieutenant," said Holmwood. He cupped his hands together and yelled. "Hey, Halloran!"

A tall, beefy man wearing a sun helmet turned to look at them. He stood at the corner of one of the revetments housing a P-39. An unlit cigar protruded from one corner of his mouth. His dirty coveralls were stained with grease. His face was pale, freckled and seamed. The eyebrows over the china-blue eyes were carrot-red.

"Jesus, Mary and Joseph," the man said deliberately as they approached. "You've come down from on high, have you, Holmwood? With a wee little lamb in trail?"

"A present just for you and the 18th Squadron, pal. Lieutenant Ardana here doesn't have any P-39 time. Captain Groves says get him started on cockpit drill."

"Hm," said Halloran. He narrowed his eyes and shifted his cigar from one side of his mouth to the other. "Did he, now. And I suppose soon enough the good Captain will desire that this young lamb shall actually fly the airplanes me and my boys have worked long and hard to repair."

"I hear that's what happens in a war," Holmwood said helpfully.

"Yes. Thank you, Holmwood." Holmwood turned and walked back up the slope.

Halloran looked at Jimmy. "First off let's understand one another. I'm a chief warrant officer. In the Army's scheme of things that means that you do not sass me, you do not give me orders, and I do not have to salute you. Nonetheless as you see I am still a working man. My job is to see that the airplane you will probably mistreat before you learn to fly it properly will in fact fly and in general perform as the manufacturer intended. That often requires that I and my lads perform miracles, but as you will learn, we do that as a matter of course. Now if you will follow me, Mr. Ardana, I'll show you what we have."

From down on the airstrip there was a roar of engines. Halloran turned to look and Jimmy followed his glance in time to see a B-17E begin its takeoff run. He could just make out the crow-hopping mustang painted on the bomber's nose.

The bomber lifted gracefully off the runway's scarred surface about two thirds of the way down, flying straight ahead until it cleared a small hill west of the runway, and then began a climbing left turn.

"This way, then, Mr. Ardana," said Halloran.

Charlie split his attention between flying the airplane and the engine gauges as he nursed the Fort into a climbing left turn west of the town of Port Moresby, straightening up on a heading of 090 towards the Coral Sea. Between him and the copilot, Lt. Mike Deering, the flight engineer, Sgt. Kim Smith, stood between their seats. He leaned against the turn, watching the gauges as closely as his pilot.

"Looks like the oil pressure on number three is holding steady, skipper," Smith said over the roaring engines.

Charlie nodded and eased the throttles back, adjusting the elevator trim for the climb to their patrol altitude of 18,000 feet. He scanned the instruments, made another adjustment to the elevator trim, and scowled a little when he could feel the trim tab wobble a bit.

His veteran B-17E was only a little over four months out of the Boeing factory, but that was a long time for an airplane in combat. Charlie knew that this airplane had had each engine replaced at least once. Her electrical system had been rewired. Most of her hydraulic lines were patched and a trifle leaky. Her right main tire was frayed from landing on rough, unpaved airstrips. Charlie was more than a little concerned about the patch job that had been done on the left inboard fuel tank, and the radio was iffy after three months in the tropics.

Four men had died aboard this airplane, and a dozen more had been wounded, including Charlie himself.

Even the air flowing over *Bronco Buster II*'s wings and fuselage didn't sound like a factory-new airplane. Her aluminum skin had been pierced by Japanese flak, machine-guns and 20-mm cannon. That meant a lot of patches with resulting induced drag on the airframe. As a result they were lucky to get 280 mph out of her at full throttle, where a new ship would have been a little over 300.

On the other hand, the engines were running smooth as silk at the moment. This ship had a ball turret in the belly instead of that goddamned useless remote turret the early "E" Forts came out with, which most of the crews removed after a couple of missions to save on weight and drag. The gunners at their stations had an ample supply of .50-cal. ammo, and in the bomb bay forward of the auxiliary gas tank there were four 500-lb. bombs.

As much as they could be, *Bronco Buster II* and her crew were ready for anything.

"Pilot to radio operator," Charlie called over the intercom.

"Sparks here, go ahead, Skip."

"You got those frequencies the Navy is supposed to be using?"

"Sure thing."

"I'd go ahead and start listening on those and the RAAF frequencies."

"Aye, aye, Skip."

Charlie looked over the nose of the bomber at the sky ahead. This morning at first light he heard the RAAF Catalinas based in Simpson Harbor crank up and fly out to the east, and the two remaining Hudsons went as well. He and his crew would have gone then too except for the oil pump failing on No. 3 engine during run-up. Their crew chief had just buttoned up the inspection covers after replacing the pump when the air raid warning sounded.

They went on oxygen above 10,000 feet and continued climbing into the blue sky. There were a few clouds well below them. To their left they could see the mountains of the Owen Stanley Range that ran down the center of New Guinea, dwindling down to foothills at Milne Bay on the eastern tip of the island.

Supposedly there would be a half-dozen other Forts flying out of Townsville to the east, searching for the Jap invasion fleet. Charlie grimaced under his oxygen mask. That "supposedly" was conditional on the availability of spare parts and the ingenuity of the bomber and maintenance crews working together with no cover on the tarmac under the Queensland sun.

As an operating base, Townsville had two virtues: it wasn't as bad as Seven-Mile and at least you could get beer.

They reached their patrol altitude of 18,000 feet and leveled out.

"Pilot to crew," Charlie called over the intercom. "Keep your eyes peeled. I hear there's Japs around here somewhere."

Chapter Three

"Congratulations, You're Boxcar Red Leader"

Jack stayed long enough to watch Charlie taxi out before taking the truck up to the 8th. On their way up he watched *Bronco Buster II* take off and climb out to the east before making a 180 and heading out to the Coral Sea. Jack was happy to see the takeoff went smoothly. The skin of the bomber's fuselage included a hell of a lot of patches and at least two of the engines had to be coaxed into starting and running smoothly. Charlie had looked out of the pilot's window at him, smiled, crossed his fingers and mouthed "Here goes nothin'!" before starting to taxi.

He wasn't surprised by the grass shack housing Group Operations. Improvised accommodations were situation normal out here. The shack looked as if a bunch of natives threw it up overnight and let it sit empty before the Air Corps moved in, but at least it had a wooden floor. He put his bags down by the entrance and got out his orders, but the man behind the Officer of the Day's desk rose and came over to shake hands.

"Jack Davis?" he asked.

"That's me."

"I'm Ed Groves. Hand your orders to Sergeant Holmwood there and come with me. Colonel Wagner wants to see you."

"I thought Colonel Smith was in command of the 8th," Jack said.

"He is."

Davis looked at Groves and raised an eyebrow. Groves returned the look without expression. Davis shrugged.

"Follow me," Groves said.

Groves ushered him past a woven palm frond partition into a space mostly occupied by an improvised desk. There was a phone on the desk, some papers and not much else. The man behind the desk looked up as Groves and Davis entered.

"Sir, this is Captain Davis," Groves said.

Lieutenant Colonel Boyd Wagner, known as "Buzz" because of his ability to fly low enough to strip the paint off a hangar roof, looked up from the papers on his desk.

"Hi, Jack," he said, standing up and offering his hand. "Glad to see you're still in one piece."

"Thank you, Colonel." Jack shook Wagner's hand and looked the colonel in the eye. The same wavy hair and little pencil of a moustache, but the cheeks were hollow and the eyes were sunken. Wagner looked old to be the youngest lieutenant colonel in the Army at 26.

"Colonel?" Wagner grinned, and for a bare moment looked his age. "You can still call me Boyd until you screw up," Wagner said, indicating a bamboo stool. "I don't expect that to happen."

"Hope not." Jack hadn't seen Boyd Wagner since they met in Brisbane. That was last January, when Wagner was still a captain. "How's the eye?"

Wagner grimaced. He'd been wounded in the left eye in the Philippines late last December and evacuated to Australia.

"Would you believe I got hit in the same eye last week at Lae? Stings like hell but I can still see out of it."

"Maybe you should stop leading with that eye," Jack said helpfully.

"Smartass," Wagner replied, grinning. He turned to Captain Groves. "Ed, would you call down to the flight line and ask Chief Halloran to get a couple of P-39s ready? Jack and I will talk for a bit and then I think we'll put in a little air work."

"Yes, sir."

Wagner waited until Groves left. Then he said, "I pulled a dirty trick on you, Jack, and I want to apologize."

"Jehosophat. You're behind my orders?"

"Yes."

Jack shook his head. "Why?"

"You never were too bright, Jack, but that shouldn't be hard even for you to figure out. Let's put it like this. It's not just those four Jap flags I hear you're entitled to paint on your airplane now. It's a little matter of experience. Hell, you were part of Squeeze Wurtsmith's outfit in Darwin. How many flight leaders and element leaders did he inherit from the 17th Pursuit?"

Jack didn't miss the shadow that came and went over Wagner's face. Wagner commanded the 17th Pursuit in the Philippines, and the outfit that went to Java was also the 17th, staffed with veterans of Wagner's old squadron, even if its full name was 17th Pursuit Squadron (Provisional).

There were plenty of guys still fighting in the Philippines from the original 17th Pursuit.

"A half-dozen, at least," Jack said quietly. "Allison Strauss and Walt Coss. Dave Malone. Me. Among others."

Wagner nodded. "I know the 49th is defending Darwin against Jap air raids, but I could sure as hell use some of that experience right here. Do you know how many combat veterans I had last week when I led these boys up here?"

"You?"

"That's right. Me. So I hope you'll excuse me when I heard you were sort of headed this way, and I talked General Brett into letting me have you for a couple of weeks."

"Crap. I'll probably get another damned case of jungle fever before then and you'll have to send me home anyway."

"I heard about that, too. Be straight with me, Jack. Did you talk those damned Australian quacks in Darwin into letting you out of the hospital too soon?"

"I'm fine, sir."

"That isn't exactly what I asked you. Look. About 45 minutes from now you and I are going to wring out a couple of P-39s. I don't want you passing out in a tight turn and going in because you don't have enough blood in your veins to supply what you call a brain. I can't afford to lose the airplane and I can't afford to lose you. Not that way, at least."

"Boyd, the RAAF flight surgeon cleared me for duty without limitations."

"Yeah? OK, then, you'd both better be right. I don't know about you, but I've learned to care about two things since last December. Can you fight? Can you fly? I care a little less about how well you fly than how well you fight because I knew a lot of hot pilots who couldn't fight, and now they're dead. You understand?"

"Yes, sir."

Wagner nodded. "Look, Jack, you did pretty well in my squadron in the Philippines. Hell, we saved each other's asses twice, and I was there when you got your first two Zeroes. I hear you got one in Java, and another one with the 49th, so I know you can still fight. You're also here, which means you haven't run out of luck yet. Now I have kind of a problem in the 18th Squadron, and it's the same old song we've been hearing since last December. We get these kids out of flight school and evidently the Air Corps thinks we can stuff them in the cockpit of a P-40 or a P-39 and send them up against Zeros without undue losses. You and I both know that's a crock of shit." Wagner looked down at his desk for a moment. He picked up the pipe on his desk and started to fill it. "That's the problem with the 18th. They don't have a lot of experience and the losses we took at Lae last week were all in that squadron. The CO, Major Wolchek, is a good pilot and a good leader but I think he could use a good flight commander. That's going to be you."

Jack started to speak but closed his mouth. Wagner grimaced.

"Yeah, you were a green kid all of six months ago. I know. I was there. And the truth is you had what, two missions in the Philippines before you cracked up that P-40? Then maybe three weeks in Java? You were a flight leader that whole time. Bud Sprague was a good friend of mine, so I knew him pretty well. He might have made you a flight leader to see what kind of stuff you had, but if you didn't show him you were good enough you wouldn't have stayed a flight leader."

"It's not me I'm worried about."

"Sure. You're worried about the other guys. I get that. I worry about it every single day. Get used to it, Jack. You've got what it takes to be a leader. The Air Corps will use that, make no mistake."

"I didn't do such a great job in Java."

"Oh, grow up and stop feeling sorry for yourself! Maybe you didn't do a good job. When we hit Lae the other day I lost three guys. I got a couple of Japs but so what? That's still three letters I have to write to wives and mothers. So maybe I didn't do such a great job, either, or maybe that's just the way it is if the other side does their level best to kill you. Like it or not, sometimes they'll succeed. Always more often than we like. Not to mention that we're still learning this job as we go along."

Jack grimaced. "I feel like I should be better."

"You're damned right you should. Me too. But it isn't going to happen overnight. And even in peacetime this isn't the safest job in the world. Your buddy Roy Chant wasn't the only guy we lost in training."

Jack sighed and nodded. "OK, Boyd. I get it."

Wagner nodded. "Fair enough. Speaking of learning the job, I want to talk to you about Java and what you saw with the 49th. We won't do that right now, and..." Wagner hesitated. "Bud Sprague and I talked a lot about tactics. Anything you can remember about what he said on the subject, I want to know about. You understand?"

Of course I do, Jack thought. *Sprague was your friend. I'll tell you everything I can think of.*

"Officially, Colonel Sprague is missing in action," Jack said softly. "I saw at least one parachute, that morning at Den Pasar. Maybe it was him."

"Maybe. All that means is at best he's running around the jungle with the natives, dodging Jap patrols." Wagner took a deep breath. "I read the available reports from Java, not that a lot came back. Sprague was supposed to have a whole pursuit group, and he ended up with a squadron at best. So you guys got thrown in piecemeal, four or five at a time, operating against unrealistic odds. Not only that but for every guy like you with some experience, you had a half-dozen kids just out of flight school. The brass said it had to be tried. Well, that's up to them. So it's like this, Jack. I know you got chewed up pretty bad. A lot of us have, though, and I don't have time to hold your hand. Can you do the job?"

Jack took a deep breath and nodded. "I can do it, Boyd."

"OK. Good. Now what's in that bag you're guarding so carefully?"

"Booze. Cigars. Similar contraband."

"I don't remember you as much of a boozer. Change your mind about that?"

"I went on the grog with some Aussies last night. Other than that I've been a model citizen. This is a present from the RAAF, you might say."

Wagner nodded and leaned back in his chair. Then he leaned forward again.

"You had some time in P-39s, didn't you? I remember Ed Dyess saying something about that, when I shanghaied you out of his squadron."

"Yes, sir. I flew the D-model in the Carolina maneuvers last year before I came out to the Philippines."

"Get pretty familiar with the airplane?"

"So-so. I had fifty hours in it, more or less."

"Right. The main thing to remember is that the little whore hardly gives you any warning when she stalls, and when she stalls she likes to spin and then she's tricky to get out of a spin. You remember that little trick with the rudder?"

Jack thought for a moment. "She likes to oscillate in a spin. You wait until the rate slows down and put in opposite rudder."

"Ever have to do it?"

"Once. It was exciting."

"I bet." Wagner leaned forward. "The P-39 has an Allison engine like the P-40, which means that above 17,000 feet she won't climb for shit. On the other hand you may recall the roll rate is pretty good and in a dive she drops like a rock. Maybe not quite as enthusiastically as a P-40, but she'll wind up over 450 mph when she gets going."

"They ever work the kinks out of that 37-mm cannon?" Jack asked. "I remember you got four or five rounds out of it and the damned thing would jam."

"Four or five rounds? You must've had a good armorer. We're lucky to get three out of ours. Regardless, you get in close and one hit with the cannon is all you need."

Jack nodded. Wagner grimaced, looked down at his desk and looked back up again.

"For a couple of different reasons I'm being pushed to hit Lae again. You know about the Jap invasion fleet?"

"The RAAF guy we flew in with, before we tangled with those Zeroes, told me he was supposed to stay up here and join the hunt for the Jap fleet."

"What about Charlie?"

"He said pretty much the same thing."

"Well, the Japs are probably going to try to take Port Moresby. Even if they call that off they could try and hit us with a carrier strike in the next couple of days. That's why we're going to Lae. They're putting the pressure on us with bomber raids from Rabaul, and their fighter escorts are based at Lae. If we can cut those bastards down a little it's less we have to face when the Jap Navy gets here."

Jack nodded. He'd figured that angle for himself.

"That mission is on for the day after tomorrow. So this afternoon I'm gonna put your ass in a P-39, like I said, and do my best to turn it inside out. I need you out there, Jack."

"Yes, sir."

"And now for the good news. Those kids that came in with you are going to be your problem, since I'm sending them to the 18th with you. If any of those kids can land a P-39 without bending it they're going to Lae. They'll be all yours."

Jack thought about that. "Those kids aren't just green, Boyd, they're still damp from the birth. I'll go but I advise you to leave those kids here or you've got a better than even chance of losing them. All of them. Christ, one of those infants doesn't even have any time in P-39s."

"It's what we've got, Jack. Let's hope they're a little better than you think. You can report to Wolchek at the 18th after we fly. Head on down to the flight line and tell Halloran I'll be along in 20-30 minutes. Now get the hell out of here, if I don't get on this damned paperwork it's going to multiply like flies."

"Yes, sir." Jack started to stand to attention and salute, but Wagner already had his head down, reaching for a pen and looking at a form on his desk.

Jack went to the outer office. Ed Groves nodded at him.

"I've got a guy here to take you down to the flight line," Groves said.

"Thanks," said Jack. "How about a parachute and a helmet and all that handy stuff?"

"That'll be waiting for you at the airplane."

"OK."

Groves nodded at a private. "This way, sir," the private said, standing up.

"Lead on," Jack replied.

He paused on the veranda for a moment, looking out over the airstrip. Like Tiny said, you could see the macadam paving, but it looked patchy and dirty and worn. Maybe that wasn't surprising, given how often the Japs bombed it. There was a hill near the west end of the runway, uncomfortably close to the approach pattern. Scrubby, dusty-looking trees were scattered around. Revetments were spaced along taxiways leading to the airstrip. Airplanes were visible, P-39s and B-26s, with a few B-17s and a scattering of RAAF Hudsons. To the north the land rose up to the mountains, wreathed in blinding-white clouds. The slopes of the mountains were a deep dark green. As he stood watching an engine started up. Jack took a deep breath of the hot, humid air.

Home.

"Whenever you're ready, sir," said the private.

Chief Halloran took Jimmy to a revetment containing a P-39 that had every panel and inspection port off of it. The engine, the breech of the 37-mm cannon, the propeller gearbox, and the ammo feed trays for the wing guns; all of them were open to the bright glare of the tropical sun overhead. There wasn't any shade to speak of except for the dubious dappling of a camouflage net stretched on poles at the four corners.

"Simmons!" Halloran called.

A sunburned young man, slender, dark-haired, stripped to the waist, wearing shorts, boots, a web belt with a holstered pistol and a canteen, and a Brooklyn Braves baseball hat, crawled out from under the after fuselage. He looked at Halloran and then at Jimmy before replying.

"Yah, Chief."

"This thing going to be able to fly in the morning?"

"In the morning, yah. 100-hour inspection's almost done. Got to do a little sheet metal work still."

"OK, good enough. This is Lieutenant Ardana. He's going to do some cockpit drill and I think we'll let him have this airplane when you get it ready."

Simmons nodded slowly, wiping his hands on a greasy rag. "OK, Chief."

"Right, then. Anything you need to know about this airplane, Mr. Ardana, you ask Simmons. He's one of my best crew chiefs." Halloran smiled at them both and walked back up the flight line.

Jimmy Ardana looked at the P-39. A big yellow number 13 was painted on the nose and on the cockpit door was the figure of a grinning green gremlin, middle digit of his right hand aloft and extended.

"It seemed like the only thing to do, Lieutenant," said Simmons. "Take Fate by the horns, you see."

Jimmy hid his grin. His grin was toothy, just like the gremlin's, even if his teeth weren't quite so pointed.

"Well, we'll see how it comes along, Sergeant," he said. "If it doesn't bring us luck maybe we can figure out something different."

Simmons looked down at the lieutenant with approval. Not all young officers would have found that little joke amusing.

Jimmy looked up to ask Simmons a question and stood rooted to the spot, eyes going wide as he beheld what he could only think of as an apparition. It was a man, a native from his black skin and apparel. The man was shorter than Ardana's own five-foot-seven. He was dressed in a white wraparound garment and leaned on a staff of black wood. A dressed leather pouch hung from a leather belt around his waist. Through the lobe of his right ear there was a bone-white earring. Ardana had the uneasy feeling that it was actually made of human bone. Clearly the man was old; wrinkles crisscrossed his face, gathering around the corners of the mouth and eyes. The eyes were dark and looked directly at Ardana from under bushy pale gray eyebrows. The man's hair was done up in an elaborate hairdo, making his head look twice as big.

"Christ Almighty," Ardana breathed.

Simmons turned quickly but relaxed when he saw the native. "Aw, you don't need to worry about him none, Mr. Ardana. That's Evarra."

"Evarra?" Jimmy asked.

"Me Evarra," the native said gravely, coming forward. He looked straight at Jimmy the whole time. There was no recognizable expression on the old man's face. He stopped two feet in front of Jimmy and stood there, staring into his eyes. Finally he nodded.

"Youpela pailat?" Evarra asked. His voice was soft and melodious. "Youpela balus man?"

"That's pidgin English, Lieutenant," Simmons supplied. "He just wants to know if you're a pilot. Balus, that's pidgin for airplane."

"Oh. I see." Ardana nodded. "Yes, I'm a pilot."

Evarra nodded, continuing to look into Ardana's eyes. Then he nodded again, turned around and walked away without another word.

Jimmy turned to his crew chief.

"What the hell was that all about?" he asked.

Simmons scratched his bristly cheek. "Couldn't say, Lieutenant. Evarra pops up every now and then, looking things over. I think he's just curious. Father Simpson, the group chaplain, is in well with the local missionaries and he says Evarra is a great man among the natives, what they call a sanguma man. Sort of like black magic."

"He's a magician?"

"Well, not like Harry Houdini or Thurston the Great. These folks believe in that stuff, just like me sainted grandmother believed in The Gentry."

"The Gentry?"

"Well, the Little People, though no Irishman would call them that. It's bad luck."

Ardana took his eyes from the spot in the jungle where Evarra disappeared. He looked at the grinning gremlin and the big yellow 13 on the fuselage of his airplane. "Well, we sure don't need any more of that, do we?"

Simmons grinned. "No, sir."

Jack Davis recognized Chief Halloran when he got down to the HQ Flight area. He had met Halloran once, years ago, and knew that the old warrant officer began his Air Corps career doping fabric on SPADs with the 94th Aero Squadron in France when he was 17, having lied about his age to enlist for the War to End All Wars. Halloran knew Jack and Charlie's father, who had flown SPADs with the 94th. Over the years Halloran busted wrenches on good airplanes and bad, in all kinds of weather, from the Aleutians to the Canal Zone. Halloran had a devout, unshakeable belief, shared in common with most mechanics, that all pilots were insane and their only wish was to take up his beloved flying machines, turn them inside out, pop the rivets, stretch the fabric, run out the oil and the coolant, and then expect him to have everything ready and in impeccable condition for their next f.

But Halloran, like most mechanics, recognized that there were pillightots, and there were pilots, and he had served with Jack's father in the last war.

"She may not look like much, Captain, but she's a pretty good ship," Halloran said, looking benevolently down at Jack.

"Jesus, Chief, are you sure you aren't going senile? That god-damn piece of tin was at the Carolina Maneuvers in 1941. I can still see the blue cross. No one bothered to paint it out before shipping it over here."

"The airframe is a little beat up," Halloran acknowledged. "But look at this."

Halloran nodded to the airplane's crew chief, who unbuttoned the cover over the engine. In the P-39, unlike more conventional airplane, the engine was in the fuselage behind the pilot to make room for the 37-mm cannon in the nose of the airplane where the engine would normally be. The cannon fired through the propeller hub. The drive shaft from the engine traveled beneath the pilot's seat and between his legs to turn a gearbox in the nose.

Davis could see from where he stood near the left wingtip that the V-1710 Allison engine was in good shape. He walked closer to inspect the engine. The shiny parts, the lack of grease on the block, the clean wiring …

"That's a brand-new engine," he said.

"Yes indeed. Brand-new, and slow-timed. It was in an airplane whose wing got blown off in yesterday's air raid. This here airplane's engine went to engine heaven prematurely, having taken a 20-mm cannon shell in the block. But she stayed together long enough to bring the airplane home, and what more can you ask of an engine?"

"That's plenty," Jack agreed.

He began to walk around the airplane.

The P-39 was a neat-looking little machine, just as he remembered. The visibility out of the canopy was great in all directions; a good thing in combat. He ran his fingers lightly over the drum-taut fabric control surfaces on the elevator.

There were freshly doped and painted patches in the elevator fabric and unpainted aluminum patches in the aft fuselage. When the former engine was mortally wounded the rest of the airplane had been damaged as well, mostly by Jap 7.7-mm machine guns bullets.

"Lt. Fritsch took a couple of slugs in the right leg, but he'll be OK," Halloran said. "The other 20-mm put some splinter holes in the coolant tank and dinged some control lines but we've replaced the tank and the lines."

"I thought you guys had a problem with spare parts."

"We do. But there's a couple airplanes out there that can't be patched up this easy, so they became our supply depot."

Jack grimaced and continued his walk-around.

Firepower was one thing the P-39 had for sure, but even that came at a price. It carried four .30-caliber machine guns in the wing, two .50-caliber machine guns in the nose, and a 37-mm cannon firing through the propeller hub. One major problem with all that firepower was that the ballistics of each projectile were wildly different, and that made picking a point of convergence for aiming nearly impossible. The .50s in the nose were synchronized to fire through the propeller, which slowed their rate of fire, and when you pulled the trigger you'd better be wearing your oxygen mask or the propellant fumes would choke you, because the gun breeches were inside the cockpit. As for the .30s in the wings, well, they'd be useful for strafing troops in the open. They were useless against another airplane except at spitball range.

Jack came around the nose to the left side of the airplane, where the crew chief had the access door open to the gun compartment. The 37-mm cannon could blow a Zero to bits with a single hit, but it only carried thirty rounds and tended to jam after 3 or 4 shots. But the weapon was clean and lubricated just enough to work without enough oil to gum up in the cold at higher altitudes.

"They ever fix the feed problem on this bastard?" he asked Halloran, indicating the cannon.

"A lot of that you can eliminate by careful loading, but it's still kind of delicate," the Chief replied. "You want some advice?"

"Sure."

"You got to shoot at something, just do what that Frenchie, what the hell was his name? Nungesser, yeah, you just do what Nungesser did back in the Great War."

"Stick the guns in the other guy's cockpit and pull the trigger," said Jack with a nod.

"That's right," Halloran said, with a nod of his own. "That way, you don't got to worry about the ballistics or much of anything else. Even those peashooters in the wings will do the job."

Jack nodded. His first kill had been a lucky deflection shot, more desperation than skill. On the second he closed to twenty yards, close enough to count rivets, before opening fire. For just an instant a vivid image of the Zero's pilot, looking over his shoulder at Jack as the bullets struck his airplane, flashed before Jack. There was a *splat!* of red inside the cockpit as the Zero pilot's head disappeared, and a gush of flame as Jack's tracers ignited the Zero's fuel.

Jack blinked. Halloran was looking at him, but not with any question in his eyes.

"That's good advice, Chief," Jack said. "Got a parachute handy?"

The crew chief, a sandy-haired kid named Terraine wearing cut-off shorts, boots, an Aussie bush hat and nothing else, reached inside the pilot's compartment and brought out a seat-type parachute. Jack nodded and reached for the harness, carefully adjusting the crotch straps, tightening the chest straps, making sure of the D-ring and the quick-release fittings. Then he hobbled up on the wing, crawled through the door, and sat inside the cockpit.

All the familiar smells, the odors of hot aluminum, gasoline, oil, hydraulic fluid, dried blood and oh yes, eau de vomit, overlaid with a little bit of mildew and hot wiring and tubes from the radio set behind his armored seat, all of them made themselves at home in his nostrils. Jack took his time, touching the switches, calling them up from memory until he was confident he remembered what went where. He reviewed the start procedure with Terraine, going over it twice until he asked for the Form 1 and signed it. He closed the automobile-style door and rolled down the window.

"Be sure the ignition switch is in OFF position, sir, and we'll pull the prop through a couple times," Terraine said.

"OK, ignition OFF," Jack answered. Terraine gestured. The two ground crewmen pushed on the propeller blades in relays until the propeller made two complete revolutions.

Jack went through the rest of the checklist. Gun switches: OFF. Flap control switch: OFF. Generator switch: ON. Parking brake: ON. Jack rested his feet on the rudder pedals. They seemed a bit short so he lengthened them with the adjusting lever on the outboard side of the pedals. Then he checked the rudders, ailerons and elevators. Everything moved freely as he watched.

"Your guys clear?" Jack asked Terraine.

"Yes, sir," said Terraine. Jack had seen the ground crew move clear before he asked. He nodded in satisfaction when he saw Terraine actually look before answering.

"OK, let's start that pretty new engine."

The checklist: Battery to ON. When he threw that switch small rising whines began behind the instrument panel as gyroscopes spun up. Then ignition switch to BOTH. The fuel gauges read full. Jack turned the fuel selector switch to the reserve tank. Mixture control lever to IDLE CUT-OFF, crack the throttle open. Fuel pump to ON, three strokes of primer to the engine, fuel pump to OFF.

The energizer pedal was by his right heel. He pushed down on the pedal with his heel. There was a whine from the engine that started low and built up as the starter flywheel increased RPMs. When the whine leveled out Jack pushed the pedal forward with his toe. Behind him the Allison engine coughed once. The propeller twitched. Then the engine coughed, spat and rumbled. Jack opened the mixture control to Automatic Rich. The airframe shook and shimmied with the engine vibration. Jack added some throttle and the engine evened out and began to sing that even regular one-note song.

While he waited for the oil and coolant temperatures to move into the operating range he cycled the flaps, watching the indicator set in the upper surface of the left hand outer wing panel, making a note to remind his new kids that it was just like the AT-6, only in a different place.

He watched the oil pressure and cylinder head temperatures climb into the operating range, keeping an eye on the engine RPM indicator. He was aware of Halloran and Terraine on the wing, looking at the engine gauges with him.

"What do you think?" he yelled to Halloran over the roar of the engine and the blattering wind of the propeller.

"She looks good," Halloran yelled back. "You've been flying P-40s, right? Engine overheat is a worse problem in this airplane than in the P-40. Soon as you get off the ground throttle back a little and run level to let it cool off some before you climb out. You'll see what I mean when you taxi this bitch. It's 97 degrees and 90 percent humidity out here, Captain. That's hell on men and worse on Allison engines."

Jack nodded. Halloran clapped the canopy twice for luck and climbed off the wing, walking to the back of the fighter and then left out of the propwash. Terraine stayed an instant longer, watching the gauges, and then nodded to Jack and followed Halloran. Jack leaned out the window and signaled to the ground crew to remove the chocks.

When they backed away displaying the chocks he rolled up the window and turned on the radio.

"Seven Mile Tower from Army Two Four Seven, ready to taxi for local familiarization flight."

"Roger, Two Four Seven, cleared to taxi to the active and hold for Brickbat Leader."

"Roger, Seven Mile, Two Four Seven is taxiing to the active."

As he went down the dirt taxiway he saw what Halloran meant about the engine overheating. By the time he got to the active runway his engine temps were uncomfortably high and still rising.

Wagner turned onto the taxiway behind him. Jack heard him call over the radio.

"Seven Mile, this is Brickbat Leader with a flight of two, local familiarization."

"Roger, Brickbat Leader. Cleared for takeoff."

Without further ado Wagner taxied onto the runway and began his takeoff roll. Jack stayed on his right wing, just out of the dirt and dust, one hand on the throttle, the other on the stick, feeling the airframe in the seat of his pants. He remembered the thing about the P-39, you just had to think about it and the airplane would do it. So when the nose of Wagner's airplane lifted off the ground he thought about it and his own lifted off a fraction of a second later. He leveled off when Wagner did at 100 feet, tucking it in tight off Wagner's right wingtip. They screamed down what was left of the runway like that and as they crossed the threshold Wagner began a gentle right turn.

Jack followed Wagner and the airplane came back to him as he did, like the way it needed only the gentlest of pressures on the controls. The controls were delicate and balanced to a hair, a virtue and a vice all in one. The good pilot could make the airplane talk. The average pilot would be all over the sky.

"Two from Lead," Wagner radioed.

"Go ahead, Lead," Jack replied.

"We'll climb to six on a course of three five zero. Then we'll see how much you remember about flying this airplane."

"Roger, Lead," Jack said. He snugged his P-39 a few feet closer to Wagner's airplane, stopping only when he felt the turbulence off Wagner's right wingtip tapping his own left wingtip.

"Ooookay, Two," Wagner drawled. "Keep it tight."

Jack moved in another foot. "How's that, Lead?"

"Guess it'll have to do, Two."

They flew like that for a few minutes, passing through four thousand feet. The air grew noticeably cooler but still warm. Jack sweated freely inside his flight suit and the unfamiliar straps of the seat and parachute harness found novel places to chafe and wear his skin as a result. But here it is, he thought, the sun, the wind rushing over the canopy, the roar of the engine and that damned banshee screaming from the propeller gearbox, the cotton-ball clouds in the endless blue of the sky, the green and dun earth falling away below, and the strange unfamiliar peaks of the Owen Stanley Range slowly growing closer to starboard. He looked around when he could, knowing he would never see any of this for the first time again.

They reached six thousand feet.

"All right, Two, let's see what you got," said Wagner. Quite abruptly he stood his P-39 on its left wing and pulled into a hard left turn. Jack was right with him, grinning.

Chapter Four

"A mother hen and three chicks"

Jimmy watched the two P-39s accelerate down the runway. They lifted off in formation and their gear came up almost as if one pilot flew both airplanes. The P-39s stayed low enough while their gear came up that dust from their propwash flew out behind them. Number Two tucked it in even tighter as the pursuits climbed to clear the trees at the end of the runway.

"Sensitive to pitch," Jimmy thought to himself.

From the apparent ease with which Col. Wagner and Capt. Davis took their P-39s off the ground one never would have known it.

Jimmy became aware that his right hand was twitching and his toes in his shoes pressed into the dirt, ever so slightly, on imaginary controls. He watched the P-39s climb away, drinking in every detail of their flight.

As the roar of engines faded with distance Jimmy realized Danny Evans stood next to him.

"Jesus, Ardana," Evans said. He mopped his streaming face. "This place is hell."

"Won't hurt you to sweat off a few pounds."

"I've always been this size. This is my training weight."

Jimmy looked at the big beefy guy, standing there pouring sweat under the equatorial sun.

"If you say so, Evans."

"Wish I had a nice cold Coke."

Jimmy wiped the sweat from his eyes with his khaki sleeve and peered up at the sun almost directly overhead, a pale, pale-yellow white, pouring intense light and heat down on them and the airstrip. It was hard to imagine a Coca-Cola in a frosty, sweat-beaded glass, tinkling with ice, in the cool interior of a soda shop on a late Saturday afternoon.

"Yeah," said Jimmy. "Good luck with that. I bet the nearest refrigeration plant is back in Australia. But it's always cold at 17,000 feet."

"What are you talking about? Swiping a plane just to cool down a Coke? That's against regulations."

Jimmy looked at him again. "Are you really an officious prick, Evans, or is this just an off day for you?"

"Fuck you, Jimmy."

"That's Ardana to you, Evans. Why don't you keep standing in the sun for awhile? If you got sunstroke maybe they'd send you back to Australia. And if you tell me 'fuck you' again I'm going to put my fist down your throat."

Evans looked at Jimmy for a long moment, then stalked back to his airplane, where he could be heard yelling at the crew chief.

Jimmy shook his head. "Loser," he muttered.

"What's that, Jimmy?" asked Bellmon, walking up.

Jimmy indicated Evans. "Him," he said. "He's sweating like a pig and he stinks like one."

Bellmon looked over at Evans, who was pointing to some imagined flaw on the cowling of his P-39.

Jimmy frowned, still looking at Evans. "Looks to me like he's gonna piss his ground crew off. That's not smart. My guys seem pretty good and I definitely want them on my side."

"They're enlisted men," Bellmon said tentatively. "Won't they just follow orders?"

Jimmy looked at Bellmon. Finally he said, "I'm sure they will, Gerry. What are you down here for?"

"I thought I'd see if there was a spare airplane. You know, sit in the cockpit."

Jimmy nodded slowly. "Go find Chief Halloran and ask nice, Gerry. That's my advice."

Jack Davis taxied along, relaxed and alert, with a little smile on his lips. While watching the engine gauges he played the flight back over in his mind, particularly the rat-racing. Neither he nor Wagner gained a decisive advantage over the other and Jack, in the process of wringing out the P-39 against an experienced adversary, learned new things about himself and about the airplane.

Wagner, from that very first tight turn, had shown him that you had to feel the airplane when you sucked that stick back in the turn. Jack knew that, in his mind, but in that first turn he had pulled the stick back a shade too far, enough to feel the first faint judder of an accelerated stall. The first turn, then, taught him the most. The P-39 was an airplane you had to fly smart; you couldn't rely solely on the seat of your pants. You had to *know*, ahead of time, what the airplane would and wouldn't do and when it was about to do it. Jack was sure he had a lot left to learn about the airplane and he considered that a good thing. The day you stopped learning about an airplane was the day you quit flying in it or it killed you.

He reached the 18th's dispersal area and taxied past a revetment where the ground crew was assiduously polishing a P-39. A lieutenant in a new although sweat-stained flight suit stood watching them, hands on his hips, and from the way his lips flapped was either shouting advice or abuse. Jack recognized the lieutenant as Evans.

Jack taxied to his own revetment, three bays down. Chief Halloran and Sergeant Terraine were waiting for him. He shut the airplane down, safed the gun switches and the controls, and let Terraine help him out of the airplane.

"Terraine, give me a minute, will you? I need to talk to Halloran. Airplane did good. Engine purred like a sewing machine. We'll go over the details when I get back."

Jack unbuckled his parachute and left it in the seat pan. Then he jumped off the wing. Halloran came to meet him.

"What's the problem, Captain?" the line chief asked.

"Who's the crew chief on number 28, that's three bays down?"

"28? That's Joe Forrest. He's a good kid and so's his crew. Why?"

"Not the kind of crew chief to let his airplane get dirty? I mean, within reason?"

"Hard to keep 'em shiny and bright in this hole, but no, sir, Forrest is a good kid, conscientious. He might be as good as Terraine here."

Jack nodded. "OK. That's what I needed to know. Terraine, I'll be right back."

"Yes, sir," Terraine replied.

Halloran fell in step with Jack as he strode down the taxiway. "Captain, you seem like a man with a mission."

"You got it, Chief,"

"Something about Forrest?"

"Probably not. I think this is more my problem than yours, but we'll see."

They passed Ardana and Bellmon, who straightened up.

"Come with me," Jack said to them, and they fell in behind Jack and Halloran, exchanging a puzzled look as they did.

Evans could be heard describing the shortcomings of Sergeant Forrest, the armorer and the assistant crew chief as Jack approached. He paused for a moment. Evans had his back to them.

After a moment Jack glanced at Halloran. The older man had a certain look on his face Jack had learned to recognize, the look of a veteran, senior enlisted man dealing with a very young, very inexperienced and possibly slightly stupid second lieutenant.

"Lieutenant Evans," Jack said.

Evans stopped his tirade and turned around. When he saw it was Jack he came to a position that might be thought of as standing upright, if not exactly as attention.

"Yes, Captain?" Evans said.

"Lieutenant Evans, you are assigned to my flight. I am your flight commander." Jack turned to look at Ardana and Bellmon. "Who's got a half-dollar or a quarter?"

Bellmon shook his head. Ardana reached into a pocket and took out an old silver dollar with a dent in its center.

Jack hardly looked at it. "Jimmy, you're my element leader. We're going to toss for our wingmen. You ready?

"Ah, yes, sir."

"Heads you get Bellmon, tails you get Evans."

"Now wait a minute!" said Evans. Bellmon looked at Jack, confused.

Jack flipped the dented old coin into the air, caught it, and turned it upside down on his left hand, covered with his right. He lifted his hand.

"Heads," Jack said. "OK. The squadron call sign is Boxcar. We're Red flight. That makes me Boxcar Red Leader. Evans, you're Red Two, and Bellmon, you're Red Four. Jimmy, you're Boxcar Red Three. Any questions?"

Ardana hesitated before he spoke. "No, sir."

"Bellmon? Evans? No? Good!" Jack turned to Chief Halloran. "Chief, d'you think you can scare up some airplanes for us?"

"I believe so, Captain."

Jack nodded. "Thanks, Chief. Bellmon and Evans here have some time in P-39s, so I'm going to start with them. What can Mr. Ardana fly?"

Halloran nodded. "He can use the Colonel's airplane."

"Wagner won't mind?"

"No, sir."

"All right." Jack turned to look at his lieutenants. "Bellmon, Evans. You two are coming up with me as soon as Chief Halloran can get a couple of ships ready for you. Go get your flight gear together and be back here in what, Chief?"

"Fifteen minutes should be plenty, Captain."

"Very well, then, fifteen minutes."

"Yes, sir," Bellmon said. He turned to leave and hesitated when he saw that Evans didn't move.

Evans stood staring at Jack, who returned the stare without expression. Evans opened his mouth once or twice. His face was red.

"Now wait a minute, Captain! How come Ardana gets to be an element leader? He doesn't even have any time in a P-39!"

"Well, that's easy, Evans. You sat in your chair in that Hudson while Ardana saved our asses." Jack turned to Ardana. "Ardana, don't be offended, but I would have preferred someone a bit more experienced for my Number Three. Seems there isn't anybody. I think you can handle the job and I'm going to be right behind you, helping you learn the ropes."

"Yes, sir," Ardana said.

"We'll go up after I finish with these two. Halloran will show you the airplane you'll fly today."

"Yes, sir."

"This way, Mr. Ardana," said Halloran, and the two of them walked off down the taxiway.

Jack looked from Evans to Bellmon. "Gerry, why don't you go along with Chief Halloran?"

"Yes, sir," Bellmon replied. He turned and walked away.

Then he turned to Evans.

"OK, Evans, I know you're not through. Spill it now because you won't get another chance."

"So I sat in my seat! I've never been in combat before!"

"Neither had Ardana. Don't make excuses. Some guys it takes awhile. But we don't have a hell of a lot of time and right now Ardana looks like a better bet to me."

Evans' mouth worked for a moment. Then he said, "And we can't just go into combat like that! Hell, don't we get to ease into it? Or at least get a little more orientation than that?"

"Get this through your head, lieutenant," Jack said. "Day after tomorrow you'll fly your first combat mission. Sorry you don't get to go a little better prepared. None of us were too well prepared back in the Philippines, or in Java, either. Too bad. Now, any other problems?"

"I...how come you made me your number two? Why not Gerry?"

"I'll be blunt. It scares the shit out of me to have you flying my wing. I'd rather have Ardana, as a matter of fact, because I think he'd at least try to do his job, which is covering my precious ass."

"Jesus, you think I'd run off and leave you? I've never run from a fight in my life and I'm not running from the Japs!"

"I didn't say anything about running from a fight, Evans. Sometimes that's the smartest thing you can do."

"Aw, that's a coward's excuse!"

Jack felt anger rise up inside him. He remembered Bud Sprague back at the hut the 17th used for an operations shack at Ngoro, telling them they had to fight smart, and fighting smart sometimes meant running from a fight. If you were dead you were out of the fight, and what good were you to anyone then?

Jack knew the anger was still building inside him, because he felt his hands clench into fists. For a long moment anger warred with self-control, and anger very nearly won.

Some of that struggle must have been plain to Lt. Evans, whose face and eyes reflected a sudden unease, that look of having stepped in something deep, smelly, and highly unpleasant.

Jack made himself relax. He took a deep, slow breath. Then he knew what to do.

"Help me out with something, Evans. What were you saying to the ground crew of that P-39 over there?"

Evans hesitated before speaking. "Well, sir, that airplane is a sorry piece of shit, and it's the one that Chief Halloran assigned me. It's got dirt all over it. And the crew didn't salute me."

"Mm. That's a terrible breach of discipline." Jack kept his face expressionless. The Philippines had been hot, but New Guinea was a sauna, and the ground crews were working their asses off to keep these planes flyable. But Evans was oblivious to the obvious.

"Oh, yes, Captain," Evans said earnestly. "I explained that to the crew chief. Very unmilitary."

Jack looked at Evans.

"Very unmilitary indeed. Let's see, there's what looks like someone's undershirt and a pail of water. Polish that airplane, Lieutenant."

"What?"

"You polish that airplane yourself, Evans, and you do it now. You put some elbow grease into it, too, because I want you to learn what's important under a tropical sun at Seven-Mile Drome before you give an order. Get to it, Lieutenant, right now."

Evans actually opened his mouth again.

Jack repeated, very quietly, "Now."

Evans closed his mouth, stepped back, and went to work.

"I'll be back in fifteen minutes," Jack said. "I expect this airplane to shine before you fly in it, Lieutenant. I'm going to spend a little of that fifteen minutes considering what to do with you if it doesn't. So work hard. You like military chicken shit, maybe I can scrounge up a white glove somewhere."

Jack turned his back on Evans and walked up the taxiway. He passed a pursuit with a big yellow "19" painted on its nose. Gerry Bellmon was deep in conversation with a man Jack took to be the airplane's crew chief. Number 19's engine cover was off and the chief was pointing to something inside the engine compartment. Jack nodded to himself and kept walking.

Maybe there was hope for Bellmon.

If he lived long enough.

When he got to the next revetment he had to cover a grin at the gremlin painted next to the number 13 on the nose of the P-39. Ardana stood beside the left wing talking to the crew chief.

"Ardana," Jack said.

Ardana looked up. "Yes, sir?"

"Are you superstitious?"

"No, sir, not particularly."

"Good. I wondered. That silver dollar looked like a lucky charm to me."

Ardana smiled. "My grandfather gave that to me when I started flying. Said it had to be lucky, since it stopped him getting killed by some tin-horn gambler with a Derringer."

"Guess I could see that one. When did you start flying?"

Ardana hesitated, then shrugged. "I've been flying since I was sixteen, sir. My uncle flew SPADs in the last war. He taught me, and we had our own plane."

Jack nodded slowly, thinking. "How many hours d'you have?"

"Officially, sir, two hundred and some, more or less."

"Officially?"

"My uncle isn't an instructor. The rules say I can't log that time."

Jack nodded. "What kind of airplanes?"

"Uncle Kurt got a TravelAir Sportster with the 215-hp engine three years ago. We did a lot of flying in that."

"What sort of flying?"

"Mostly taking hunting parties up into the Montana Rockies. Or low-level stuff around the ranch looking for stray cattle and horses."

"OK. So how many hours of that? Just as an estimate?"

"Oh…a couple of hundred, anyway."

Jack nodded slowly.

"So I take it you're comfortable in the air?" he asked.

"Yes, sir."

"Good. Let's talk about Bellmon for a minute. I pushed this element leader thing on you, but that's sort of the way things are right now. You follow me?"

Ardana nodded. "Yes, sir."

"OK. I'll help you however I can, but I can't hold your hand. You'll be on your own a lot of the time. Just remember this. Your job as element leader is to hunt for targets. Your wingman's job is to watch for people who think you guys are targets. It's not quite as simple as that but that's the basic idea."

"Yes, sir."

"Just remember that being an element leader isn't exactly a promotion. You're pretty junior, so you're going to have to pull this off by character. You understand?"

"Yes, sir, I do."

Jack nodded slowly. "Well, I hope so. You're going to have to rely on Bellmon, and I can't help wondering if I've put you on the spot."

Ardana shrugged. "What can you tell me about this mission?"

"Nothing much. Evidently it's some sort of maximum effort thing. Other than the target being Lae I don't know anything else about it. I guess we'll find out soon enough." Jack shrugged. "Try not to worry about it too much. Get on up to HQ Flight. I'll meet you up there in a few minutes."

"Captain Davis."

Jack looked up. Colonel Wagner stood by the edge of the revetment.

"Jack, when you've finished here we have a few more things to discuss."

"Go on, Captain," Ardana said. "I'm on my way up to HQ Flight."

"Hold up a second," Wagner continued. "You're Ardana? The one who landed that Hudson?"

"Yes, sir."

"Good work. But you're also the one who doesn't have any time in the P-39."

"Yes, sir."

"Don't believe everything you hear about this airplane, Ardana. It's just another flying machine."

"Yes, sir."

"You know when to keep your mouth shut, don't you, lieutenant?"

"Yes, sir."

Wagner grinned and punched Ardana on the shoulder, lightly. He turned to Jack. "Let's have a little talk," the colonel said.

Jack walked up the hill beside Col. Wagner.

"Jesus, Jack. You told me they were young and you weren't kidding, were you? You want to take him up now?"

"I'm going to take the other two up first, give Jimmy there a little time in the cockpit to learn the switches, at least. But he had a pretty rough morning, so, yeah, I'm taking him up as soon as I get back."

Wagner nodded slowly. "Get him right back in the saddle, eh? OK. What about the other two?"

"Boyd, what I'd really like is to put Jimmy on my wing where I can maybe teach him something and let the other two go to hell, because I think that's what will happen anyway."

"But you aren't going to do that."

"No, sir, I'm not. I've got Evans as my wingman and I made Jimmy an element leader. Bellmon's number four."

Wagner shook his head slowly. "Evans. He's the tall beefy one? Looks like a football player?"

"That's him."

"You're not being easy on anyone, are you? OK. So you're going to take them up and get a feel for what they can do. That's today. What about tomorrow?"

"Tomorrow I figure we'll concentrate on low level stuff. Do we have a map of Lae I could look at? Or is there a place around here that looks kind of like it?"

"What we have are some old Kraut nautical charts drawn before the last war. Pretty good for the coastline but the blue-water types aren't too concerned about anything inland, unless it's a river they can float on."

"Hold up, Boyd." Jack gestured at the mountains to the north. "You mean those peaks up there aren't charted? I thought having no maps was just a Java thing."

"Afraid not. As for those peaks, no one knows exactly how high they are or where they are. My advice is if you get caught in the soup up there and have to go on instruments, do a climbing turn to fifteen thousand feet. That might get you over the worst of it. If you don't find rocks in the clouds while you turn."

"Might?"

Wagner nodded.

"Jehosophat."

"It is a kind of a screwed up war," Wagner agreed. "But it's the only one we have. Now, let's talk about you for a minute."

Jack nodded.

"Your flying is good," Wagner told him. "You're still kind of a hot dog, but that's all right. And I guess you can handle yourself."

The colonel stopped, looking up the hill at the operations shack. He shook his head.

"Do you see what I mean about accelerated stalls in the P-39?"

"Yes, sir."

"What did you feel in the stick?"

"Not much. Bit of a twitch, that's all."

"Any other ship would give you more warning, but that's all you'll get from a P-39. And no one who's ham-handed and over-controls will ever be able to fly that airplane, not smoothly, not safely."

Jack grimaced, thinking about Evans. Wagner saw the grimace and matched it with one of his own.

"Here's what I want from you, Jack. I figure all you really need to do is support Major Wolchek and be your calm, competent, and aggressive self. Set an example for the rest of them. You've got four Japs. Paint kill flags on your airplane. Those kids will look at you like you're God. Understand me?"

"Where do you get all this confidence in me, Boyd?"

Wagner grinned a little. "What, Jack, don't you believe in yourself?"

"Hell, yes."

"There you are, then. That's all you have to do. Go do it. Wolchek's tent is down that way. It won't hurt any of your kids to have a few more minutes of cockpit drill."

The 18th Squadron's operations shack was the canvas tent Major Steve Wolchek, the squadron commander, shared with his operations officer, Captain Leonard Barnes. Wolchek had the standard Port Moresby office equipment set up outside his tent with a scrap of canvas for some shade over it. He looked up as Davis approached and got up to meet him.

"You Jack Davis?" Wolchek asked, putting his hand out.

"Yes, sir," Jack took Wolchek's hand. Wolchek looked to be a year or two older than Boyd Wagner, maybe 5'10" and 160 pounds with gray eyes and dark black hair.

"Colonel Wagner told me he was sending you down. I'm glad to have you, Captain. Look, you call me Steve and I'll call you Jack, OK?"

"At least until I screw up, right?"

Wolchek laughed. "You got it. Now, what can you tell me about these kids that came in with you?"

"Green as grass. One of them has zero time in P-39s. The other two have about ten hours each."

Wolchek pursed his lips. "Well, that seems about par for the course out here. And I guess Boyd told you about the mission?"

"A little, yes, sir."

"What do you think?"

"I'll tell you what I told Boyd. I think we should leave those kids here, Steve. Having said that, given our orders, I'll do what I can to bring them back."

Wolchek nodded slowly. "Fair enough. What would you like to do between now and then in terms of training?"

"Today I'm going to take my flight up for familiarization with the airplane. Boyd said the 18th will supply the strafers for the mission, so tomorrow I thought we'd concentrate on coming in at low level, over the ocean, and shoot up some coconut trees or something."

"OK. Well, I understand you've already got an airplane. By tomorrow Halloran tells me we should have enough for everyone. Losing four airplanes in 48 hours put the squeeze on the mechanics."

Jack watched Wolchek as he mentioned the losses. For just a moment the major's eyes went blank and dead, but it was only a moment and then it was gone.

"That sounds fine, sir," Jack said. "With your permission, then, I'll get going."

Wolchek held out his hand again. "Glad to have you, Jack. Let me know what I can do to help, and good luck with your kids."

Jimmy sat in the cockpit of the P-39 from HQ Flight. It was the same one Buzz Wagner had just flown. The mechanics were refueling the airplane and doing a quick check on the systems.

He settled back into the seat on the hard parachute pack. He buckled the Sutton harness tight, as it would be in flight, so he could see how hard it was to reach different items.

The flight instruments themselves weren't that hard. He let his eye wander over them, looking over his shoulder as if checking his tail, then back to the panel and focusing straight ahead, down the long nose of the airplane that looked over the airstrip. Then to the other side and through the top of the canopy, holding the stick without moving it in a light three-fingered grip, then eyes back to the panel. There's the airspeed indicator, the artificial horizon, the turn and bank indicator, the gyrocompass, now look to the left and behind you, look above. Back to the panel. Oil pressure gauge, coolant pressure gauge, RPM indicator. Look to the right and behind, look below, look above. He did that for awhile and then he went to the gun switches. There were three of them, one for the four .30-calibre wing guns, one for the twin .50-calibre nose guns, and one for the 37-mm cannon firing through the propeller. He didn't flick the switches but he did touch them, one at a time, repeating their function under his breath.

Where were the switches and knobs for the landing gear, the propeller, the fuel tank selector, the flaps? He found them, closed his eyes, reached out and touched them, opened his eyes to be sure he touched the right switch.

Back to the flight instruments, the same routine over again.

Jimmy had both cockpit doors open for whatever breeze there might be but the metal fuselage and the curved Plexiglas canopy overhead focused the sun and the heat. He was running with sweat and beginning to realize that this would be a normal condition in Port Moresby. He thought for a moment of how many times during the long Montana winters he'd longed to escape to somewhere tropical and warm and smiled wryly.

One thing was sure, he wasn't going to freeze to death here.

Jimmy was still going from needle-and-ball to airspeed indicator to flaps lever and looking over his shoulder out the cockpit when someone called his name. He looked up. Evans stood at the left wingtip of his P-39.

"You got any rags?" Evans asked when Jimmy looked his way.

"Rags? I don't know." Jimmy started to add that his crew chief might have some and then thought, those rags are for *this* airplane, not for whatever Evans is doing to *his* airplane. "Why? What are you doing?"

"None of your business." Evans turned and walked back to his own revetment. Jimmy watched the retreating figure in the sweat-dark flight suit, noted the hunched, drawn shoulders.

Evans was what Jimmy thought of as a frat boy. Ardana wondered if Evans joined the Air Corps because in some ways it was like a fraternity.

Only Jimmy didn't believe the mission coming up would be anything like a football game. Even without the Zeros that shot the hell out of the Hudson this morning, Jimmy could feel that in his bones, absorbed with his grandfather's stories of his Texas gunfighting days and his Uncle Kurt's stories of flying over the Western front in the last war. The eyes of a man recalling good times didn't look like those of a man standing on the edge of a grave, looking down at a bloody, bullet-riddled corpse. And a football game was something for a cool fall afternoon with a lot of cheering and beer and if you were lucky a couple of pretty girls. At the end of the day the winners shook hands with the losers and everyone went home for dinner.

This mission sure as hell wouldn't be anything like that. Ardana got out of the airplane and walked over to the revetment where Evans' P-39 sat.

The beefy lieutenant was polishing the airplane's nose. There was a pail of water beside him. As Ardana watched Evans reached down into the pail of water, wet the rag down, and began wiping down the airplane. Ardana understood what was happening. Davis sent the airplane's ground crew away and put Evans to the task of polishing his airplane, just as Evans had been after his ground crew to do.

Jimmy watched how Evans was wiping down his airplane. The guy was misdirecting his energy, pure and simple. There was enough of a breeze blowing that the red dust from the airstrip and taxiways stuck to the damp area Evans wiped down. The tropical sun heated the aluminum of the airframe to the point where the water on his rag evaporated almost at once. The dust streaked and dried between one swipe and the next, so all Evans accomplished was to make the airplane look muddy and dirty. Ardana frowned. It wasn't only the mud. There was the extra weight, probably not much, but on an airplane where every ounce was considered, you had to wonder. And you also had to wonder, Jimmy thought, how much drag the dirt and mud added to the airplane. Again, it probably wasn't a lot, but what if it slowed you down two or three mph when you had a Zero chasing you?

That couldn't be good.

More to the point was that Evans hadn't figured any of this out. Ardana saw why Evans wanted the extra rags. He figured if he could slop more water on the airplane it would take off the mud before the water dried.

Then he looked across the taxiway. In the shade of a tree sat Evarra, the old sanguma man. He had a fan made of long white feathers. He fanned himself slowly as he watched Evans curse and wipe down his airplane. Ardana thought there was something of a smile in the complex wrinkles at the corners of the man's eyes and mouth.

The old bastard's laughing his ass off at Evans, Jimmy thought. *And I can't say I blame him.*

Evarra turned to look at Jimmy. The old face broke into a gap-toothed grin and Evarra pointed the fan at Evans. Then Evarra pointed to the north.

Jimmy followed the gesture.

Great gray clouds rolled down off the mountains. There was a crack of thunder in the distance.

"Hey, Evans," Ardana said.

"Buzz off."

"You might want to look up at the mountains, pal."

"I'm busy."

Ardana looked at him and then looked back at the mountains. The rain would be here in minutes.

"It's gonna rain, Evans. In about ten minutes."

"I got work to do."

Jimmy watched a moment longer and then walked back to his airplane. He closed the doors, walked around the wings to be sure the airplane was chocked and tied down, then looked at the grinning gremlin. He could have sworn the cartoon gremlin had the exact same gaptoothed grin that Evarra sported.

There was another far-off peal of thunder. Halloran came up the path from the squadron area.

"Reckon it's gonna rain, Mr. Ardana."

"Reckon so, Chief. I checked the chocks and tiedowns but maybe you should be sure I got everything secure."

"Never hurts to check," Halloran agreed. Then he looked over at Evans, still working on his P-39. Jimmy looked for Evarra, but the sanguma man had vanished once again.

"What's he doing?" Halloran asked, pointing at Evans.

"Washing his airplane," Jimmy replied.

"But it's gonna rain."

"Yup. I told him."

"Oh."

"Yup. What's a New Guinea rain like?"

"It's the tropics, lieutenant. You can get two feet a day, sometimes more in the wet."

"The wet? Oh, you mean like monsoon season?"

"That's right. That's what the Aussies call it, the wet."

"Got you."

"Come with me, Mr. Ardana. We got a little shelter not far away. These rainstorms are real frog-stranglers."

Halloran led the way up the taxiway to where the mechanics and ground crew stretched canvas tenting between some trees. The canvas was ripe with the stink of mildew and tar. There was a little hump in the ground so the rain would drain away from the shelter.

Bellmon was there, talking with his crew chief. Captain Davis arrived just as Jimmy and Halloran did.

"Jimmy, you reckon you know your panel by now?"

"No, sir. I think there's a lot of circuit breakers still to learn."

"Good. Keep at it. Where's Evans?"

"Washing his airplane."

"Jehosophat. Doesn't he know it's going to rain?"

"Yes, sir. He said he was busy."

"Well, let's not interfere with his work. I guess he'll be up in a few minutes."

Another peal of thunder, much closer, echoed from the sky.

"I guess he will, sir," Jimmy agreed.

A few drops of rain hit the dust, raising puffs like the impact of bullets. There was a pause and another blast of thunder. The wind hit the tops of the trees and set the leaves and branches roaring. They could see the rain coming down the mountain like a solid wall of water. Thunder rolled and cracked, the wind roared louder, and then the rain hit them in great sheets. In moments torrents of water ran down the taxiway and among the trees. The rain front swept by them, down the line of revetments, headed towards the sea seven miles south.

Then they saw the vague outline of a man running towards them. The mud was already thick enough that he wasn't running very fast, and he kept slipping and falling face first. It was Evans, and when he reached the canvas he crawled under it, soaking wet and daubed with mud. He lay there gasping.

Jimmy felt a part of him wanting to laugh at Evans, but the rest of him couldn't do it. Jimmy thought that a man wet, bedraggled and covered in mud made a pitiable spectacle. He'd seen it happen in Montana sometimes during cattle roundups. He took a handkerchief and held it out in the rain, then offered it to Evans.

Evans hesitated, looking at Jimmy. Then he took the handkerchief and began to clean his face.

"Thanks," he said.

"Keep it," Jimmy said. "You might need it."

Jimmy stood up and looked at Halloran. "How long is this likely to last?"

"Oh, twenty minutes or so. Then the sun will come out and we'll have a nice steam bath."

"Jesus, what a place," Jimmy said.

One of the crew chiefs shook his head mournfully. "I thought I was going to England. Instead they shipped me here."

"Who the hell did you piss off?" Davis asked. Everyone laughed.

Evans got his face wiped clean and sat on the ground looking out at the rain.

"Hell," he muttered. He got up and stood out in the rain, holding his face up to it, eyes shut against the battering drops, and brushed at the mud that coated his flight suit. He got it mostly clean before the rain eased up and the sun broke through the clouds.

In moments the sun turned the wet ground and air into Halloran's promised steam bath.

"Well, you're either soaked with sweat or soaked by the rain, but either way you're soaked," said Davis. "Evans, how does your airplane look?"

"I reckon she's clean now, Captain."

"I guess so. OK, Bellmon, Evans, with me. Jimmy, we'll be back in about an hour and a half. Be ready."

"Yes, sir," Jimmy replied.

Jack sat in his P-39 at the edge of the runway. He took off first when the tower gave him the green light, sucked up the gear and the flaps, then climbed to 1000 feet and circled in a leisurely pattern, scanning the surrounding sky carefully for marauding Japs.

Evans was halfway down the runway and repeated the same mistake he told Jack about, earlier this morning. He pulled back on the stick way too far and way too hard for the P-39, which promptly ballooned up into the air, then pushed over and dove, then up again a foot or two above the runway, yo-yoing down the field as Evans cleaned up the gear and the flaps and Jack winced, watching him, half-convinced he'd see the P-39 smash into the ground and burst into bright yellow flame and flying metal bits. But Evans managed to stay clear of the ground. Once he got the gear and flaps up he climbed out and circled around to rendezvous with Jack.

Bellmon's takeoff was smoother but he still climbed out at an angle that Jack thought too steep. Jack wondered what the engine cylinder head temps looked like in Bellmon's ship and wondered if Bellmon was keeping an eye on them.

Jack looked around the sky but they were the only airplanes over Seven-Mile for the moment.

"Boxcar Red Leader to Red Two and Red Three, close it up," he radioed. "Two, get on my right wing, Three, on my left."

"Roger, Lead, Three's on your left."

"Ah, roger, Two's on right."

Jack kept up a standard rate climbing turn to the right. It made him cringe, kept him looking around at the sky and the ground. This was crazy, conducting training flights in a war zone. Not having any choice about it, when Zeros might pounce on them at any moment, made it worse.

Evans joined up on his right and oscillated between thirty feet low or high, alternately surging forward and falling back, most of which Jack figured was poor pitch control. Jack looked over his shoulder at Bellmon, who held tolerable formation, but only just tolerable, off his left wingtip.

"Right, Lead coming out of the turn on heading 180," he radioed. "We'll climb to angels ten."

"Roger, Lead, Three copies 180 and ten," Bellmon affirmed.

"Two understands 180 and ten," Evans called.

"Two, close it up," Jack radioed.

For a moment Evans did nothing, and then he skidded towards Jack's airplane, dropping below and behind as he did. Jack lost sight of him.

"What the hell, Two? Three, do you see Two?"

"Ah, Lead, Two is rejoining," said Evans. His voice was harsh and thick over the radio.

Jack looked over his right shoulder and saw Evans at least two hundred feet back and sixty feet low.

"Jehosophat," he muttered. Then he keyed the radio. "Three, we're turning onto 160, now."

Jack continued to climb but rolled out onto a heading of 160. He looked over to the left and saw Bellmon, still ragged and too far off Jack's wing, but at least more or less where he should be.

"OK, Two from Lead, join up on my right. Tuck it in."

"Ah, roger, Lead," Evans radioed, breathing heavily over the radio.

Jack looked around and cleared the sky around him, then checked his engine and instruments.

So far so good.

He looked back at Evans, still trying to catch up, and sighed.

It was going to be a long hour.

Jimmy was going over engine start and propeller control procedures with Number 22's crew chief when he heard the moaning snarl of Allison engines overhead. He and the crew chief looked up at the three-ship formation of P-39s in the traffic pattern.

"Jeez," the crew chief said, shading his eyes.

Jimmy assumed Captain Davis was in the lead, and knew from experience the lead slot was the easiest when flying formation – that was one of the first things he had learned in advanced flight training. But flying a three-ship "vee" formation wasn't that hard, and that formation was, more or less, what the formation seemed to be.

Except that the left wingman was perceptibly out of position and the right wingman was both out of position and doing some sort of up-and-down motion way the hell out on the right side of the leader's wing.

The lead airplane peeled suddenly up and away. The wingmen continued on, right wing going into trail behind left wing, fishtailing to put some distance between them. To Jimmy, the fishtailing incorporated something of a Dutch roll.

The first P-39 put its gear and flaps down, rolling onto final approach, nose a little high, making one bounce as it landed and coming down harder than it should from the bounce, then settling down, speed bleeding off.

The second P-39 wobbled on final, flaps down, gear coming down at the last second, ballooning up in the landing flare until the airplane almost stalled, a great burst of power coming in just in time to pull the airplane out of the stall. Nose down, power off; too close to the ground, nose yanked up, main gear slamming into the runway not quite hard enough to bounce the P-39 into the air the same way Jimmy had bounced the Hudson to clear the B-26.

"Jeez," the crew chief breathed again. He kept looking, and Jimmy followed his eyes.

The flight leader came downwind and turned into the break, a hard left turn that pulled streamers of condensation off the wingtips for a moment. Gear and flaps came down on crosswind, speed dropping off visibly, and when the pilot turned on final Jimmy could all but see a rigidly straight track in the air that the P-39 would follow to a landing as the power came off the engine and the nose came up, just enough to stall the airplane as the main wheels touched the airstrip with the merest puff of dust, propeller idling in coarse pitch.

Number 22's crew chief sighed. "That guy can fly a P-39," he said. "Mind a little advice, Mr. Ardana?"

"Not at all."

"Whatever that guy tells you to do, you do it."

Jimmy nodded. "You bet."

The P-39s taxied up from the runway to their revetments and shut down one by one. Jimmy continued his cockpit drill but from the corner of his eye he could see Evans and Bellmon gather in front of Captain Davis. Davis was barely as tall as Gerry Bellmon, and nearly a head shorter than Danny Evans, and he couldn't be more than two years older; but something in his manner reminded Jimmy of the old-time Air Corps sergeant who greeted his incoming class of cadets with something less than open-armed enthusiasm.

"Yep," said the crew chief, watching Captain Davis. "You do whatever that guy tells you."

Jimmy went back to his cockpit drill. A few minutes later the P-39 staggered as someone's weight came on the left wing. Jimmy looked up to see Captain Davis kneeling on the wing and rolled the car-style window down.

Davis did not look happy. It was in the muscles under his eyes and at the slightly-turned down corners of his mouth. In fact, Jimmy thought, Davis looked pretty pissed off.

"How's it coming, Jimmy?" Davis asked.

"I might know this airplane in a year or two, sir," Jimmy replied. When Davis looked sharply at him he returned the look.

"Yeah," Davis said. "Run through the engine start procedure with me."

Jimmy walked through the sequence required to start the engine, taxi, takeoff, go into cruise climb, and then land. He stumbled a couple of times but caught himself. After ten minutes of close questioning Davis nodded.

"You're right," Davis said. "In a year or two you might know this airplane, but that's good enough for now. As soon as my guys check the fuel and oil in my airplane, you and I will have a go at it."

"Yes, sir."

"You nervous?"

"Yes, sir."

Davis nodded. "Good. You should be a little nervous, flying this bitch. You saw Evans doing his yoyo imitation? That's because he was trying to fly the airplane as if it were an AT-6 trainer with a hell of a lot of elevator travel to control pitch. I've had a talk with him about that but you should learn from his mistakes. Now look, the P-39 has really finely balanced controls, maybe a little too good. On pitch, you only need to move the stick a little bit. So be careful when you use the ailerons that you aren't also feeding in back or forward stick. That's another reason Evans was all over the sky. This is your first flight in the airplane so I'm not expecting miracles. Just feel her out, keep alert, and you'll be OK."

Jimmy nodded. "What about Japs, sir?"

For the briefest moment Davis looked at Jimmy. "What about 'em?"

"Well, we sure as hell know they might show up any time."

"Yeah. You have any gunnery training?"

"No."

"OK. I want you to do three things when we fly today. The first thing is, concentrate on flying the airplane. You do that, you've got a fair chance. The second thing is, keep your eyes open and moving all around. You see the little bastards before they see you, you've got an even better chance. Finally, if we do see Japs, you stick with me. Stay with me and keep your eyes open, and if you see Japs, no, skip that. If you see any other airplane at all radio where and how many. Got it?"

Jimmy blinked, looking into Davis' eyes. There was something hard and flintlike in them, something that reminded him of his grandfather.

"Yes, sir," Jimmy said quietly. "I'll do that."

"Good. See that you do. As far as shooting goes, remember what the guy said at Bunker Hill and don't fire until you see the whites of their eyes. You do that, you ought to by God hit something." Davis smiled, a very tight, contained smile, and looked over his shoulder. A fuel truck was parked in front of his P-39, and his crew was filling its tanks.

"We'll go in about ten minutes," Davis said. "Your call sign for this flight is Boxcar Red Two. You taxi ahead of me and take off first. I'll join you in the pattern."

Davis climbed off the wing.

Jimmy took a deep breath and tried to disregard the sudden hammering of his heart.

"Show me the gunsight and armament panel one more time," he told the crew chief.

Fifteen minutes later Jimmy taxied past the revetment where Captain Davis sat in his P-39. From the corner of his eye Jimmy saw Evarra, sitting just inside the trees, fanning himself with the fan of white feathers and watching Jimmy as he taxied past.

Davis taxied out of his revetment and followed behind Jimmy. The radio crackled into life as Davis called the tower for clearance.

Jimmy watched his engine gauges. Just as the crew chief warned him, as he taxied the temperatures were already high and getting higher.

Then he was at the edge of the runway, running up, checking magnetos, then lining up on the runway heading; the green light from the tower, the dusty pockmarked runway ahead of them, the dun and green hills on either side, the heat and dust in the cockpit, the sweat streaming off him, his heart going like a crazy snare drum and the adrenaline singing in his blood.

"Let's go, Two," said Captain Davis over the radio.

"Boxcar Red Two, rolling," Jimmy heard himself say as he advanced the throttle, checking the propeller pitch. The P-39 rattled and bumped over the uneven surface of the airstrip, gathering airspeed, the engine howling out an exultant note of full throttle.

And Jimmy relaxed. After all, as Col. Wagner told him, it was just another airplane, and he wiggled his ass against the parachute pack, took a deep breath, and felt the shimmy of the airframe in his body, the increasing rush of air over ailerons, rudder and elevator in the stick and rudder pedals. He didn't know exactly what everyone meant when they said if you wanted to take off in a P-39 you just thought about it, but it was almost like that, the merest beginning of back pressure on the stick; the P-39's nose lifted and the mains rumbled for another half-second before going silent as the airplane came off the ground. The stick was firm in his hand as he leveled out a few feet above the runway, cleaning up the landing gear and the flaps as the speed increased. He eased back a little on the throttle and the RPMs, watching the temperature gauges. The end of the runway flashed below him. There was a hill ahead and to the left. He was still below the hilltop, but there wasn't anything directly ahead of him. He began a climbing turn to the left, toward Fairfax Harbor and Port Moresby. The engine temperatures started going down into the normal operating range.

Jimmy wiggled the stick a little, noting how the ailerons and elevator responded. He checked his airspeed, which was pushing 200 mph, and his altitude, which was 1100 feet ASL.

His radio rattled to life. "Two from Boxcar Red Leader, don't fly over the harbor. Like as not they'll shoot at you."

"Roger, Lead." Jimmy lowered his nose and turned sharply to the left, feeling the response of the

P-39 in the turn. He was amazed at the g-forces that piled on him with the lightest back pressure on the stick. He realized Captain Davis was right. This airplane had to be flown every second.

Being just a little nervous about the airplane was the right way to fly this little bitch.

Jimmy smiled and patted the throttle quadrant. "That's OK," he said. "You and me, sweetie. You and me. I think we'll get along just fine."

He started scanning the sky around him, and when Davis called for him to join up on his right wing Jimmy rendezvoused neatly and snugged it in.

"Oookaaay, Two," Davis drawled. "Keep it tight."

Jimmy looked at Davis' right wing tip and Davis' head in the P-39's cockpit. He moved in closer, just a little, but felt like that was enough for a first flight.

"Not bad, Two," Davis radioed. "Stay with me."

"Roger, Lead."

Jimmy relaxed into his seat, scanned his panel, attention on Davis as the flight leader began a standard rate turn to the left that had them heading towards the mountains north of Seven-Mile.

"We'll climb to 17,000 feet and do some air work," Davis radioed. "Check your oxygen system. We'll go on oxygen above 10,000 feet."

"Roger, Lead."

Jack shut down in his revetment and opened the left-hand door of the cockpit. His crew chief helped him out of the seat straps and Jack climbed out onto the wing, shrugging out of the parachute harness.

"Terraine, gas and oil, and check her over. No problems to report. I hope to go up again once more before dark."

The crew chief nodded. "Cap'n Davis, the Chief told me that first chance we get we should paint four Jap flags on your airplane."

Jack grimaced. "How long will that take you?"

"Oh, heck, maybe fifteen minutes." Terraine grinned and indicated the armorer. "Joey here has been practicing painting Jap flags. Ain't that right, Joey?"

"Yes, sir," the armorer said enthusiastically. "Would you like to see a couple?"

Jack shrugged, but smiled. "Let's have a look."

The armorer produced a piece of scrap sheet aluminum. There were two Jap flags on it, both about the size of a picture postcard. One was the red-orange meatball centered on a white background, the other was the "rising sun" motif, the red-orange meatball with the rays streaming out from it, with the meatball offset to the left. The edges were crisp and clear.

Jack nodded at the "rising sun" flag. "That's good work, Joey," he said. "Put 'em on at the end of the day if you have time, or whenever you get to it."

Jack walked out of the revetment and met Ardana, walking towards him on the taxiway.

"Not bad, Jimmy," Jack told him. "How'd you like to go up again in a bit?"

Ardana smiled. "Sure thing. I like that airplane."

"Yeah? Most pilots don't."

Ardana shrugged. "I like the controls. The elevator takes a little getting used to, but that airplane does exactly what you tell it to do."

"Make sure your guns are armed for this next flight. We'll shoot the guns just so you can see what it feels like. Go grab a bite to eat. We'll go up again in an hour."

Jack found a truck full of Aussies headed across the airstrip and hitched a ride. The Aussies dropped him off at the tent that served as the 19th Bomb Group's operations shack at Port Moresby. He was still in his flight suit but had taken off his Mae West and his leather flying helmet.

The enlisted men looked up for a moment and then went back to what they were doing. One of the men sat in front of a radio set, tuning the dial, listening in on a pair of headphones. A major stood next to him. There was a ruled blackboard on the left as Jack went in and among the others he saw the number of Charlie's Fort, 41-34544, along with Charlie's name in the "A/C CMDR" column.

The major looked up at Jack, frowning, and then smiled. "Hey, Jack," he said. "I heard you were dead."

The major held his hand out. Jack shook it. "Good to see you too, Sammy," he said. "Thought I'd see how Charlie's doing."

"Yeah, us, too. Lemmons here has been trying to call him for the last ten minutes."

"Voice no good?"

"Aw, it's the tropics. Radio's not for shit out here."

Lemmons, the radio operator, pulled one of the headphones off his ear and looked up at the major.

"Sir, still not getting through on voice," he said. "I'll give Morse a try."

The major nodded and the radioman bent over his telegraph key, tapping out a brief message in Morse.

On the third try the radioman tensed, put a hand to his left ear, and grabbed a stub of pencil and a pad of paper. He wrote down a string of letters, then tapped out a reply before turning to look at the major.

"They're OK, sir. Major Davis reports his position is approximately two hundred miles due west of Rennell Island."

"Where the hell is that?" asked Jack.

The major grinned at Jack. "The innocence of you pursuit guys. Rennell Island is about a thousand miles more or less northeast of Townsville."

Jack snorted. "And the only reason you know that, Sammy, is because your navigator told you."

"Hey, that's what they're for." The major turned to Lemmons. "Nothing else? Just the position report?"

"That's all, sir."

"So no sign of the Japs?" Jack asked quietly.

"No, sir. Not yet."

Charlie breathed rubbery air through his oxygen mask and looked out the cockpit window at the sea 20,000 feet below. Somewhere nearby half the Jap Navy was supposedly steaming towards Port Moresby. But there was a lot of ocean spread out below them, with just enough cloud cover to keep things interesting. And it was amazing how often the whitecaps on the ocean would combine and look like the wake of a ship.

He looked inside the cockpit and swept his gaze over the engine instruments. The even rumble of the four Wright Cyclone engines told him most of what he needed to know, and the gauges revealed the rest. For a miracle the engines were behaving themselves.

"Navigator to pilot."

"Go ahead, Al."

"One minute until we reach the eastern limit of our search sector."

"Yeah?"

"Yeah. Then, ah, you know. We turn north for about an hour."

"North? Oh, you mean, turn left? OK."

"After that can we go home?" came the plaintive voice of the ball turret gunner. "It's plumb cold out here in the South Pacific."

"Plumb cold at 20,000 feet about anywhere in the world," said someone else.

"Yeah, you bums will be warm enough when we get back to Townsville."

"Much less Seven-Mile."

Charlie smiled under his oxygen mask, listening to the good-natured bickering over the intercom. Like the rumble of the engines, the bickering told him his crew was in good shape, despite bad chow, equipment failure, rotten living conditions, tropic heat and stratospheric cold, all within hours of each other. Oh yeah, and too god-damn many stinking Japs.

The bickering died away naturally as he and Lt. Deering turned *Bronco Buster II* to the north.

"Radio operator to pilot."

"Go ahead, Sam," Charlie replied.

"I got through to Seven-Mile and gave them our position. Joey says someone named Jack says hello."

Charlie shook his head. "That's my pesky little brother, the pursuit pilot," he said.

"Jeez," said Lefty. "The same one we almost shot down when we got to the Philippines last December?"

"More like he almost got us," said Al Stern. "That guy knows what he's doing. How many Zeros does he have now, Charlie?"

"Four so far," the airplane commander replied. "But I told him not to do anything stupid."

That provoked a chorus of catcalls and sarcastic comments on the notable lack of brains exhibited by pursuit pilots, regardless of the excessive size and brass content of their balls.

Then Mike Deering's voice cut through the chatter. "Hey! Are those ships out there at two o'clock?"

"Bandits, bandits four o'clock high!" A clatter and hammer of machine-guns vibrated the airframe. Yellow and red tracer swept by in front of the cockpit, followed by a gull-gray winged shape that barely missed the nose of the Fort. More tracer

swept by and cannon shells chewed into the right wing.

"Al! Work up a position report! Sam, tell Seven-Mile we're under attack approximately twenty miles north of our last position, ships in sight ten miles to the northeast, accompanied by at least one carrier."

"Roger, Charlie, twenty miles north, ten miles northeast, one carrier!"

The guns hammered again. "Bandits coming in, eight o'clock low!"

Charlie looked over his shoulder just in time to see the round-nosed Zeros climbing up at them, nose and wing guns winking, tracer arcing up and flying past them, then the *Wham!Wham!* of cannon strikes. The left wing jolted.

"Skipper, left waist, we got fuel venting from the left wing tank."

"Roger, Lefty. Sparks! Come up front and transfer fuel to the right wing from the left."

"Got you, Skipper, transferring fuel from the left wing," said the radio operator.

"Sparks, you remember where the transfer switches are?" asked Kim Smith. The flight engineer manned the upper turret gun.

He was a little bit busy at the moment.

"Yeah, I got it, I got it!" said the radio operator.

The machine guns hammered again. The nose gun got into the act, sending tracer out after a Zero that pulled in front of them after attacking from 8 o'clock low. It looked to Charlie like the Zero took some hits but the Jap fighter kept going, rolling hard right and diving away from the stream of tracer.

Charlie put the Fort into a turn to the right, headed in the direction of the contact, and there they were, a whole hell of a lot of ships steaming in formation.

"Pilot to bombardier, let Al have the gun. We got Japs dead ahead. Pick something big and drop on it."

"Got it, skipper."

"Zeros coming up our ass!" called Emmons.

The right waist and tail guns fired.

"Got one! Got that bastard, he's burning!"

"Two more of 'em coming in," drawled the ball-turret gunner.

Charlie straightened out.

"Steady, steady on this heading and altitude," called the bombardier. "I got a big sonofabitch just coming into the bombsight."

Charlie and Deering steadied on the controls. Hitting a moving target on the ocean called for equal measures of skill and luck even if the bomber flew on rails.

"Thirty seconds to target," called the bombardier. "Opening bomb bay doors."

"Right waist, Zeros coming in, 5 o'clock level."

Charlie felt the drag as the bomb bay doors opened.

There was a mad tattoo of bullet strikes just behind them on the flight deck and a Zero screamed over the cockpit, diving away to the left. Two more followed it, one of them trailing dark gray smoke.

"Bombs away! Closing bomb bay doors!"

Charlie felt the lift as the bombs released, relieving the Fort of a ton of dead weight.

"Radio operator, has anyone acknowledged our position report yet?"

Burning yellow tracer passed close to the cockpit. Machine guns hammered and chattered, then the Zero passed by over the left wing, the Jap fighter's wings and fuselage barely clearing the propeller arcs of the left engines. The nose gun fired as the Zero flew in front of the Fort. Tracer licked out from the nose gun, smashing into the Jap as the Zero rolled right and down. Bits came off the wings and canopy. A bright thin stream of yellow flame licked out of the right wing root, broadened, and then the fighter vanished from Charlie's field of vision.

"Good shooting, nose gun!" Charlie called.

Deering leaned out to the right. "Hey, that's a kill! That's a kill, his wing just came off!"

Charlie heard the heavy clunk behind him as the bomb bay doors finished cycling into the closed position.

"Ah, radio operator to pilot, Seven-Mile confirms our sighting report. Trying to reach Townsville."

"OK, well done, keep trying." Charlie turned the Fort away from the Jap fleet and started a shallow dive, advancing the turbo controls for maximum power. The Fort's airspeed crept up, pushing 210 indicated, and they steadied out on a heading of 270.

"Flight engineer, how's our fuel?" Charlie could tell from the controls that the Fort was flying right-wing heavy.

"Sparks got what he could out of the left wing, skipper, but we lost a lot of it. I think we have about seven hundred gallons."

Charlie exchanged a worried glance with his copilot. They'd lost over a third of their remaining fuel.

"I heard that, skipper," said Al's voice. "Seven-Mile's about five hundred fifty miles away. It'll be tight."

"OK," said Charlie. "Get me a course to Seven-Mile, then."

"Roger," Al replied.

"Skipper, right waist, looks like the Zeros are breaking off."

"Skipper, upper turret, they're all headed back to the ships."

"Can anyone tell if we hit anything?"

"Skipper, ball turret, I saw some splashes around a ship but nothing else."

"OK."

"Hey, Charlie, if you can give me cruise settings on a course of 279, we ought to hit Seven-Mile in about three hours."

"We might make that, skipper, but it'll be on fumes," said the flight engineer.

"Acknowledged," Charlie replied. He settled himself in his seat.

They'd either make it or they wouldn't.

Chapter Five

"Jimmy the Kid"

Jimmy thought Captain Davis looked worried when he came back from the other side of the airstrip, where the bomber guys pitched their tents. But all he did was ask Jimmy if he was ready to go, and Jimmy said he was.

"OK," Davis replied. "We'll go to 17,000 feet so you can see how the airplane handles at altitude. Then we'll do a dive from altitude and some more formation work. Same rules otherwise, especially about keeping your eyes open."

Passing through 10,000 feet they went on oxygen. At 13,000 the radio crackled in their ears.

"Boxcar Red Leader from Seven-Mile, say your position and altitude."

"Seven-Mile, this is Boxcar Red Leader, fifteen miles west of the field passing base plus 5."

"Roger, Boxcar Red Leader. We have a raid warning. Fifteen plus Japs passed over Dobodura ten minutes ago. Can you intercept?"

Jimmy looked over at Davis' airplane. The flight leader didn't hesitate.

"That's affirmative, Seven-Mile."

Oh shit, Jimmy thought. He looked to his armament panel and flipped the gun and cannon switches to the ON position, then he turned on the gunsight. *I've got an hour twenty minutes total time in this airplane and I'm taking it into combat!*

"Two from Lead," Davis called.

"Roger, Lead."

"Keep your eyes astern of us. Move out a little bit, stay loose. We may need room to maneuver. Just keep your eyes open, let me know if there's anything on our ass, and stay with me. Got it?"

"Roger, Lead." *What the hell else do I need to do?* Jimmy thought. He reached out and turned the gun sight on full bright. Then he pulled back the charging handles for the machine guns on either side of the instrument panel. Hell, what about the wing guns? Those charged from the ground. Had Simmons charged them before takeoff? Jimmy remembered Captain Davis said something about it, but had Simmons actually done it?

Oh shit. Jimmy looked over his shoulder to the right and to the left, but saw nothing behind them.

Jack kept his eyes on the northern horizon as they climbed. Now and again he looked to the rear, if only because he had that crawling feeling between his shoulder blades. Their engines were laboring above 20,000 feet, climbing at only 500 feet per minute. Jack wanted to make it to 24,000 feet but he'd take what he could get.

Holy Christ, he thought. I'm taking a total infant into combat again.

Then he saw the glitter of sunlight on metal, just above their altitude, still fifteen miles away.

Jimmy checked six, fishtailing a little to clear the blind spot on his tail.

"Bandits," he heard Davis call over the radio. "Boxcar Red Leader has bandits at eleven o'clock."

Jimmy started to acknowledge the call and then something attracted his attention. He felt his throat constrict a little and he had to swallow before he could make the call.

"Lead from Two, three bandits at 9 o'clock high." Jimmy couldn't believe his voice sounded so normal. He also couldn't believe he'd seen the three little dots.

Zeros. Oh holy howling shit. The Zeros were flying the opposite direction, staying high, trying to come around to dive on their tails.

Jack looked to his left and up. Jehosophat, the kid had good eyes. He looked back at the main formation. Yep, hammer and anvil time.

The Zeros wouldn't attack for another minute or so. Jack thought about diving away from the fight. The odds weren't there. Three Zeros moving into position from behind and above, plus the Zeros he could see covering the bombers, ahead and to the left of the Jap formation. He looked up and over at the Zeros, who flew serenely along on their opposing course.

God damn Jap bastards, he thought coldly. Jack felt the anger and distrusted it. But the sight of those Zeros really pissed him off.

"Roger, Two, keep an eye on 'em," Jack radioed.

There was a little time. He wasn't going to give up yet.

Jimmy felt his mouth sag a little. He had been watching the Zeros and keeping his eye on their own six o'clock as well.

Back in flight school he wondered what he'd feel in his first dogfight. Well, technically this was his second. But he didn't feel anything like he'd expected, not at all. His first sight of those Zeros told him those guys were very, very bad news and that he was going to need some luck to live through the next few minutes, much less make it back to Seven-Mile.

Jack leveled out of his climb and held his course for a moment, watching the airspeed creep up. They were still at full military power, 3000 RPM and 44.5 inches of manifold pressure. Those guys in the Zeros would notice the speed change any second, and when they did they'd turn and dive into the attack.

The Zeros turned in formation, elegant, smooth and graceful, like performers at an air show, and began to dive in pursuit.

"Hard left, Two," Jack called. "I've got the three at 9 o'clock. You watch the Zeros with the main formation."

"Roger, Lead."

Jimmy stared at the Zeros diving on them as he turned left on Jack's wing. He had to force himself to look away from them to the Zeros still with the main formation.

"Ah, Lead from Two, those guys are staying with the bombers," he radioed.

"Understood, Two. Stay with me."

Jack's fighter nosed down and began to accelerate. Jimmy gulped, looked at the Zeros on his left diving on them, looked at the Zeros with the bombers on their right, and looked back to clear their tails.

Jack watched the Zeros curve inside the turn he made but they were still way out of range and his P-39 was accelerating, indicating 240 already, which meant his true airspeed was over 300 mph at this altitude. He was trading that hard-won altitude for airspeed, and airspeed was life.

The Zeros stopped overhauling them at about 350 mph. When the Zeros began to fall behind Jack leveled out. The P-39 didn't have the acceleration of the Zero but he remembered it would top out at about 360 mph on the straight and level at 17,000 feet. They had more than that already, trading altitude for airspeed. The Zeros chased them until they were over the mountains and then turned back toward the bomber formation.

Jimmy had never been more thankful in his life than when the Zeros turned away. He looked at his engine instruments and fuel gauges. The engine temps and pressures were looking good, and a little mental arithmetic told him they weren't more than fifty miles from Seven-Mile. They could almost glide home from here at this altitude.

"Jimmy, throttle back to 2600 RPM and let's have best climb speed," Jack radioed.

"Ah, roger, Lead," Jimmy replied, reaching for the throttle.

And suddenly Jimmy knew what Davis planned to do. He throttled back, following Jack into a climb, trading their airspeed for altitude now. At that throttle setting their fuel flow was reduced, increasing their endurance.

Jimmy grinned then. He was still scared, still had that adrenaline flowing through his veins, still felt shaky and a little weak in the bladder, but he grinned as their airspeed bled off to 160 indicated and Jack began a gentle turning climb to the right.

They had twenty minutes to get above the Japs, ten minutes for the bombers to reach their target and turn away, then ten minutes to get here.

Where he and Jack would be waiting with the altitude advantage.

Maybe. If the Japs didn't figure it out.

Jimmy's grin faded. He looked back over his shoulder, around the sky above them, then back over his other shoulder.

Where was the relief tube on this thing, anyway?

At 25,000 feet the controls were mushy and Jack had the feeling that his ship was poised on the most delicate of balances. He treated it that way. A look to his left showed Jimmy in good position, not too far out, not too close, nice and loose. Jack looked around, head on a swivel, head on a swivel all the time. The sky was a dark blue up here and they could see impossibly far, to the Solomon Sea on the north coast of Papua New Guinea, to the Coral Sea and the Gulf of Papua to the south. And smoke started rising from Seven-Mile five minutes ago.

"OK, Jimmy," he radioed. "Time to earn our pay. Turning south."

Jimmy followed Jack's lead, breathing the rubbery oxygen through his mask, turning the cockpit heater knob up again. *Christ*, he thought, *an hour ago I was wishing for the cold!* He shivered.

"Two from Lead."

"Go ahead, Lead."

"Those Zeros won't figure we just ran off, Jimmy. They'll have their eyes peeled. We're going to make one pass on the bombers, just one pass. Ignore the Zeroes. Pick one bomber. When it fills the outer ring in your gunsight, start shooting. Use short bursts. The cannon will probably jam after a few shots. Don't worry if it does. Just keep diving and stay with me. One pass and we head for home. Got it?"

"Ah, roger, Lead."

"Remember, whatever you do, don't try to turn with those bastards. Dive, shoot, keep diving, and get the hell out. Here we go."

Jack turned south and cracked on the throttle. Airspeed picked up. He looked anxiously at his fuel gauge. They'd been up for about an hour, running at high RPMs much of the time. Maybe another half-hour of fuel left. At least they were headed in the right direction now.

Head on a swivel, keep your head on a swivel, he reminded himself, looking around. They were at 25,000 and it didn't mean the Japs were below them, or that those Zeros with the bombers were the only Zeros around.

And then there they were.

Below them, and headed right for them.

"Tallyho, Two, tallyho, formation is dead ahead about thirteen miles."

Jimmy looked. The twin-tailed Japanese bombers – Nells? – were in five vics of three airplane each. Beyond them he could see smoke rising from Seven-Mile. There were the Zeros, one set to either side, a little higher than the bombers.

Jack nosed over at a shallow angle. Jimmy swallowed and checked his gunsight and armament switches. He felt twitchy inside and had to fight his breathing. For a minute he shook and he thought, he truly did, that he would piss his pants. Or shit himself. It wasn't like the Hudson. That happened so fast he didn't have time to be scared. Not like now. Not seeing it coming like this.

Then he thought about the Colt Peacemaker strapped in the shoulder holster. Jimmy took a deep shuddering breath, and then another. It helped. Adrenaline still yelled in his veins but he calmed down. He touched the Colt for luck.

Jack watched the Zeros. The best thing the escorts could do now was to pull up, try for a head on pass and catch the P-39s in a cross-fire. The Zeros wouldn't have long to act.

He lessened his dive angle. The wind howled and screamed around the canopy as the bombers approached.

Jimmy watched the bombers approach, swelling from dots in his gunsight to actual airplanes. The Zeros clawed up at them, almost standing on their propellers, and the guns in their wings and cowlings spat tracers at his airplane. Jack was jinking and weaving to avoid the fire, yeah, never fly straight and level, he'd heard that, and as soon as Jack jinked Jimmy did too, not in unison, but slightly away, not too far, but not the same direction, either. Something hit his wing with a *Wham!* and his ship staggered a little. Then they were past the Zeros and the bombers swelled in his gunsight.

I'm gonna do this, I'm gonna do this, I'm gonna do this, he thought, as the green-painted bomber with the big red meatballs grew in his sight. The bomber's wings filled the sight reticle and his finger twitched, *wait for it*, he thought, *I don't see Jack shooting yet*.

Then he was close, close enough to see the men in the cockpit looking up at him, and he held down all the triggers on the control stick.

There was a jack-hammer roar from the .50s in the nose. Smoke from the gun breeches made his eyes smart. The cannon fired twice and quit. Jimmy saw the tracers reach out from his nose and wing guns, saw the sparkle of hits dance across the nose of the Jap bomber, saw them reach across the nose and the left engine and wing and then oh shit *oh shit!* Too close, way too close!

Jimmy rolled to the right, scraping by the Nell as smoke and fire erupted from its left engine. To his left he saw Jack pulling level, firing at another Nell and then rolling over and diving away.

Jimmy looked frantically over his shoulder. Two Nells were on fire and as he watched smoke and flame blossomed from another. And holy sweet loving Jesus, there were the Zeros, diving through their own bomber formation, hot on their tails.

Jack looked over his shoulder at the Zeros. Above and beyond them one of the Nells stopped burning but still trailed smoke.

"Two, shallow up your dive a little more," he radioed.

"Roger, Lead," Jimmy replied. He could see that. They were ahead of the Zeros, they had the edge on speed, no need to surrender more altitude to stay ahead. Then he looked at his fuel gauge.

He wished he hadn't. And with the Zeros right behind them they didn't dare throttle back.

Jack looked at his fuel gauge as they overflew the field at 15,000 feet. He figured the Zeros were mad enough to stay and play, and the Zeros could out-range the P-39s.

"Stay tight, Two," he radioed.

He pulled his airplane into a hard left bank, as close as he dared to an accelerated stall, nose down to keep his speed up in the turn.

Jimmy watched the Zeros, as he tried to breathe against the g-force of the turn. He was starting to feel tired. That scared him back into alertness. He'd heard about this airplane, how it would stall and spin with little or no warning. Oh no, not on me you won't, he vowed. He held the turn and looked at the Zeros.

The Zeros were falling *behind* them.

Jack calculated how long they could stay in this turn. To keep their airspeed above 320 mph indicated they had to use up their altitude and burn gas, but they were slowly pulling in behind the Zeros. He bared his teeth behind the oxygen mask. Yeah, everyone said you couldn't turn with the Zero, and you sure as hell couldn't outclimb it, but the Zero turned tighter at lower airspeeds than it did at higher.

It was a race.

His radio crackled. "Boxcar Red Leader, this is Brickbat Leader, come in."

"Go ahead, Brickbat Leader."

"We're climbing out, passing seven thousand. Maintain your turn."

"Roger, Brickbat Leader."

Jimmy didn't know who Brickbat Leader was. He didn't care. The cavalry was coming over the hill and that was just fine with him. He could see the needle on his fuel gauge flickering towards empty, the engine at 3000 RPM drinking it down at 145 gallons per hour.

"Jimmy, break right, break right now!"

Jack's P-39 rolled right and reversed its turn, Jimmy hanging on, turning against the g-force to watch the Zeros, who followed them into the turn and ran right into four P-39s. Tracers crisscrossed as the Zeros and the P-39s fired together. One P-39 staggered and tumbled, then spun down trailing thin smoke. One P-39 went head-on with a Zero, avoiding a collision only at the last moment. The Zero trailed smoke and turned to the north.

The other two Zeros spun around in that impossibly tight Zero turn and caught the three surviving P-39s as two of them tried to turn with them.

Another P-39 took hits across a wing, which separated from the fuselage. The other P-39 rolled over and dove for the deck, away from the Zeros.

Then Jimmy was very busy indeed, because the yellow low fuel light came on, and the engine coughed. It steadied out again but it was a clear warning. In minutes he would be flying a glider.

He looked around. A P-39 and a Zero were going at each other in another head-on pass. The Zero that had been hit was still egressing to the north. There was one more somewhere.

Jack grimaced at his fuel warning light. Then his engine sputtered and backfired.

Oh, hell.

But the field was a half-mile away and he had four thousand feet altitude. Then he saw Jimmy, lining up for the approach to the runway.

With a Zero coming up his six o'clock.

Jimmy pulled his throttle back as far as he dared, keeping the airspeed up around 130 mph. If that was a little fast, that was fine with him. OK, lined up with the runway, flaps coming down, gear coming down.

Tracers started reaching up from the ground, flying all around him.

Jesus Christ, they're shooting at me! My own guys!

Something slammed hard against his tail. There was a crack and a screech of metal from the engine. The prop jerked to a stop.

He pushed the nose down and saw tracer flying *above* him.

Jimmy dove for the ground. He didn't need to look to know there was a Zero sitting on his tail. He had to get this bitch on the runway *now*.

Smoke filled the cockpit and flame licked up around the seat.

Jack gritted his teeth as ground fire reached all around and past his airplane, thankfully missing himself and Jimmy, but also missing the Zero, which fired into Jimmy's P-39. Bullets and cannon shells struck Jimmy's after fuselage. There was a small explosion and fire smeared out of the engine compartment behind Jimmy's cockpit.

Jack put the gunsight pipper on the Zero and squeezed the triggers.

Jimmy stalled the P-39 in the last few feet as he scrunched behind the armor plate. The main gear hit hard but the airplane didn't bounce back into the air. He sucked the stick back into his gut and hit the release catch on the door. Oh shit oh hell, he was going to have to dive out on that wing and hope the fucking engine didn't explode.

Something roared over his head. He looked up to see the light grey underside of the Zero not ten feet above him, smoke and fire pouring out of its engine. The Zero fell out of the sky and pancaked on the runway in front of him in a billow of fire, smoke, and dust.

Jimmy stood on the brakes. He wanted out of this thing, he wanted out right now, and he hit the quick-release catch on his Sutton harness, ready to jump out of the door. He steered the fighter to one side of the runway and the left gear caught the lip of a bomb crater. It slewed him to the left as the gear broke off. The airplane ground-looped to a halt.

Jimmy hit the main switch, shutting off electrical power, and was out of the cockpit and rolling off the wing root as the burning P-39 shuddered to a stop. He shut his eyes and breathed out against the fire from the engine. The wind blew heavy oily smoke at him when he breathed in. He hit the ground in a ball, rolled, came to his feet and started running, trying to cough the smoke out of his lungs.

There was a *bang!* and something whipped past his ear. Ardana looked up, still running.

Right ahead of him the Jap Zero sat on the runway, burning merrily. Its canopy was open.

The Zero pilot was running straight at him. He had a pistol in his hand and as Jimmy stood there the Jap shot at him again, rapid fire, bullets whistling and snapping around him. Something tugged at his pants leg and there was a sting of pain in his calf.

For the longest of slow-motion moments Jimmy watched the Jap run at him, firing his little automatic. Jimmy could even see the spurt of flame from the pistol muzzle and the man's mouth working as he screamed something inaudible over the cracking antiaircraft guns and the roar of airplane engines.

Then he heard his grandfather speaking to him, from years in the past. They were out riding, looking for stray cattle, and came across a coiled rattlesnake on the trail. Jimmy froze, fascinated with the fear of the snake, looking right into its black eyes. Just like the black eyes of the Zero pilot, who fired once again.

"Reckon you better draw, son," his grandfather's voice drawled casually from somewhere behind him, exactly as it had that day on the trail.

Jimmy reached up. His thumb swept aside the safety strap holding the Colt revolver in place in the holster. He did exactly as his grandfather taught him. He didn't hurry. There was no need to hurry. There was only the need to shoot straight. The Colt's grip filled his hand and the pistol's long blue barrel cleared the holster while Jimmy's thumb slid over the hammer spur, his index finger going into the trigger guard, hand holding the barrel slightly up.

The Zero pilot was less than ten yards away, still running, screaming something at the top of his voice. Jimmy pulled the hammer of his Peacemaker back and brought the barrel in line with the Zero pilot's chest and squeezed the trigger. The .45 lead slug took the Jap in the breastbone and blew his heart out behind him.

The man stumbled and went to his knees. He looked thoughtfully at Jimmy. He tried to bring his pistol up. He kept trying for a long moment, until he fell face forward onto the runway and was suddenly, terribly still.

Chapter Six

"You had to have guys you could rely on"

Jack taxied up to the revetment and shut down his engine, looking down at the runway.

In the smoke and dust from the crashed airplanes he couldn't see much. He went numb, trying not to think, but he remembered guys in his squadron in Java, men he had known for less than a week or sometimes less than a day, who died in flames or a hail of machine-gun bullets, screaming over the radio and then going abruptly silent, falling from the sky and smashing into the ground in a welter of exploding gasoline and metal parts while the Zeros danced overhead.

Jack opened the cockpit door and noticed the silence. The fire of the antiaircraft guns had stopped. There wasn't even a hum of engines on the field until a truck drove by, headed to the airstrip, full of mechanics. It made him angry. Christ Almighty, Jimmy Ardana was lying dead on the airstrip and those fucking ghouls were going down there to strip his airplane!

Jack cursed as he struggled with the fittings of the Sutton harness and the parachute, shrugging off the chute as he climbed out onto the P-39's wing. Then he looked around again. Where the hell was Terraine? He had to get gas and oil and refill the ammo trays.

He looked down at the airstrip and saw men gathered around the smoking wrecks of the Zero and Jimmy's P-39. Three men split off from the crowd and began walking up the slight rise to the squadron flight line.

The man on the left was tall and lanky and almost had to be Chief Halloran. But the smaller figure in the center wore a flight suit and as Jack watched took off his leather flying helmet and goggles, running his hand through his hair. Jack sagged against the wing of his airplane, almost weak with relief. It was Ardana. He was all right. He was walking, even, so if he was hurt it couldn't be bad.

Wolchek hurried down the hill and motioned to Davis as he passed the revetment. Jack fell in beside him.

"What happened, Jack?" the major asked.

"We hit the bombers on their way back," Jack replied. "Then the Zeros chased us home. We were way low on fuel. I shot one off Jimmy's tail but I was sure he'd bought it."

Wolchek looked at him curiously. He nodded towards the Zero, smoking at the side of the airstrip.

"You shot that one down?" the major asked.

"Well, yeah, I..."

Jack became aware of the Wolchek's expression. He was looking at Jack in a strange way, as if Jack had suddenly grown wings or acquired a halo or something.

"That makes five, Jack," said Wolchek.

It made Jack irritable but at least he understood the looks Wolchek kept stealing him as they started down the hill again.

"Yeah, well, maybe I can go Stateside and sell war bonds," Jack said. "We've still got a hell of a lot of Japs to kill. Five of the little bastards isn't much more than a good start."

The words made Wolchek nod. "You're right," he said. "How did you do with the bombers?"

"Can't claim anything. Maybe some damage. Twin engines and twin tails, probably Mitsubishi Nells. I shot up two of them. Jimmy got a piece of one too, but they were still flying along the last time I looked back. We were running from the Zeros by then."

Wolchek nodded. "Looks like Ardana came through it OK. But I wouldn't have pegged him for a white scarf guy. Not in this heat, anyway."

Jack looked from the major to Jimmy, coming up the hill between the two mechanics. Then he noticed that Simmons carried Jimmy's parachute, and Jimmy did indeed have a white scarf wound loosely around his neck. He carried some kind of leather belt in his hand.

Jack didn't remember Jimmy wearing a scarf when they took off.

And then Jack noticed the way Simmons and Halloran were walking, or rather marching, almost as if they were on parade, keeping step with Jimmy Ardana, who looked tired and almost spent.

"What's up with those two?" Wolchek wondered aloud.

When they were close enough Halloran stopped and came to attention, as did Simmons. Ardana took a pace beyond them but stopped himself, looking puzzled as Halloran snapped an extremely sharp salute at Wolchek.

"Sir, it is my duty to report that there's a dead Jap on the airstrip," Halloran barked. He held the salute.

Wolchek came to attention and returned the salute. "A dead Jap? What are you talking about, Chief?"

Halloran relaxed and grinned. He clapped Jimmy on the shoulder. "Christ, Major, you should've seen it. Captain Davis here shot down the Jap that got Jimmy. Jimmy put his P-39 down and the Jap crash-landed just beyond him. They both got out of their airplanes and went gunning for each other like it was the OK Corral or something. Lieutenant Ardana here shot the Jap. Killed him deader 'n hell."

Wolchek looked curiously at Ardana. Jack took a second look at the leather belt Ardana held. It was actually a pistol belt, he saw, for some sort of small automatic. Then he looked at the scarf loosely wound around Ardana's neck. It hung around him in big loops and must have been twelve feet long. Davis picked up an end of it and looked at it curiously. There were characters in Japanese calligraphy stitched onto it.

"Damn," said Wolchek, looking at the scarf. "I had a parachute once that had less silk. Are you OK, Lieutenant? You look a little singed."

It was true. Ardana's flight suit had soot on it and he reeked of burning gasoline.

"I'm fine, sir," Ardana replied.

Jack looked at him. He thought Jimmy looked a little out of it.

He turned to Wolchek. "Steve, if you don't mind, I'd like to take Ardana up to my tent so we can hash out the mission."

"Sure, sure, Jack. You going to try to fly any more today?"

Jack looked at Wolchek and blinked. "Oh. Right. My other two chickadees. If it's all the same to you, sir, it might be better to fly at first light tomorrow morning."

Wolchek nodded.

Halloran looked from Davis to Ardana and nodded. "Simmons, come on. Let's have a look at old number 13. Looks like you've got a real gunfighter on your hands. We're going to have to make sure he's taken care of."

In a moment Jack stood with Ardana on the taxiway. Around them the mechanics returned to work. Somewhere down the line an engine started up, running at idle.

"Come with me, Jimmy," Jack said. He led the lieutenant up to his tent and got the barracks bag full of liquor out from under his bunk. Jack uncorked the first bottle he came to and held it out to Ardana.

"I don't know what it is," Jack said. "But take a good long swig."

Ardana looked at the bottle. Then he looked down at his right hand, which held the Zero pilot's pistol belt. He took a deep, shuddering breath and tossed the belt onto Jack's bunk. Then he took the bottle from Jack and put it to his lips. He took two deep gulps before he had to stop and cough.

He handed the bottle back to Jack, who took a swig and coughed himself. It was some kind of cheap Australian whisky that clawed its way down your throat and set off a fire in the gut.

"Well," Jack gasped. "That's smooth."

He handed the bottle back to Ardana, who took another, more cautious drink. Then Ardana unwound the scarf from his neck and bundled it up before tossing it into the bunk by the pistol belt.

Jack looked at the holster. It wasn't very big, not much larger than a man's palm.

"You mind?" he asked. Ardana shook his head and sat down on the edge of the bunk.

Jack sat down and took the Jap pistol out of its holster. Jack had heard of the Nambu pistol but this was the first one he'd ever seen. It looked like a skinny Kraut Luger. It had the look of a carefully kept weapon, though, clean, with a light sheen of oil still visible, as if the owner had wiped it down just before taking off. Jack examined the grip and slide, then extracted the clip and ejected the cartridge in the chamber. He picked up the cartridge and looked at it. It was a little bottle-necked thing that might have been .32-caliber. 8mm, he guessed, since the Japs used meters and kilograms same as the Krauts. When he pushed the remaining cartridges from the clip he found only two there.

"That guy managed to take a couple of shots at you," Jack said. "He hit you?"

"Grazed my leg. Nothing to speak of."

"Well, hell, that's a wound received in combat. You should get the Purple Heart for that."

Jimmy pulled up the leg of his flight suit. There was a purple discoloration on his leg. A little blood had welled out of it and crusted over.

"It's just a scratch."

Jack shrugged. "It's up to you." He juggled the pistol idly in his hand, then tried it for balance. "A little light, but good balance. Not much of a bullet, though. What you got in the hogleg?"

"Colt 45."

"Jesus. That'll stop an elephant."

Ardana shrugged. He picked up the scarf and wound it through his fingers, looking curiously at the odd characters. "I wonder what these mean."

"Something inscrutably Oriental, I'm sure. Why did you take it?"

"I didn't. I was standing there looking down at the Jap when Halloran and Simmons and some other guys came up, whooping and hollering. Halloran took the pistol belt and the scarf off the

Jap, picked up the pistol and shoved it in the holster, and gave them to me. One kill, he said. Confirmed."

"No fucking shit," said Jack. One kill, confirmed. He took a swallow of whisky and handed the bottle to Ardana. Ardana had a swig and handed the bottle back to Jack, who replaced the cork and put the bag back under his bunk. "How did you do with the Nells?"

"The who? Oh, those Jap bombers? Well, I'm pretty sure I got a piece of one. I started firing and saw hits across the canopy and left wing. Thought I saw his engine stream smoke. If the cannon had fired more than twice I might've gotten the bastard, but I guess I opened fire too soon."

Jack nodded. "Did you ever look back?"

"Hell yes. You told me to watch our tails, remember? Looked like fire coming from at least two of the Jap bombers, but all I could really see were those six Zeros coming down on us."

"Yeah. They have a way of getting your attention all right. What did you make of the fight over the airstrip?"

"Captain, I was so scared all I could do was stay with you. I did notice we were pulling ahead of the Zeros in the turn. I didn't think you could do that."

"You can in a diving turn above 300 mph. Take a look at the ailerons on that Zero once they push it off the runway. They're huge. Above 300 mph the control forces on those ailerons must be really high."

Jimmy frowned. "So you're saying we can dogfight with a Zero?"

"Sure, if you want your mother getting one of those deeply-regret letters from the War Department. The truth is we were lucky as hell, and it didn't hurt that Buzz and some of the other guys came up to hell out."

"They weren't so lucky. I saw at least two of them go down."

Jack nodded. "Yeah. And you saw what they were doing."

"Dogfighting with a Zero."

"Yeah. So don't do it. The only real advantages we have over the Zero is we're a little faster and we can dive away from them."

"That's why you hit them the way you did."

"Right. And we still almost got our asses handed to us by those little yellow bastards."

Ardana shook his head slowly and looked up at Jack. "I didn't even realize he was there, you know. That Jap pilot on the airstrip. First I knew about it was when a bullet went by my head. I looked up and there he was, running at me and shooting, screaming something. And I just stood there. I couldn't believe it. He was shooting at *me*. What the hell did I ever do to him?"

"Nothing," Jack said. He frowned at Ardana. "Some crazy Jap bastard runs at you, screaming and shooting, and all you do is stand there? You're lucky to be alive, kid."

"I know," Ardana said. "If he'd just taken careful aim instead of running at me he might have gotten me."

"You did finally shoot the bastard. What happened?"

"Well, I heard my grandfather tell me he reckoned I'd better draw, so I did."

"Your grandfather?"

"He was from Texas. Came to Montana after some kind of gun trouble down on the Texas border he'd never talk about. Not to me, anyway."

"Damn. Well, I'm glad you listened to him."

"Me too."

"Hungry?"

Ardana thought about it for a minute. "I'm starving."

"Let's get some chow, then. It's Aussie stuff. I hear it's really terrible."

"It couldn't be any worse than that whisky."

"Pilot, radio operator."

"Go ahead, Sparks."

"Goddamned Japs are bombing Seven-Mile again, Skipper."

"OK, acknowledged. Thanks, Sparks." Charlie grimaced.

"Jeez," said Deering. "D'you think we'll ever land at that place when it hasn't been bombed, or about to be bombed, or being bombed?"

"Doubt it," Charlie replied.

"Bet the RAF doesn't have to put up with this shit anymore. Just go bomb some Kraut city flat and come back to a nice civilized beer on a nice civilized air base."

"So join the RAF, Deering."

"It's just that landing on a bombed-out runway is so rough on the airplane, skipper. And my nerves."

"Your nerves? Your little delicate nerves, Mike?"

"Oh, hell, yeah, skipper. Very small, extremely delicate."

Charlie suppressed a grin as the crew, listening in on the intercom, expressed various opinions concerning the co-pilot's delicate nerves.

"Hey!" Deering said indignantly. "I'm talking about my nerves, not my man-parts here! You guys keep it clean!"

"Hey, Lieutenant, keeping it clean is your problem," said Lefty. "No medics and no pro station on this here airplane."

"OK, guys, take it easy on poor Mike," said Charlie. "He's turning pink up here."

"Thanks, skipper," Mike said as more hoots and howls of amused derision filled the intercom. The merriment gradually died away and the Fort flew on over the ocean east of New Guinea, past green islands ringed with white surf in the blue whitecapped sea.

"Navigator to pilot."

Charlie shifted uncomfortably in his seat. After seven hours it was getting damned hard. "Go ahead, Al," he said.

"There's our next landfall, skipper, about one o'clock. Milne Bay."

Charlie and Mike Deering craned up to look over the nose of the bomber. Stern popped up in the navigator's astrodome ahead of them and smiled cheerfully before disappearing back down into his compartment.

For the last hour they flew at ten thousand feet over seas of every shade between blue and green, with plenty of that pale turquoise denoting shallow water around the green islands ringed with the white foam of breakers. Charlie relaxed a little. With Milne Bay in sight they were maybe an hour to an hour and a half from Seven-Mile. The Australians were at Milne Bay, anyway, so even if they had to crash land the Fort on a beach nearby at least they'd be rescued pretty quickly. And from now on they'd have the beach of eastern Papua New Guinea on their left, within easy gliding distance of their base course.

As they passed the west end of Milne Bay Stern came up on the intercom again. "Aaaand...mark! Within three minutes of my prediction. It's good to fly with a pilot who can follow directions, isn't it, boys?"

"You were three minutes off?" Charlie retorted. "You're slipping, Al. Mike here says he's going to study navigation. He could do a better job than that."

"Yeah, but skipper, you always told me I can't add two plus two and get five reliably," Deering replied. "I thought that was a prerequisite for being a navigator."

"Go on, laugh it up," Stern said. "Next time you two want to know where the hell we are I'll multiply when I should divide and you can see how you like it."

"Pardon me, gentlemen," came the voice of the flight engineer. "Thought you might like to know we have 400 gallons of useable fuel remaining."

"Well, Al?" Charlie asked.

"Just a sec, keep your pants on...OK, 220 miles to Seven-Mile, indicating 170 mph at 9000 feet, we'll be there in, oh, hour twenty minutes – what's your throttle setting, skipper?"

"2100 RPM."

"OK, so burning 265 gallons per hour, we'll use about 350 gallons getting there, so we should have enough to taxi off the runway."

"OK. Thanks, Al."

Charlie thought about it. The tables for fuel consumption had some wiggle room built into them, usually 10%. Also, they would burn a little less fuel at 5000 feet than they would at their present altitude of 9000 feet, but if they had to glide in with the last of their fuel, altitude was money in the bank.

"What do you think, Mike?" he asked his copilot.

Deering shrugged. "Fifty gallons gives us what, another ten minutes? We could lighten the ship, throw some guns and ammo overboard. Hate to do that, though. Closer we get to Seven-Mile the more likely it is we'll see Japs. Gliding to a landing on the beach versus being shot down out of control because we can't defend ourselves? Think I'd take a chance on running out of fuel on approach."

Charlie nodded. "Pilot to crew," he said on the intercom. "Looks like we'll make it to Seven-Mile but it's going to be close. Everyone check your chutes and emergency equipment."

"OK, Mike, next question," he said. "Land on the beach, in the jungle, a swamp or the ocean just off the beach?"

"Jeez, Skipper, what's with the Twenty Questions? I thought you were the brains of this outfit."

"Lazy bum. I might get shot. My oxygen mask might fail. God forbid, you might get your own airplane. What would you do?"

Deering sighed. "The beach might be OK if it was wide enough, long enough and free of obstacles. Not many like that I recall seeing. No way I'd land in the jungle, not when those trees are fifty feet high or more. The swamp might be OK, again if it was long and wide enough but hell, there's plenty of swamps near the coast. Water landing might be the best bet. Land a little off the coast, get the rafts out and paddle ashore."

"Yeah. There was a crew tried that in the Philippines. Took 'em forever to make it in."

"But they did make it in," Deering pointed out.

"Fair enough. Any landing you walk or swim away from, I guess."

"You guys aren't really gonna put us in the water, are you?" said the ball turret gunner. "Y'all know ah cain't swim."

"What the hell, Reb, you can always learn," said Lefty. "I'll help you. Nothin' to it."

"Nothin' to it, he says. Ah ain't seen nothin' bigger than the Mis'sippi River before Ah joined this heah Army, and now I don't see nothin' but ocean and more ocean and little bitty islands heah and theah. Even that damned Australia ain't no proper continent, jes' an overgrown island."

"They got women and they got beer, so how big do they need to be?" asked Lefkowicz.

The intercom fell silent. Behind Charlie, Kim Smith rotated his turret slowly, searching for Japs, and off their right wing the mountains of the New

Guinea interior climbed above their height and grew clouds.

"Pilot, radio operator."

The radioman's brusque, business-like tone instantly silenced the intercom chatter.

"Go ahead, Sparks."

"Skipper, I'm listening to some pretty confused radio chatter from Seven-Mile. Sounds like a dogfight or something over the field. Brickbat and Boxcar squadrons are fighting the Japs, and it sounds like at least one and maybe two guys got shot down."

"Well, hell. Al, what's our position?"

"One hundred ten miles east of Port Moresby."

"OK, Sparks, you got that?"

"Yes, sir, one hundred ten miles west of Moresby. Shall I send a position report?"

"Affirmative. Let them know we're headed in, and we're low on fuel."

"Got it, boss."

"Flight engineer, pilot. How's our fuel, Kim?"

"About 150 gallons."

"OK, thanks. Pilot to crew, you all heard Seven-Mile is under attack. Let's keep a sharp lookout for Zeros."

There was a businesslike chorus of "Rogers" over the intercom and then quiet.

Fifteen minutes later Deering pointed ahead of them, between the banks of towering cumulus in the late afternoon sun that was just low enough to start being a nuisance. "Look there, Charlie, isn't that smoke?"

"Looks like it," Charlie replied. "Sparks, we heard from Seven-Mile yet?"

"No, sir, not yet."

"OK. Flight engineer, check the flare loading and be sure we have the correct colors of the day."

"Roger that, skipper." A moment later the engineer said, "We're good. Green, red, green."

"OK, thanks."

"Hey, skipper, it's Sparks. I've got Seven-Mile on voice. They say the runway is foul right at the moment but we should be able to land in thirty minutes."

"Tell 'em we've got fuel for about twenty minutes and we're coming in, unless they want us to try the beach."

There was a pause, and then Sparks said, "They say they'll do their best and good luck."

And then it was only the waiting, as the miles slipped by below them and the 100-octane aviation gasoline was sucked from the tanks and burned by their four thirsty Wright Cyclone engines.

"Navigator to pilot."

"Go ahead, Al."

"Bootless Inlet at one o'clock."

Charlie and Deering looked over the long nose of the Fort. Al Stern, looking out the clear Plexiglass nose, had an unobstructed forward view. But sure enough, there it was; the coastal plain indented, with some low hills on a peninsula to seaward forming the southern side of the inlet, and the hills marking Fairfax Harbor and Port Moresby beyond that. They looked at the still-visible pall of smoke and dust, including one small fire sending up a cloud of black smoke, and at its base was the airstrip.

"OK, Sparks, tell Seven-Mile we have the runway in sight and we're coming straight in. Be ready to fire the flares."

"Roger, Skipper."

Charlie settled back in his seat. Deering began their landing checklist. In a moment they were over the beach at the western end of Bootless Inlet, with the runway visible ahead.

"Gear down, flaps down," Charlie called.

Deering pulled the levers. The gear and flaps came down. Charlie steadily reduced the power to maintain the rate of descent, scanning the runway ahead as the damage became visible. It really wasn't too bad, only one crater on the right side about the middle of the runway. There were two burning airplanes on the runway, creating the smoke they had seen. There were trucks off to the side nearby.

Charlie edged a little to the left to avoid the crater, pulled the power off to almost idle. The Fort sank gently to the ground, stalling in as Charlie pulled back on the yoke. As soon as the mains began to rumble over the runway he and Deering were on the brakes, the yokes firmly in their stomachs to keep the bomber on the ground. A moment's touch of left brake and they were past the crater. As they flashed past they could see one burning airplane was a P-39 and the other a Zero.

They came nearly to a halt and Charlie applied power to taxi to their dispersal area. Just as he cleared the runway Number 3 engine missed, coughed and died. Number 2 quit without notice, followed by Nos. 1 and 4.

Bronco Buster II rolled a few yards and came to a quiet halt on the taxiway.

"Told you we'd have enough gas," said the navigator.

Jimmy noticed that when Jack walked in to the mess tent there was a brief lull in the conversation. Heads turned their way, studied Jack for a moment, and then turned back to their neighbors.

Jack was an ace. But he was still going to have to drink the lousy coffee or tea being served for lunch, and eat the food, too, which deserved the word "mess" as far as Jimmy was concerned. It was something Australian all right, a ration they called "M&V" for "meat and vegetable." Jimmy was pretty sure the "meat" part was questionable and the same went for the "vegetable." It didn't sit well on top of Jack's rotgut whisky, either.

Evans and Bellmon ate with them. Bellmon kept looking at him throughout the meal. Jimmy couldn't figure out the look and he wished to hell Bellmon would look somewhere else. It finally occurred to Jimmy that Bellmon was envious. He couldn't for the life of him figure out why Bellmon would envy him. He'd never be able to tell anyone what he really thought, that he wished to hell he could take it back. He kept seeing the light go out of the Jap's eyes. Even if the crazy sonofabitch was doing his level best to shoot holes in Jimmy's own sweet posterior, Jimmy wished he hadn't had to kill the man.

As for Evans, he kept quiet and choked down the food. Finally Bellmon asked about the flight schedule for the next day.

"We'll do a little formation work in the morning," Davis replied. "We'll spend an hour or so going over maneuvers, then we'll come back and gas up. Then we'll get in some low-level practice and shoot the guns."

"Low level?" asked Bellmon. "Isn't that for bombers? The mediums, anyway?"

Jimmy watched Davis. Davis didn't answer Bellmon right away. Some sort of shadow passed over the captain's face.

"We're going in as strafers," Davis said. "You got a problem with that, Bellmon?"

"Yes, sir, I do. I've never done any low-level work."

"Oh, gee. It's just not fair, is it? You want to blame someone, blame Tojo for starting this war."

Gerry suddenly acquired an interest in the unidentifiable stuff on his plate.

Evans muttered something. Jimmy saw the captain's eyes flicker over at Evans, who kept his head down, staring at the food he was shoveling into his mouth despite the swarming flies. Jimmy thought about the loudmouthed Evans of this morning, spoiling for a fight.

Davis looked at Evans for a long moment, and then looked back at Bellmon.

"Do you think we'll see any Japs in the morning?" Bellmon asked.

Davis scowled. "You'll see all the Japs you want, Bellmon. Maybe not tomorrow morning but soon enough." Davis stood up. "My advice is, you boys get some rest. Sunrise is at 0615. Be on the flight line at 0545. All of you. It's likely to be a long day."

The captain walked off, dumping his plate in a tin tub of greasy water.

"What did I say?" Bellmon asked.

Jimmy shrugged. "Don't be so god-damn eager, Gerry, not with Captain Davis. That's my advice."

Bellmon frowned and looked away. "I was just asking," he muttered.

Evans snorted and got up.

"What's wrong with him?" Bellmon asked.

"Probably scared."

"Yellow?"

"No. Just scared."

"Are you scared?"

"Shitless."

Bellmon darted a look at him. Jimmy kept his face deadpan. It wasn't any effort to do it. He was telling the truth, after all.

"So what was it like?" Bellmon finally asked.

"You were in the Hudson this morning. Hell, you were in an air raid this afternoon. What was that like?"

Bellmon shrugged but the look in his eyes was a man looking at something a thousand yards away, just for a moment. "The air raid wasn't much. We were in a slit trench with a bunch of other guys. The bombs hit about a mile away. There was a hell of a lot of noise. You could feel the earth shake. It was scary but not too bad, not that far away. Some of the mechanics told us to wait for the Japs to drop close by. Don't think I care for that idea."

"Yeah. Think I'd rather be flying. My Dad told me about being trapped in a shell hole in No Man's Land during an artillery barrage in the last war."

Bellmon looked at Jimmy again. "I guess what I really meant was, what was it like when you shot that Jap?"

"Jesus Christ, Gerry."

"I mean it. I mean, I have to ask. I have to know."

"You'll get the chance to do it yourself, day after tomorrow. You tell me when we get back."

"It's just, I don't know if I can do it."

"Oh, hell. I was scared, and that Jap on the airstrip, that just sort of happened. I can tell you all about how scared I was and brother, that wouldn't be half of it. And shooting that guy? Jesus, Gerry, I don't know how the doughboys do it. I don't know how my grandpa did it. I don't know how I'm going to do it again, when I have to do it."

Jimmy got up and put his dishes in the greasy water. Bellmon came with him and they walked to Tent 7.

Canvas has its own stink. When it rots and mildews it has a heavy fungal odor that cut its way right through all the other smells of Seven-Mile. Ardana raised the tent flap and walked in.

Someone had deposited their bags and footlockers in the middle of the floor of the tent.

"What did that Captain say about the tent being cleared out?" Bellmon asked.

"Just that. I guess the guys who were in here before won't be coming back. Do you care where you sleep?" Ardana made a vague gesture around the tent. It was about ten by ten. Mosquitoes and flies swarmed inside it.

"Jesus, do you think we can sleep in here?" Bellmon replied. He waved his hands in front of his face as a particularly determined swarm of insects attacked. "I don't care. I'll take this one." He indicated a bunk on the right-hand wall and dragged his footlocker over to it. "Hey, Jimmy, look at this."

Bellmon reached under the bunk. Jimmy watched him pull a field scarf out from under the bunk.

"Guess they forgot something," Jimmy said.

"I guess."

Jimmy chose the bunk nearest the door and put his bags on the bunk and the footlocker underneath it.

"These sides are supposed to roll up. Look, there's mosquito netting along the walls," he said. "Let's see if we can at least get some air moving through here."

He and Gerry were rolling up the walls of the tent when Evans trudged up. He was still in his slightly muddy flight suit, but the mud was in streaks where his sweat washed it further down the fabric. Here and there the sweat had dried and left salt incrustations.

"What, you guys moved in here without me?" he growled.

Jimmy looked up. "Where the hell were you, anyway?"

"Out. Walking."

"Whatever. Make yourself useful and help us roll up the tent sides."

"You'll let the rain in."

"It's not raining right now. Come on."

"Fuck you, Ardana. You aren't my boss."

Jimmy turned to face Evans. "Danny boy, d'you remember what I told you I'd do if you said 'fuck you' to me again?"

Evans scoffed. "You think you're a big man. Try anything, Ardana, anything at all, and I'll pin your ass up around your ears."

Jimmy jabbed and caught Evans on the nose. He purposely didn't put a lot of force behind it, just enough to make it hurt. Evans staggered back two steps, hand going to his nose, and then he brought his fists up.

"OK, Jimmy, you and me," Evans said.

Jimmy stood there, watching how Evans moved. What Evans did next almost caught Jimmy by surprise just because it was so stupid. Evans cocked his big right fist back and aimed a powerful roundhouse swing at Jimmy's jaw. Jimmy ducked under the blow in time and hammered his left fist into Evans' exposed lower ribs and then his right fist deep into Evans' gut. Jimmy danced back a step as Evans' left fist came around in that same swooping powerhouse swing, then jabbed again to Evans' chin in a quick one-two that staggered the man. He shook his head, breathing heavily, and looked at Jimmy.

"Knock it off, Evans," Bellmon said. He went to stand by Jimmy. "You're out of line."

Jimmy was surprised by how cold Bellmon's voice was.

"You're in this too?" Evans growled. He shook his head again.

"You're damned right," Bellmon replied. "Don't you get it? This is no good. You were a football player. Don't you know a team has to work together?"

"Yeah, and every team has a boss. Ardana ain't gonna be my boss."

"I'm not your boss," said Ardana. "Captain Davis is. But it's like this, Evans. If I have to pound you into liquid shit so I can sleep easy tonight I'll do it. But Gerry's right, too. I don't like you and you don't like me. We don't have to like each other to work as a team. So what's it going to be?"

For answer Evans took that same long roundhouse swing at Ardana's head. This time Jimmy moved in with a left-right to the gut that caught Evans exactly right, and when Evans' breath whuffed out and he doubled over, Ardana brought his left up under Evans' chin. Evans' head snapped up and he fell to the floor, unconscious.

Jimmy stood looking down at him, breathing a little hard and unconsciously flexing his fingers. The knuckles were cut and bruised on his right hand.

"You a boxer or something?" Gerry asked quietly.

"Yeah. In college. Learned more in cow camps during the summer, though."

"Is he OK?"

"I don't know. You hear about guys taking a hit like that and it breaks their necks or something."

At that moment Evans groaned, curled into a ball, and vomited. Gerry and Jimmy jumped back before the noxious fluid splashed their boots.

"Christ," Jimmy said in disgust. "Come on. We have to get him on his bunk, head down."

"Why?"

Jimmy grabbed one shoulder as Gerry moved to take the other. They dragged Evans to his bunk and dumped him on it with his head hanging down over the edge. "My Dad was county sheriff. He and his deputies always had a lot of fun with the miners and cowpunchers on Saturday night. They'd get a skinful of rotgut whisky and most of them would head on home singing and laughing, but there's always a few that Dad had to tap on the head. When he put them on a bunk in the jail he'd be sure they were face down with their heads over the edge, 'cause they always puke and he said a man drowning in his own puke was no way to die."

"Evans isn't drunk."

"Yeah, but he's out cold. I don't like him, but I don't want to see him die like that."

They picked Evans up, straining with effort, and put him face down on a vacant bunk. Jimmy sat down on his bunk. There were little pinholes in the canvas and the sun dotted the room with little pinpoints of light.

"Call me if there's an air raid or something," he said. He lay back on the bunk and fell asleep.

Jack stood outside his own tent. The whiskey he drank with Jimmy Ardana was roiling around with the greasy M&V rations and for a moment he thought he'd lose whatever was in his stomach to the dusty downtrodden bushes near the mess hall. The moment came and went and the image of his tracers slicing into the Jap Zero on Ardana's tail replaced it.

He looked up at the clouds and the blue sky.

I'm an ace, he thought to himself. It was every pursuit pilot's dream, like being knighted back in the old days or something like that. I'm an ace, Jack thought, and wondered why he wasn't elated.

He started walking down the path. In the distance he could see the mechanics still working to strip parts from Ardana's P-39 and the Jap Zero. A crane truck was getting ready to lift the P-39 and cart it off to the boneyard, while a bulldozer stood by to push the Zero clear. Another bunch of engineers filled in the bomb crater with rocks and gravel. He kept looking down the runway and saw a B-17 being hauled down a taxiway, and recognized it as Charlie's airplane.

Jack hitched a ride across the field and went looking for Charlie in the Ops tent for the 19th.

Charlie waved at him from across the tent, where he sat with Al Stern and two guys he didn't recognize. One guy wasn't wearing a flight suit, which meant he was probably an intelligence officer, and this was a debrief.

"Take a chair, Jack," Charlie said. "Symington, you don't mind if my brother sits in, do you?"

The officer thus addressed turned to look at Jack. "Hm. A pursuit pilot. Aren't you afraid he'll learn all our secrets, Major?"

"I already know you bomber guys shave your legs," Jack scoffed. He sat down. Charlie punched him on the shoulder, not too hard.

"You aren't supposed to know that," Charlie said. "Besides, I swore I'd never say anything about you pursuit guys wearing women's underwear."

Al Stern rolled his eyes. He looked at Bob Frye. "Is this something I should know about, Bob? All this Air Corps humor?"

"It probably isn't serious until they start singing or something," the bombardier advised. "And they usually have to be drunk for that."

"Don't count on it," said Jack. He looked at Charlie. "You guys run out of gas or something? I saw your ship being towed off."

"Aw, it wasn't that bad," said Charlie. "We made it home, didn't we?"

Al Stern scoffed and shook his head. "That song about coming in on a wing and a prayer should have a line about coming in on fumes," he said.

"Al, I thought you were taking better care of Charlie than that," Jack said. "How do you explain letting him almost run out of gas?"

"Not my fault," Stern said. "Japs hit the gas tank in our left wing. We were lucky it didn't start a fire."

Jack looked at Charlie and raised an eyebrow.

"Well," said Symington. He sat up, gathered his papers together, and stood. "Guess I'll leave you kiddies to catch up. Some of us have real work to do."

"Yeah, don't sprain a finger typing," Charlie shot back. Symington made a rude and unsympathetic gesture as he walked off.

Charlie chuckled. Then he looked at Jack. "My radio operator said there was a pretty good fight over the airstrip," he said. "What happened?"

Jack shrugged. "Air raid. I was up for some of it with that kid you met yesterday, Ardana."

"Are you a Brickbat or a Boxcar?"

"Boxcar Red Leader."

Al sat up straight. "Up for some of it, eh, Jack?"

"Yeah."

"OK. If you say so." Al sat back, a smile playing around the corner of his mouth.

Charlie looked at his navigator, then he looked back at Jack, who scowled suddenly.

"What?" Charlie asked.

"It's kind of all over," Stern said. "You saw that Zero on the airstrip? The guys on the ground crew claimed they saw the whole thing. The Zero shot down the P-39, then another guy in a P-39 shot down the Zero, which pancaked in front of the first P-39. Then the pilots got out and had an old-fashioned Hollywood gunfight, right there on the airstrip, and the P-39 pilot killed the Jap with one shot. Said it was the gol-darnedest thing they'd ever seen."

"Yeah," said Charlie." Like they saw anything from where they were hiding like sensible men at the bottom of a slit trench, during an air raid."

"Well, it's true, pretty much," said Jack. "In fact that gunfighter is Jimmy Ardana."

"No kidding?" said Charlie. "Pretty talented kid."

"Jimmy the Kid," said Stern.

That took the scowl off Jack's face. He laughed, a little ruefully. "Or the 7-Mile Kid," he said. "I didn't see it myself, but Jimmy told me about it after it happened."

"Where were you during the big gunfight?" Charlie asked.

"Landing my ship," Jack said.

Charlie sat silently for a moment, looking at Jack. Then he sighed. "You shot the Zero off Ardana's tail, didn't you?"

"Wait a minute," said Al. "Doesn't that mean..."

"It does," said Charlie. He studied Jack's face. Then he stood up. "Come with me, Jack."

The brothers left the tent and walked down the dusty path.

"Where are we going?" Jack asked.

"I want to check on my airplane," Charlie replied.

"You're not going to lecture me, are you?"

"Hellfire, no," said Charlie. "In the first place, what good would it do? In the second place, what else could you do? I just want to be sure you're OK."

"I'm fine. I'm more concerned about Jimmy."

"Well, he's had one hell of a first day. I think maybe you should talk to Wagner about putting him in for a medal. Silver Star, or a DFC, anyway. Landing that Hudson, that was DFC material for sure."

"Not sure I want to talk to Boyd right now."

"No? Why is that?"

Jack was silent.

"Just because you're the second ace of the war? I don't think Wagner will mind that at all. He doesn't strike me as the jealous type."

"That's not it."

"OK. I'm not psychic, and I'm not going to drag it out of you, little brother. Tell me what's eating you."

"People went crazy over Wagner being an ace. I don't want that. I just want to keep flying."

Charlie shook his head and laughed. "Jack, I don't think you have anything to worry about on either score. You're the *second* ace of the war. People went crazy over Boyd Wagner because he was the *first* ace. So don't think anyone's going to buy you any drinks over it."

"You think?"

"I'd be pretty sure, yeah. As for flying, well, here you are, and I don't think you'll have to worry about it. You ever wonder why the Air Corps decided to ship you home?"

"Not really."

"Your lack of curiosity is exceeded only by your endearing naivete. Jack, they're going to make you a major and put you in command of a squadron, maybe not all at once, but before the end of the year. I'd bet on it. Now that you're an ace it's even more certain. Why, you might even make colonel before I do. Look at your buddy Wagner. I was a captain when the war started, and he was only a first lieutenant."

"I don't know if I want a squadron."

Charlie put a brotherly arm around Jack's shoulder. "You ever meet Hap Arnold? You know, General Henry H. Arnold? The guy in charge of the whole Air Corps?"

"No."

"I did, once. Now that's an impressive guy, a real operator. But he's an operator with a problem. He's got this brand new air force, see? Back home they're building thousands of planes a month and training pilots to fly them. That means all sorts of new groups and squadrons being formed and guess what? All of those new groups will need colonels to run them, and since there are three squadrons to the group, every new group will need three majors to act as squadron commanders. That's a bunch of colonels and majors, Jack, and where do you think good old Hap is going to find them?"

"Aw, hell."

Charlie laughed. "Look at it this way. If the Jap navy doesn't invade Port Moresby and you live long enough, you'll get to go back Stateside, marry that incredibly gorgeous girl you're engaged to, and then you'll have six months to a year training your new squadron, during which time no one will be shooting at you, and you can enjoy a state of wedded bliss. So if you think I'm going to feel sorry for you, Jack, you're wrong. I know guys that would cut their left nut off to be you."

It was on the tip of Jack's tongue to say they could have it, then, until he saw the look on Charlie's face. It was a blend of amusement, concern, affection, and brotherly exasperation.

"Well, if you put it that way," Jack said.

Charlie let his arm fall away and punched Jack on the shoulder again. "I do," he said. "Look. What's your real job, right now? I'll give you a hint. It's not all about being a famous ace."

"You must be talking about those kids I got saddled with."

Charlie nodded. "Sounds to me like one of those kids has the stuff to be a real winner. If he lives long enough. So look on the bright side and start from there."

Chapter Seven

May 7, 1942

"Low enough over the water to count the fish"

It rained before dawn. Jack and his pilots walked through the mud and the little freshets of water draining down the slope back to the flight line. Jack's P-39 had been refueled before the rain and Halloran was working on another airplane in the revetment next to it. Jack stopped in front of the revetment.

"OK, here's the drill. Bellmon, you and Evans take a few minutes and go over the startup checklist with your crew chiefs. They're the ones who have to take care of your airplanes so they might know some tricks you don't. Clear?"

"Yes, sir," said Evans in a sullen tone. Davis decided not to take notice. He figured there was a good chance that tone was normal for Evans. Besides, he was being very careful not to notice Evans' swollen jaw or the raw skin on Jimmy's knuckles.

"Yeah. Jimmy, I talked to Halloran a few minutes ago. He said Number 13 was ready to go. All of you, one more time, we're Boxcar Red Flight. I'm Lead, Evans is Two, Jimmy is Three and Bellmon is Four. Unless your airplane won't start we take off in fifteen minutes. Come up on the radio with your call sign when you're ready to taxi. Any questions?"

Jack looked at the three other pilots, who shook their heads.

"All right. Let's get started."

Jimmy ran his hand over the left wing of the *Gremlin* where cannon holes gaped the day before. Now freshly painted sheet metal covered the wounds. Jimmy walked around the airplane, feeling that same sense of unreality he felt yesterday as the Hudson took off from Townsville.

Jesus God, that was only yesterday. He'd been in combat twice and seen men die all around him. He'd been sure he was going to die himself. Jimmy took a deep breath and looked around him.

The sanguma man, Evarra, stood on the other side of the taxiway. He watched Jimmy with those same calm, knowing eyes. Jimmy lifted his right hand and waved. Evarra nodded and waved back.

This is his world, Jimmy thought. Me being here waving at him has to be almost as unreal to him as this world is to me.

The sun's light gilded the tops of the trees around the revetment. Simmons and Jones, the armorer, crawled out from under the wing.

"She's ready to go, Mr. Ardana," Simmons said. "How does she look?"

"Really good," Jimmy replied. "You guys must have worked like hell to get this ship ready. Anything I need to know?"

"You've got full ammo trays and Jones and I charged the wing guns. Hope you don't need them, but they're ready if you do." Simmons hesitated and started to say something, then stopped.

"What's up, Simmons?"

"Look here, Mr. Ardana…"

"Reckon you better call me Jimmy." Jimmy put his right hand out. "I mean, here in this revetment at least."

Simmons took Jimmy's hand and shook it. "My friends call me Don," he said, and grinned. "At least, in this revetment they do."

Jimmy grinned back. "OK, Don. So what did you want to say?"

"You kind of had a rough day yesterday, Jimmy. But the boys and I think you did all right. We think you might be our kind of pilot."

"What's that, exactly?"

"Well, we don't want you to take any stupid chances, but it would sure be nice to be able to paint a couple of Jap flags on the side of the *Gremlin*."

Jimmy nodded slowly, reluctantly. He remembered the light going out of the Zero pilot's eyes. "Yeah. No stupid chances, but if I shoot, I'll shoot straight."

"Good enough, sir."

"OK, Don, since this is only the third time I've ever started an Allison engine, would you kind of look over my shoulder?"

The crew chief grinned. "Sure thing, Jimmy."

Jack lined up on the dirt strip feeling increasingly pissed off at his Number Two. Evans had charged out of his revetment as if he were going to drive right into the brush on the other side of the taxiway. When he hit the brakes to slow down Evans compressed the nose wheel strut to the point where Jack actually thought the prop tips struck the taxiway. Evans finally got behind him but he was either lagging behind or his prop was scant inches from Jack's rudder. Evans caused Jack enough concern that he had little attention to spare for Jimmy and Bellmon, taxiing behind them as Boxcar Red Three and Four. And God damn it to hell, Evans lined up on the runway at an angle. Jack thought about telling him to straighten up his airplane but Evans was still way too close to him. Jack was forcibly reminded about what Colonel Wagner said about no one who was ham-handed on the controls would ever fly a P-39 safely.

He gritted his teeth as he looked around the sky to check the pattern. No one was inbound so he keyed his radio and said, "Boxcar Red Leader with a flight of four ready to depart the active at Seven-Mile."

The tower flashed him a green light. Jack pushed his throttle forward, gently at first so that Evans could get the idea, increasing throttle until it was at takeoff power. The P-39 accelerated, reaching 100 mph indicated in seconds. Jack eased back on the stick with the merest suggestion of pressure and the P-39 lifted smoothly off the runway. He looked over his shoulder just in time to see Evans ballooning up like an elevator.

Then Evans pushed forward on the stick and his P-39 headed for the ground at full takeoff power with the gear still down. Jack winced as Evans yanked up on the stick and his P-39 yoyo'd back into the air. Eventually Evans was flying more or less straight and level. But he still hadn't retracted his gear.

"Gear up, Two," Jack radioed. Three seconds later, just as Jack was about to radio again, the gear came up on Evans' P-39, which began to accelerate as the drag decreased.

"Two, reduce your power to 2600 RPM and 34 inches of manifold pressure," Jack radioed. He was sure Evans was still at takeoff power, and the Allison wasn't supposed to go more than five minutes at that setting.

A moment later and the other airplane stopped accelerating. Jack bumped his throttle a little to stay ahead of Evans' airplane, giving it some elbow room, because Evans was still gently bobbing up and down. He even threw in a Dutch roll from time to time, cross-controlling on rudder and ailerons. Jack watched him. Gradually Evans got control of the airplane.

Jack looked around. He suddenly wished he had someone else with him, someone with a little more experience who could be watching the sky and keeping their tails clear while he tried to teach Evans how to fly a P-39.

Jimmy watched Davis and Evans accelerate down the runway, leaving a cloud of dust in the early morning air. Davis lifted out smoothly but Danny did that same pogo-stick thing with his gear down. Then he looked up at the approach to the runway, but there was no traffic visible.

He looked over his shoulder at Bellmon and kicked his rudder as a "follow me" signal, then moved onto the runway, waited for Gerry to line up behind him, and fed in the throttle.

The Allison responded with a steadily increasing howl of power and Jimmy's P-39 accelerated down the airstrip. Jimmy darted a look over his shoulder to be sure Bellmon was with him and then watched the runway and the airspeed indicator. The airplane wanted to fly at 100 mph but he held it down an instant longer before pulling up ever so gently on the stick. The P-39 responded with a smooth break from the ground. The wheels instantly stopped their rumbling and rattling. Jimmy moved the gear switch to UP and looked around, and that saved his life.

Just above him and settling on top of him was Bellmon's P-39, gear down and inches above his canopy. Jimmy sawed at the rudder pedals, fishtailing to bled off speed, and put the nose down, ever so gently, because he was less than a hundred feet off the ground.

Bellmon's landing gear started coming up. Jimmy moved out to one side, until he could climb level with his wingman. He could see Bellmon in the cockpit, looking around, and when Bellmon's head came around he waved cheerfully at Jimmy.

Jimmy realized he was holding his breath. He let it out in a whoosh.

Gerry has no idea he almost killed us both, Jimmy thought. *And now I have to fly formation with him.*

Bellmon was flying slightly in front of Jimmy but started to drop behind as he throttled back to let his engine cool. Jimmy waited until Bellmon was behind him and then moved over so that Gerry was off his right wing. Then he looked around and saw Jack and Danny a couple of miles ahead of them, turning in a circle, obviously waiting for them.

Jimmy looked around again. This might be a training flight, but they were training in a combat zone. Zeros had chased him in this part of the sky only yesterday. They could come anytime.

Maybe it was only his third flight in a P-39, and maybe he was scared, but he was damned well going to do his job.

Jack held his breath, even forgot Evans inching up on him from out on his right wing, watching the two P-39s nearly merge into each other. When he saw the lead P-39 abruptly move out from under the other he exhaled sharply, then evaded Evans, who was evidently doing his best to kill him as he slid closer and closer to Jack's elevators with his propeller. Jack looked around the sky, continuing his turn to let Jimmy and Gerry join up. When they were close enough he straightened out of the turn, slowly, but even so Evans cut across behind him and had to reverse to get back into position.

"Boxcar Red Three from Lead," Jack called. "Close it up."

"Roger, Lead."

There was a different note in Jimmy's voice. Davis knew Jimmy had been scared yesterday. He'd heard that over the radio. But now Jimmy sounded pissed off, and that made Davis grin. He knew how Jimmy felt. He had to suppress a chuckle, imagining how pissed Jimmy would be, trying to fly formation off Danny Evans' right wing.

But Jimmy surprised him. After the first attempt to get in close to Danny, who was still pretty much all over the sky, Jimmy moved out a little and stayed there, just as if there was one more airplane in the formation, and Jimmy was on that airplane's wing. And, Davis noted, the imaginary airplane Jimmy was flying with was flying pretty damn good formation on Boxcar Red Leader.

Davis nodded. Good enough, under the circumstances.

"Boxcar Red Flight from Lead, follow me," he called over the radio, and began some elementary formation work. He didn't dare try anything else with Bellmon and Evans in his flight.

Jimmy was sweating from more than the heat and the humidity as he taxied into his revetment and shut the airplane down.

Simmons climbed up on the wing root as Jimmy opened the door. He reached in and helped Jimmy with his harness.

"Jeez, Jimmy, Captain Davis really put you guys through the wringer, hah?" Simmons said.

"You could say that," Jimmy replied grimly. "Gas and oil, Don, I understand we're going back up after we grab a bite. And God help us, we're going to shoot live ammunition at something."

"Ah...sure thing, Jimmy."

Simmons raised an eyebrow. Jimmy shook his head. "Don't ask. Let's just say we had way too much fun up there. However, the *Gremlin* did fine. She's a sweet ship, Don."

"Thanks."

Jimmy climbed down from the P-39 and stretched. Davis had landed first and appeared now at the entrance to the *Gremlin's* revetment

"Well, Jimmy my lad," he called. "How are you doing?"

"Swell, skipper, just swell."

"Yeah. That's what I thought. Come on."

Jimmy fell in with Davis. They walked to the edge of Bellmon's revetment. He was just getting down from his airplane with a sheepish look on his face.

"Uh, sorry about that, Jimmy," he said.

"Save it," Davis replied. "Follow me."

Bellmon ducked his head a little and walked with Jimmy, just behind Davis, who was striding towards the revetment that housed Evans' airplane.

Danny Evans was leaning against his wing root, looking very pale indeed.

Jimmy looked at Danny and suppressed the urge to walk over and beat the living daylights out of him. Danny looked up at him and flinched.

"Ah, guys...I'm sorry."

"Lieutenant Evans, come with me," Davis said in a quiet, even tone.

Once they were out of earshot of the mechanics Davis chewed Bellmon and Evans up one side and down the other. Jimmy grew up on the range in Montana around cowboys, miners and various other sorts not known for their sheltered lives and gentle habits, so he thought he knew a little something about the manly art of profanity. But somewhere Captain Jack Davis acquired a mastery of the vernacular that would have aroused the admiration of any range boss or Army drill sergeant. And not once, it seemed, did he take the Lord's name in vain, and some of it sounded odd, like Shakespeare or something.

What the hell was a fulminating pustule, anyway? Jimmy wasn't sure. He was glad it wasn't directed at him, though.

The truth was, though, that Gerry and Danny deserved every bit of the attention that Davis lavished upon them.

Evans never did master the art of the crossover turn. He overcontrolled so badly that he had flown across Jimmy's nose twice, almost within the *Gremlin's* propeller arc, and once Jimmy was sure Evans dinged the skipper's right aileron, after which Danny, in a panic, turned hard right away from Davis and nearly took out both Jimmy and Gerry. Jimmy had called for Gerry to break down and pushed hard on his stick. For once Gerry was right with him, but even so Evans flew just over their canopies.

It was almost the only thing Gerry Bellmon did right during the flight, as far as Jimmy was concerned. Gerry wouldn't close up his formation and was generally slow to obey commands. Still, except for nearly killing him during the takeoff, he hadn't come anywhere near as close to killing him as Evans had.

"And you, Evans," Davis concluded. "You give me one good reason why I shouldn't go to Colonel Wagner, right now, and have you grounded."

Evans muttered something.

"Speak up, asshole. I didn't hear you."

"Because I'm here, Captain, and I want to fight the Japs."

"You want to fight the Japs! Hell, you can do that in the infantry!" Davis turned away. He balled his hands into fists and put them on his hips.

Jimmy took a step back. He figured Davis was going to slug Evans and he didn't want to be in the line of fire.

But Davis turned back after a long moment and said, very quietly, "You're right, Evans. That's a good reason. Not because you want to do it, but because you are here. And right now that does count for something. Now get out of my sight. You too, Bellmon. Go get something to eat. We fly again in one hour."

Bellmon and Evans scurried away, up the path to the mess tent.

Jimmy stood where he was.

"You still here?" Davis asked.

"Sure."

"You hungry?"

"Thirsty as hell."

Davis looked at him and glowered. Jimmy shook his head. "Water. Let's go find some that doesn't smell like shit or whatever that crap is they put in it so it doesn't give you the shits."

Davis scoffed. "Good luck with that."

But he started walking up the trail to the mess tent. Jimmy sighed and walked with him.

Jimmy Ardana concentrated very hard on the water and the horizon. The water was only fifty feet below him and he was very, very conscious of the fact, as well as the reading of his airspeed indicator, which showed him he was flying at 320 mph. At that speed, if he hit the water he might as well hit solid rock.

Ahead of him Davis as Boxcar Red Leader flew 20 feet lower than Jimmy. Evans, as Boxcar Red Two, bounced around in the general vicinity of his leader's right wing. Jimmy, as Boxcar Red Three, gritted his teeth and eased the stick a mere fraction of an inch forward, pulling up almost immediately. He found himself slightly below Davis and Evans.

"Boxcar Red Four, close it up," Davis said.

"Ahh...Roger, Lead," Bellmon replied. Jimmy flicked a look over his shoulder. Bellmon was a good forty feet higher than any of them.

Ahead of them a small island loomed. Davis eased up and over it. Jimmy looked over his shoulder again. Bellmon was lower but still ten feet too high.

Davis flicked his ship into a hard right turn. Evans ballooned out high and to the left, crossing behind Davis' tail. Jimmy followed Davis but realized that Bellmon had done almost as poorly as Evans.

"Two and Four from Lead, get back in position."

Bellmon moved back to his position on Jimmy's right wing but stayed fifty feet higher. Jimmy flicked a look over his left shoulder and saw that Evans was inching up slowly into his slot off Davis' right wing. He stopped when he was more or less abreast of Jimmy.

Evans looked over at Jimmy and then looked back at Davis' airplane.

"Two from Lead, what's the problem back there?"

Evans looked over at Jimmy again and quite suddenly Jimmy understood that Evans thought he was much too close to Jimmy and couldn't safely join up with Davis. Evans evidently wanted Jimmy to move over, to break formation, so that he could slide in.

Jimmy grimaced and decided he was damned if he'd break formation without orders just because Danny Evans wasn't enough of a pilot to fly formation.

Apparently Davis, looking back at his Number Two, had sized up the situation as well.

"Two, if you want to keep your wings, you've got three seconds to get into formation."

Evans gave it way too much throttle. He scooted ahead, missing Jimmy's left wing and almost colliding with Davis, who rolled left and climbed to get away from him. Evans then pulled his throttle back too far, forcing Jimmy to break right to get away from him. When Jimmy broke right Bellmon stayed fairly close to Jimmy's wing.

"Ooookay," Davis drawled over the radio. "Two, form up on my left wing."

Jimmy sighed with relief. Davis had been working them up to fly in right echelon. It was one of the first formations taught to cadets in flying school.

"Boxcar Red Flight, let's keep it loose for now. Three, move out a little to my right. Two, try to stay somewhere near my left wingtip."

Jimmy moved out a little, watching Gerry as he did. Bellmon wasn't really smooth but he was at least maintaining a passable formation this time.

They were flying in the vicinity of Daugo Island to the southwest of Port Moresby. Daugo Island was forty or fifty acres of flat sand and scrub brush with a little indented bay at the west end.

"OK, Three, you see that little bay?"

"Affirmative, Lead."

"Make a strafing attack on the end of it. Keep your dive angle shallow."

"Roger, Lead. Follow me, Four."

"With you, Three," Bellmon radioed.

Jack orbited at five hundred feet as Evans worked to stay on his wing. He watched Ardana and Bellmon swing out about a mile and then turn back towards the island.

Ardana opened fire too soon but it was only a short burst with his machine guns. The bullets hit the water short of the target and kicked up a lot of spray. A second later Davis saw smoke trailing back from Jimmy's wings. Bellmon opened up a little behind Jimmy, and then there was a half-visible puff of smoke from Jimmy's 37-mm cannon. Fountains of spray from his bullets striking the water marched up the beach and across the sand at the end of the inlet, along with at least one larger fountain indicating a cannon hit. Jimmy and Gerry stopped firing at about the same time and pulled up in a graceful chandelle to the left.

"Three's off," Jimmy radioed.

"Four's off," Bellmon called.

"Roger. Two, follow me. Lead's in."

Davis looked to his left to be sure Evans was with him, at least more or less. Evans was at least thirty feet farther to the left than he should have been and about twenty feet too high. Davis turned left and rolled out on his attack heading. He looked over his shoulder again and Evans was still there.

The arms of the little bay got closer, separated, grew. Davis added a little left rudder, straightened, and started firing. Tracers went by his left wing as Evans fired. Davis gave it one burst and started his pull out.

"Two! Two, pull out pull out *pull out!!*"

Davis dipped his wing in time to see Evans just miss the surface of the ocean. The water of the little bay was roiled from the machine gun fire and dust from the sand drifted in the air.

Davis took a deep breath and let it out.

"Two, join up," he said tiredly.

That was it. Davis watched Evans fly and decided when this flight was over, assuming Evans didn't kill himself landing, he was going to Colonel Wagner and have Evans grounded.

As Evans pulled into his volume of air off his left wing Davis hit the radio again. "OK, Three, form up."

"Roger, Lead."

When Jimmy was back off to his right Davis turned west for a minute, then made a diving 180-

degree turn, leading his flight right down to the water again. Except for Evans, of course, who was now fifty feet higher than everyone else. Davis sighed and looked over at Ardana and Bellmon. Ardana was right where he should be and Bellmon was flying lower, almost right where he should be. OK, fair enough. Bellmon was showing signs of improvement, at least.

"Boxcar Red Flight, we're going to attack Daugo Island," he said. "Our target is that same peninsula we attacked initially. Wait for me to fire and then open up."

"Two."

"Three."

"Four."

Then they were down on the deck with the palm-tree studded beach off to their left. Daugo Island appeared above the horizon. Jack looked for the target and skidded over a bit to line up with the northern arm of the bay. He opened fire and watched his tracers flying out, the bullets striking sand and water and flinging up spray and dust. Jack ceased fire and climbed up a little over the island, checking left and right to be sure his flight was in position.

"This is Lead. Let's go around and do it again. Same routine."

Jimmy shut down the engine and leaned back in his seat. He replayed the strafing attacks on the island in his mind as Simmons came up on the wing. Jimmy opened the door.

"Everything OK, Jimmy?" Simmons asked.

"Pretty good," Jimmy replied. He hit the quick-release on the harness. "We shot off some ammo, though."

"How'd the cannon do?"

"Jammed after four shots. I tried to clear it the way you said but it didn't work."

Simmons shook his head. "Chief Halloran swears it's how you load the shells. I'll ask him to come down and watch Dave reload."

"OK."

Jimmy climbed down, stretching, and went to the water jug his ground crew kept under a scrap of canvas for shade. He drank long and deep out of it, gasped for breath, and drank again.

"Hey, Jimmy."

He looked up. Captain Davis beckoned to him.

Jimmy went to join him. "Yes, sir."

"Keep Bellmon here. I'm taking Evans up to Operations."

Jimmy opened his mouth and shut it. "Yes, sir."

Davis walked over to Evans' revetment. Evans stood there waiting for him.

"You're taking my wings, aren't you?" Evans asked.

"I don't have that authority. But Colonel Wagner does, and he'll do it if I ask him to."

"Captain, give me one more chance. Look. I know I'm not the best pilot in the world. But please, if you take my wings I ..."

"What?"

Evans looked away. "Nothing, sir."

"Evans, my concern isn't just for you. It's for the safety of everyone in the flight. Why should I give you another chance? When I think there's a good possibility you're going to kill someone along with yourself?"

"Captain, look, I don't know what to tell you except I'm begging you."

"Aw, hell," Davis said in disgust. He turned away and looked at the jungle on the other side of the taxiway without seeing it.

"All right, Evans, come with me."

Davis took Evans to Bellmon and Ardana.

"OK, first the good parts," Jack said. "Jimmy, you and Gerry didn't do too badly, about what I'd expect for pilots of your experience. Gerry, you still need to work on your formation flying, but I see improvement. Work harder. Now, Evans."

"Yes, sir." The voice was husky and hardly audible.

"Evans, I'm at a loss as to what to do with you. Bluntly, I don't see how you graduated from flight school. I don't see that you even have the basic skills I would expect you to have at this point. Look. Are you afraid of the airplane?"

"I'm not afraid of anything, sir."

"Bullshit. You're afraid of losing your wings."

"Yes, sir. But nothing else."

"Nothing else. That makes you either stupid or insensitive. Are you stupid and insensitive, Evans?"

"What? No, sir!"

"Well, you should be a little bit afraid of the P-39. She's a delightful little bitch to fly but she will bite you on the ass if you give her any chance at all. That's one airplane you need to be on top of every second. And Evans, you weren't. You were high when we were flying low, you were out of position on the turns, and you didn't obey orders. All of those are symptoms of inexperience or inability to fly the airplane. You want to transfer to bombers, Evans? I hear the 19th can always use a new copilot. Maybe you'd like B-17s better than P-39s."

"I'm a pursuit pilot, sir!"

"Well, even if that's true, you're a sorry excuse for one. Here's what I want you to do. Run up to the operations shack and put in for some more flight time. I want you to go up solo and just have some fun. Get to know the airplane. Push the envelope a little bit, but not too much. Understand? Maybe if you aren't worrying about other airplanes nearby you'll settle down."

"Uh, yes, sir."

"OK. Go on now."

Evans turned and trotted up the taxiway to the Ops shack. Davis watched him go, shaking his head.

"Ardana," he said.

"Sir."

"Good job. A little too good. A bit of hot-dogging is all part of the game but you don't have to impress me with how good you are. Impress the Japs. That's what we're here to do."

"Yes, sir."

"And another thing. This formation flying is all very well but I don't expect we'll do a lot of that stuff. Mostly it's for bombers. Bombers fly in a tight formation so the gunners have interlocking fields of fire while you fly straight and level towards the target. We're pursuit pilots. Our protection is getting out of the way. You can't do that easily if we fly too close together. We're going to fly a loose formation, sort of like the fingers of your hand spread out. The Germans developed it before the war, the Brits picked it up, and we learned it from them." Davis held up his right hand, thumb tucked in, fingers spread wide. "There you have it. I'm the middle finger, and Evans the index finger. Jimmy, you and Bellmon are the outside fingers. We'll practice that if we have more time, but keep it in mind." Davis paused, thinking. "Radio chatter. We were talking a lot today but on an actual mission I don't want you on the radio at all unless you're reporting an emergency. That could be your engine quitting or Zeros about to crawl all over us. There's no time for anything else. I might be trying to warn you about that Zero on your ass when you open your mouth to comment on the pretty clouds and jam the frequency. You guys get me?"

"Yes, sir," said Ardana. Bellmon nodded.

"OK. Have your crews rearm and refuel your airplanes. We'll see about another flight this afternoon, but let's take a break for a couple of hours and we'll see how Danny does after his solo flight."

Evans didn't like flying alone. He never had.

The Allison engine purred behind him and then snarled as he advanced the throttle to takeoff power. The prop screamed, air flowed over the wings, in two hundred yards she was light on the wheels, bouncing a little on the nose, eager to fly, and Evans pulled back on the stick with a light three-fingered grip, just enough pressure to feel it. The P-39 soared up and off the ground and he leveled out to let the engine cool a little while he sucked up the gear and the flaps. Then he turned left out of the pattern and headed towards the ocean. He circled around the town of Port Moresby, giving the harbor and its trigger-happy antiaircraft gunners a wide berth as he climbed.

At ten thousand feet above ground he leveled out and looked down at the map-view layout of Port Moresby. He could see the aerodromes pushing out into the jungle from the sea. There was a smaller strip called Three-Mile nearer the harbor. The bombers and transports mostly flew out of Seven-Mile with its longer runway. There were a couple of freighters in the harbor with boats going back and forth to the docks. He shook his head. It was one primitive place to fight a war.

Evans cracked the canopy and let cool air scream through the cockpit. He sighed with relief as the sweat dried and chilled his skin.

Then, as he flew straight and level at ten thousand feet and two hundred fifty mph indicated, the thought popped into his mind that he hated being alone, and he was all alone up here, and even if the Japs didn't come any further south than Port

Moresby, he'd seen for himself they definitely came this far south.

Adrenaline popped into his blood and the sweat popped out cold on his skin. Gasping he fishtailed the P-39, peering over each shoulder to see if some goddam Nip was on his tail, but there was nothing, nothing, not even any chatter over the radio. Evans looked up into the sun but it made him squint and he gasped again, wondering if there were Zeros up there, looking him over like so many sharks trying to decide if he was chum. My God, Evans thought, when a bullet or a piece of shrapnel rips into you, what does it feel like? Is it agony or is it so sudden, so total, that you feel nothing at all because your brain can't handle it? Evans tipped his left wing up and banged the rudder over and quite suddenly the P-39 was headed for the blue ocean almost two miles below. Speed, yeah, speed, everyone said you could dive away from a Zero, if those bastards were out there he'd just run the hell away! In seconds the airspeed indicator was pushing 400 mph, into the speed range where sudden maneuvers might tear off a wing. His chute! Had he checked his chute properly before he got in the airplane, was it snug and tight or would it crush his balls into pulp if he had to bail out?

At six thousand feet the airspeed was pushing 460 mph and he knew he had to pull out, pull out, pull back on the stick, *easy easy you idiot!* Fear ate at him, growing with the g-force pushing him into his seat and crushing the breath from his lungs, pull back, a little more, a little more, Jesus, that was seven gees on the meter! The edges of his vision began to gray and he saw the instrument panel through a tunnel whose opening got narrower as the blood pulled out of his brain and the g-forces distorted his eyeballs. Oh Jesus Oh Jesus I don't want to die.

The P-39 bottomed out and began climbing for the sky at nearly 500 mph, prop and engine screaming and howling and all Evans could see was the blue sky over the nose as he gasped breath and life back into his lungs and his vision cleared. He leveled out at two thousand feet and fishtailed again, looking for Zeros that weren't there.

"I'm alive," he said to himself. And then, just to hear it again, he repeated "I'm alive."

Without thinking he did a barrel roll, an Immelmann turn and a Cuban eight. He didn't think about anything except the airplane after that. He did high-g turns, wingovers, loops, chandelles, all the flight school maneuvers and the tricks he'd heard about from different pilots.

He only turned for Port Moresby when the yellow warning light for low fuel began to flash.

Davis watched the performance. Someone outside the mess tent had said, "Jesus, look at that fucking guy."

The comment, along with the far off echo of a prop run to high RPMs and rising in pitch, made him turn and look, thinking, oh, hell, that's almost got to be Evans. He watched as the P-39 began to pull out of the dive and he thought, he really did, that the P-39 was going into the drink. But then the airplane made it, climbed up, and began an aerobatic series, one thing flowing into another, not smoothly or with any great skill, but not too bad.

Finally the exhibition ended.

Davis met Evans as he taxied up, engine coughing and sputtering. The captain nodded to himself; he had thought the P-39 must be running on the fumes in the tank. Evans taxied into his revetment, watching the hand signals of his crew chief, and shut it down at the cut signal. The propeller whirled a few more revolutions, the Allison engine spit once, and then the propeller began to wind down until there was relative silence, broken only by engines running up here and there around the airfield.

Evans sat in the cockpit, head back, eyes closed. His crew chief climbed up on the wing beside him.

"You OK, Mr. Evans?" the crew chief asked.

Evans opened his eyes. They were bloodshot from blood vessels broken in high-g turns. The pilot blinked.

"Yeah," he said thickly. "I'm OK." With slow fingers he began to unbuckle his harness. The crew chief reached in to help him. Evans unbuckled the chute harness as well and slid out of it as he climbed out of the door. The crew chief backed down off the wing. Evans slid off and stood leaning against the fuselage as if listening to the *pop!ting!* sounds of the cooling engine. Then he saw Davis standing at the corner of the revetment and tried to come to attention.

Davis waved a hand at him and walked to stand looking at him. "What was that all about?"

"Zeros, sir," Evans husked out from a parched throat.

"Zeros? You saw Japs?"

"Well, no, sir. But I got to thinking about it, when I realized I was by myself."

"OK. So you kicked it into a dive to get away from the Japs hiding up-sun."

Evans looked at Davis, mouth opening. "How...?"

"If you thought you saw Japs, or thought they might be there, it makes perfect sense."

"It does?"

"Absolutely."

"But I was afraid."

Davis stood looking at Evans. "So? You think you're the only asshole ever been scared in an airplane? Fear can be a friend. You just have to understand what it's trying to tell you and not let it take control. An airplane isn't a jungle. You can't just react. You have to think about what you do. You have to adapt your instincts to a situation they didn't evolve to handle."

"Ah...OK."

"You aren't too bright, are you, Evans? Either that or you didn't take biology or psychology back at RahRah U?"

"I majored in English, sir."

"I see. How did you pass ground school? That's a lot of engineering and math for an English major."

"It wasn't easy, sir."

Davis looked at Evans thoughtfully. "OK. Go get yourself some chow and something to drink. Water, I mean. You've lost a lot of fluids. Don't want to dehydrate. Bad for you."

"Yes, sir. Thank you, sir."

Evans shambled off. Davis watched him walk away for a moment before turning to the crew chief.

"Check all the stress points and rivets," Davis said quietly. "If you see anything you don't like, anything at all, down-check the airplane until you can fix it."

The crew chief nodded. "Yes, sir."

"Thanks, chief."

The chow was bad at lunch. It had been bad yesterday, too, so Jimmy felt this meant it would probably be bad all the time. Jimmy had been in the Air Corps nearly a year now and the food served in base mess halls was usually pretty good. In Australia before they left they were warned that conditions in Port Moresby weren't like Stateside. But knowing things would be bad wasn't the same as being served some sort of unidentifiable meat, stringy, tough and gristly, boiled potatoes, stewed vegetables and hardtack, with stewed apples for dessert, washed down with water that tasted of chlorine and purifiers and ever so faintly of shit.

Bellmon excused himself and belched with gusto. "Damn, that was almost as bad going out than going down," he complained.

"You gonna do that all night?" Jimmy inquired. "Sleep might be scarce if you do."

With that Jimmy let out a sonorous fart.

"Makes you miss that Australian steak, doesn't it?" Bellmon sighed.

Evans came in and went to his bunk. He sighed and sat down on the edge of the bunk with his head in his hands. His tent mates exchanged glances.

"You get some chow?" Jimmy asked in carefully neutral tones.

"I think I'm gonna be sick," Evans replied.

"Oh, then you did get some chow," said Bellmon.

"That stuff musta been left over from the Great War."

"Oh, no. I doubt it was any older than the Spanish Civil War."

"They expect us to eat that stuff and then fly?"

"I guess so. You noticed the old guys tucking into it without too much complaint." Jimmy smiled. "Maybe you get used to it. Especially if there isn't anything else."

"I don't want to get used to it."

"Me either, but I guess we won't have any choice." Jimmy shook his head.

"What?" asked Bellmon.

"Well, earlier I remembered how cold it got in Montana during the winter, and how I'd wish I could go somewhere warm, like Texas or Florida or California. But after a day in this place I reckon I'll be happy to get back to a nice cold Montana winter. Now there's something else about Montana. It's mostly ranches out there. And deer hunting, or elk or even cougar if you think you're up for it." Ardana shook his head as his stomach rumbled. "That means meat. Fresh killed and slaughtered and fire roasted. Oh, I don't even want to think about it, and I apologize to you guys for even bringing it up."

Evans rose and sprinted out the door, moving fast for a man of his bulk. He could be seen running between the tents to an edifice whose sign, "Latrine," proclaimed the function its stink advertised a hundred yards off.

"I'm starting not to like him much," Bellmon said. "But you got to admit he's had a hard day."

"Yeah. Finding out you ain't God's gift to the Universe is pretty tough."

They saw Captain Davis walking up the path between the tents.

"You guys find the chow to your liking?" he asked.

"Oh, yes, sir," said Ardana.

"Went back for thirds," claimed Bellmon.

"Where's Evans?"

"Shitting his brains out in the latrine from the way he ran out of here a minute ago."

Davis frowned. "It's a little early for dysentery."

"Dysentery?"

"Also known as Montezuma's Revenge. Mostly but not solely caused by drinking water or food carrying some sort of bug or parasite or something. Speaking of which, you guys take your Atabrine?"

"Yes, sir," they chorused.

"The stuff tastes horrible and turns you kind of yellow, I'm told, but rumors regarding its effect on your virility are no doubt exaggerated."

"I thought that's what the saltpeter in the food was for, sir," Ardana volunteered.

Davis laughed. "You haven't been in the Army long enough to know about that, Jimmy."

"My dad told me about it, sir. He was in the Great War."

"Yeah. So was mine. I guess guys our age, about all of us had dads or uncles in that war. Look,

I came over to tell you we're on alert for a mission tomorrow morning. Briefing at 0400, so be ready and dressed and in the mess hall about 0330. Someone will come by to wake you up but I'm advising you to make it an early night and sleep as much as you can."

"Thanks, Captain."

Davis nodded. "There's a meeting of flight leaders up at Group. I'll see you in the morning." He grinned. "Bright and early. Be sure and let Evans know."

"Yes, sir."

Davis walked away. The two young lieutenants carefully avoided looking at each other. Then Bellmon walked over to his footlocker and took out a .45 automatic and a cleaning kit.

Jimmy got his own cleaning kit from his footlocker and started in on his revolver.

"Where'd you get the cowboy gun, anyway?" Bellmon asked.

"Aw, my grandfather bought it for me," Jimmy replied. "He said the .45 automatic was a good pistol but nothing ever beat the old Peacemaker. For five shots, anyway."

"How much ammo you got?"

"Fifty rounds. Guess if I run out I'd better get an automatic."

Bellmon laughed. "Plenty of those around."

They were still cleaning their pistols when Evans returned. "You guys know something I don't?" he asked.

"Mission tomorrow morning," Bellmon told him. "Brief at 0400. Remember?"

"Where we going?"

"Captain Davis didn't say. Not too many places we can hit with a P-39. Rabaul's out of range. Maybe Lae."

"Lae?"

"Yeah. You remember, Amelia Earhart took off from there on her way to Howland Island."

"She never got there," Evans said.

Bellmon looked at him. "That's right. But she still took off from Lae. I remember seeing a newsreel about it."

"What did it look like?" Jimmy asked. "The airstrip, I mean."

"All I remember is a dirt strip out in the jungle with a bunch of natives and white guys in floppy hats standing around. Probably pretty much the same now except for the white guys."

"And a lot of flak guns."

"And Zeros," Bellmon said. "Probably a hell of a lot of Zeros."

"Would you guys mind not talking about Zeros?" Evans said. "I don't feel so good. I'm going to sleep."

"OK. We'll wake you for the mission."

"OK," Evans said. He crawled into his bunk in his skivvies and passed out cold. Ten minutes later he was snoring gently.

"Well, ya gotta hand it to him for getting to sleep," Jimmy said as he put his pistol away. "Doubt if I will."

"What, you got the willies?"

"I'm a bit nervous, yes, if you must know."

"Don't be. I've got second sight. We'll live through the war and become famous aces."

Jimmy laughed. "In a pig's eye. Seriously, though, you want to be an ace?"

"Hell, yes. Don't you?"

"I think I'll settle for living through tomorrow for now. Then maybe we'll see about the famous ace part."

Gerry nodded. "Yeah, maybe you're right."

Chapter Eight

"We will win this war"

The sun touched the mountains to the west. Jack walked up to the 8th Fighter Group's Operations Shack for a meeting of squadron and flight commanders as well as group staff and intelligence types. They were going through the plan for the mission in the morning to finalize the pilot's briefing.

Three men stood in front of the shack. Jack recognized Boyd Wagner, who was in conversation with two older men Jack didn't know. One of the older men was an Army colonel. The other man was in an Army uniform without insignia or cover.

"Jack," said Wagner. "Let me introduce you to Congressman Matt Snyder of Montana, and Colonel James Carollton from FEAF."

Jack saluted the colonel and shook hands with the Congressman. "Of Montana?" Jack asked. "One of the kids in my flight is from Montana."

"I'd be happy to meet him," said the Congressman. "What's his name?"

"James Ardana from Choteau, Montana."

"Oh my stars. Jimmy Ardana? I stopped by Choteau on my way out here from Washington. His folks have always been supporters of mine. You say he's in your flight? How's he doing?"

"Pretty well," Jack said. "I think he's got promise."

The Congressman positively beamed. "Well, that's always good to hear."

"Gentlemen, let me have a minute with Jack before we start the meeting," said Wagner. "Go on in if you like."

The Congressman, still smiling, shook Jack's hand again and went into the Ops shack with the colonel.

Jack turned to Wagner.

"What is it, Boyd?" he asked quietly.

Without speaking Wagner handed Jack a message flimsy. There was enough light to make out the teletype strips pasted onto the paper. It was from FEAF HQ in Brisbane.

It said, in terse officialese, that the surrender of remaining US Army forces in the Philippines to the Empire of Japan was expected at any time.

"Jehosophat," Jack breathed. "I wonder how many of our guys got out of Del Monte Field."

Wagner said, "No way to know right now. Look, Jack, that colonel who's with the congressman handed me this. General Brett at FEAF wanted me to know, and since we served in the Philippines, I didn't want you to hear it from anyone but me. And this isn't surrender. Not yet."

"You think there's any chance?"

Wagner's lips compressed. He looked away for a moment as the sun slipped below the mountains, and the light faded on his face.

"General MacArthur says he'll return to the Philippines. He left the when a bit vague, is all."

They stood there as the other officers filed up the hill and into the Ops shack. Finally they went in. Wagner walked to the front. Jack sat with the other squadron and flight commanders, squadron ops officers and group types in a crowded, stuffy room barely big enough to hold them. It was lit by a pair of gas lanterns whose mantles threw off an eerie pale green glow. No air flowed through the room because the doors and windows were tightly closed due to blackout regulations.

"Before we begin I have an announcement to make," said Wagner. The Director of Fighter Operations, the combat commander of the 8th Fighter Group, when all was said and done, suddenly grinned. "Mostly because I know the pilot in question is painfully shy and girlishly modest, this duty falls to me. Captain John T. Davis, rise."

Aw, hell, Jack thought. *What's Wagner up to?*

He stood up.

Wagner came down from the podium. The colonel held something in his hand, and Major Wolchek, grinning hugely, fell in behind him.

"Attention to orders," said Wolchek. To Jack it sounded like Major Wolchek was imitating the lordly tones of President Franklin D. Roosevelt giving a radio speech. "Whereas, on the 7th of May, this year of our Lord 1942, a day that shall live in infamy in the annals of the Mikado, at a godforsaken airstrip on a godforsaken tropical island, Captain John T. Davis did engauge in aerial combat with the forces of said Mikado, and was in fact successful in such enterprise, in that he shot down one Jap Zero, whose carcass came to rest on the aforesaid godforsaken airstrip. This kill being thus unquestionably confirmed, it is hereby and forthwith added to the tally of the aforementioned Captain John T. Davis, and therefore, be it known to all and sundry, he is from henceforward added to the roll of aces of the United States Army Air Forces."

Wolchek snapped to attention. Wagner held up the object he carried under his arms.

"I will mention, gentlemen, that that roll of aces is so far very short indeed, and its members are confined to this very room. And now, by the power vested in me by Congress, the Constitution, and the Great Jehovah, I hereby confer upon Captain John T. Davis the Order of Winged Death."

"Aw, crap, Boyd," Jack groaned.

"Be silent, Captain Davis," Wagner intoned sternly. "I was there when you were wet behind your ears and got your first kill. I never would have thought you would come this far alive, yet here you are."

Laughter and applause and a few cheers erupted as Wagner unfolded a loop of silk apparently cut from a parachute. An attempt had been made to dye it red, but the dye job was splotchy. A winged bronze device the size of a dinner plate hung from the splotchy red silk. In the round center a black enamel scythe was interleaved with a bold red 5. Wagner draped the loop over Jack's head as the applause and cheers grew to a crescendo.

Jack heard something in the acclaim of the other officers in the room that had nothing to do with triumph or humor. The laughter was too forced, the cheers had an edge. Then he recognized the pent-up fear and frustration, and he looked up into Wagner's eyes.

The older man held his look for a moment and nodded, just a little. Then Wagner grinned deliberately, pantomimed an outrageous Frenchman's kiss to both of Jack's cheeks, and held up Jack's hand as the cheers and laughter changed to a roar.

The moment altered and stretched for Jack. It was only a moment, and so many things crowded into it. It was as if he heard the clashing of spears and swords on shields in some far-off dawn before battle.

He raised his other hand and joined the baying chorus. It went on and on, and finally began to diminish. Wagner gave one final shout and shook Jack's hand.

"Looks good on you," he said loudly. "Go forth and kill some more!"

"Count on it," Jack said grimly.

"On that note, gentlemen, let's get back to business," Wagner said briskly. He clapped Jack on the shoulder. Wolchek winked at Jack, shook hands quickly, and followed Wagner.

Jack sat down. Jehosophat, that medal was heavy.

Wagner turned to a map of the northern New Guinea coast tacked up on the wall.

"The purpose of this mission is to neutralize, for as long as possible, the Jap air base at Lae," Wagner began. "It's a combined operation with the 22nd Bomb Group. No B-17s this time. FEAF needs those to help the Navy hunt the Jap fleet, which is supposed to be somewhere east of us in the Coral Sea."

Wagner paused and looked around the hot, airless room.

"The mission concept is pretty simple," he continued. "One squadron goes in on the deck, strafing anything they see, preferably Zeros. One squadron stays at medium height to deal with any Zeros that manage to get off the ground. The B-26s come in three minutes behind our strafers and hit the runway and taxiways. We'll have one other squadron at 17,000 feet, orbiting five miles south of Lae, to cover our withdrawal. Steve?"

Major Wolchek stood up. "My squadron's part is to supply the strafers. I'll lead with Boxcar Yellow flight. Jack here will lead Boxcar Red Flight, and Ed Groves will have Boxcar Green flight. One flight will go straight down the runway, the next, five seconds behind, will extend right and strafe the first half of the runway. The third flight will be ten seconds behind the lead flight. It will extend left and strafe the second half of the runway. All flights will turn south and head back to Seven-Mile after one pass."

"One pass," Wagner repeated deliberately. "All other considerations aside, we won't have the fuel for more than that."

Wagner indicated a major Jack didn't know.

"Some of you may know Major Tommy Rhodes from the 22nd Bomb Group," he said. "Major Rhodes?"

"Yes, sir," said Rhodes. He stood up, looked around the room, and shook his head. "Jeez. I thought my boys were ugly, but your bunch takes the cake for ugly, Boyd."

Wagner suppressed a grin. "Play nice, Tommy. I hear your airplanes look a lot like a Jap Betty bomber. Wouldn't want any mistakes to be made."

"That's assuming you can hit anything," Rhodes muttered. Someone threw a wadded-up piece of paper at him, which bounced off his head. "Oh, all right, all right! So the 22nd will have a half-dozen bombers ready to go tomorrow morning. And honest, you guys aren't any uglier than my Daddy's mule, back in Iowa."

The major sat down, grinning.

"And thank you, Major Rhodes," said Wagner drily. "Very well, gentlemen, let's get to the questions. Wolchek, what would you like to know?"

"Jap antiaircraft guns," said Wolchek promptly.

Wagner looked at another man, a captain. The man stood. "Captain Fred Gallardo. I'm the intelligence officer for the 19th Bomb Group. As of our reconnaissance flight over Lae this morning there are no changes in disposition of Jap antiaircraft guns around the airfield. Two big guns at the end of the runway, facing out to sea, probably 75mm. A half-dozen dual 25mm and the same number of tribarrel 25mm automatic cannon spaced around the field. Count on small-caliber automatic weapons, unknown number. Your best defense against the AAA is to stay low and stay fast."

"Well, you're just a ray of goddamned sunshine," someone muttered. "How many Zeroes?"

"We count thirty, with maybe another fifteen under nets or in hangars."

"Hey, Tommy, how many Zeros up at Vunakanau?" Wolchek asked.

The B-26 pilot shrugged. "Fifty, sixty maybe. They seem to ship them in by the squadron every few weeks. Too god-damn many, anyway. Why?"

"Just curious. They can reinforce Lae pretty quick from Vunakanau, then," said Wolchek.

"Let's fight one battle at a time," said Wagner. "If we can keep the Japs busy filling in holes and clearing wrecks off the runway and taxiway, even only for a day, it's worth it. Now, Dave, suppose you brief us on the route."

Jack looked at the map Wagner tacked to the wall. Dave Schuster, squadron commander of the 88th, got up and went to the map. He tapped a long curving finger of land on the north New Guinea coast.

"This is the Salamaua Peninsula," Schuster said. "We'll go over the mountains at 17,000 feet, heading more or less due north. When we get over the peninsula we'll be twenty-five miles from the target. Steve's Boxcars will put their noses down, turn a little to the west, and get down on the deck at high speed. We'll follow the same route back and hope the weather holds."

"On that score, gentlemen, we won't bother assembling into formation until we're over Salamaua," said Wagner. "When we take off it'll be dark. Try to stay in elements at least, flights if you can. Don't worry about anything more than that. There's too much risk of collision and more to the point, we'll burn too much fuel."

Jack nodded and said nothing. He had never been over Lae but he could see in his mind how it would be. The reconnaissance photos showed a single runway oriented east-west. The rising sun would shine straight into the eyes of the gunners at the seaward end of the runway. The strafers would come in four abreast in three flights. The range was too great for the P-39s to carry bombs, so the strafers would spray the field with machine-gun and cannon fire, then exit the target area and turn to the southwest, where the high cover squadron would be waiting to pounce on any pursuit from the advantage of altitude. It wasn't that far to Lae, about an hour at the cruising speed of a P-39. They'd have enough gas to get to the target and return, plus maybe ten minutes of fuel at full throttle to mess around with over the target, and that would be it. Some of the wingmen would have less than that. Jack squirmed in his seat, thinking about Evans.

Wagner paused, looking around. "OK. That's the basic idea, anyway. I don't see any more information coming in in the next ten hours, but if it does we'll deal with it at the mission brief in the morning, along with navigation and weather. Any questions?"

At that moment a captain came through the light-locked door. Wagner looked at the newcomer and said, "This is a secure briefing, captain."

"Colonel Wagner, I'm sorry, but I have a priority message from FEAF for Colonel Carrolton."

The congressman's chaperon stood and came forward.

"Colonel Wagner, please continue your briefing. I'm sorry for the interruption," the older man said smoothly. He walked out of the room with the captain in tow.

Wagner looked after them for a moment, but before he could resume the briefing the colonel came back in.

Jack saw Wagner's eyes widen. He turned to look.

The older colonel stood just inside the door, standing stiff, ramrod straight, but not like a soldier at attention. His stance was that of a man receiving an electric shock. He walked slowly forward towards Wagner.

When he reached Wagner he leaned forward and whispered in Wagner's ear. Jack knew the truth from Wagner's response. Wagner's eyes closed and his shoulders sagged. Jack had seen that exact response from Wagner before, and that memory flooded back to him, of Wagner standing on the ramp at Nichols Field the day the Japs started the war, being told by yet another colonel that the Japs had bombed Clark Field and wiped it out.

Jack snapped back to the present as the colonel leaned away from Wagner, who looked at the other man and nodded once.

No one spoke. The only noise was the soft hissing of the gas lanterns. When Wagner spoke it was with the same even, controlled voice he used during the briefing. But he didn't begin the way Jack thought he would.

"You all know by now about the Jap invasion fleet headed this way. The Navy will take care of them, or not, but either way whatever losses we inflict on the Japs at Lae tomorrow morning will be worthwhile. But maybe some of you..." Wagner stopped speaking for a moment to get himself under control.

"We just received a message from FEAF HQ confirming that General Wainwright, on Corregidor, has ordered the surrender of all US forces in the Philippines."

Jack felt the air leave his lungs without any exhale from him. He felt his heart beating in his toes. Something hot and wet burned like acid in his own eyes and dripped down his cheeks. He got his breath back and looked down, blinking against the tears in the pale green light of the lanterns. He had balled his hands into fists.

Wagner continued speaking. "First we never thought it could happen. Then we never thought it would. Then we hoped it wouldn't. Now it has." Wagner paused and looked around the room.

Jack took a deep breath, remembering guys he knew in the 17th and 21st Pursuit Squadrons, back in the Philippines. Most of them were dead now, in the Philippines or in the fighting around Java. He wondered about Ed Dyess and the other guys he'd come out with back last November. If they weren't dead, they were POWs, or at best running through the jungle trying to escape the Japs.

"We will win this war," Wagner said. "Make no mistake about it. But we're going to have to fight harder and smarter than we have been. Make it your business to do that, starting now."

Then Colonel Wagner indicated Congressman Snyder, sitting in a corner of the room with Colonel Carrolton.

"Gentlemen, I'd like to introduce Congressman Matt Snyder of Montana. He's here at the personal request of President Roosevelt to get an idea of conditions in this theater. Congressman Snyder, would you care to say a few words?"

The congressman looked as stunned as any of them by the news of the surrender in the Philippines. But after a moment he stood. "Thank you, Colonel. Boys, I'll keep this short, as I figure every one of you wants to get some rest before going out to do such an important job tomorrow. Being here has given me some small idea of what that job is, but I can't and won't pretend I understand what you go through. So I want to say thank you for the job you're doing, thank you all, and please pass that on to the brave men who serve with you. When I get back to Washington I will see what I can do to improve conditions out here. That's all I have to say except the very best of luck and God speed to each of you."

The congressman sat down, leaning over to speak quietly into Colonel Carrolton's ear. The colonel nodded.

"See you back here at 0430," Wagner said. "Like the Congressman said, get some rest."

Jack walked out of the Ops shack and found himself standing by the rickety steps below the porch. The other guys moved past him, talking among themselves. He pulled the parachute ribbon over his head and wrapped it around the brass medallion. He hefted the medal again, wondering who Wagner found to make the thing on such short notice.

"Captain Davis, could we have a moment?"

Jack turned to see Colonel Carrolton, with Congressman Snyder close behind him.

"Certainly, sir."

"I had no idea you were an ace when we met earlier," said Snyder, pushing forward. "Congratulations, young man! Now I'm sure young Jimmy is in good hands. His uncle Kurt was an ace, too, you know, in the Great War."

"No, sir, I didn't know that. But thank you, congressman."

"I want you to know I meant what I said in there, about seeing what I can do about helping you boys out here," Snyder went on. "What's tops on your list, Captain?"

"Now, Matt, I don't think the captain..." began Carollton.

"A group of P-38s," said Jack.

"P-38s?" The congressman frowned. The colonel opened his mouth and started to speak. Snyder raised his hand in an imperious gesture; the colonel closed his mouth but glared at Jack, who ignored him, keeping his eyes on Snyder instead.

"You mean the Lightning, that Lockheed airplane? I thought they were having real trouble with it, something about the tail coming off in a dive."

"Yes, sir. But that was six months ago, and it's also the sort of problem engineers tend to work out. I'll bet that work is pretty well in hand. We need a fast airplane with better range and rate of climb out here, and the P-38 will do that and more."

The congressman nodded slowly. "So it's not better chow or accommodations you want," he said. "It's a better airplane to fight with."

"Yes, sir. And I expect you've eaten in our mess hall, so you know the chow out here could stand a whole lot of improvement. I'd still rather have a P-38 to fly, and I doubt I'm alone feeling that way."

Jack held up Wagner's medallion. "Don't get me wrong, Congressman. We'll fight with what we have, just like we've been doing since last December. We'll do our best and more. But get us some P-38s and you'll see a lot more aces out here."

The congressman nodded again. A slow smile spread over his face. "All right, Captain Davis, that's the sort of language an old Montana cowhand can understand. I'll see what I can do. You know the President thinks we should go after Germany first, but surely to God we can get you fellows some good airplanes."

"Thank you, sir."

The colonel stepped forward. "Congressman, you wanted to meet with the boys over in the 19th Bomb Group," he said.

"So I did," said Snyder. He looked at Jack and held his hand out. Jack shook it. "Good luck in the morning, Captain, and tell young Jimmy I'll see him when you boys get back."

"I will, sir."

The colonel ushered the congressman away. Jack saw the pale flash of the colonel's face as the man turned back to glare at him.

"Don't think you made a friend there, Jack," said Wagner, standing by Jack's shoulder.

"Guess not," Jack replied. "But if that guy actually gets some P-38s out here, I'll move to Montana and vote for him the rest of my life."

Wagner chuckled. Then he said, "You've done something like this before, haven't you, Jack? Tomorrow's mission, I mean. You went up to Palembang with Bud Sprague and some of the other guys, back last February."

"Yeah. Yeah, I guess there are some similarities. A long trip at low level to the limit of our fuel. At least we've got better intelligence this time. We got sent in blind at Palembang."

"Hairy trip?"

"You could say that. The whole thing was supposed to put some heart in the Brits at Singapore. How we were going to do that with a handful of P-40s and two bombs each was sort of beyond us, but hell, what else could we do? We refueled at Batavia and spent the night. That's when we found out the Brits had surrendered Singapore."

Wagner sighed. He pulled out a handkerchief and mopped his face. "Bet Bud Sprague liked that. What did he say?"

Jack thought about it. He remembered standing on the sod ramp at Batavia, where he and Grant Mahony spent the night with the P-40s while the other guys tried to find a place to sleep in town. He hadn't slept well, and when Sprague and the rest of the guys got there, just before daybreak, they told him Singapore had fallen.

"Sprague said, let's go kill some Japs."

Wagner nodded, looking away. "That sounds about right," he said.

He kept his voice low but Jack heard the rough edge in his words. He remembered what Wagner said about being friends with Sprague.

At that moment the air raid siren went off. To the south, towards Port Moresby, a battery of searchlights flicked on. Shafts of grayish-silver light speared up into the heavens, like the spotlights at a movie premiere.

Wagner sighed. "God-damned Japs," he said. He sounded weary. "Come on, Jack, I'll show you a nice muddy slit trench. If we're lucky we won't have to share it with snakes and centipedes."

Jimmy woke in the darkness to the sound of a ripsaw hacking through a pine knot. He sat upright in his cot and realized that buzzing roar was someone snoring. He looked around in the pitch-black tent.

"You awake, Jimmy?" Bellmon asked.

"I am now. Damn, is that Danny?"

"Yeah."

"I've been in a bunkroom full of drunken cowhands that all together didn't snore that loud."

"I can't sleep anyway. Let's go for a smoke."

"OK." Jimmy threw on a pair of pants and stuck his feet into his boots. He followed Bellmon out under some trees.

A mosquito bit him, then three more. He bit off a curse, waving his hands in front of his face when something insectile flew into his mouth.

Bellmon shook a cigarette out of a pack and offered it to Jimmy.

"No, thanks. Don't smoke."

"No? Why'd you come out here then?" Bellmon took the cigarette from the pack and stuck it between his lips.

"Are you kidding? Listen to that."

From their tent came the long, drawn-out screech of Evans snoring.

"Yeah," said Bellmon. He lit up and slapped at a mosquito.

"On second thought give me a cigarette anyway," said Jimmy. "Maybe the smoke will help keep off the mosquitoes."

Bellmon offered him the pack. Jimmy took a cigarette and the pack of matches offered with it. He lit up, cupping his hand over the match flame and the glow of the cigarette lest Jap night intruders see the betraying light.

"D'you really think a match flame can be seen thirty miles away?" Bellmon asked. Before going overseas this point had been unceasingly drilled into them.

Jimmy shrugged. "Who cares? Why take a chance?"

"I guess that's the point."

They smoked in silence for a moment.

An air-raid siren went off across the field, a rising, ululating wail. Another, closer by, joined in. There was a confused hubbub of voices.

"Aw shit, not again," said Gerry. "Where the hell is the air-raid shelter?"

"Where did you go last time?"

"A slit trench, but I'm not sure where it is."

"Well, we aren't that close to the field. Let's just stay right here unless it looks close."

"OK," Bellmon said dubiously.

The sirens trailed off and high overhead they heard the drone of engines. From closer to the field there was an enormous cracking *wham!* as a heavy antiaircraft gun fired. They looked up but the trees kept them from seeing anything. In a moment there was a hollow echoing *boom* from altitude, and then the antiaircraft barrage began in earnest.

Jimmy found Bellmon's shoulder and pulled on it. They backtracked and found the trail and went to stand in front of their tent. It was clear of the trees and high above them they could see the flashes of exploding shells, but still they couldn't see the Jap bombers, despite the weaving searchlight beams reaching up into the sky.

"We'd really better find some cover," Bellmon yelled over the gunfire. "There'll be shrapnel coming down from altitude."

"Will the tent canvas keep shrapnel off of us?"

"I don't know. Better than standing in the open, anyway."

Jimmy nodded. They went back inside the tent, standing just inside the doorway. They watched the barrage from the guns and then, over the *crack-boom* of the barrage came another noise, a shuddering wail; then a stick of bombs exploded down by the runway, flashbulb-bright explosions that shook the ground underneath them. Another stick of bombs landed, then another, and this one fell in the jungle close by. The last bomb fell very close indeed but Jimmy and Bellmon were on the floor of the tent, hands over their heads, making a very intimate acquaintance with the dirt and splinters of the wooden floorboards.

Then the bombing stopped. They didn't move. The AA barrage continued for a few more minutes and stopped. One final round was fired. They became aware of another noise, like rain pattering on the roof and in the jungle, the shrapnel falling from the AA shells exploding 25,000 feet above them.

The sirens sounded the all-clear. Only then did they look up.

"Well," said Bellmon. "I don't think I pissed my pants."

"My bladder felt a little weak there, once or twice."

"Hey, look." Bellmon pointed.

There was a cluster of three tents not far away. They could tell because one of them was burning merrily. Men could be seen in silhouette as they ran in front of the fire.

Jimmy and Bellmon ran down the trail to help, but it turned out the fire was not a big one. By the time they got there a dozen shadowy figures fought the flames with blankets and shovels. Bellmon and Jimmy stood back from the firefighters, looking for a blanket or a shovel to use, but the blaze was nearly out. In a moment there were only smoldering embers outlining what had been the floor of a tent.

"Anyone hurt?" asked a new voice.

Jimmy turned to see Captain Davis and Colonel Wagner standing with a major he didn't know. Another man, standing just visible as an outline in the starlight, said, "I don't think so, Major."

"How did it start, Blaine? Stray incendiary?"

"Probably a stray cigarette butt," another man said. There was laughter.

"Kerosene lantern turned over when that last stick of bombs hit," said the first man. "That's my guess. And, maybe, like Pete said, a stray cigarette butt."

"Goddam Jap saboteurs," someone called, raising more laughter.

"All right, all right. Pete, this your tent? You and McAllister? Where the hell is McAllister, anyway?"

"Here, sir, and yeah, that's our tent. We saw the fire from the slit trench and got most of our stuff out."

"Good! You saved your booze, then?"

"Well, er, sir, you see, I got a brand new flight suit in my footlocker, and you know, Pete there has that collection of girlie magazines."

More laughter.

"OK. You guys bunk down in the Ops Shack tonight. Not to cast a damper on the festivities here, but mission briefing is in seven hours. Believe me, you guys need your beauty sleep."

"After that?" Bellmon muttered to Jimmy.

"I reckon," Jimmy muttered back. They went back to their tent. Evans was still sound asleep, snoring.

Chapter Nine

May 8, 1942

"Over the mountains and down on the deck with the Boxcars"

After the briefing Davis led his flight members down the dark taxiway to the revetments. On impulse Jimmy put his hand out, and Bellmon shook hands with him as a still-drowsy Evans stumbled alone to his P-39.

"See you later," Bellmon said.

"Couple hours," Jimmy replied. "Piece of cake."

Bellmon turned and walked off. Jimmy turned away and looked at his P-39. The grinning gremlin was just visible inside the shadow made by the airplane's nose and the number 13 stood out for a moment in his mind as if it were bathed in neon light.

Terraine appeared in the gloom beside him. "She's looking good, sir. We started the engine about an hour ago, got everything warmed up. She should start right up for you."

"Thanks, Don."

As Terraine helped him buckle into his parachute and seat harness Jimmy felt as if he were receding from reality, as if things he had done a hundred times before – at least, in other airplanes in other places -- were suddenly unfamiliar and disconnected. He took a deep breath.

"You OK, sir?" Terraine asked.

Jimmy turned to look at Terraine, whose face was less than a foot away from him. Terraine's face was shadowed and ghostly in the dim yellow light of his flashlight.

"Yeah," Jimmy said after a moment. "I'm OK."

Terraine gave Jimmy's shoulder harness an extra tug. "Look, Jimmy, don't worry about bringing us back some Jap scalps. I hear it's going to be a long war." The crew chief hesitated. "We'd rather you come back in one piece."

"That's what I'm aiming for."

Terraine chuckled. "Good luck."

Jimmy nodded. "Thanks, Don."

Up and down the flight line came the sound of energizers and starters before being drowned out by cough and rumble of Allison engines. Jimmy went through his own startup checklist. The engine rumbled and sputtered. With a cough and a roar the propeller spun and prop wash blasted through the open cockpit door. Terraine watched the engine gauges for a moment with Jimmy, clapped him on the shoulder and flashed a thumbs-up. Jimmy nodded and made an "OK" gesture with his right hand, since his left was on the throttle. Terraine leaned back and closed the door for Jimmy, who latched it closed. Then Terraine climbed off the wing and moved in front of the airplane, holding the flashlight in front of him so Jimmy could see him. Jimmy looked left and right for the rest of his ground crew, but they had moved away from the danger of the spinning prop. They, like Jimmy, knew all the grisly stories of what happened to men who walked into a turning propeller.

Terraine stood at the entrance to the revetment, still holding the shielded flashlight in his hand. Terraine looked to his right, where Captain Davis and Danny Evans would be the first of their flight to move out. Jimmy saw dim blue exhaust glows and now and then the flash of formation lights, but the strongest light in his little darkened universe was the shielded flashlight in his crew chief's hand. Jimmy flicked a look at the oil and coolant gauges and when he looked back Terraine was pointing to his right with the flashlight in the signal to begin taxiing.

Jimmy eased the throttle open until the P-39 moved forward. He eased it back a hair and stood gently on the left brake pedal to turn onto the taxiway. Fifty feet ahead of him he saw the glow of the exhaust from Danny Evans' P-39, flaring up and back suddenly and rocking up and down as Evans rode the brakes and the throttle. Jimmy shook his head, and then looked behind him to see Terraine's dim shadow with his right arm cocked up in a salute, and beyond him Gerry Bellmon's Airacobra edged out of its revetment.

In the dim glow of their formation lights the pursuits taxied to the runway. There were no radio calls. Everything was done with hand and light signals. The briefing specified that they would take off by twos and stick together, not bothering to form up in larger groups since it was too dark to see except by formation lights and the blue glow from the exhaust stacks. After takeoff they would begin climbing to clear the mountains and go on oxygen above ten thousand feet. They would clear the mountains above fifteen thousand feet, but all the raiders would level off at seventeen thousand and stay at that altitude until the sun came up. Each element would navigate independently until, hopefully, dawn found them over the north coast of New Guinea slightly to the east of Salamaua. That would at least save fuel, and the plan was to join into attack formations in the twenty miles of open sea between Salamaua and Lae.

Jimmy thought the scheme was too dependent on luck. Leaving the briefing, he heard the more experienced pilots discussing the unpredictable weather over the Owen Stanley Mountains that lay between Port Moresby and the north coast of Papua New Guinea. There wasn't anything significant reported in the weather briefing but that just meant it would be the usual, which meant thunderstorms as bad or worse as the one yesterday afternoon. This was the tropics, after all. Everyone said it rained all the damned time in Papua New Guinea.

Aside from the weather there was the prospect of spending an hour on instruments in an airplane he had only flown for six hours, and none of that on instruments. That was one thing Uncle Kurt had been a little weak on, but hell, needle, ball, gyrocompass and airspeed, right? That was all you really needed to keep the airplane straight, level and on course.

Just like back at Kelly Field in training.

Jimmy felt the sweat break out in his armpits.

Ahead of him Boxcar Yellow Flight, the first flight of strafers, made it to the taxiway. Jimmy looked at the control tower, which flashed a dim green light at the flight leader, Major Wolchek. Wolchek flashed his formation lights in reply. Jimmy couldn't see much except the formation lights running down the runway after that, just ahead of the blue fire from the exhaust stacks.

One by one the elements took off, Boxcar Yellow, then Boxcar Green, and then Jimmy was at the runway threshold. Dimly he could see the P-39s carrying Evans and Captain Davis move onto the runway, and then once more the green light from the tower, and the roar of the engines audible for a moment over the rumble of his own. Jimmy saw their formation lights speeding down the runway and soaring up into the black sky.

He flexed his hand on the throttle and took a firm grip on the levers. Then Jimmy fed power to the engine and moved onto the taxiway.

Jack Davis leveled off at seventeen thousand feet. Above and ahead of him he saw stars in all the profusion of a clear, pitch-dark tropic night, and that was reassuring because it meant no clouds, and no clouds meant no adverse weather. He was sure that Major Wolchek, several miles ahead of him and flying as Boxcar Yellow Leader, was breathing a sigh of relief. Good weather was by no means certain, and this was already good luck for the mission.

Ahead of him he could sometimes see the exhaust flames of Boxcar Green Flight. Behind him he could see the bulk of Lieutenant Evans's pursuit, right down to the occasional reflection of his exhaust in Danny's windscreen. He scanned his instruments and the sky around them. The ground was black and featureless for the most part; once he thought he saw a fire burning far below, a native village maybe, but who knew? By his dead reckoning they should be halfway over the mountains, and in twenty minutes the coast should be in sight. Off to the right against the horizon and a few thousand feet below him a mountain bulked against the horizon, blotting out some of the lower stars.

It was amazing how many stars there were. Davis loved night-flying for just such nights as this, when you could turn the cockpit lights down low and pick out the unfamiliar southern constellations and the navigational stars.

Jack's engine purred even and sweet and powerful. The rush of the air over the cockpit was like a symphony, with the even rhythm of his breathing through the oxygen mask providing a slow tempo against the roar of the prop and the constant scream of the gearbox. He checked his instruments and gauges, noted his fuel consumption, looked again at the clock on the panel and out to the right, to the east where the sun would come over the horizon in thirty minutes.

So far, so good.

From time to time Jimmy Ardana looked at the stars, but mostly he searched for the telltale signs of other airplane. airplane headed south were likely to be Japanese bombers or even Zeros headed to Port Moresby. Those would pass them by at a combined speed of over four hundred mph. The lights that were more or less stationary, those were the Boxcars and the Brickbats of the raid. Off to the left he thought he saw the dwindling lights of another group of airplane. He figured those were the P-39s of the Rattlers, flying high cover, making for their orbit point over the Markham River delta five miles south of Lae.

He looked over his shoulder at Bellmon. Gerry was almost glued to Jimmy's wingtip, and Jimmy thought he could see the ghostly outline of Bellmon's head in the lights from his instrument panel. Forty minutes ago Jimmy would have been willing to bet that by this point in the mission he'd be alone.

Off to the east there was a hint, a mere suggestion of rose and salmon pink from the rising sun on the horizon. Jimmy looked at his clock. By his dead reckoning they should be ten miles inland from the north coast, near Salamaua, and it was time to begin their letdown. He flashed his lights twice and got the same from Bellmon. Ahead and around them he could see other pairs of lights flashing on and off. Jimmy pushed over and began a letdown at 1500 feet per minute, still holding his course north.

The radio crackled to life for the first time during the mission. "All Boxcars from Boxcar Yellow Leader, arm 'em up, arm 'em up."

Jimmy looked carefully at his armament panel. He flipped the switches that armed the machine guns in the wings and the guns and cannon in the nose.

Jack Davis looked at the coastline below them. He wasn't sure, this being his first trip north, and there wasn't a hell of a lot of light from the sun peeking over the horizon, but it looked like there'd been a bit of wind from the west during the flight.

Well, that was only to be expected, he thought. Everything had been going too smoothly.

But they were over the coast because you could tell the difference between being over water and being over land on what was still a clear starry night. And the point was that since the north coast of New Guinea ran more or less east and west before making a sharp turn to the north at the west end of the Huon Gulf, that meant they were east of Lae. He looked at his altimeter. He and Evans were down to 12,000 feet now and descending as their speed built up to 400 mph.

Jimmy was sure he had a glimpse of two airplane maybe a mile ahead of them. He debated for a moment whether he should try to close them. It meant using a little more fuel and he'd been warned to hoard his fuel. Instead he increased his rate of descent a little, which meant his forward airspeed also increased. He'd hold this for a bit, pull close to the other pursuits, whom he devoutly hoped were P-39s, and see if they turned west at the appointed time. Then he'd know they were Boxcars, at least, hopefully Captain Davis and Danny Evans, and he could join up then.

Jack had been aware of the two airplanes behind and below them for a minute or two when the sun began to gild and paint the mountains to the south and east of them. It was only the tops of the mountains and the clouds around their peaks, but the sun would reach the deck in a few minutes. As the sunlight reached them he could tell they were P-39s.

The radio crackled again. "Boxcars, turning, turning now."

Davis began a standard rate turn to the west, still descending, with Danny Evans a lot closer to his wing than he liked, wobbling up and down but still there. Jack was amazed that the dumb kid had managed to stay there in the dark for the last hour. Maybe Evans was better at night.

Ahead of them it was still dark, and behind them the sun was still the least ember on the horizon, but that ember grew rapidly. Jack realized he could see whitecaps on the waves below them.

He stayed in a shallow dive towards the Huon Gulf as they straightened out to a heading of 350. The two P-39s joined up with them off Jack's right wing, and in the light Jack made out the grinning gremlin on the nose of Jimmy Ardana's P-39.

They continued descending to one hundred feet above the Gulf at 450 mph. Davis saw the sun lighting the top of a hill north of Lae, and he thought he could see the reflection of the sun on the wings of the Brickbats flying top cover.

Off to the left he saw another flight of P-39s, but they were too far away to see markings or figure out who they were. They were in the right position to be Boxcar Yellow flight, which, again, was nothing short of remarkable.

Everything looked like they were only ten miles from the target.

Jack keyed his radio. "Boxcar Red Leader with four, inbound to the target."

"Roger, Boxcar Red Leader, this is Boxcar Yellow Leader. Is that you about a half-mile north of us?"

"Roger, if you're a half-mile south."

"Glad to see you. OK, Boxcars, go to full throttle."

"Boxcar Yellow Leader, Boxcar Green Leader is in trail with four. Going to full throttle."

"Roger, Green."

Jack eased his pursuits in behind Yellow flight. The coast was visible ahead, but where the hell was the airfield? It wouldn't look like much, the only way they could even see it was to pick out a little hill just north of the field and stay to the south of that and hope for the best.

Then the flak started and he knew they were in the right place as his balls tried to clutch up inside his abdomen.

"Boxcars, take it to the deck," Wolchek radioed.

The strafers eased their pursuits towards the whitecapped surface of the sea as their airspeed indicators hovered around four hundred mph.

Jimmy flew over the surface of the Huon Gulf, so low he didn't dare look at his altimeter. Tracer from Japanese 25mm AAA soared past him and among the Boxcars. Heavier stuff exploded around them with red flashes and black puffs of smoke that appeared as if from nowhere. Something pinged against his tail. It sounded just like he'd been told it would, like pebbles rattling against a tin roof. As they approached the field Jimmy made out the AAA emplacements between the end of the runway and the seashore. And they were going to fly right over them when they turned to sweep down the runway. He checked his machine guns and cannon armament switches again.

Jimmy knew he was a dead man. He knew it. He wanted to make little whining noises and do anything but what he was doing right this instant, which was to stay here in the Number Three slot off Jack Davis's wing, flying into the tracers that walked across the water, sending up splashes that flew higher than the Boxcars and spattered his windshield with spray.

Something exploded ahead of them with a godawful *whump!* Jesus Christ, cannon fire, the goddam bastards are shooting honest to God cannons at me!

The Boxcar Yellow P-39s were within a mile of the beach when black smoke streamed from the airplane in the number three slot.

"Three's hit," someone remarked over the radio, at the same moment Boxcar Yellow Four exploded, simply exploded in an orange flash edged in black smoke and flaming, streaming metal bits.

"Four's gone," said that same insanely calm voice.

Two heartbeats later they flew through the smoke where Yellow Four died and ahead of them the three remaining P-39s of Yellow Flight were over the beach, with smoke puffing back in their slipstream. Jimmy could see the flashes from the Jap AAA now and a line of a half-dozen Jap Zeros on a taxiway, propellers glittering in the sunlight as they prepared to take off.

Jimmy looked over his shoulder at Gerry Bellmon one last time and then Davis turned sharply left to come across the runway to get at the Zeros lining up to take off. Two of the Zeros began their takeoff runs with two more right behind them.

Jimmy fired. He saw smoke blowing back from the airplanes in the lead and their tracer smashed into the AAA emplacements. There were small explosions on the ground from the cannon shells fired from the lead airplane. The P-39s swept over the Zeros at the end of the runway as something exploded underneath them. Tracers went past Jimmy's right wingtip; Bellmon, firing away at something. They completed their turn on the runway heading. Jimmy fired his guns at a Zero parked in a revetment and saw the tracers sink into its wings and canopy. Ahead of them the two Zeros on the runway lifted off. Davis jinked and skidded, firing at the lead Zero. Evans overshot Davis and started firing at random. The lead Zero dropped a wingtip and cartwheeled, spreading debris before exploding into flames. Davis rolled and fired at the other Zero, which puffed smoke and broke to the right, straight into the tracers from Danny's P-39, which danced over the cowling and cockpit of the Zero. The Zero's nose dropped and it went into the jungle at the end of the runway in billow of smoke and fire. Then they were past the runway and over the jungle with a few tracers flying past them, then nothing. Davis led them into a hard turn to the left with their wingtips brushing the treetops. Jimmy looked over his left shoulder at the Lae airfield. There were a half dozen plumes of black smoke boiling up from Lae. As Jimmy watched two more Zeros got off the runway and turned towards them.

"Boxcar Red Leader to Brickbat White Leader, at least two Zeros off the runway."

"Roger, Boxcar Red, we're coming down. You guys head for home."

"Affirmative, Brickbat. Boxcars, you heard the man. Let's go home."

Jimmy looked all around, watching the Zeros behind them. He saw the Brickbats at twelve o'clock high, falling like thunderbolts on the Zeros taking off from Lae.

Jack finished with the debrief and went looking for the other members of his flight. He found Gerry Bellmon and Jimmy Ardana watching in bemusement as Danny Evans described the fight to a debriefer who was very clearly trying to escape.

"And it was like magic!" Evans said. "That damn Jap flew right across my sights as I pressed the trigger and bam, zammo! Down he went!"

"OK, OK, lieutenant," the debriefer said. "That's a half-kill anyway, because Captain Davis put some bullets into that one and caught it on fire."

"A half-kill! But I'm tellin' ya, it came apart when I shot at it!"

"Evans," said Jack. "It's a half-kill, and that's a good start."

Evans looked up at Davis. Muscles worked on his face and around his mouth.

"Evans," Jack said. "You come with me. Bellmon, Ardana, you guys come along too."

"But..."

"Evans, now."

Ardana got up, with Bellmon right behind him, and followed Jack, who didn't look around to see if Evans followed.

They went to Jack's tent, where he sat them down and pulled a bottle out from under his bed, along with some mess cups. Jack passed around the cups and poured them each a tot of the Australian whiskey. He raised his cup.

"Here's to us," he said. "There's a longer version, but that'll do for now."

"To us," said Jimmy. "To us," chorused Bellmon and Evans.

They tossed down their whiskey. Bellmon gasped.

The whiskey burned down their throats and clawed their stomachs with liquid fire.

"Hoo," said Bellmon. "I've had raw stuff but this is something else again. Australian?"

"All I could find in Townsville," Davis said, tilting the bottle to his lips again.

Ardana said, "Damn, I've tasted cowboy rotgut in my time, but that stuff ain't for the young."

"Then it shouldn't be for you," Davis replied. "Have a little more."

"Little flowers," sneered Evans. "I've drunk worse stuff than that. It ain't so bad."

Jack poured more whiskey.

"OK, boys, here's the thing. Evans, you surprised me. You did pretty well out there, from being on my wing when the sun came up to staying there on that run into the target. Good work with that Zero, too. Don't get a swelled head. You damned near cracked up landing and if you kill yourself on the landing you've just done the Japs a favor."

Evans scowled.

"Jimmy, Gerry, how did you do?"

Jimmy shrugged. "I got bullet strikes on a couple of Zeros. Maybe one of them was smoking a little."

"Gerry?"

"Ah, Captain, I don't know. I got so excited it was all just a blur. Sorry."

"Don't be sorry. Just do better next time. Did you shoot, at least?"

"Yes, sir."

"Then maybe you hit something. You helped scare the hell out of the Japs, anyway."

Evans chortled, looking from Bellmon to Ardana. "You mean I did better than both you guys? Ha! Ha! Still think you're some punkins now, Jimmy boy?"

"Danny, you were firing blind," said Ardana evenly.

"I was not!"

"I was off your right wing. You followed Captain Davis into a left and then a right turn, we all did, when he started shooting at that second Zero. Bits came off and it started to smoke. You couldn't have seen the Zero until it flew right in front of you because of the angle of your bank. The only reason you hit him was because you were already holding your triggers down."

Evans stood up abruptly and balled his fists, looking at Jimmy.

Jack said, "Evans, sit down. Jimmy's right. I saw your tracers shooting holes in the air two seconds before that Zero flew in front of you."

"But, Captain…"

"You don't agree? Prove it, next time. Because you can count on there being a next time. But right now, sit down and drink up."

Jack watched the tableau for a moment, gathering his feet underneath him. He saw that Bellmon flicked a glance between Ardana and Evans, and that Ardana sat relaxed, not quite looking at Evans. Then Jack saw that Ardana's apparent relaxation was deceptive. His canteen cup full of whisky was tilted ever so slightly towards Evans, and there was something about the way Ardana held his legs. Then it hit Jack that Ardana was ready to throw the whisky in Evans' face and drive his booted foot right into Evans' midriff.

Jack chuckled and shook his head. "Danny, take my advice. Sit down, or I'm going to let whatever happens next happen, and claim afterwards you tripped over your own big feet. Nobody will think twice about that, either."

Evans stood a moment longer, breathing hard, not taking his eyes off Ardana, who maintained a totally expressionless look on his face, relaxed and ready to strike.

"Christ, Danny, just sit down," said Bellmon.

"I'll remember that, Gerry," Evans growled. "I thought we were pals, but I guess you've decided who your friends are."

Jack felt the anger rise up in him again. "Evans, sit down and shut up. Do it now, and if I have to make that an order, I will."

Evans stood a moment longer, then sat down abruptly and tossed down the whisky in his cup. "You need me for anything else, Captain?" he asked.

"No. Go for a walk. Cool off."

Evans stood and left the tent. Jack watched him walk down the path between the tents.

Ardana sighed and sipped at the whiskey in his cup. "Damn, Gerry," he said. "What's with that guy?"

"Danny played ball in college."

"So?"

"Well, he was good. He was *really* good, like in the running for the Heisman Trophy good. He didn't make it, but he has a hell of a lot of other trophies and awards."

"This is what he said?" asked Jack.

"Sir, I know Danny is kind of a blowhard..."

Ardana snorted.

Bellmon gave him a pained look before he continued speaking. "And he talks a lot about himself, and he tends to exaggerate a little, like anyone might, but I don't think he's dishonest."

Bellmon looked in his cup and took a sip of the whisky. "Was it only three days ago we got shot up by Zeros, coming in here?" he asked quietly. "On top of everything else, I think it might be the longest three days of my life. And Danny? I think, until those two guys were shot to pieces right next to us, that Danny thought this was another football game, and he'd be a big shot on this playing field like he was back home. I guess that was in my mind, too."

"What do you think now?" Jack asked.

"Now?" Bellmon shuddered. "Now I just want to do the best I can and come back in one piece. To be honest, I think I'd settle for the coming-back-in-one piece part."

Jack nodded. "You can build on that, Bellmon," he said. "Especially since it isn't easy to do, as you've seen."

Bellmon nodded. Jack poured a little more whisky in Bellmon's cup, then held the bottle out to Ardana, who shook his head.

"No, thanks."

Ardana sipped from his cup and looked up, past Jack. His eyes narrowed.

"Here's that colonel from FEAF, and…"

Ardana set down his cup and ran out of the tent. Jack turned, surprised, to see Ardana running towards Colonel Carrolton and Congressman Snyder.

"Uncle Matt!" he heard Ardana shout, just as he came to attention and saluted the colonel, who returned it in time for Ardana to seize the congressman's hand.

"Hello, young James," boomed the congressman. "How the hell are you, son? It's good to see you still in one piece!"

"Not half as good as it is to be in one piece," said Ardana.

Jack stood in the tent entrance, watching. "Hey, Jimmy," he called.

"Yes, sir?"

"Perhaps your uncle and Colonel Carrolton would care for a drink?"

"You're damned right I would!" said Snyder. "Come along, Colonel, I'll be dipped in shit before I miss a chance to drink with these young men."

"After you, sir," said the colonel. He rolled his eyes at Jack, his ill-humor of the night before evidently forgotten.

Jack said, "Jimmy, we didn't know you kept such famous company. "

"Oh, I'm not famous, Captain, not at all," said the congressman. "It's only my second term and the only reason I'm in politics at all is to see that the folks in my district get a fair shake. Actually it was James' dad that put me up to it. He's been in politics all his life."

"Oh?"

"He's the county sheriff," said Jimmy.

"That's so," said Snyder comfortably. "And a county sheriff knows as much about politics as anyone in Washington. And Joe Ardana is a smart man. Too damn smart to go to Washington himself. That place is no more than a small town writ large as far as I can see."

Jack found another cup, rinsed Danny's cup out with a little whiskey, and filled them both.

"Careful, Uncle Matt," Ardana said, as Snyder lifted the cup to his lips. "This stuff reminds me of what your brother used to make."

Snyder winked at Ardana. "Well, here's confusion to Hirohito," he said, and everyone drank.

The congressman gasped a couple of times. "Whew! You were right, James, that stuff kicks worse than lightning! How is it you're drinking it? Should I tell your mother you're drinking this stuff?"

Bellmon grinned. Jimmy blushed and said, "Go ahead, Uncle Matt, but she's likely to bend a rolling pin over your head for letting me do it."

That brought a laugh all around.

"It was my idea, sir," Jack said. He held up the bottle, and the congressman extended his cup.

"What are you celebrating?"

"Being alive," Jimmy said.

Snyder looked up at Jimmy's tone. Then he looked at Jack.

"How did it go this morning?" he asked.

"Pretty well," Jack said. "We caught the Japs by surprise, which isn't easy to do, shot them up, and got the hell out. That isn't always easy to do, either."

Snyder nodded. "Not to put you on the spot, Captain, but how did Jimmy do?"

"Uncle Matt…"

"James, you know your Dad will ask when he thinks your Mama isn't listening."

"This was Jimmy's second combat mission," Jack replied. "Jimmy's a good pilot, and I think he'll make a pursuit pilot, too. That's not necessarily the same thing."

"Second mission?" Snyder looked from Jack to his nephew.

"Yes, sir. You want to tell them about your first mission, Jimmy?"

"I got shot down," Jimmy said.

"Great God! But it couldn't have been too bad. You look all in one piece."

"Jimmy's right, he got shot down," Jack said. "But you might say he had his revenge."

Snyder looked suddenly at the Colt revolver Jimmy wore. The congressman grinned, then, and the grin surprised Jack. It was a hard, wolfish, knowing grin.

"Old Tom's present came in handy, did it?" Snyder asked softly. "How did that happen?"

Ardana nodded towards Jack. "Captain Davis shot the Zero off my tail…"

"A second too late," Jack said.

"Maybe, but that Zero crash-landed on the airstrip ahead of me. I was trying to land, but that sonofabitch shot up my engine. It got a bit hot in the cockpit and as soon as the airplane stopped rolling I was out the door. Next thing I know there are bullets flying around me, and with all the smoke and noise and guns going off it took me a second to realize the pilot of that Zero was shooting his pistol at me."

Snyder nodded, leaning forward a little. The grin faded, but the wolf was still there in the lines of his face. He nodded.

"Well, I was surprised as all hell, and for a second I watched that Jap run at me, shooting. And about then I heard my grampa's voice."

"What did he say?" Snyder asked.

Jack was surprised at the matter-of-fact tone in Snyder's question. As if he had no problem believing that a dead man spoke to Jimmy on the airstrip.

"He told me he reckoned I'd better draw, so I did."

"Ha!" Snyder leaned forward and clapped Ardana hard on his shoulder. "Good! You killed that Jap, then?"

Ardana shook his head. "Yes, sir."

"What?" Snyder asked.

"I didn't like it," Jimmy said.

"It's good you shot that Jap before he shot you," Snyder said bluntly. "It's better you don't like it. You did your bounden duty, young James. You keep doing that, and you won't ever be afraid to look your folks or anyone else in the eye when you get back. And you will get back, because we need you back home."

Ardana looked at Snyder. His brow furrowed and he chuckled as he shook his head.

"Thanks, Uncle Matt," he said. "Tell you what, can you take something home for me? For Dad?"

"Sure. What is it?"

"I'll go fetch it."

Ardana left the tent, but was back in less than a minute. Jack figured he would have the Zero pilot's holstered Nambu pistol, and that was in the hand he extended to Snyder.

The congressman took it and looked at it curiously. He opened the holster and took the pistol out, hefting it in his hand before pointing it across the tent. The move surprised Jack. Watching the way Snyder handled the pistol convinced Jack the congressman not only knew his way around firearms, but had used them at some point.

"Were you in the last war, sir?" Jack asked.

"Jimmy's father and I were in a Montana militia regiment that went over to France," Snyder said. "All that French mud was quite an experience for us. Not like the mud in Montana, I must say."

"Where were you, congressman, if you don't mind me asking?" Colonel Carrolton inquired. "I was with the 126th Infantry in the St.-Mihiel salient."

"Oh, what a lovely place! I remember it in my dreams to this day," Snyder replied. He held up his cup and clinked it with the colonel's.

"Me too," said Carrolton quietly, and they drank.

"Congressman, if you don't mind me asking…" Jack began.

"You call me Matt, Captain Davis. You're looking after my nephew here."

"How is it that you came to know Jimmy's dad? Because you were in the same outfit?"

"Well, we're both from the same town in Montana, Choteau. You've probably never heard of it, it's barely even a whistle stop, so you know, small town, everyone knows everybody else. Cow country and mining, mostly, with maybe a few trappers still up in the mountains. Not all that different from when the Sioux and the buffalo roamed all over it. Joe Ardana and I grew up together, huntin' and ridin' and punchin' cows when we were old enough. When the last war came along we figured it would be sort of like the Spanish war, you know, and maybe we could join something like Teddy Roosevelt's Rough Riders. But when we mustered in we were told to leave our cow ponies home, because it was going to be an infantry war, foot-soldierin' all the way."

The congressman grinned. "Now that was me an' Joe, but Joe's younger brother Kurt joined the Air Service. You get enough red liquor in him and he'll tell you all about fighting the Red Baron."

Jack exchanged a glance with Ardana, who grimaced and looked away.

"Now, young James, no need to blush! You know your uncle Kurt might like to stretch the truth a bit, but he came home with the scalps of a half-dozen Huns and a chestful of medals. I reckon he's entitled to some stretchers, now and then."

A private came down the path, stood in the doorway, came to attention, and saluted.

"Begging your pardon, sirs," he said.

"What is it, private?" Carrolton asked.

"Colonel, Colonel Wagner sent me to tell you your plane back to Townsville is ready when you are."

"Very well, private. My compliments to Colonel Wagner, and we'll be on our way up to Operations in a few minutes."

"Yes, sir." The private saluted again and left.

"Well, Matt, that's our cue," the colonel said.

The congressman turned to Davis. "Captain, congratulations again on your fine work this morning, and thank you for taking care of my nephew. Be careful, but let us hear more from you."

"I'll do that, congressman."

Snyder smiled benevolently and turned to Ardana.

"James, you take care, you hear?" He embraced the younger man. "I'll tell your folks you're doing OK."

"Thanks, Uncle Matt." With a last handshake, the congressman left with the colonel and the major.

After they left Davis sat on his bunk and poured another round for everyone. Then he drank most of what he had poured off at one draft. "Crap," he said. "I didn't know your family was in politics, Ardana."

Jimmy shrugged. "Just Uncle Matt, really. Dad's the county sheriff, which is sort of like Uncle Matt said, you get to know where the bodies are buried and what deals to do and all that kind of thing. But that's all Dad wants. If I remember right Uncle Matt ran for Congress the same year I went off to college."

"Hm," said Davis. He shook his head. "Screw politics. I just want to fly."

"Like my uncle Kurt," said Jimmy. "He and dad argue about that all the time. Dad wants to know when Kurt is going to settle down, give up flying and build a real life. Kurt says he's too old to change now and he has too much fun."

Jack laughed. "Was your uncle in the last war?"

"Yeah. He flew SPADs in Eddie Rickenbacker's squadron. Or so he always says." Jimmy grinned. "Uncle Matt is right, though. Uncle Kurt claims he shot down the Red Baron if he gets enough whisky in him."

"Huh. So was my dad. In the 94th Aero Squadron, I mean."

"Oh?'

Jack grimaced.

"Wait a minute," Ardana said. "Frank Davis? Was that your dad?"

Jack looked at Ardana and said, "Gerry, why don't you go find Evans. Tell him to go paint a half-flag on his airplane."

"Yes, sir."

Jack waited until Bellmon left. "Want another snort?"

"No, sir. I'm fine."

Jack capped the bottle and put it back in his footlocker.

"Did I say something wrong?" Ardana asked.

"No. Both my grandparents were in Congress." Jack grinned. "The way my mother told it, they were arch-enemies. Grandpa Beauregard was a Democrat from Georgia, Grandpa Davis was a Republican from Connecticut. When my brother Charlie was born it did a lot to end that particular rivalry."

"Damn. I didn't know your family was so well-connected."

"My dad wasn't really interested in politics, not after flying got into his blood. If it weren't for the war he might have run for Congress, but there you are."

"How about you?"

"Me? I'm with Dad. I'm a pilot, and that's what I want to do. What about you, Jimmy?"

"I know how to run a ranch and fly an airplane. The truth is, I don't know who I'm going to be when this is all over."

"What do you mean?"

"Well...something my Dad and my Uncle Kurt told me about the last war. They weren't really the same when they got back. They said a lot of the guys were even worse."

"Crawled into a bottle?"

"Yeah. Some of them."

Jack nodded. "So maybe not worry about the future further ahead than a week or two."

"If that." Ardana hesitated. "Look. Was I right about Evans?"

"You mean, about him holding his triggers down and shooting blind? Yeah, you were. Don't count on luck, Jimmy, but don't underestimate it, either. I hope to hell Evans knows he was lucky, but I doubt it. Now tell me, how do you really think you did today, Jimmy?"

"Hell if I know. I got a piece of a Zero, I think, one sitting on the taxiway." Jimmy grimaced and said bitterly, "I can't hit shit."

Davis looked up at him. "Evans was lucky. You know it. I know it. Besides, you left one of those bombers smoking the other day. So you can in fact hit shit."

Jimmy studied Davis. "Why are you telling me this?"

"I meant what I said to your uncle. You've got the makings of a good pilot, Jimmy. You're smart and you've got the right moves. If you stay alive long enough you might even be a good pursuit pilot, and it really isn't the same thing."

"I don't get it."

"I know you don't. You will, if you live long enough. Don't worry about Danny Evans getting a half-Zero today. You did fine."

Jimmy grimaced.

That was when the air raid siren went off.

"Aw, hell," said Davis. "Guess the Japs want revenge."

"Do you know where the slit trench is?" Jimmy yelled as they ran out of the tent.

"Follow me."

They joined a slit trench already crowded with men, most of whom sat on the edge of the trench looking up at the sky. Suddenly three gull-gray shapes with red meatballs on their wings roared overhead, low enough to throw rocks at. Another trio of Zeros roared past further away, and down towards the airstrip came the rattle of machine-guns and cannon, along with the cracking boom of heavy-caliber AAA. They could see the Zero fighters strafing the revetments along the airstrip. Something exploded with a yellow and orange flash of gasoline and then the *WH-WHUMP!* of exploding bombs. Another flight of Zeros came down the taxiway, strafing the dispersed P-39s in their revetments. A fire and a column of smoke boiled up. Nearby an automatic weapon chattered, the deep jackhammer slamming of a quad-mounted .50-caliber weapon. A Zero flew into a line of tracers and fell apart in a gout of flame and burning aluminum, with the engine spinning out like the head of a comet. Three Zeros in a beautiful vic flew overhead, in a formation like they were in an air show. Another weapon opened up on them and the lead Zero staggered but flew on.

The Japanese raid was over in minutes. The all-clear sounded and the men in the slit trench stood up and began to go to the airplane dispersal areas to check their airplanes.

Jimmy got to the *Gremlin* first but other than the holes she picked up in the morning raid on Lae there didn't appear to be any new damage. Terraine came running a few minutes later. The two of them went over the airplane together.

"What do you think?" Jimmy asked him.

"Just the same holes you picked up this morning, Jimmy. We'll get to work patching her up right now."

"Thanks, Don."

While they were opening panels to the engine compartment aft of the cockpit the other two members of the ground crew came panting up. Jimmy looked over Terraine's shoulder while the crew chief inspected the engine and began tracing back to the holes in the after fuselage.

"How did that happen, sir?" the armorer asked.

"Damned if I know. There was a hell of a lot of shooting going on over that runway. Kind of like what went on just now, only us instead of them. And sorting out who did what to whom, well, ask me in a couple more trips. It was everything I could do to stay with Captain Davis and shoot where it looked like it would do some good."

"Reckon you got a piece of them Jap bastards anyway, sir. That's not bad for a second mission."

Down on the runway there was the sound of a twin-engined airplane taking off. In a few moments they saw a C-47 rising above the runway, sucking up the gear and making a left turn to the south, the sea and Australia.

"Guess Uncle Matt got off OK," Jimmy murmured. He watched as a couple of P-39s flew southward above the C-47 to act as top cover against marauding Zeros.

Chapter Ten

May 9-10, 1942

"How's the war going?"

The RAAF had the only clubs at Seven-Mile, one for the officers and one for the enlisted. Jack got cleaned up after dinner and headed to the Officers Mess. The beer was the piss-warm Aussie brew, but at least it was liquid and relaxing. After this morning he wanted to relax. He just hoped no one started any crap about him being an ace. Regardless of Charlie's opinion, Buzz Wagner could have the famous ace part.

The RAAF Officers Mess was doing a roaring business. American aircrew outnumbered the RAAF types, but the RAAF made up for it with sheer noise and exuberance. Jack got a beer from a sweating barman and looked around. He spotted his brother Charlie with a couple of other majors, one of whom looked familiar from the Lae mission briefing. Charlie spotted him at the same moment and waved him over.

"Jack! Come meet some low characters!" Charlie shouted above the din. "Guys, this is my brother, the famous ace."

"Jehosophat, Charlie," Jack scowled. "Don't start that shit."

"What? You aren't a famous ace?"

"I doubt anyone outside Seven-Mile even knows," Jack replied. He sat down in the chair Charlie dragged out. "I'm sure as hell not famous."

"Are you sure he's a pursuit pilot, Charlie?" one of the majors asked. "He seems kind of modest."

Charlie laughed. "Jack, you know Sammy Keith. This other guy is Tommy Rhodes from the 22nd Bomb Group."

"Marauders?" Jack asked, extending his hand.

"The Baltimore Whore herself," said Rhodes cheerfully. "Or the Flying Prostitute, if you prefer."

Jack drank his beer. "Why d'you call it that?"

"Martin forgot to put enough wing area on the damned thing, so it has no visible means of support."

Jack grinned. 'No visible means of support' was a legal phrase implying that a woman who had no job was probably supporting herself as a member of the oldest profession, or the second oldest, depending on how one felt about priests.

"Guess that makes takeoffs kind of interesting," he said.

"You got that right, Davis," Rhodes said. "Although if you fly P-39s, I'm sure you know all about interesting airplanes."

"Yeah, she'll keep your attention, all right."

Rhodes offered his beer mug, Jack clinked glasses with him, and they drank to interesting airplanes.

"You were at the meeting the other night," Jack said to Rhodes.

"Sure was. What did you do with that gorgeous bauble Wagner bestowed on you?"

Jack groaned inwardly. Charlie looked at him, his eyes alive with brotherly malice.

"A bauble, little brother? What sort of bauble?"

"About the size of a dinner plate," Rhodes said cheerfully. "With wings on it and a huge silk ribbon, for suspension from the necks of heroic aviators."

Charlie laughed. "I thought you said you weren't famous, Jack. What did you do with this treasure?"

"It's at the bottom of my footlocker, if you must know," Jack replied.

The majors laughed. Then Sammy Keith leaned forward and clapped Jack on the shoulder.

"All kidding aside, Jack, congratulations and good work and I hope you bag a couple dozen of those bastards before it's over."

"Hear, hear," said Rhodes. Which made it another occasion to clink glasses and take a healthy swig of beer, healthy enough that Rhodes offered to buy the next round and went to the bar to collect.

"When did you get in, Charlie?" Jack asked.

"An hour ago."

"How's the war going?"

"My part, or in general?"

"Both."

"Me and the boys have a job tomorrow morning, weather permitting. Can't say where," said Charlie cheerfully.

"Of course not. Well, then, how's the war in general going? No one tells us pursuit types anything."

Charlie gestured with his stein towards Major Keith. "What do you say, Sammy? You recon guys always have the scoop."

Keith scoffed. "Well, the Krauts are kicking Russian ass on the other side of the world. Or maybe it's the other way around, depending on the day of the week and who you ask. Closer to home, our Navy isn't talking much about the Jap Navy, but I gather they had a pretty good fight of some kind."

"Oh? The Japs still coming this way?"

"Doubt it. Don't take a deep breath just yet, though. Not until we figure out where the little yellow bastards went."

Jack looked at Charlie. Charlie returned the look, then gave him the slightest nod.

Rabaul.

Jack had noticed that no one, especially the bomber crews, talked about Rabaul as if it were a normal place, because it wasn't. Since the Japs took the place over in January, they shipped in Zeros and bombers by the squadron and antiaircraft guns by the battalion. The Jap air raids on Seven-Mile came from airfields around Rabaul and the only thing the RAAF and USAAF, between them, had to hit back with was a handful of B-17s and B-26s, plus the odd Catalina and Hudson from the RAAF, hitting Rabaul and Simpson Harbor at night. It was the same old story, just like it had been from the start of the war. The Air Corps was trying to put out a three-alarm fire by pissing on it.

Jack guessed Charlie was going to Rabaul to have a look in at Simpson Harbor, because the US Navy wanted to know if the Jap Navy was there. You didn't have to be a G-2 genius to figure that one out.

Rhodes came back with a pair of mugs in each hand which he passed around.

"Thanks, major," said Jack.

"Call me Tommy. Drink up."

"Damn, do you Marauder guys always drink like this?"

"Like what? This is perfectly normal for anyone who flies that bitch."

Jack grinned wryly. "Sometimes I envy guys who fly nice, stable airplanes," he said, pointing at Charlie with his beer mug.

"Yeah, but somehow I can't see you flying a B-17," Charlie said. "Too nice. Too stable. I know you, you're like Dad, you want a little crazy riding with your wings."

"Well, speaking of crazy, are you likely to bring any friends back from wherever you're going?" Jack asked. "Seems like the Japs might not want folks taking pictures of something they want to keep hidden."

"You could say that," Charlie relied. "And to answer your first question, sometimes we do. Persistent little bastards."

Jack nodded. He looked at the other two men at the table. They both wore blank, preoccupied looks that focused on something in the far distance.

Rabaul.

Jehosophat.

"Well," said Jack. "If someone wanted to join the party, where and when do you suppose they might meet?"

Keith looked at Jack, and then at Charlie. "Now, if I understand your kid brother correctly, Charlie, that might be a good idea."

Charlie nodded. "You think Wagner would go for it?"

"Probably. I'd have to ask."

"Can you set it up? Or do you need some support? Like maybe I go visit Wagner with you?"

Jack thought about it for a moment. "No, I don't think so. I can think of a couple of good reasons to go and do it."

"OK," said Charlie. He looked at Keith. "Sammy, maybe Jack could come to our briefing tomorrow morning?"

Major Keith nodded. "That might be helpful. Who knows what the weather will do in this shithole, anyway. We might not even go."

There was a lull in the conversation, one of those moments that happen in the noisiest bars, and in the comparative quiet Jack heard the voice of Danny Evans.

"And you shoulda seen it! I shot his wing right off, and down that Jap went, screeeee-pow!"

The conversation picked up to its former level. Jack turned to look at Evans, who was in full-on pursuit-pilot mode, hands cocked up to show just how it had been when he shot that Jap down, screeeee-pow.

"Ah," said Rhodes. "No doubt that *he's* a pursuit pilot. Is he famous, Jack?"

"I'm told a lot of college sports writers thought so, a couple years back."

"Indeed? A football hero! Did it happen the way he says?"

Jack frowned. He didn't like Danny Evans or his big mouth, but God help him, Evans was one of his boys.

"I was there," Jack said shortly. "And yeah, it happened like that. Pretty much."

Charlie looked at Jack. "Tommy, you played football at the Point, didn't you? I seem to remember you even if you were a year ahead of me."

Rhodes looked at Charlie and then back at Jack. The major held his hand up hastily. "Davis, if I spoke out of line, I apologize."

Jack relaxed and shrugged. He held up his mug, and Rhodes touched his glass to Jack's. "No sweat," Jack said. "The guy rubs me the wrong way, too, but he's in my flight."

Rhodes nodded. "You seem to have a pretty colorful bunch. Don't you have a real live gunslinger, too?"

"What's this?" Charlie asked.

"Aw, Tommy here is talking about Jimmy Ardana. You met him the day I got here. He flew the Hudson."

Charlie shook his head. "Did you see that, Tommy? The Hudson that jumped over one of your B-26s, three days ago?"

Rhodes looked at Jack. "That was this Ardana kid?"

"The one and only."

"Well, damn. He seems like a certifiable loon. Think he might like to fly a B-26?"

"Hands off, Major. Ardana's going to be a really good pursuit pilot if he lives long enough."

Charlie said, "Besides, the 19th gets first crack at him if he decides to leave pursuit flying. I already asked."

Jack woke up the next morning feeling the drag of too much beer the night before. He sat up, head swimming and stomach roiling for a moment. He drank some foul-tasting water from the canteen by his cot and felt better. Another swig and he reflected that a beer belly and a slight headache were a small price to pay for blowing off a little steam.

He swung out of his bunk and got dressed. He checked the glowing radium hands of his watch, which pointed to 0545. He was supposed to meet Charlie at the 19th's Operations shack at 0630.

Jack stood in the entrance of his tent for a moment, looking at the stars through the branches of the trees. Then he started down the line to Tent 7, where Jimmy Ardana and his pals were quartered.

When he got there he noticed a blur of white on the other side of the path, near the tree line. He frowned, puzzled, before he made out the outline of a man, one of the natives, squatting by a tree in front of Tent 7. Jack stopped and looked at the man.

"Hello," he said. "Who are you?"

The native stood up, still barely visible in the early-morning darkness.

"Me Evarra," the man said. "Youpela pailat?"

"Pailat?"

"Balous-man, like Jimmy," said Evarra helpfully, pointing at Tent 7. "Youpela bosboi balous-man?"

It took Jack a moment to puzzle out the man's meaning.

"Flight leader," Jack replied. He pointed to his chest. "Jack Davis. Bosboi balous-man. Flight leader."

Evarra nodded. "Flight leader," said the sanguma man. Then he walked away, fading into the darkness in three steps.

"Jack?"

He turned to see Jimmy standing at the entrance to Tent 7.

"Morning, Jimmy. You up for a little walk?"

"Sure. Where we going?"

"Over to the 19th's Operations shack. I have something in mind but I need to check their schedule first. I want you to come along to see how things work."

"One minute."

One minute later they were walking down the path. Jimmy skipped on one foot for the first ten feet as he got his left foot in his flying boot. Then he walked beside Jack in silence, yawning.

"So what's up?" Jimmy asked. He stomped his left foot down to settle his foot in his boot.

"You up for a some flying, later this morning?"

"Sure."

"I had a talk with my brother last night. He and his crew are headed north a little later this morning, and I thought we might meet him when he comes back."

"Think he might bring friends back with him?"

"Could be."

"OK."

"So who is this native I saw standing outside of your tent?"

"Evarra? My crew chief told me he's what the locals call a sanguma man, kind of like a witch doctor. What was he doing?"

"I don't know. Watching your tent. You owe him money or something?"

"Not that I know of. I met him the day we got here. Wanted to know if I was a balous-man. 'Pailat' I get. It sounds like 'pilot'. Wonder where the hell they got 'balous-man' from?"

"Maybe one of these missionaries knows." Jack paused. "Look, I haven't even talked this idea over with Wagner, yet. He may not like the idea, but what the hell, let's see what happens."

The sun broke over the eastern horizon as they walked into the Operations shack for the 19th Bomb Group. Major Keith was there with Charlie, looking at the operations schedule. There were two airplanes listed there. The pilots were listed as "MAJ S KEITH" off at 0700, with "MAJ C DAVIS" slated to take off at 1000.

"Good morning, gentlemen," Jack said. They exchanged salutes. Keith grinned, shaking Ardana's hand.

The major indicated Ardana's Colt revolver.

"You like the old six-gun?" he asked.

"Yes, sir," Ardana replied.

"Well, I hope you never have to make any more good Japs with that."

"Me, either," Ardana said. "Hopefully I can stick to a P-39."

Al Stern came in with another officer Jack didn't know. Both of them carried identical satchels, which meant the other guy was Keith's navigator.

"What's the scoop on the weather?" Keith asked. "By the way, this is my navigator, Lt. Frank Wellman."

"Pleased to meet you," said Wellman. "The RAAF weathermen think we'll be OK if everyone is back on the ground by 1500 at the latest, as far as it goes here at Seven-Mile. As far as points north go, we're on our own."

"As usual," Keith muttered. "So nothing on the weather north from the coastwatchers or submarines in the area?"

"No, sir."

"OK. What about the course?"

"Straight in, straight out."

"Keith, you're flying over New Britain," Charlie said. "That whole island is crawling with Japs. Aren't you afraid they'll see you in time to launch an intercept?"

"We'll be at 27,000 feet. They won't see a thing unless we start throwing a contrail."

Charlie nodded. Jack, watching his brother's face, saw that Charlie didn't think much of Keith's plan.

"Well, other than that, skipper, we're wheels-up in an hour," Wellman continued. "Don's finishing the fueling and I talked to the crew chief. We should be ready for engine start in a half-hour or less."

"OK. Meet me at the airplane, Fred. I need a minute with Charlie."

"Yes, sir." The navigator picked up his satchel and walked out.

Keith offered his hand and Charlie took it. "So you'll follow along at 1000?"

"Yes," said Charlie. "Don't stir up a hornet's nest, OK?"

"I sure hope not. See you later."

Charlie watched Keith leave. When the major was out of earshot Charlie turned to Al Stern.

"You plotted our course out to sea, right?" Charlie asked.

"Yes, sir," said Stern.

"Out to sea?" Jack asked.

"Keith wants to fly the short, straight course. That's OK, but his route takes him over the length of New Britain. I don't like his odds of being spotted and putting the Japs on alert before he's halfway to Rabaul. So we're going to fly out to sea, well to the east of New Britain, and swing in to approach Rabaul from the east. It adds a hundred miles to the mission, but it reduces the chances that the Japs will spot us until we're pretty close, maybe close enough that we can drop a couple of bombs, take our pictures, and start heading for home before the Zeros can climb up and intercept us."

"How fast can a Zero get up to your altitude?"

"Ten to fifteen minutes."

Jack nodded. "You carrying extra ammo?"

"You bet. Look. You talk to Wagner yet?"

"No."

Charlie nodded. He went to a nearby desk, picked up the phone, and asked for 8th Fighter Group Operations.

He looked up at Jack and covered the mouthpiece. "We'll see what he has to say, then."

Jack leaned against the desk.

Ardana said, "Danny and Gerry coming in on this?"

Jack thought about that. His first thought was to keep this flight between Jimmy and himself, and leave the other two out of it. He could even justify that on the basis that they had more time in the P-39 than Jimmy did, and Jimmy needed to build experience.

On the other hand, Jack was Boxcar Red Leader. This might be a chance to strengthen the flight as a whole, not just one man.

"Jimmy, that was my first thought. Truth is, though, it might be better to take everyone. That puts a little more responsibility on you, though, because you don't get to goof off playing wingman."

Ardana scoffed and said something under his breath that sounded suspiciously like "jee-hoso-fucking-fat."

Jack repressed a grin and said sternly, "Do not mock the great Jehosophat, you pitiful sinner."

"Great howling jumping Jehosophat, then."

"Better," said Jack. "Besides, that leaves Danny Evans on my wing. Maybe I'll put him on yours. I could use the rest."

Charlie held up a hand for silence. "Colonel Wagner? It's Major Davis, sir, at the 19th Bomb Group. Could I have a few moments? Thanks. Look, I wonder if you'd mind a suggestion for a mission this morning? Well, why don't I let Captain Davis explain it?"

Jack rolled his eyes and reached for the phone. "Colonel?"

"Don't 'colonel' me, Jack. What's up?"

"Boyd, the 19th has two B-17s going up on a photo-recon at different times this morning. I'd like to meet them on the way back."

"Where are you thinking?"

"The coast, maybe about one hundred miles northeast." Jack looked at Charlie, raising his eyebrows. Charlie nodded.

"I presume they're going to Rabaul?" Wagner asked.

"Yes, sir."

"You think the Japs will follow them far enough south to make this worthwhile?"

"The recon guys over here seem to think the Japs want to keep their movements secret. Might raise the stakes a little."

"Could be. OK, Jack, tell you what. I'll call Steve Wolchek and square it with him. You coordinate with Charlie on the timing."

"Yes, sir, will do."

"Good. Talk to you in a few."

Jack handed Charlie the phone, then looked at his watch. It read 0615.

"You're wheels-up about 1000?" Jack asked.

Charlie nodded. "Here's how I see it. Keith and his boys will be over Rabaul about 0930. Maybe they'll get away with it. Keith isn't carrying bombs, so they won't tip off the Japs by blowing something up, even if it's just fish in Simpson Harbor."

"So if they don't get spotted, they probably won't be intercepted," said Jack. "What odds do you give them?"

Charlie shrugged. "You heard Keith. He's going right over the island, and the island is occupied by the Japs. We've had guys flying up there for the last two weeks, and we lost three crews doing it. They were alone, and all we got were radio messages saying they were under attack and going down."

Jack nodded slowly. He'd shot down Jap bombers, and he could make the jump to imagining what the scene looked like as Zeros swarmed over a B-17 and shot it to pieces along with its crew.

"Don't," Charlie said quietly. His eyes were on Jack.

"OK," said Jack, equally quiet.

"Nice to know you care, though," Charlie said. His mouth quirked a little.

"Jerk," said Jack. Charlie chuckled.

Al Stern sat watching in silence. Now he spoke to Ardana. "It's Jimmy, right? I'm Al Stern."

Ardana shook hands with Stern. "Glad to meet you," he said. "Are those two always like this?"

"Pretty much," said Stern.

"You been up there?" Ardana asked. "To Rabaul?"

"Yes."

"It's bad?"

"Yeah, well, Java wasn't any fun either."

"Java?"

"It's a long story, Jimmy," said Jack.

Ardana nodded. "Well, let's all get together tonight, and you can tell me about it."

"Count on it," said Stern.

"Let's go get some breakfast," Jack said. "These guys have work to do."

Jack walked out of the ops shack and started up the path to the mess tent. "What d'you think they'll have for breakfast?"

"Bacon and fresh eggs," Jimmy said. "Fried antelope steak. Fresh-baked bread and new churned butter."

"Antelope steak?"

"That I shot myself."

"Damn. Where'd you have that breakfast?"

"Came home from a hunting trip."

"Can I visit your place sometime?"

"Sure. Mom would feed you up until you couldn't fit in an airplane."

Jack laughed.

"But you know, Boss, maybe you had a good idea."

"What's that?"

"Switch Danny and Gerry. Put Danny on my wing."

"You think so? Why?"

"Call it a hunch."

"OK. But you know he'll scream bloody murder."

"So what?"

Jack was a little surprised at the cold overtone in Ardana's voice.

"Then that's what we'll do, Three. It'll be up to you to make it work."

"Yes, sir."

Three hours later Jimmy sat in his P-39 at the edge of the airstrip, watching his engine temps edging up as they waited for the green light from the tower. Ahead of him Jack Davis and Gerry Bellmon, flying as Boxcar Red Leader and Boxcar Red Two, sat with their engines idling.

Jimmy looked sourly over his shoulder at Boxcar Red Four, Danny Evans, who scratched his nose in Jimmy's direction with his middle finger. Jimmy nodded.

The green light came. Red dust whirled back from the P-39s ahead of them. Jimmy pushed on the toe brakes and applied full throttle and manifold pressure. Jack's rudder kicked back and forth, and a moment later he and Gerry rolled down the runway. Jimmy moved forward and turned onto the runway heading.

One minute later Jimmy joined up in a loose formation behind and above Jack and Gerry. When Captain Davis said they'd fly loose to conserve fuel, Jimmy saw the look of relief, instantly suppressed, on Danny's face. Danny suppressed nothing when Davis told him he'd be flying on Jimmy's wing.

They made a half-circle around the field, climbing through 5000 feet before turning on heading 045. Jimmy double-checked that his Aux tank was set on the fuel selector, then checked that his armament panel was set to safe.

He looked back to check on Danny Evans, who was nowhere to be seen.

"Boxcar Red Four from Three, where are you?"

"Under your tail, Three," Evans replied.

"Four, this is Lead. Quit screwing around and get in position."

"Four to Lead, roger."

Jimmy looked over his shoulder again. Evans eased up about seventy feet off Jimmy's wing, bobbing and weaving.

Well, Jimmy thought, *at least he won't be an easy target.*

He checked his watch, looked at his fuel gauge, and glanced at his airspeed indicator. One hundred sixty-seven mph, right where it should be for best rate of climb. They'd be over the northern Papuan coast in thirty minutes. They'd fly another half hour, then, almost halfway between Papua and New Britain, along the course Major Keith's B-17 would follow, returning home. One hour out meant no less than one hour back, plus the climb to 21,000 feet, and, given the probable fuel consumption of an Allison V-1710 engine, that meant only about fifteen minutes of fuel to deal with any Japs that might happen along in the B-17's wake.

Jimmy scanned the sky, checked Evans, and looked suspiciously at the thunderheads starting to gather over the Owen Stanleys. Those thunderheads might hide Zeros.

The next time he looked at Evans, Jimmy shoved his stick full down, because Evans almost had his wingtip in Jimmy's cockpit. Evans kept going right over Jimmy's airplane, and Jimmy pulled back on his stick, getting right on Evans' tail, close enough to feel the propwash and see the slightest movement of Evans' control surfaces.

"Ahhh, Lead to Three, say your intentions."

"Four to Lead, I've lost Three!"

"Lead to Four, check your six."

Jimmy stayed just below and behind Evans, who frantically kicked his rudder, trying to see Jimmy.

"Three to Lead, I'm checking Four's oil cooler for leaks."

"God damn it, Jimmy, get out of my tail!"

"Four, shut up. Three, ease off."

"Roger, Lead."

"Lead to Four, you don't watch your fuel consumption, you'll walk home," Davis radioed.

"Roger, Lead."

Jimmy looked over at Evans, who looked back. Jimmy could see Evans' eyes over his oxygen mask.

They passed over the Papuan coast, which stretched out of sight to left and right. Ahead of them the island of New Britain appeared on the horizon, with a long stretch of water between them.

Suddenly Jimmy's earphones crackled to life. "Primrose 4, Primrose 4, this is Boxcar Red Leader. Come in, Primrose 4, over."

There was no reply, and the flight continued on over the sea, with the Papuan coast falling behind.

"Primrose 4, Primrose 4, this is Boxcar Red Leader, come in, come in, Primrose 4."

Silence.

Jimmy scanned the deep blue sky above and around them, then ahead towards New Britain, and there was a dot in the sky, or maybe a smudge.

A smudge, and in the right direction to be Primrose 4.

"Lead, Three, bogey at 11 o'clock."

"Roger, Three."

Davis turned to the left until the smudge was at 1 o'clock. He didn't change speed. Jimmy watched the smudge resolve itself into what he was sure was an airplane trailing smoke.

"Primrose 4, Primrose 4, this is Boxcar Red Leader, come in, over."

The radio crackled and howled in Jimmy's earphones and then a voice came over the air.

"Boxcar Red Leader, Primrose 4, glad to see you. We brought some friends back from up north, think you can show them the way home?"

The voice was cool, even laconic, but in the background machine-guns hammered and there was an explosion during the transmission.

"Primrose 4, that's affirmative. We have you in sight at our one o'clock."

"Boxcar, we're a-headin' that way. Primrose 4, out."

Jimmy looked at his airspeed indicator and did a little mental arithmetic. He was indicating 230 mph, with the B-17 maybe 20 miles away and making maybe 150 mph. They'd meet in a little over three minutes. He looked around, tightened his safety harness, and looked over at Evans, who was trailing well behind.

"Red Four from Red Three, close it up, Four."

Jimmy looked ahead. Davis didn't call for an increase in speed, and Jimmy figured he knew why. Right now, at cruise settings, the Allison engine burned 40 gallons of fuel per hour. In combat that would go to maybe 140 gph, meaning they could fight for 15 minutes before burning through their fuel reserves. Plus they still had a few gallons in their aux tanks, meaning the drag caused by the tank was now a liability exceeding the asset of fuel remaining.

On the other hand the 230 mph they were flying at now was far too slow. Davis would have to call for them to accelerate within the next two minutes.

Jimmy's hand curled over the throttle and manifold pressure controls. *2600 RPM,* he thought. *38 inches manifold pressure.*

"This is Boxcar Red Leader. Pickle your aux tanks, be sure to switch tanks first."

"Two."

"Three," said Jimmy.

"Four."

Jimmy saw the aux tanks tumble from the leading P-39s, spewing a brief white plume of fuel as they fell away. His own airplane picked up speed as the drag abruptly decreased when the tank came off.

"Reds, let's go to full throttle," Davis radioed. "Check your armament panels, guns hot."

Jimmy watched the smoking bomber ahead of them grow wings, and the smoke trailing behind it became billows rather than a smudge. Then:

"Bandits!" he called. "Three has Zeros behind the B-17, eleven o'clock high!"

"Got 'em, Three."

As Jimmy watched the Zeros made another attack on the B-17, six of them in two waves of three. The B-17 was maybe a thousand feet lower than his altitude. He checked his airspeed, which edged up over 300 mph.

It came down to timing now. The Zeros made their attack on the B-17, and the two elements split up, one element climbing to meet the P-39s.

For three seconds Jack studied the Zeros climbing up at his flight. The other element of Zeros curved up in what looked like the beginning of a chandelle, prelude to another diving attack on Primrose 4.

Jack had one hand on the throttle and the other on the stick. He pushed the nose down to meet the climbing Zeros, and looked over his shoulder at Gerry Bellmon.

"Two from Lead, move out a little. Pick one but don't shoot until you're almost on top of him."

"Roger, Lead."

Jack looked to the left at Ardana's element. Jimmy was right where he should be but Evans was doing his usual imitation of a crazy yoyo, bouncing around off Jimmy's left wing.

The Zeros came into range. The Zeros held their fire, and Jack felt his fingers closing around the triggers for his guns. The airspeed indicator unwound, pushing 360 mph. Jack picked the lead Zero, centering the gunsight pipper just above the engine as the Zero's cowl guns began to wink.

Wait, he thought. *Wait...*

He squeezed the triggers. His tracers crossed those of the lead Zero, and on his left tracers flew past his wingtip from Bellmon's guns. There was a sudden *winkwinkwink* of hits across the Zero's cowling and cockpit. Jack heard the rattle of hits along his wing, a bullet slammed through his canopy and buried itself in the armor plate behind his seat, then he roared over the Zero, pulling back hard on the stick with the g-force piling onto him.

"Two, break left," Jack ordered as they came to the vertical. He looked through the top of his cockpit and found the Zeros, coming out of their own climb and trying to maneuver on to their tails. He looked left and saw Bellmon in position, sticking with him as they ruddered over, out of the vertical into a hard left turn.

The Japs were coming down at an angle, now, and from the angle and the speed the Zeros would be on their tails before Jack and Bellmon got their own speed back up.

Jack chopped his throttle and dropped his flaps, slowing radically. Bellmon pulled ahead of him before he could follow Jack's lead. Jack watched the Zeros and when they began to overshoot he retracted his flaps and pushed the throttle all the way forward. The engine howled, the gearbox screamed, he pulled back gently on the stick. The Zeros flicked to the right, diving away, before Jack and Bellmon could get on their tails. Jack turned after them, but the Zeros were on their way back north.

Jimmy picked the left-wing Zero, waiting as it filled first the inner and then the outer ring of the gunsight, aware of Danny's tracers pouring past his left wing. He pressed the triggers. The guns hammered, tracer slashed out, he was so close he couldn't possibly have missed, but the Zero flew right over his canopy, apparently untouched. Jimmy cursed to himself. He couldn't see how he'd missed that close!

"Red Four, follow me," he said. He looked over his shoulder at the Zeros, but they were engauged with Jack and Gerry, and Jimmy continued his dive, taking Danny Evans down on the Zeros attacking Primrose 4. As he watched, the B-17's smoking No. 3 engine blazed a streamer of flame. The flame went out but the smoke got worse. The Zeros turned to the right away from the B-17. Tracer arced out of the top turret and right waist guns, reaching for the Zeros

"Stay with me, Red Four," he radioed. "Turning right."

The Zeros kept turning and began to climb. Jimmy rolled right to follow them, pulling back gently on the elevator to tighten the turn, tightened it as much as he dared, knowing the onset of an accelerated stall was only a few miles per hour away. He sagged into his seat against the hard parachute pan as the g-forces piled on. The Zeros kicked top rudder and dove away. Jimmy rolled hard right, diving after the Zeros, and looked right to check his wingman.

Evans wasn't there.

"Red Four, Red Four, this is Red Three, where are you?"

Nothing.

Jimmy continued after the Zeros, who dove towards the B-17. The range closed. One of the Zeros pulled up and over while the other two continued their attack on Primrose 4. Jimmy pulled up, meeting the Zero head-on, pressing the triggers on his machine-guns. Tracers raced past his canopy, and his own tracers streaked into the Zero. Then they blew past each other, and Jimmy closed on the other two Zeros.

The Zeros broke left. Jimmy looked over his shoulder to see the first Zero coming down off the top of a loop. Jimmy checked his airspeed, which pushed 350 mph, still accelerating in the dive. He looked again at the Zero behind him and saw he was pulling ahead. He turned hard after the Zeros, straining against controls stiff with the forces of the air piling over them.

"Red Three, Red Three, this is Red Leader, we're coming down."

"There's one above me, Lead, keep him off me."

"Got him, Three."

Jimmy stayed in a tight diving turn, reversing right when the Zeros broke that way, back towards Primrose 4. He pulled up, trading airspeed for altitude, then back down on the Zeros closing on the B-17. They were nearly in range when Jimmy started shooting at them, short snapping bursts with the machine guns, one finger on the cannon trigger. The Zeros broke right, away from the B-17. Jimmy broke with them, closing the range, firing as the Zeros began to pull away in the turn. His tracers ate into the lead Zero, bullets sparking up the length of the fuselage and into the wing root. Flame streaked out of the Zero's wing, which separated from the rest of the airplane. The Zero tumbled wildly, going down in flames. The remaining Zero rolled out of the turn and pulled up in that impossible Zero climb, almost hanging on its prop. Jimmy rolled level and pulled back hard on the stick, getting the Zero in his gunsight and squeezing both sets of triggers. The machine guns rattled and hammered, the cannon fired three times and quit, and Jimmy's machine gun bullets and cannon shells blew the Zero apart.

He looked around, flicking his head left and right and kicking his rudder to clear his tail. Primrose 4 was still headed for the New Guinea coast, smoking from two engines and losing altitude. Jimmy looked at his fuel, gritted his teeth, and looked around again. Two P-39s above him chased a lone Zero, heading north towards New Britain. As Jimmy watched the two P-39s turned away to the south.

"Red Leader from Red Three, come in, over."

"Go ahead, Three."

"Have you seen Red Four?"

"Negative, Three."

"Boxcar Red Leader, this is Primrose 4. We saw a P-39 spin out of the fight when your low element attacked. We lost track of him."

"Thanks, Primrose. Think you can make it home?"

"Negative, Red Leader. We're losing fuel and altitude. We're going to try and make the beach."

"Understood, Primrose. We're headed that way. We'll stick with you as long as we can."

"Thanks, Boxcar."

Jimmy joined up with Davis and Bellmon.

"How's your fuel, Three?"

"Forty gallons, more or less."

"OK. I've got about the same. Two, say your fuel."

"Not quite forty gallons."

"OK. By the way, good shooting, Three. I saw two Zeros going down."

"Roger," Jimmy said.

Jimmy took a long, deep breath through his oxygen mask, then another. A sudden wave of fatigue swept over him, leaving him blinking and yawning. He shook his head and checked his oxygen flow meter. The feeling passed in a moment.

They flew on, above and behind the mortally-wounded Primrose 4, until Sammy Keith bellied her in on the beach west of some place called Gona. Then the Boxcars turned for Seven-Mile.

Bronco Buster II turned west towards Rabaul at noon, cruising at 27,000 feet in the cold thin stratospheric air. The sky was clear; so far, they were above the contrail layer, where the whirling propeller tips would condense the water vapor in the air and leave a trail behind them betraying their exact location. Below and around them on the earth below green islands, fringed in turquoise, lay on a dark blue sea.

Charlie Davis looked over at his copilot, Mike Deering, who was flying the airplane at the moment. Deering looked relaxed and confident, as much as Charlie could tell from the copilot's eyes above the oxygen mask. The copilot's eyes flicked over the instrument panel, lingering on the engine gauges before resuming his scan. Charlie looked at the gauges himself, but temperatures and pressures and RPMs were where they should be. It was a long haul to altitude, and the engines, not to mention the rest of the airplane, were showing signs of poor maintenance and the stresses peculiar to flying in tropical conditions, especially in Papua New Guinea.

"Pilot, navigator."

"Go ahead, Al."

"Charlie, maintain this heading. Estimate we'll be over Lakunai in twenty-four minutes."

"Roger, thanks, Al. Crew, pilot, you heard the man. We're likely to have company anytime now. Keep your eyes peeled."

After the chorus of acknowledgment died away Charlie looked ahead. The island of New Britain was visible, as was Simpson Harbor, flanked by volcanoes, at the northern end. North of New Britain, off the right wing, the long narrow island of New Ireland stretched nearly to the horizon, running east and west.

Charlie knew they'd find out soon enough what was in store for them. Sparks caught intermittent radio transmissions from Keith's B-17, and, two hours ago, garbled voice transmissions which sounded like a dogfight. So maybe Jack's idea worked after all.

Which was great and swell and all that, but left the question of what the Japs would do when yet another Yankee bomber came sailing along on a high-altitude sightseeing tour.

Charlie looked at the engine instruments again, then checked the fuel gauges and his oxygen flow meter.

"Crew, navigator, check in."

"Bombardier OK."

"Copilot OK."

"Pilot OK."

"Top turret OK."

"Radio OK."

"Ball turret OK."

"Right waist OK."

"Left waist OK."

"Tail gunner OK."

"Right, thank you, gentlemen. Pilot, be advised we are ten minutes from the coast-in point."

"Thanks, Al. OK, boys, showtime. On your toes and stay there."

Five minutes later black balls of smoke appeared ahead of them. That was exploding flak from the warships in and the defenses around Simpson Harbor, reaching for their altitude. It also meant the alert had gone out in the last few minutes that another recon ship was inbound. Charlie checked his seat harness, tightening it a little more, and looking out the windows and all around his airplane.

"Pilot, bombardier."

"Go ahead, bombardier."

"Looks like a lot of ships in the harbor, boss. If I see something that looks like a carrier I'll drop on that, otherwise I'll pick the biggest ship I see."

"OK, Kim. Put one down a smokestack. You got your camera ready?"

"Yes, sir. She's set to automatic."

"OK, thanks."

Charlie shook his head, remembering his first recon trip when the 19th had its finger in the dyke, trying to hold back the Japanese flood advancing on Java. FEAF ordered them to conduct aerial reconnaissance of the Dutch port at Balikpapan, a place recently occupied by the Japanese. Charlie had to borrow a hand-held camera from the Dutch colonial air force to do it.

Now at least they were set up to do a proper job of photography.

Ahead of them he could make out details of Simpson Harbor. Looked like a hell of a lot of shipping there, and from the flash of the guns most of them were warships, and they were firing a hell of a lot of flak their way. Most of it looked to be below their altitude, but that might mean the Japs hadn't set their fuzes properly.

Yet.

And where were the Zeros?

"Navigator, pilot, have you got eyeballs on Lakunai?"

"Affirmative, Charlie. Doesn't look like anything's moving there, at least not yet."

"Check Vunakanau."

"Can't make it out yet. I'll keep looking."

"Roger, Al."

As far as Charlie was concerned if the Zeros wanted to stay asleep in their revetments that was fine with him. The flak was danger enough, not to mention flying at high altitude.

They flew over the coast-in point and passed over the Jap airfield at Lakunai. Then they were over the harbor, with the flak reaching up to their altitude, bursting higher and closer, finally rocking them with roiling air and explosive turbulence. Shrapnel pinged through the hull and wings, and once a shell burst under the right wingtip, tossing the bomber on its side and shredding the right aileron.

"Mike, check the starboard-side fuel tanks and the No. 4 engine," Charlie ordered.

"Don't see any signs of fuel leaks, boss. No. 4 doesn't seem to be leaking anything."

"Damn, that's too much luck. Crew, check in, everyone all right?"

From the chorus of rogers they all sounded fine.

"Kim, you see anything worth a couple of bombs?"

"I didn't see anything that looked like a carrier but there's a couple of big bastards down there I'll take a crack at."

"OK. We'll swing wide over Rabaul so you can set up the bomb run."

"Roger."

Charlie turned wide of the town, almost flying over the coast to the west, and then allowed Sgt. Smith to coach him onto the right heading.

"Oh, yes, there's one big bastard riding at anchor down there. OK, opening bomb bay doors. Steady, pilot. Steady."

The flak waited for them, reaching up to slam the air and create eddies and pools of turbulence that tossed them up and down with more shrapnel pinging through the fuselage.

"Right, steady, hold her steady...bombs gone, closing bomb bay doors."

Charlie felt the lift of the airplane as one thousand pounds of bombs fell away from the bomb bay. He pushed the controls forward to keep the airplane level.

"OK, keep an eye out on the harbor, guys, see where the bombs fall."

Charlie banked right, flying over the south shore of the harbor, taking up a heading to pass over the airfield at Vunakanau. The flak dropped off to nothing until a cluster of shells from the AA defenses at Vunakanau burst around them as they passed over the field.

"Ah, pilot, ball turret gunner."

"Go ahead, ball turret."

"Skipper, I see dust trails at Vunakanau."

"Pilot, tail gunner, I see 'em too."

"Swell. OK, keep an eye out for Zeros. They'll be here soon."

Charlie looked at the instruments. The engine gauges looked solid, all the needles pointing right where they should.

"Mike, you see anything coming out of the starboard engines?"

"No, nothing, no oil leaks or anything else."

"OK. Mike, let's bump up the RPMs to 2400. Trim the airplane for a 50 feet per minute descent."

"Yes, sir."

"Radio operator, pilot."

"Radio operator, go ahead, pilot."

"Sparks, tell Seven-Mile we're headed that way. Al! When do you estimate coast-in over New Guinea?"

"Ninety-seven minutes at our present speed. Call it 1400."

"You copy that, Sparks?"

"Got it. Coast-in at 1400."

"Tail gunner, pilot."

"Go ahead, Emmons."

"Boss, we got maybe a dozen Zeros coming after us. They're still climbing but they'll reach our altitude in five minutes or less."

"OK, thanks, Emmons. Everyone, you heard Emmons, keep your eyes peeled. We'll have company soon."

"Pilot, radio operator. Seven-Mile acknowledges our transmission. They say we can expect to be met north of the coast-in point."

"OK, thanks, Sparks."

Charlie looked at the airspeed indicator, which showed their airspeed was still increasing. At fifty feet per minute they'd lose one thousand feet of altitude every twenty minutes, three thousand feet in an hour. More important was their speed through the air, accelerating as they traded the energy of altitude for the energy of airspeed.

Now the real fun begins, Charlie thought.

When Jack led his flight into the break at Seven-Mile he saw a wrecked P-39 being picked over by the mechanics at the edge of the runway, and when he landed he recognized the numbers and markings on the P-39. It was Danny Evans' ship.

It was a relief that Danny made it this far, but the P-39 was pretty torn up, evidently from a misjudged and nearly disastrous landing. Jack turned off onto the taxiway, followed by Bellmon and Ardana, up to the revetments among the sparse trees and scrub brush.

He waved at Jimmy as he taxied past, then he got his harness off, opened the door, and climbed out onto the wing, shrugging off his parachute harness.

"Gas and oil and ammo," he said to his crew chief. "Check for damage, but I don't think you'll find anything."

"How'd you do, sir?"

"Got a piece of one but I don't think I did more than frighten him."

"Better luck next time, then. By the way, sir, Major Wolchek wants to see you."

"OK. Thanks."

Jack climbed down from his P-39, stretched, and walked to Ardana's revetment. Ardana was drinking from the water can the mechanics kept on a nearby tree. His mechanics already had the inspection covers off the engine and the guns, feeding ammunition into the trays for the wing and cowl guns.

Ardana drank three cups of water, then pulled the leather helmet off his head and poured water over it. He scrubbed his fingers through his hair and shook his head vigorously before pouring another can of water and drinking it slowly.

"Jehosophat, Jimmy, are you part camel?" Jack asked.

Ardana looked at him over the can's edge, finished drinking, and put the cup back.

"Thanks, Don," he called to his crew chief, who waved, smiling.

Ardana came over to Jack, taking off his Mae West and unzipping his flight suit down almost to his waist.

"I see Danny made it back," Jack said. "What happened?"

Ardana shook his head. "When we started in for our initial attack I made a pretty hard turn. I checked to see if Evans was still with me, and he was gone. I made a radio call but never got any response."

"You think he left you?"

Ardana looked Jack in the eye. "No. I think he pulled too hard on the elevator and went into an accelerated stall. Then he went into a spin."

"I figured it was Danny that Major Keith saw," said Jack. "Well, Major Wolchek wants to see me. Why don't you come along, in case Wolchek wants to know about Evans."

"Lead on," said Ardana.

They went up the hill to Wolchek's tent and found him sitting under a scrap of canvas, trying to fan himself with some kind of big green leaf. He wasn't having too much luck with it.

"Jack," he said, waving. "And you brought Jimmy the Kid. Excellent. How'd it go?"

"We intercepted Primrose 4 and chased away the Zeros in pursuit," Jack said. He laid a hand on Jimmy's shoulder. "And Lt. Ardana here got two Zeros. Better than me, all I can claim is a damage. Primrose 4 made it to the beach west of Gona and crash-landed. We saw the crew get out."

Wolchek nodded. "Evidently FEAF is hot to know what's going on at Rabaul, because they've asked the RAAF to send a couple of Catalinas up there to pick up the crew of Primrose 4."

"Any news from Charlie? I think he's Primrose 6 for this mission."

"Not that anyone told me. But I suspect we're going to fly cover for the Catalinas and see if Charlie needs any help."

Jack looked at his watch. "It'll take us a half-hour to get up there once we get off the ground. It'll take the Catalinas over an hour."

Wolchek nodded. "We'll take the squadron and head north in forty-five minutes. Will your airplanes be serviced by then?"

"Yes. We were lucky. Not a scratch."

"Good." Wolchek looked at Jimmy and grinned. "Two Zeros on one mission? Not bad, Ardana. Don't get a swelled head, though."

"No, sir."

"Right. Jack, I'll come along, but since you've been up there I want you to lead the mission. You're short a man, so if Lt. Ardana doesn't mind, I'll fly as Boxcar Red Four."

Jack looked out of the corner of his eye at Ardana, whose eyes widened. "Er, Major..."

Wolchek held up his hand, smiling. "Jimmy, I hope you don't think I'm not good enough to be your wingman."

"Oh, no, sir, it's not that."

"Good! Then I think you'll find I'm a fair pilot. Why don't you go and check on your flight's airplanes for Jack? I need to speak with him for a minute."

"Yes, sir!"

Ardana saluted and trotted back down the path to the revetments. Wolchek shook his head, smiling, as he watched Ardana go. Then the smile faded as he turned to look at Jack.

"He's got skill. I hope his luck holds," Wolchek said. "Now let's talk about Danny Evans."

"Yes, sir."

"When he came in to land he made one good hard bounce, tried to recover, and stalled in. Then it was blood, guts, and feathers halfway down the runway. The only reason he didn't burn was because he was nearly out of gas. The medics pulled him out of the cockpit with a gash on his head, out cold. The hospital called a few minutes ago. They don't think there's much wrong with him. Something about his skull being too hard for a concussion."

"Probably true," Jack said.

"How did he get separated from the rest of you?"

"Jimmy said he lost Danny in the first turn they made after the Zeros." Jack frowned, remembering the same thing happening to him over Den Pasar last February. "Primrose 4 saw a P-39 spinning out of the fight."

"Accelerated stall with a spin," Wolchek said. "Came back too hard on the elevator."

"That's what I figure. At least he recovered from the spin. Evans could stand a lot more training."

"So could half these kids. Looks like Jimmy is coming along. How about the other kid? What's his name, Bellmon? Gerry Bellmon?"

"Bellmon's not likely to be a hot pilot, but he stuck with me and did his job. No complaints."

"Good. You mind me coming along as your Number Four?"

"No. You tell me how well I'm doing as a flight leader, and I'll tell you how you're doing as a wingman."

"You will, eh? Don't let those six Jap flags go to your head, *Captain*."

"Oh, no sir, *Major* sir. Never."

They laughed.

"OK, back to Evans. When the doctor certifies him fit to fly you'll get him back. I'll cover his slot today, but we'll find you a replacement tomorrow. Supposedly we're getting some new pilots."

"Seems to me I remember something about better the devil you know."

"Remember all you like, Jack. It's going to be the luck of the draw."

Jack nodded. "I'll get back to my boys, then, Steve. We'll see you in a few."

"Wouldn't miss it."

Before they took off Major Wolchek held a briefing in front of his tent.

"Most of you know Jack and his boys bounced some Zeros attacking one of our B-17s this morning," he said. "That B-17 went down on the north coast about here."

Wolchek pointed to a map spread out on the boards between the two fuel drums that constituted his desk. It was an old maritime chart, and the squadron commander pointed to a spot on the coast west of a place marked "Gona" on the chart. Wolchek moved his finger and tapped the southern coast of New Britain, marked "Cape Gloucester" on the chart. He moved his fingers back and forth over the strait between New Guinea and New Britain.

"We'll intercept Major Davis' B-17, call sign Primrose 6, about halfway between the coast and Cape Gloucester," Wolchek said. "Watch your throttle settings. You'll see we're going about as far on this mission as we did to reach Lae yesterday, and I know some of you boys came back on fumes. If we meet Zeros we'll burn through our reserve fuel pretty quick."

There were nods among the gathered pilots, all of whom appeared grave and several a little glum, looking at the point Wolchek indicated on his chart.

"Groves, once we get to the coast, you head west and cover the Catalinas while they pick up that B-17's crew."

Groves nodded, looking around at his pilots, who gathered around him.

"Jack, I'm flying with you and your boys, but I want you to lead us north." Wolchek looked at Captain Ward, the Blue Flight leader, who nodded. "So, if you wouldn't mind?"

"No, sir, not at all," he said.

"What shall we do about tactics if we meet Zeros?" Wolchek asked.

"Don't try to dogfight with the bastards. They can out-turn and out-climb us, but they aren't as fast as we are, diving or on the straight. Hopefully we'll have the altitude advantage like we did this morning. So dive, pick your target, make one pass, and keep diving away from the fight until you're clear. If your fuel permits climb up to make another pass, but only if you can get an altitude advantage. And keep your speed up, over 300 mph. Do I need to remind anyone about staying in elements? Element leaders are the shooters, wingmen protect the leader's tail."

Jack looked around. "Basically, keep your speed up and don't be sucked into a turning fight. When you shoot, get in close before you open up. Watch your fuel. And finally, the most important thing, live to fight another day."

That brought grins all around. Not very amused grins, but grins nonetheless.

"Damn right," said Wolchek. "Any questions? No? All right, start engines in ten minutes, begin takeoffs in fifteen. Mount up, gentlemen."

Jimmy was getting used to takeoffs in the red dust of Seven-Mile. He took one look over his shoulder at Major Wolchek, who smiled from his cockpit and made a shooing motion with his right hand. Then they taxied out to the runway, pushed the throttles forward, and climbed up out of the dust into the sky, with the mountains on their left and the Coral Sea glittering in the sun on the right. All the Boxcar P-39s got off the ground quickly and formed up, making one turn over the airfield and turning north.

For the first ten minutes Jimmy looked over his right shoulder to be sure Major Wolchek was in his assigned slot. The fourth time he did that Wolchek waved at him, and Jimmy realized Wolchek was an experienced pilot who at least knew how to fly the airplane, unlike Danny Evans. He relaxed and concentrated on keeping his own formation and searching the sky for Zeros.

At 23,000 feet they were north of the peaks of the Owen Stanley Mountains, with the north coast before them, and the sea stretching away north to the island of New Britain. The sweat from the tropical jungle five miles below had long since dried and even with the cockpit heat full on it was cold.

"Boxcar Red Leader, this is Boxcar White Leader, peeling off."

"Roger, White Leader. Good luck."

"Thanks, Red Leader. See you in a bit. White Flight, switch to the rescue frequency."

Groves, leading White Flight, waggled his wings and turned north, followed by his pilots.

Jimmy swept a look over his engine instruments and then back out to the north, scanning the sky a sector at a time, the way his grandfather taught him to search for game or hostile Indians. Then he looked back at his tail and above them. The sun was past zenith, just over his left shoulder; he held his thumb over its disk to check for enemy fighters diving on them, using the sun's glare to mask their attack.

Nothing. *This time*, Jimmy thought to himself. Then he checked his engine instruments again, took another deep breath of rubbery oxygen, settled his ass on the hard parachute pack in the seat pan, and began his scan all over again.

At the head of the formation Jack looked north as they passed over the coast. Then, like all the other pilots with him, he checked his flight and engine instruments before scanning the sky again.

Best to keep quiet for now, but it didn't sit well with him. He wanted Charlie to know he was there, that help was on the way.

Then, on the horizon to the northeast, there was something. Just a glint or a speck, maybe something on the canopy. He focused in on the Plexiglas, but the speck vanished, and when he focused back out again there was the speck.

He keyed his radio. "Boxcars, Boxcar Red Leader has a bogey at eleven o'clock low. Check your armament panels, be sure your guns are hot."

Jack looked left and right. "Boxcar Blue Flight, maintain this heading. Boxcar Red Flight, follow me."

He turned left, watching the bogey as it approached. Finally he keyed his radio. "Primrose 6, Primrose 6, this is Boxcar Red Leader, come in."

Charlie winced as something whanged into his seat armor. For a moment the B-17's cockpit was full of bullets, smashing up the Plexiglas windscreen and the instrument panel.

Behind him it sounded like every gun was firing at the attacking Zeros. The intercom was filled with terse warnings, the voices of his gunners pitched up with adrenaline and fear. In the nose ahead of him two guns chattered, which meant, at least, Sgt. Frye was on the nose gun and Al Stern was going back and forth between the cheek guns.

He darted a look at Mike Deering in the seat beside him. Deering was hit bad in the left arm, which hung useless at his side. He kept passing out and coming to, trying to help on the controls, and passing out again. Deering had been hit ten minutes south of Vunakanau, which meant he'd been bleeding badly for over an hour while the rest of Charlie's crew, every one of them, manned the bomber's .50-cal. machine guns, fending off an attack by a dozen Zeros.

They were passing over Cape Gloucester now, still descending. The New Guinea coast was in sight ahead of them, and at worst maybe they could crash-land on the beach with some hope of being rescued by the RAAF.

Another storm of bullets screamed and howled through the cockpit. Charlie saw the Zero off their left wing, firing at them. Something seared past his calves and buried itself in the throttle quadrant next to his seat, and something white and hissing flashed in front of him, through the holes already in the Plexiglas, touching nothing in its flight. The upper turret guns hammered above and behind him, the concussion rattling his teeth. The Zero roared overhead, and another one turned in, taking its place. Charlie looked left and right again, checking his engines to see if they were leaking oil or smoking, because most of his engine instruments were shot out.

"BANDITS! Bandits, eleven o'clock high, one o'clock high, coming down!"

Charlie looked up through the roof window and saw four dots, flinched away as a cannon shell went off somewhere behind him, and looked again.

"Negative, negative!" he called over the intercom. "Pilot to crew, bogeys at eleven and one are P-39s, repeat P-39s! Don't shoot at 'em!"

Charlie swept the instruments he had left, checked his throttle controls and RPM settings.

There was a yell of pure raging triumph over the intercom. "Right waist to crew, look at those beautiful bastards!"

Charlie looked right across Deering's body in time to see a Zero explode and four P-39s scream past them in a high-speed dive. He looked to the left and saw four more P-39s, one element catching a trio of Zeros between the other element and lacing the Japs with tracers. One Zero spouted flame from its engine before its wings peeled off and the Jap went down in pieces.

For a couple of minutes there was a swirling dance of pursuits around his bomber, P-39s pulling up from dives into zoom climbs before diving again, Zeros turning away from attacks and coming around on the tail of the P-39s, who dove away and turned in their dives. Then the fight fell away behind them.

"Tail gunner, pilot, what's going on back there?"

"Kind of confused, boss. There's another smoke trail but I can't tell who went down, one of ours or one of theirs. Wait, there's a couple of them breaking away and turning north. A couple more, yeah! That's it, the Japs are going home!"

Charlie heaved a sigh. "You sure, Emmons?"

"Yes, sir. They're headed north, and the P-39s are headed this way."

"OK. You guys keep your eyes open in case the Japs decide to come back. Navigator, pilot."

"Go ahead, Charlie."

"Al, come up and give me a hand."

A moment later Stern crawled up through the tunnel from the nose and leaned over Deering, checking his arm.

"Charlie, I'm going to try and bandage Mike's arm, but it's about shot off. Are you OK?"

"Yeah. Pilot to radio operator, Sparks, get up here and give Al a hand."

"On the way, skipper."

In a moment Al and Sparks had the copilot's now-limp form pulled from of his seat and laid out in the narrow space between the seats and the upper turret turntable. Charlie checked the altimeter, which was about the only instrument he had still working. They were passing through 12,000 feet. He took off his oxygen mask and breathed deep of the cold air inside the B-17.

It was the things he could smell that crawled inside him and made themselves at home, the familiar airplane smells of oil and aluminum and exhaust gas, but laid on top of that was the nearly-overwhelming cordite stink from the machine-guns and the smell of blood.

Stern touched his shoulder. "We've done what we can for Mike, Charlie, but it doesn't look good. Want me to help you?"

"Thanks, but no." Charlie indicated his instrument panel. "You got a compass and airspeed indicator still working?"

"Yes."

"OK. Go back up front and get Frye up here to help me. I'm going to need you to tell me where to go."

"Don't I always?" Stern said. Charlie looked over and exchanged a brief grin with his navigator, who gripped Charlie's shoulder and disappeared back down the tunnel.

Frye came up and climbed into the co-pilot's seat. He buckled in, looked around, and said, "Want me to take it for a bit, give you a break?"

"Thanks, Bill. Just keep her straight and level until Al has a new heading."

The bombardier nodded, looked left and right again, and put his hands and feet on the controls.

"My airplane," he said.

"Your airplane," Charlie confirmed, taking his hands and feet off the wheel and rudder pedals.

A wave of fatigue washed over him, leaving him blinking and gasping in its wake. He shook his head a couple of times and everything came back into focus.

Frye punched his shoulder lightly and pointed to the left. Charlie looked and saw a P-39 sitting there, off the B-17's left wing. The pilot waved, and for a moment Charlie had a weird feeling of deja-vu. Then he saw the six Jap flags painted under the cockpit and waved back at his brother, who waggled his wings and climbed away to the left, rejoining his formation.

Charlie looked up. There were eight P-39s out there, a couple of hundred feet higher in altitude.

"Pilot, radio operator."

"Go ahead, Sparks."

"Boss, the P-39s say they'd love to stick around and hold hands with us, but they don't have a lot of fuel left. They want to be sure we can get home, though. They also say they've sent for friends to meet us."

Charlie shook his head.

"Pilot, navigator."

"Go ahead, Al."

"Charlie, we're good for gas. We should have a thirty-minute reserve when we get home."

"OK. Sparks, tell them we think they're awfully cute but they're not really our type, and we can make it home from here."

"Will do, Skipper."

A moment later Charlie watched as the P-39s pulled ahead of them and headed home.

"Crew, pilot. Check in."

"Bombardier OK," said Frye from the seat beside him.

"Navigator OK."

"Pilot OK, copilot down," said Charlie.

"Top turret OK."

"Radio operator OK."

"Ball turret OK."

"Left waist OK."

"Right waist OK, but those little bastards shot my boot heel off."

"Tail gunner OK."

"All right, thanks, guys. Let's go home."

The afternoon thunderheads built over the mountains as the Boxcar P-39s entered the pattern at Seven-Mile, watching constantly, even in the pattern, for marauding Zeros. They had time enough to land and get off the taxiway into their revetments before *Bronco Buster II* entered the pattern.

Charlie's number 3 engine was feathered and trailing a thin stream of smoke. A ragged hole, the size of a man's head, behind the left waist gun marred the patched, mottled fuselage, a souvenir left by a Jap 20-mm cannon shell. As the bomber turned on final red flares burst out of its fuselage, signaling wounded aboard. But dead engine, battle damage, wounded, and all, the big bomber slid down the final approach as if on rails, remaining power coming back smoothly, both mains kissing the ground gently in as near-perfect a touchdown as any pilot could wish, at least until the left main tire blew. *Bronco Buster II* started to slew hard into the dead tire but the left wing lifted slightly and hard right rudder and a burst of power to the left wing engines, immediately taken off, corrected the skid for the moment. The lift bled off with the airspeed and when the left main touched again the pilots of the bomber were ready with hard right brake. The airplane headed for the edge of the forest on the south side of the runway, bordered with the wreckage of other airplane, but stopped with its Plexiglas nose just inside the foliage.

Jack exhaled, only then realizing he had been holding his breath.

"Damn," said Jimmy Ardana, standing next to him. The profanity had the tone of a reverent prayer. "That was a hell of a landing. You're brother's pretty good."

Jack scoffed. "Charlie? I taught him everything he knows about flying."

Ardana chuckled.

Jack started walking down towards the runway, where men climbed out of the B-17E. A couple of jeeps and an ambulance headed down to the airplane. By the time they got there a repair truck stood next to the bomber and a group of mechanics with a jack were preparing to raise the wing and replace the blown left main tire.

Charlie stood next to the mechanics, running his hand over the tire strut and peering up into the landing gear bay. Jack stood next to him, looking up at the dirty gray underside of the wing, streaked with oil and engine exhaust. A group of punched holes, too irregular to be machine-gun bullets, peppered the underside of the wing, a gift of shrapnel from some Jap antiaircraft gunner.

"Jehosophat, Charlie," Jack said. "Don't you bomber guys know how to land any better than that?"

"Aw, look," Charlie said, still peering up into the landing gear bay. "I was trying to see how close I could come to that tree over there. My bombardier was helping me on the controls. He bet me I'd hit it."

"Did not, skipper," said a sergeant. He wore a baggy, much-patched flight suit and a blue baseball cap. "I think what I said was something I wouldn't repeat in front of my mother."

Charlie grinned and straightened up. "Yeah, come to think of it, so did I." He winked at Jack and turned to the group of mechanics. "The pivot looks like it took a pretty good beating, Sarge."

"Lucky it didn't come clean off," said the mechanic. He looked up into the gear well.

"We'll jack it up, replace the wheel, and tow it to your revetment nice and slow, Major. Then we'll see what we can do with her. She's pretty well shot up, though, so it might be awhile."

"Thanks, Sarge." Charlie turned and looked around. "Al! Where are you?"

Jack saw Al Stern leaning against the right main gear. The navigator looked tired. He bent over and picked up a satchel.

"Right here," Stern said. "The medics got Mike off OK. They'll get him up to the hospital."

"Good. Where's Frye? Does he have the film?"

"Right here, Boss." The bombardier hefted a metal canister. "Got the pix right here."

"Find anything?" Jack asked.

"Well, let's see. A bunch of Zeros. How many Zeros would you say, Al?"

"Twelve, at least," Al drawled.

"There were definitely a lot of ships in the harbor," Charlie mused. "Hard to tell how many through all the flak. Damned if I can tell a battleship from a destroyer anyway."

"Battleships are bigger," Al said scornfully.

"Don't airplane carriers kind of look rectangular?" Ardana asked with such diffidence that Jack and Charlie both turned to look at him.

"What?" he asked, the picture of innocence wronged.

Al snickered and cleared his throat as Charlie turned a look on him.

Jack said, "Kids. Take 'em out, teach 'em how to fly, and just look at 'em."

"It's a disgrace," Charlie agreed.

They reached the grass-roofed hut that doubled as the reconnaissance squadron's operations shack. There was a lieutenant colonel and a major inside the hut, seated at yet another plank and drum desk. The colonel looked up from his paperwork as they came in. Jack recognized the major as Tommy Rhodes, from the 22nd BG, who was probably quite as interested in what Charlie found at Rabaul as the US Navy, since the 22nd was probably headed up to Rabaul in the near future.

"Charlie!" the colonel said, beaming. "Did you have fun?"

"Oh, sure, Geoff," Charlie replied. "We took pictures and everything."

"I'm certain the Navy will be ever so grateful. They've been ever so worried about you. Why, in the last two hours I've had three radio messages from some admiral or other in Brisbane. He's so very concerned about you."

"I'll bet," Charlie said drily. "But I bet he was ever so much more worried about those pictures of Simpson Harbor."

"Well, that did come into the messages," the colonel said, "Did you have a look-in at Vunakanau?"

"Sure did, but we couldn't see much but dust trails from 25,000 feet. There were Zeros down there, though, because they decided to come up and play."

The colonel dropped the banter. "So, in sum?"

"Zeros out the ass, twice as much flak as last time, and three-tenths cloud over the harbor. We had a dozen on us all the way to the coast north of here before the Boxcars chased 'em off. Hey, Jack, who got those Zero? We saw two go down."

"Don't know. Someone in Blue Flight."

"You guys didn't get any?"

"Jimmy here collected two this morning."

Charlie smiled and offered Jimmy his hand. "Good work, Jimmy."

"Thanks, Major."

"Hell, you call me Charlie. I told you that the other day."

"Sure thing, Major Charlie."

Charlie shook his head in mock disgust. Jack laughed. "How did you guys do, Charlie?"

"I think my boys got a couple of Zeros. Al?"

The navigator shrugged. "Frye and I were all over the nose, going from one gun to another. I saw pieces fly a couple of times. Frye hit one pretty solid. The guys in back claimed at least three."

"Jesus," said Rhodes. "I saw you lost an engine."

Charlie nodded. "Yeah. It wouldn't have been that big a deal but flak shredded the left main gear. The tire blew on landing. Added to the sheet metal work, engine replacement, and who knows what else the mechanics will find, the *Bronc*'s in bad shape. Don't know how long she'll be down."

"You're kind of hard on airplanes, Charlie," said the colonel.

"Oh, hell, Geoff, I'm easy on airplanes, it's the Japs that are hard on them."

"Yeah. Well, it's like this, we're out of airplanes until we can get your ship repaired. Tell you what, we'll get it airworthy enough to get you down to Townsville, then you guys are probably up for some leave."

"Leave? In Townsville?"

"You could probably spend a few days in Sydney if you wanted."

"That sounds good. I don't think my boys will complain, either." Charlie looked at the operations schedule. "Any word on Sammy Keith and his crew?"

The colonel nodded. "They're OK. The RAAF picked 'em up off the beach. They have a couple of guys in bad shape, but no one dead, and they're bringing back their film. Could've been worse, but that means we're down two airplanes."

Charlie sighed and nodded. "Yeah."

"Hey, Charlie, do me a favor," Jack said.

"What's that?"

"If you make it to Sydney buy me some Scotch."

Charlie laughed. The colonel joined him.

"I doubt you can find any Scotch worth drinking, not in Sydney, not at any price," the colonel said. "Or any Scotch not worth drinking, for that matter. But one can always hope."

"Sure thing," said Charlie. He shook hands with Jack. "Behave yourself while I'm away, little brother."

"Never," Jack replied, and ducked the mock punch Charlie threw at him.

Chapter Eleven

May 11, 1942

"Youpela bilip ensel?"

Sergeant Holman looked up as Jimmy entered Operations and pointed back at Colonel Wagner's office. Wagner looked up as Jimmy entered.

"Well, Lieutenant, have you ever heard that no good deed goes unpunished?"

"Er...Yes, sir, I believe I've heard that."

Wagner grimaced and gestured with his hand at the other man in his office. "This is Major Rhodes from the 22nd Bomb Group, Ardana. He's looking for volunteers."

Ardana looked at the man Wagner indicated. He waved at Ardana and yawned, then extended his hand. "Hiya, lieutenant. I hear you're a natural born multiengine pilot."

"Oh? Well, it was only the one time, Major."

"Call me Tommy. Look, we need copilots. Usually the RAAF lends us a few if we need them but right now things seem to be a little tight. Day after tomorrow we have a mission headed to Rabaul. Buzz here says it's up to you if you want to volunteer to fly with us. How about it?"

Jimmy looked at Wagner, who grimaced and shrugged. "Like the man said, Ardana, it's your call. But you know by now these guys don't go on milk runs. In fact, why don't you take a walk and think it over? You don't need an answer right this second, do you, Tommy?"

"Nah. Take your time, Lieutenant. But if you decide to go you need a check flight. The Marauder isn't exactly an easy airplane to fly, any more than the P-39."

"Hour or so be OK, Tommy?"

"That's fine."

"Go on, Ardana, get the hell out of here," said Wagner. "And congratulations on bagging those Zeros yesterday."

"You're out of your mind," Davis said bluntly. "Don't you know enough about the Army to never volunteer?"

"I think I've heard that, yeah," Jimmy replied.

"You've already made up your mind to go, so why are you asking?"

"I hoped you'd have a good argument. Something to talk me out of it."

"OK. I'm your flight leader. I'm older, smarter and more experienced than you. I think it's a bad idea. Don't go."

"Yeah."

"Get out of here, Jimmy. You make me tired." Jimmy turned to go. Davis scowled. "Hey. Jimmy."

"Yeah, Jack?"

Davis got up. "I know some of those guys at the 22nd. Let's go talk to them before you make up your mind."

Jimmy nodded. Davis opened his B2 bag and took out a bottle. He looked at it and sighed.

"Come on, before I change my mind," he said. They found a jeep no one was using and drove down the hill to the dispersal area used by the 22nd Bomb Group (Medium).

The 22nd flew the B-26 Marauder. The B-26 was a fast, hot medium bomber, almost as fast as a P-39 or a Zero. These bombers had been in theater for two months now and that was a long time for an airplane flying frequent combat missions.

They passed a group of mechanics working on the port engine of one of the B-26s. The nacelle aft of the engine mount was blackened with soot and oil. The port engine had caught fire in flight. Ugly holes from exploding 20-mm cannon shells dotted the wing and the nacelle.

"Jesus," said Jimmy, looking at the damage.

Except for a slight glance the mechanics never paused in their work. Over to one side there was a crate with a new engine in it. The mechanics were going to change the damaged, burned-out engine for a new one. Then they would patch the holes and check the hydraulic lines and the electrical system and the fuel tanks, the bomb shackles and the gun turret and the control runs, and this battered, beaten-up bomber would be ready for war once again.

"I don't know how they do it, myself," said Davis. "Just flying straight and level into flak and fighters. No real chance to take evasive action. Those B-26 guys have guts, no doubt about it."

"Yeah," said Jimmy.

Davis put the jeep in gear and went up a trail among some trees until they came across a ramshackle hut with the sign "22nd Bomb Group." Officially, like the 8th Pursuit Group, the 22nd was stationed in Townsville, where their major repair and overhaul facilities were located to preserve them from Japanese attack. That meant every mission began and ended with the flight from Townsville to Port Moresby, adding additional wear and tear on engines, airframes and aircrew.

They parked the jeep and Davis took his bottle. They went inside to where an orderly sat.

"Where can I find Captain Phillips?" Davis asked.

"He's in the back, sir, with Major Rhodes. I don't think he'll be long if you'd like to wait." The orderly indicated a couple of homemade bamboo chairs in one corner.

"We'll wait outside in the jeep," said Davis. "Tell him Jack Davis would like a word."

A few minutes later a short, stocky captain in cut off shorts and a uniform shirt with the sleeves hacked off stepped out of the shack.

"Jack, you sonofabitch," he said, coming forward with his hand extended. "I heard you were out of the hospital. Or was it a psycho ward?"

"Aw, who'd know if I was crazy or not in the middle of all this shit, Phil? Wanna take a little ride?"

"Sure."

Phillips got in the back of the jeep and Davis drove down towards the runway. He found a shady spot and parked. Then he pulled the bottle out and handed it to Phillips, who regarded the bottle and Davis with suspicion.

Phillips looked at Ardana. "I don't know you, kid, but if you've hung around this guy for long enough you've found out this means he wants something."

"Well, Captain," Jimmy began hesitantly. "Actually I'm the one who wants something."

"Oh? What's that?"

"I've been asked to volunteer to fly as copilot on this next mission with you guys. What can you tell me about it?"

Phillips scowled. "What the fuck kind of question is that? We're going to Rabaul. You guys wouldn't know about that because you can't fly that far. Last time we were there we bombed the Jap airfield at Vunakanau south of Simpson Harbor. There was a hell of a lot of flak and fighters. I spent most of the mission trying to keep from pissing myself. What else do you want to know?"

Phillips took the bottle from Davis and took a long, long pull at it. When he put it down he took several gasping breaths. "Jesus, Jack, if that isn't just like you to buy cheap whisky. You might at least have brought Scotch."

"If you can find Scotch at any price anywhere in Australia, you let me know. I'll bankroll you."

Phillips handed the bottle back and looked at Ardana. "You ever fly multi-engine airplane? Know anything about a B-26?"

"It's an airplane, ain't it?"

"Fucking pursuit pilots think you know everything. You know what the takeoff speed of a B-26 is at the density altitude we operate at, here at Seven-Mile?"

"I'm guessing it's pretty high. You lose an engine, an engine even coughs on takeoff when you're full of bombs and gas, and you go in."

"That's right. A big expensive airplane and seven crewmen you can't set a price on. OK, hotshot, orders are one thing, but you're crazy to volunteer for this."

"I've been trying to tell him that," Davis said.

"Yeah? Well, Jack, you may be crazy, but no one ever said you were stupid," Phillips replied. He turned back to Ardana. "Kid, how long do you want to live?"

"I'd like to die in bed, a long, long time from now."

"Well, you either like wishful thinking or you've got a lot of faith."

"No point in believing you're going to die," said Ardana.

"No point in believing you're going to live forever, either," Phillips retorted. "OK. Tell you what. You saw the mechanics working on that B-26 in our dispersal area?"

"Yeah."

"That's Bob Zeamer's plane. He and his crew caught a little grief over Lae day before yesterday, but their ship ought to be OK for a test hop this afternoon. So how about it, Jack? Can Ardana here go up with Zeamer and see how he likes the airplane? Or do you guys have something important to do, like play sitting ducks with the Zeros?"

"Screw you, Phillips."

Phillips laughed. "You can't help it if the P-39 is a piece of shit. Maybe they'll let you guys have a good airplane one of these days." Phillips turned to Ardana. "How about it, kid?"

"Sure thing. Where do I show up and when?"

Phillips shrugged. "They'll be another couple of hours at least. If the Japs don't bomb the crap out of us this afternoon, we'll probably schedule the maintenance test for about 1600. Why don't you show up about 1530 and even if they aren't done Bob will probably be glad to sit in the cockpit with you and show you the all the dials and switches and doodads. What do you say, Davis?"

Jack shrugged. "How much trouble do you guys get in on test flights?"

"Depends. Three weeks ago I ran like hell from some Zeros on a test flight. Lost an engine, controls all shot to shit, had to crash land, and then some crazy Aussie bounced a Hudson over me."

Jack laughed. "That wasn't a crazy Aussie. It was this idiot right here."

"Aw, bullshit."

"Hell, no. Tell him, Jimmy."

Jimmy shrugged. "The Hudson's pilot got shot up. Jack here was already in the turret, holding off the Zeros. Me, I figured there was nothing to lose by trying."

Phillips smiled reluctantly. "Well, you've got the basic idea, all right. Come on, let's go find Bob Zeamer."

"Jesus," Davis muttered. He put the jeep in gear and followed Phillips' directions.

Zeamer was a tall skinny guy with close-cropped dark hair and sunken green eyes. He looked straight at Ardana. "You're crazy," he declared.

"Yes, sir," Ardana said.

"OK. We're all sort of crazy in this outfit. You ever fly multi-engine?"

"Not really, sir."

"I hear he's got about a half-hour," Phillips said. He told Zeamer the story.

Finally Zeamer shrugged. "OK. We'll get you a cockpit check. Don't want you pushing the gear down button when I call for full flaps."

"Makes more sense to get a practice flight in this afternoon, too," said Phillips. "You guys have a test flight scheduled, right, Bob?"

"Yeah. Usually that's just me, my copilot, the flight engineer and maybe half-tanks. One more guy won't make a lot of difference." Zeamer rose from his seat in front of his tent. "My crew chief thinks late this afternoon."

Phillips nodded. "I told Jimmy here to show up about 1530."

"Sounds about right. I'll see you then. I'm going to get some shuteye."

Zeamer went into his tent. Phillips looked at the bottle and Davis handed it to him.

"Cheap whisky, Jack, but at least you're a generous soul," he said, saluting Jack with the bottle.

"I'm just a friend to all mankind. Maybe I'll open a bar after the war. Most of the pilots who survive are gonna be drunks anyway."

"Amen, brother," Phillips said reverently, tilting the bottle to his mouth. Davis and Phillips passed the bottle back and forth. Ardana refused any more.

"Good man," Phillips said with approval. "You'd better be either drunk as a skunk or stone cold sober to tackle that bitch."

"Is the Marauder as bad as that?"

"Look. In one sense she really is just another airplane and a pretty good airplane at that. You won't believe what it will take in terms of punishment. Last week we got back with fifteen holes from 20-mm stuff and about three hundred from those little seven-seven guns the Zeros use. Not counting shrapnel from flak hits over the target. Shot the port side elevator to rags, wounded the tail gunner but he's OK. Kept shooting the whole time." Phillips drank from the whisky bottle, which was becoming sorely depleted. "Anyway. We're maybe 120 feet above sea level here which is good, nice dense air. But it's hot as hell and that raises the density altitude, which is why we like to take off early in the morning or late in the evening when it's relatively cool. But then the humidity doesn't do a hell of a lot for the engines, either, and that goddam runway is kind of short for a fully loaded B-26."

"I noticed you guys don't seem to clear the trees by much."

"Yeah. You don't really get a good maneuvering speed on that airplane until you're up around 165 mph, especially when you're loaded. So you stay low, build up a little speed, got it? Maybe two hundred or so, then you can start to climb. But

Zeamer will go over all that with you." Phillips looked at Davis. "You gonna hold onto that bottle?"

"Here, keep it. You sound like you need it more than I do."

"Brother, you've got that right," said Phillips reverently. He tilted the bottle to his lips and drank.

It was intensely hot in the cockpit of *Bugs Buggy*, Zeamer's B-26. The Marauders were parked in revetments whose only shade came from camouflage netting stretched over the airplane. The sun shone freely through the netting and the temp gauge set in the cockpit Plexiglas read 110 degrees Fahrenheit. The cockpit was a lot bigger than a P-39 but that only seemed to give the heat room to grow in.

The ground crew stripped back the netting while Zeamer and the engineering officer, Cardenas, who was acting as copilot for the test flight, buckled in and began going through their preflight checklist.

With a bang and a sputter some sort of engine started in the after part of the airplane, making Ardana jump. Cardenas saw it and laughed.

"That's the auxiliary power plant," he told Jimmy. "We use that to generate electricity to start the left engine. After that the main generator's on line and we shut it down."

Jimmy nodded in reply. He was a little bewildered at first by all the extra dials and gauges in the center of the panel for the two Pratt & Whitney R2800 engines flanking the fuselage. But he listened to the patter and realized it was fundamentally the same as a P-39, a little more complicated and with different speeds and operating ranges. In the end it really was just another airplane.

"Left hand booster pump to ON," said Cardenas.

"Priming," said Zeamer, holding the booster switch down. Zeamer looked out the window at the left engine and the crew chief standing near it with a fire bottle. "Clear prop!" Zeamer shouted.

After a few seconds – Jimmy, looking over Cardenas' shoulder, saw that the checklist required ten seconds of prime for a cold engine start – Cardenas said, "Energize left."

"Energizing." Zeamer pushed the energizer switch to LEFT. Inside the left engine there was that familiar rising whine of an inertial flywheel building RPMs. It took a good half-minute to build up but that was a big four-bladed prop on that engine, with a lot of inertia to overcome.

Then Zeamer primed for a couple of seconds and pushed the starter, which whined and groaned and that big four-bladed prop started to turn, even more reluctantly than the prop on a P-39, one blade, two blades, three, and there was a burst of smoke and a blattering roar from the engine. Zeamer fiddled with the throttle and mixture controls and after a little coaxing the engine ran smoothly.

"Well, that's the easy one," Zeamer shouted to Cardenas, who nodded. "Ready starboard."

Cardenas nodded again. "Right hand booster pump to ON."

The two pilots started the right engine while Cardenas looked outside. Ardana had been told prior to entering the airplane that this was the engine that had been replaced, and that while the ground crew consisted of top-drawer professionals they were working under difficult and improvised conditions, so if the engine should, say, catch fire, Ardana might want to immediately exit the airplane through the entrance hatch behind the pilot's seat that opened into the nose wheel well. "And you'd better get out first, 'cause if you don't we're gonna trample you on our way out," Zeamer drawled.

Jimmy looked down at the hatch and back at the right engine, whose propeller had begun to rotate. But the professionals of *Bugs Buggy's* ground crew had done good work, and the engine settled down to deliver its one-note song of power with much less persuasion than the port engine needed. Cardenas and Zeamer watched the gauges for a moment and then Zeamer made a gesture with both hands, thumbs pointing outward, to signal the crew chief to take away the chocks holding the tires in place. The ground crew darted under the airplane and in a moment came out, holding up the wheel chocks to indicate that the airplane was now free to move.

During the taxi to the runway Jimmy noticed that both pilots kept scanning the engine instruments. He leaned close to Cardenas and asked, "What are you guys looking for when you scan the engine gauges?"

"Anything that starts looking out of the ordinary," Cardenas yelled back. "See how they're just sitting there, RPM steady, oil and fuel pressure steady, temps climbing but that's normal?"

"Yeah."

"That's what it's supposed to look like. If anything moves too quick one way or the other then what we try to do is shut down the engine before something tears loose."

Ardana nodded and leaned back.

Zeamer spoke to the tower and held short of the runway, revving up the engines to takeoff power and watching the gauges intently. Ardana looked back at the approach path to the runway, checking for airplanes on approach to landing, then looking at the traffic pattern to be sure it was clear.

"Well, everything looks good," Zeamer said. He keyed his radio and asked for takeoff clearance. A moment later the tower replied with a green light and Zeamer taxied onto the runway.

"Takeoff flaps," he said. Cardenas flipped a lever and there was a groan of metal and a whine of electric motors and hydraulics. Then there was a thump as the flaps extended to 30 degrees and locked into place.

Zeamer looked his instruments over one last time and shoved the throttles forward with a firm smooth motion.

At first the bomber hardly seemed to move. Then it rolled forward at a walking pace. Ardana looked at the engine instruments for a moment and when he looked back the B-26 had accelerated until the trees on the side of the strip started fading into one another. The roaring of the engines and the pounding of the props assaulted Ardana's ears. The slipstream roared through the open windows at the sides of the cockpit. Zeamer eased back about an inch on the yoke and the nose of the airplane rose. Some of the rumbling and rattling from the landing gear diminished as the nose gear lifted. Jimmy watched the flight instruments, especially the airspeed. Takeoff speed was about 140 mph at this density altitude and airplane weight.

Zeamer held the airplane on the ground as the end of the runway approached and the airspeed passed 140 mph. Jimmy looked from Zeamer to Cardenas but neither man showed any sign of strain, just looks of the most intense concentration, darting from their instruments to the runway ahead. Finally Zeamer pulled back a little more on the yoke and the rumble of the mains ceased almost at once.

"Gear up," Zeamer called. Cardenas flipped a lever. There was that same rumble and whine as the gear raised up into their nacelles and the covers sealed over them.

"Flaps up," Zeamer said.

As the flaps came up the airspeed increased rapidly. The B-26 indicated 180 mph and increasing. Jimmy nodded to himself. Whatever its reputation, the seat of his pants told him the B-26 was a solid airplane. He began to wonder what she'd feel like on the controls.

Zeamer pulled back on the throttles and the engine RPMs came down. The airplane climbed through fifteen hundred feet. Zeamer turned to Ardana and shouted, "We'll climb to five thousand and you can switch seats with Cardenas."

Jimmy nodded. At five thousand feet Cardenas took off his earphones and climbed out of the co-pilot's seat, squeezing past Jimmy in the narrow space behind the seats. Jimmy got into the seat and buckled in, somewhat gingerly settling the earphones over his officer's hat, from which he had removed the stiffener. *Now I really look like a Hollywood pilot,* he thought to himself.

"Take the controls and try a few standard rate turns to get the feel of her, then we'll run through some slow flight and engine-out procedures," Zeamer said.

Jimmy rocked the yoke left and right, back and forth, and pushed left rudder, then right rudder. Zeamer was looking at him with one eyebrow raised sardonically as Jimmy looked over his shoulder and banked the B-26 in a standard rate turn to the left. The ball on the turn and bank indicator stayed centered and the needle lined up exactly with the mark for a standard rate turn. Jimmy continued through a full turn and as the compass came through on their original course he turned smoothly into a standard-rate turn to the right. Without thinking about it his left hand went to rest lightly on the throttle and he looked around. The B-26 had a generous greenhouse of a cockpit, but the pilots' visibility was severely restricted by the bulk of the engines just in back of the flight deck.

"OK, hotshot, climb to seven thousand and take up a course of one eight zero," Zeamer called. "Engine RPMs for the climb should be 2200. Watch your cylinder head temps. They'll climb a little. You may have to crack the cowl flaps for cooling."

"Roger, climbing to seven thousand, turning one eight zero, RPMs to 2200," Jimmy said. He had noticed the elevator trim wheel while Zeamer was in his takeoff roll. Now he cranked in some nose-up trim as he advanced the throttles until the engines showed 2200 RPM. The cylinder head temps climbed a little but stayed relatively cool. At seven thousand he leveled out and reset the elevator trim for level flight.

They spent the next two hours flying above the Coral Sea ten miles south of Port Moresby. Zeamer explained what he was about to do and Jimmy followed through as they feathered first the port and then the starboard engine, restarted them, did approach to landing stalls with and without flaps and gear, and finally turned back to Seven-Mile.

"Let's see if you can land this bitch," Zeamer said. "I'll work the radios but you've got the airplane. What's your landing configuration?"

Jimmy rattled off engine RPMs, approach to landing speed and flap settings.

"Right, then, here goes nothing. Seven Mile Tower, Army Three Four Two Four requesting landing instructions."

Jimmy listened to the clearance instructions from the tower. There was a flight of P-39s taking off and another landing. A C-47 was holding short of the runway and would take off after the P-39s got down. The tower cleared the B-26 to land after the C-47 took off. Jimmy nodded and entered the downwind leg as the P-39s touched down. He recognized Jack's voice as Boxcar Red Leader in one of the P-39s. For just a moment he wondered if Boxcar Red Two was the new guy, Slim Atkins, and how he had liked his familiarization flight. Then he concentrated on landing his own airplane.

The airspeed indicated 165 mph as the B-26 neared the end of the downwind leg. Jimmy pushed the landing gear lever to DOWN and fed in a little throttle to maintain 165 mph as the drag increased with the gear and flaps hanging in the slipstream. He darted a look at the flap and gear indicator in front of Zeamer, which showed the mains and the nose gear down and locked and the flaps down. Jimmy turned onto the base leg of the approach, watching the end of the runway and the airspeed indicator.

"Make sure you keep the nose down. Don't let the airspeed go below 150 on final," Zeamer cautioned Jimmy. Then he picked up his mike and called the tower. "Seven Mile, Army Three Four Two Four is on final approach."

Jimmy watched the end of the airstrip approach over the nose of the bomber. At the far end the C-47 rose over the trees. So far the B-26 had acted just exactly as he expected, something like a big P-39, sensitive on the controls, needing a firm touch that already knew what it would do before it happened.

Which was when the port engine burst into flames and came to a shuddering, grinding halt accompanied by a rending crack from inside the nacelle. Out of the corner of his eye Jimmy saw Zeamer's hand dart to a switch marked "FIRE XTNG." Red lights flashed on the left side of the engine instruments panel. Jimmy pushed down on the yoke and fed power to the good right engine, pushing right rudder to compensate as the airplane tried to skid into the dead engine.

"Feathering port," Zeamer said, actuating the feathering control that would turn the port propeller blades knife-edge to the wind, but nothing happened. The propellers were in coarse pitch, causing almost maximum drag.

Zeamer slammed his window shut as flame licked in through it.

Jimmy dropped the left wing a little and kept the nose down. Airspeed was everything now, it was life itself, but they were losing altitude faster than they should. He knew Zeamer was looking at him and shouting something but he couldn't hear what the man was saying. He righted the airplane as it drifted crabwise, but there was the end of the runway and the glide angle looked good, airspeed was holding with the other engine at full throttle with Jimmy's hand holding it against the stop as he fought the port wing's tendency to drop, and then the ground was coming up. He held the nose-down descent attitude and rotated just as his ass began to bite buttons out of the seat cushion. When the mains touched he cut the power to the starboard engine.

The fire extinguishers hadn't done a thing for the fire in the port engine, which burned back towards the main wing spar. Zeamer jammed on the brakes and Jimmy added his weight to the effort. The brakes squealed and the nose of the bomber came down hard on the nose gear.

"Get the hatch open!" Zeamer yelled to Cardenas.

The airplane slowed. Jimmy could feel the heat from the engine now. Zeamer was shutting down the starboard engine and cutting the switches for the electrical system.

"Go on!" Zeamer yelled at Jimmy. "Go with Cardenas!"

Jimmy sat where he was, holding the bomber's brakes down.

"Asshole!" Zeamer yelled.

The bomber came to a shuddering halt and Jimmy had his belt unbuckled. Zeamer hit his belt with practiced ease and Jimmy slithered out of his seat with one quick, adrenaline-fueled motion, feeling Zeamer's hand on his shoulder. As soon as he saw them coming Cardenas dropped through the hatch and disappeared. Jimmy dropped through the hatch and instinctively turned from the heat of the burning engines. Zeamer piled down almost on top

of him and the two collapsed in a heap on the
runway.

"Fucking idiots!" Cardenas yelled as he grabbed
them by the shoulders and urged them up. "Run!
The fucking fuel tank will go any second!"

They ran, pelting down the runway with the
searing heat of burning avgas at their backs.

There was a soft *whoomp!* Jimmy staggered,
kept running, but did not look back. That was the
fuel on the left side and there was still the tank on
the right...

WHOOOOOSH-Boom!

The exploding fuel knocked all three of them to
their knees and shoved their noses in the dirt. Heat
washed over them, intolerable for just an instant and
then past them. Jimmy sat up and looked back. *Bugs
Buggy* was a mass of flames on the centerline of the
runway, main spar already burned through on the
port side, fuselage sagging down tiredly, bright
yellow fire and billowing black smoke licking up
into the sky.

"Hey, Ardana," Zeamer shouted over the roar of
burning fuel. "You still want to go to Rabaul with
us?"

"Well, hell, it couldn't be much worse than
that," Jimmy yelled back. "That's if you've got one
of those deathtraps that will actually make it to
Rabaul."

Zeamer and Cardenas began to laugh as the
crash trucks and meat wagons came down the
runway towards them.

Jimmy Ardana sat on his bunk staring at his
hands. They were steady. He turned his hands,
looking at his fingers.

When he closed his eyes he could see from the
corner of his left eye the engine exploding into
bright yellow flames, silhouetting Bill Zeamer's
head as the glow of the fire filled the cockpit.

Zeamer started yelling something but even now, in memory, he couldn't remember what it was. Probably something like, give me the controls. Jimmy opened his eyes again, to the stinking canvas tent in the New Guinea hills.

Why didn't I give him the controls? Jimmy wondered. But that was an easy question to answer. They were already halfway down the final approach, and Jimmy had control of the airplane. He could feel what the airplane was doing, right from the first fatal tremor that shook the airframe when the port engine failed. There was the airplane and that was the airspeed and hell, all I really did was land the friggin' airplane, so what's the big deal? He could see exactly what was going to happen next and he knew exactly what he had to do and when to do it.

Now, was that a weird thing? Jimmy knew he was a good pilot but there were guys who did a lot better in flight school. He'd always felt comfortable in the air. But this was something a little different. It was as if time and space had taken on different properties inside his mind.

Something white moved at the corner of his eye. He looked at the entrance to the tent.

Evarra the sanguma man sat there, squatting on his heels, the ebony staff clutched in the crook of his right arm. The old man's eyes were upon him. They contained nothing but attentive watchfulness. The thought came to Jimmy that a scientist watching the dials of his experimental apparatus would look like that.

Jimmy looked into the old man's eyes. They were dark brown and expressionless. Jimmy didn't speak.

After awhile the old man nodded, the least perceptible movement of his head.

"Yupela savvy ensel?" the old man said.

"What?" Jimmy asked.

"Ensel," the old man said. "Yupela savvy ensel?"

"I don't understand."

The old man nodded again, the same exact minimal gesture. Then he rose and walked away. Jimmy looked at the vacant door of the tent. Then he got up and went to the path outside the door. He looked both ways but the old man had disappeared.

"Hey, Jimmy!" Gerry yelled from down the path. Jimmy turned to look at him, smiling. Gerry was walking with someone Jimmy didn't recognize, a somber looking fellow with high cheekbones, medium height and build with yellow hair. He came forward with his hand outstretched.

"Charles Atkins," he said. "But everyone calls me Slim. Don't know why."

Jimmy shook hands with him. "How do, Slim. Call me Jimmy."

"Good to meet ya, Jimmy. I hear you had some real fun today."

"Oh, yeah, fun. Well, we walked away from it. That's what counts. Were you flying my airplane?"

"The Gremlin? Oh, heck yeah. She's a sweet little piece. I can't wait to fly one of my own."

"Yeah, well, be careful what you wish for, right?"

Bellmon looked Jimmy up and down. "Why d'you want to fly with the 22nd , anyway, Jimmy? That's not a game, flying up to Rabaul or wherever it is those crazy bastards are going next."

Jimmy shrugged. "Don't know what to tell you, Gerry. That major, Tommy Rhodes, asked if I'd go, and I didn't have any better sense than to say yes."

Gerry looked at Jimmy. "You're serious. You're really going."

Jimmy sighed. "Yeah."

Bellmon shrugged. "OK. If you don't make it back, can I have your booze?"

"Sure thing, asshole."

Jimmy was half awake when he walked into the briefing for the Rabaul mission. He found Zeamer and sat with him and his crew. They welcomed him with nods and made a space for him on the bench.

It wasn't much different from the briefings for missions he'd already flown except it seemed to go on a lot longer and went into more detail about the target. Jimmy figured that made sense. He understood in a general way that bombers usually went for specific targets.

When the briefer named the target as the shipping in Simpson Harbor no one said anything but Jimmy felt a quiver of tension pass through the room like a jolt of electricity. He looked around. It was the lack of expression or the purposeful control of it that scared him.

These guys had been up north to Rabaul before.

They didn't want to go back.

They'd go anyway.

Oh, *shit*.

Zeamer and his crew had found an airplane to replace the one lost yesterday. It was still pretty dark when the truck pulled up in front of the revetment among the palm trees. There was the painting of an old hillbilly with a corncob pipe on the nose and the letters *MOB*. "What's that mean?" Jimmy asked.

"Miserable Old Bastard," Zeamer replied. "No one wants to fly this piece of shit. People keep dying in it or getting shot up bad. But it's the only airplane available so it's the airplane we fly."

Jimmy looked at the B-26. The airplane had been bare aluminum once, then painted olive-drab, poorly, because streaks of aluminum were visible here and there along with the dull aluminum of patches over holes made by machine gun bullets, cannon shells and flak. There was a list in the way the bomber sat on the ground, detectable more by instinct than by sight. This was one tired airplane.

"I hate to ask, Bob, but will this thing fly?"

"I flew it late yesterday afternoon, actually," Zeamer replied. "Everything works."

The crew chief came up and handed Zeamer the Form One. Zeamer signed it and motioned everyone aboard. From down the line came the whine and snarl of an R2800 engine starting, coughing, and settling into an even rumbling idle.

Jimmy followed Zeamer up onto the flight deck. It was different from the check ride. There were more people, more things happening. He put on headphones over his hat with one ear free. Almost at once Zeamer began the prestart checklist. In a moment they had the electrical system online, the instruments whirring, pumps and motors whining into life. Zeamer hit the switch to the port engine, which came to life with a rush and a gush of gray-white smoke, quickly blown away by the propeller. Jimmy exchanged a look with Zeamer.

"Whaddaya know," Zeamer yelled over the blattering scream of the prop. "It works. For now anyway."

"Swell," Jimmy said. "Ready on starboard."

They taxied out behind a herd of other Marauders in the predawn darkness, so much like that first mission to Lae that Jimmy had to shake off a feeling of unreality. That mission had been more of a stunt for the P-39 drivers, but it was something the B-26 crews did every day, almost as a matter of course. As they taxied to the runway with squealing, moaning brakes, watching over their engine temp gauges, Jimmy thought he saw the first hint of light in the east, a slight waning of the brilliant stars above.

When they were next in line for takeoff, after a half-dozen other Marauders flung themselves down the runway and over the trees into the still-dark sky over Seven-Mile, Zeamer tapped his shoulder and Jimmy leaned towards him.

"You did good the other day and I think you're a natural," Zeamer shouted into his ear. "But if things go to shit in the next few minutes, you let me fly the airplane and you follow my lead. You got it?"

Jimmy nodded emphatically. "You got it, skipper."

Zeamer nodded, satisfied, and held a hand out. Jimmy shook it. Then the airplane ahead of them howled down the field to vanish into the darkness at the far end, and they taxied the *Miserable Old Bastard* onto the runway.

The sun came up off their right wing as the formation turned north and set course for Rabaul. Nine Marauders were on this mission. They would hit Rabaul in about two hours, bombing from 11,000 feet.

After the takeoff Zeamer turned the airplane over to Jimmy, coaching him into formation with the other bombers. Jimmy was fairly absorbed with the task, but the Marauder was easy enough to fly, despite carrying a load slightly in excess of maximum gross weight. The formation was briefed to fly to 16,000 feet to clear the mountains. Once they were over the coast of New Britain they would start a gradual descent to their bombing altitude of 11,000 feet.

"Pilot to crew," Zeamer said into the interphone. "Passing through ten thousand feet, let's go on oxygen. Be sure to check your flow meters and walk-around bottles."

Zeamer put on his oxygen mask and took the controls while Jimmy did the same.

It started to cool off. Zeamer turned up the cockpit heat. The Marauders climbed up to 16,000 feet and leveled out. Three miles below the New

Guinea coast gave way to the blue sea of the Huon Gulf. To his left he could see the coast trend off to the west. Lae was that way, about 120 miles. On the way back that could be an issue, according to the briefing. The Zeros at Lae could be in a good position to intercept the survivors of the mission.

They droned on over the western Solomon Sea. Zeamer talked to the navigator over the intercom from time to time, and about when the navigator, Lt. Harry Pearce, said it would, the coast of the island of New Britain came into view. All Jimmy could really see was a dark green island with clouds in the center, rising above the mountains in the center and north end of the island. They were still a hundred miles from the target, the transports and warships the B-17 recon crews found at anchor in Simpson Harbor.

"The Zeros usually hit us over the center of the island," said Zeamer over the interphone. "Navigator, how long to target?"

"Twenty-five minutes, Bill."

"OK, crew, pilot, we're liable to have company from here on out. Stay alert."

They came over the south coast of New Britain and Jimmy noticed the way Zeamer held himself. Zeamer seemed to shrink inward in a way that made him seem tighter, more controlled, more deliberate. Jimmy looked around at the formation of Marauders, and they were doing the same thing in the formation that Zeamer did with his body, drawing in like a fist closing, ready to strike. Like a boxer, Jimmy thought, gauging an opponent: shoulders a little forward, head down, fists clenched and up in a guard to protect the head and upper body from the blows to come.

"Bandits! Top turret to pilot, bandits eight o'clock low, count ten, fifteen, make it twenty for now."

"Fifteen minutes to IP," said the navigator over the intercom.

They droned on towards the northeast and just as the volcano at the north end of Simpson Harbor came into view the Zeros peeled off and dove down to the attack. The Zeros concentrated on the lead element of the group; tracers licked out from the turrets of the lead Marauders, lashed back at the Marauders from the Zeros. And then Jimmy called, "Zeros at eleven o'clock level."

A group of Zeros came at them head-on, and Jimmy saw their nose guns and wing cannon winking yellow. Tracers slipped by them and the bombardier's nose gun hammered short bursts. The upper turret joined in. Tracers from the guns of the other bombers crisscrossed with the Japanese fire. Something smashed into the cockpit and wind howled through the starred hole in the Plexiglas. There was a tattoo of bullet strikes and a *WhamWhamWham!* of exploding cannon shells. The Zeros swept past, one of them flying over the canopy, close enough to see the rivets on the underside of the Jap fighter's fuselage, close enough to hear the roar of its engine over their own.

"Crew, check in," Zeamer called.

"Bombardier OK."

"Navigator OK."

"Copilot OK," said Jimmy.

"Radio operator OK."

"Waist gunner OK."

"Turret gunner OK."

"Tail Gunner OK."

"OK. Stay loose, guys, they'll be back."

"Pilot, ten minutes to IP."

The formation leader came up on the strike frequency. "Keystones, this is Keystone Lead, the target is in sight. Keep it tight."

Ahead of them they saw the smoke of antiaircraft shells bursting over the harbor.

"Pilot from tail gunner, those little bastards are reforming astern."

"Roger that."

Jimmy looked at the airspeed indicator. It read two hundred eighty mph. The Zero was about fifty mph faster, but it would still take them a few minutes to catch up. It was a race, and coming from astern the Zeros would have a lot more time to line them up.

Simpson Harbor came into view. Jimmy knew a carrier would look rectangular from the air but other than that he couldn't tell a battleship from a rowboat. You didn't need to, to see the harbor was full of shipping, good-sized ships at that. A lot of them were warships, outlined by the flashes from their AA guns. The shells burst in the air directly ahead of them over the harbor, black flowers with red centers that appeared suddenly and drifted, gradually dissipating, replaced by dozens of others.

"Bombardier, navigator. IP in sight."

"Roger that, navigator."

"Pilot to bombardier. Your airplane."

"Bombardier's airplane."

Flak exploded in and around the formation. A near burst jolted their airplane, tilting the left wing up. The autopilot built into the bombsight corrected their course as both Zeamer and Ardana reacted on the controls, steadying the bomber on its course. Ahead of them one of the Marauders in the lead element sprayed smoke from its port engine, and then the smoke increased as fire trailed from the engine.

Jimmy watched in horror as the fire grew, but the bomber stayed on course, its bomb bay doors snapping open in unison with the others in the formation. Very slowly it began to lose speed, the other airplanes in the formation pulling back around it.

Flak burst closer and closer around them, shrapnel peppered their fuselage.

"Pilot, tail gunner, those little bastards are getting close."

"Understood, tail gunner," said Zeamer.

"Bombs away," said the bombardier. The *Miserable Old Bastard* surged up as its bombs fell free. A shell exploded almost in the nose of the B-26 with the burning engine. It staggered and fell off to the left, narrowly missing the Marauder next in formation. Jimmy could see a hole blown in the left side of the forward section of the airplane and the pilot of the airplane fell out. Half of him did, at least, the half that was still in the seat that fell out of the hole. The half-pilot hit the propeller and exploded into red mist. Tattered bloody rags were sucked from the hole and blew into red mist in the slipstream as the B-26 fell from the formation.

Behind them the fuselage shook with the recoil of the tail guns and then there was a scream over the intercom, cut short.

"Pilot, waist gun, Sammy's hit bad!"

Tracers whipped by them. The survivors of the lead element, bombs gone, turned hard to the right. Their bomb bay doors closed. The hydraulics whined in the bomb bay behind them as their own doors closed and their airspeed picked up as the drag from the open doors fell away.

The top turret fired as the Zeros turned with them away from the target. The lead element began a shallow dive, converting their altitude into greater airspeed. Jimmy watched the airspeed indicator showing the increase in speed. They were already over three hundred mph. Tracers flew past them and there was another series of tattoos beaten by machine gun bullets on airplane aluminum. Something smashed into the armor plate on the back of Jimmy's seat and punched holes in the blank panel and windscreen in front of him. Plexiglas fragments sprayed back from the windscreen and slashed across his cheek.

Right beside them a Zero drew level, firing at a B-26 ahead and to their right. The Zero's cannon fire danced across the tail section of the B-26, flashes of explosions winking across the tail gunner's compartment and the bottom part of the horizontal and vertical stabilizers. Bits flew back from the B-26. The bomber's tail gunner kept firing, yellow tracers licking into the Zero. Bits flew from the Zero, then flame burst from its engine and the Zero came apart in midair, the blazing engine falling away in a graceful parabola, the wings spitting fire and black smoke.

Jimmy looked at the B-26. He could see the tail gunner peering out from his ruined gun position, the rudder and elevator fabric around him in tatters.

"Bombardier to pilot, we got bandits at five o'clock low, climbing, maybe three miles astern."

"Roger, bombardier. Waist gunner, can you see those guys astern of us?"

"Top turret, pilot, waist gunner is trying to help the tail gunner."

"OK. Bombardier, go back and see if you can give them a hand."

"Roger, pilot."

The formation was pushing 320 mph now and descending through 8,000 feet. The controls felt stiff to Jimmy and there was an indefinable shimmy and rattle in the airframe. Bits of Plexiglas kept coming off the windscreen.

"Pilot, yaw right!"

Zeamer hit right rudder and the turret guns fired. "Yawing left!" said Zeamer, kicking the rudders. The turret went quiet until the B-26 slewed through a slight arc and then fired again. More guns hammered.

"Navigator to pilot, I'm on the tail guns," said the navigator. "Keith's got Sammy out and he's giving him first aid."

"What are the Zeros doing?"

"Catching up," said the navigator. Gunfire hammered over the interphone.

The south coast of New Britain approached; the blue of the Solomon Sea lay beyond. As the formation crossed the coast they were down to 5,000 feet, holding a steady 320 mph.

Jimmy watched the fuel gauge and wondered about the endurance of a Zero fighter with its engine at continuous full throttle. As he watched the fuel gauges he noticed the oil pressure gauge of the starboard engine falling. Jimmy looked over his shoulder at the engine nacelle. There was a thin film of oil streaking back from the cowling.

"Zeamer, starboard engine's losing oil," Jimmy said.

"Yeah. All we can do is roll the dice and hope it keeps running. There's still twenty Zeros back there."

They flew across the sea with the Zeros right behind them, the tail guns in constant action, as the Zeros worked closer and fired. Another B-26 trailed smoke from both engines, but kept in formation. They were nearing the north coast of New Guinea when the Zeros broke off and turned away.

"Bandits! Top turret to pilot, bandits at two o'clock high!"

Jimmy looked up and to the right. There was a gaggle of Zeros peeling off and diving on them, probably the Zeros from Lae that had time to climb to altitude while the Zeros from Rabaul chased them. Ahead of them was a cloud bank but it was fifteen miles away over the Owen Stanley Mountains.

Two minutes. Two minutes and they'd be in the clouds.

Then the Zeros were pulling up from the dive to hit them on a level, taking the formation from starboard. Jimmy watched them tensely as they began their run. A B-26 was hit, trailed flame from its starboard wing and then fell off in a spin towards the jungle below. Jimmy watched in fascination as a Zero targeted them. The turret gun fired, the waist gun fired, the Zero fired, bullets and cannon shells hit the Marauder. Smoke belched from the right engine.

"Shut it down," Zeamer commanded.

Jimmy reached for the prop feathering button and pulled back the throttle and mixture controls, shutting down the engine. The attacking Zeros swept past them, already turning tightly to port to come in for a tail attack.

Before the Zeros caught up with them, the formation was in the clouds.

Chapter Twelve

"To my Darling Boy, to Remind Him of Home"

They pulled the body of the tail gunner out the airplane on a stretcher with a blanket over him. Jimmy stood with the rest of the crew watching.

After the ambulance left Zeamer said, "Come on. Let's get to the debrief."

His voice was thin with adrenaline exhaustion. He looked at Jimmy. "Jesus, Ardana, you know you got blood all over your cheek?"

Jimmy reached up and felt the rasp of dried blood under his fingers. Something high up on his cheek burned when he touched it and dug into his skin.

"Ow," he said.

"Hey, you got a glass splinter," said Zeamer. "Looks bad."

"Shit. I've cut myself worse shaving."

"You want to be careful with that. It's deep. Could get infected out here in this goddamn jungle."

"And hey, you can get the Purple Heart for that," said the navigator. He and the waist gunner were daubed with the tail gunner's blood.

Jimmy looked at them. He looked after the ambulance. "Maybe next time," he said. Then he reached up and pulled out the Plexiglas shard and looked at it. It was maybe a half-inch long and an eighth-inch wide. He flipped it into the dirt and followed Zeamer's crew to the debrief, where they learned they had, maybe, hit a cruiser and some transports in Simpson Harbor.

For the loss of three B-26s and their crews of seven men each, and the two men killed and ten wounded on the six airplane that made it back.

After the debrief Jimmy shook hands with Zeamer. They were too tired to say anything. Ardana turned and started walking back to the 18th Squadron's area. Halfway there he began to feel thirsty, and then he began to feel faint. It was a goddamned hot day and the worst of the afternoon heat was yet to come.

A passing jeep picked him up and gave him a lift. The driver, a corporal with a bunch of crates in the back, offered him a canteen.

"You might want to drink it, sir," the corporal said. "You look kind of pale to me, and it's awful easy to get heat stroke."

Ardana drank most of the water in the canteen and thanked the corporal, who dropped him off in front of the Ops shack.

Davis came out of the Ops shack and looked at him. "Welcome back," he said.

Jimmy nodded. "Thanks," he said. "How did Atkins do?"

"Fine. Wasn't much of a morning. The docs let Danny Evans out of hospital. We rode around for awhile. Atkins pretty much stayed on my wing the whole time. I let Gerry take your slot."

"Bet Evans liked that."

"He didn't say a thing. Maybe that knock in the head did him some good." Davis studied Ardana. "So you want to fly Marauders for a living?"

"Not much of a living."

"I heard it was rough."

"Yeah." Ardana looked down. "But I think I'll stay here. For now."

Davis looked at him hard. "For now?"

Ardana nodded.

"Well, Tommy Rhodes from the 22nd called Wagner. He says Zeamer will take you as copilot any time you like."

Ardana nodded again.

"You sure you're OK, Jimmy?"

"I'm fine."

"Why don't you go sack out? We have a mission first thing in the morning."

"Oh?"

"Yeah. You'll love it. The group is going to Lae again but this time we get to fly top cover. We might get a shot at some Zeros."

"Good. Brief at 0430?"

"Yeah."

"See you then."

Jimmy walked off down the path to the flight line, not the tents. He wanted to look at the *Gremlin*, be sure she was OK.

Terraine was busy with the engine when Jimmy walked up. "Hey, Jimmy," he said, looking up briefly. "Glad you made it."

"Thanks. Me too. Atkins bust anything?"

"Nah. Seems he's a pretty good stick. Didn't put a dent in her."

Jimmy nodded. "You hear about tomorrow?"

"You guys going up north?"

"Yeah."

" Don't worry about the airplane, sir. The *Gremlin* won't let you down."

"OK. Good enough."

Jimmy walked up the path to the tents.

He was about exhausted. When he got to the tent he drank some more water, stripped to his skivvies, and lay down on his bunk.

He kept seeing the Zeros roll in to the attack, the tracers, the engines on fire, the smoke, the half-pilot falling out of the stricken Marauder.

Exhaustion finally claimed him and he fell into a sleep filled with burning airplanes, frantic radio calls and the roar of engines.

He awoke sometime after midnight. The sides of the tent had been rolled up and the mosquito netting was in place. Evans was snoring, so he or Gerry must have rolled up the sides of the tent. There was a rumble of thunder and a flash of lightning and the rain started, roaring on the roof and misting through the mosquito netting. Lightning flashed again and thunder grumbled.

Jimmy sat up in bed, still feeling tired, still feeling the drain of the mission on his nerves. He rolled his feet to the wooden floor and walked to the doorway, looking out into the darkness with the rain on his face. The thunder flashed again and Jimmy jumped, because Evarra the sanguma man sat under a tree across the path. Evarra's ebony staff was crooked in his arm and he had that ridiculous white frilly umbrella over his head. He looked straight at Jimmy, who walked out into the rain and across the muddy path. The lightning flashed and Evarra stood before him, staff in hand now, the silly umbrella held over his head.

"What do you want?" Jimmy asked the darkness. And when the lightning flashed again there was no one standing there. Jimmy stood for a few moments in the driving tropical rain as the lightning flashed and the thunder roared, looking around, but Evarra was nowhere to be seen. Then he went back into the tent, dried himself off as best he could, and lay back down to sleep.

His head had barely touched the pillow before Danny Evans groaned. Jimmy sat up, sighing. A thrashing sound came from Danny's bunk.

"Jesus, Danny," Gerry mumbled. "You're having a nightmare or something. Wake up and walk it off."

The lightning flashed again and in the brief blue illumination Jimmy saw Danny's face, contorted and bathed in sweat. Evans groaned again and started shivering. Before the lightning faded he could see Evans' eyes, open and staring.

He fumbled for his flashlight under his bunk and turned it on, shining the dim yellow light on Evans.

"What the hell is that on his face?" Gerry said, sitting up on his bunk and leaning forward.

"Looks like a rash," Jimmy said. Danny moaned again and shivered under the thin sheet. Jimmy reached out and touched Danny's face. "Damn, he's hot. Some kind of fever."

"Oh, hell. What do we do?"

"Flip a coin to see who goes for the doc."

"Swell. I'll go. I'd rather face the rain than sit here with Danny like this." Gerry got dressed quickly and went out into the rain.

Jimmy sat in the dark, not knowing what else to do but shine the light on Danny's face from time to time and listen to his harsh, labored breathing, as the tropical rain poured down outside. He looked at the radium dial of his wristwatch. It was 0230. He'd have to be up in two hours for the mission brief.

"Pailat?"

Jimmy nearly jumped out of his skin. He turned to see a dark figure vaguely silhouetted in the barely-visible entrance to the tent. It was Evarra.

"Evarra?"

"Yis." The sanguma man walked into the tent and squatted down beside Evans' bunk. Jimmy flicked on the flashlight and saw that Evarra had taken the sheet off Evans and was running his hand over Evans' face. Evarra touched Evans on the shoulder and the elbow and nodded when Evans flinched. He sat back on his haunches and looked up at Jimmy.

"Man, skin i hat, fiva," Evarra said matter-of-factly. "Youpela kisim dokta?"

Jimmy blinked and shook his head. "I don't understand."

"Dokta," Evarra repeated. Then he smiled, showing yellow teeth. "Dokta. Ol waitman em kalim Evarra dokta, sanguma man, youpela savvy?"

"Dokta?" Jimmy repeated dubiously. "Doctor?"

Jimmy blinked. "Yes," he said. "Doctor." Jimmy pointed up the path where Gerry had gone. "Gerry is going for the doctor."

Evarra nodded. "Gut." Evarra nodded at Danny. "Em sik, tru sik. Nidim ol waitman dokta. Yumitupela waitam dokta, yis?"

"I guess," Jimmy replied. Evarra smiled briefly and then looked at Evans.

"Em pailat?" Evarra asked.

"Pailat? Yes. Ah, ranim balus?"

"Pailat ranim balus, yis. Wanim em nem?"

"Nem?"

"Nem," Evarra repeated firmly. He pointed to himself. "Evarra." He pointed to Jimmy. "Jimmy."

Evarra pointed to Evans and looked at Jimmy.

Jimmy nodded at Evans. "Danny."

"Danny?"

"Yes. Danny Evans."

"Danny Evans. Orait. OK. Danny Evans."

They sat together in the dark as the thunder rumbled and lightning lit up the tent and rain poured down.

Then Jimmy asked, "What is ensel?"

"Ensel?" Evarra frowned. "Ihova, em gat ensel. Youpela savvy ensel? Bilip ensel?"

"Ihova?"

"Ihova," Evarra repeated. He pointed up at the sky, clasped his hands together as if praying. "Ihova."

"Oh! Jehovah. God."

"Got," Evarra said, nodding. "Got, em gat ensel. Youpela bilip ensel?"

"Do I believe in God?" Jimmy asked, puzzled.

Evarra shook his head and sighed. "Ensel. Setan, em ensel."

"Setan? You mean Satan?"

"Setan, yis. Setan, em ensel. Mikal, em ensel. Setan, Mikal, em ensel bilong Ihova, yu savvy?"

"Angels," said Jimmy.

"Ensel," agreed Evarra. He pointed at Jimmy. "Youpela, Jimmy, bilip ensel?"

"Angels. Angels, not God, not Jehovah?"

"Ensel," said Evarra firmly. "Jimmy bilip ensel?"

Jimmy frowned. "I'm still not sure what you're asking."

Evarra sighed and patted Jimmy on the knee. Then he pointed up the trail. "Dokta kam nau," he said.

Jimmy turned to look up the trail. At first he saw nothing, and then there was a brief glimmer of light, then several glimmers, men with flashlights picking their way down the muddy, flooded path. He turned back to Evarra but the sanguma man had pulled his disappearing trick again.

"Ensel," he muttered. "What the hell does the old bastard think I know about angels?"

At 0430 Jimmy yawned and sipped bitter tea with Gerry Bellmon while they waited for the mission briefing to begin.

"Christ, what I wouldn't give for a decent cup of coffee," Gerry said.

Jack Davis came in and sat beside them. Slim Atkins was with him. Nods were exchanged.

"The doc thinks Danny has dengue fever," Davis said. "It's about time for it to start showing up among the newcomers."

"Great. So what is dengue fever?" Jimmy asked.

"Also called breakbone fever, because that's what it feels like. Hurts like hell and puts you down for a week. Usually you mend and you don't get it for awhile, like a year or two. But there's even better news. Malaria will probably start showing up soon, too. And most of us will get dysentery."

"Dysentery?" asked Gerry, frowning.

"The shits. Montezuma's Revenge. Just keep drinking tea. The cooks boil the water for the tea and that kills the little critters that cause dysentery."

Gerry looked at his cup. "I still wish it was coffee. You have to boil water for coffee, too."

Colonel Wagner entered the tent. Someone called "Atten-*hut!*" The pilots rose.

"Rest, gentlemen," said Wagner as he strode to the front of the tent. "Our target for today is Lae."

To Jimmy the rest of the briefing was like *déjà vu* except that the Boxcars were high cover and the Brickbats were on the deck attacking Lae. Somewhere in the middle would be the 22nd with as many B-26s as would fly. This time the Primroses were going to stay at low level along the coast while the Boxcars were scheduled to arrive five minutes before, orbiting at high altitude, hoping to draw the Jap Zeros off the ground.

Jimmy looked at the Colonel and looked at Davis. Davis looked at the Colonel with an absolute lack of expression. Jimmy turned his eyes forward and listened to the details of course, fuel, times for rendezvous, radio frequencies, call signs, engine settings, noting all of it down on his knee board.

When the briefing was over he turned to Bellmon. "You ready for this, partner?"

"You bet, Jimmy." Bellmon smiled. "Maybe we'll get a chance to kick some Jap ass."

"Yeah, maybe."

"Just keep your eyes peeled," Davis growled. He turned to Atkins. "Slim, you're on my wing. Just stay close and do whatever I do. This is your first mission and it's going to be a long war."

The jeep dropped them off at their revetments. Jimmy got out and walked up to the P-39. Terraine and his crew were buttoning up the cowling and inspection panels. The crew chief walked up to him, wiping his hands on a rag.

"Warmed her up about a half-hour ago, Jimmy," he reported. "Everything looked good."

"Okay, Don." Jimmy shrugged into the parachute waiting for him on the wing root. Then he climbed up on the wing and squeezed into the cockpit.

It felt easy and familiar and homely, sitting in the Gremlin's cockpit, flipping the switches and listening to the now well-known noises.

"How's she feel, sir?" asked Terraine, crouching beside him on the wing.

"Just like she ought to, Don. Let's see how that engine starts."

The engine came up sweet and solid. Thirty minutes later the Boxcars were flying towards the Owen Stanley Range, climbing past fifteen thousand and higher still as the sun began to pink the horizon, and there was the Huon Gulf ahead, and the coast below with the finger of Salamaua pointing north into the Gulf. Then the Boxcars were over the north shore and turned slightly to the left. The aux tank gave out. Ardana shifted to the mains and pickled the aux tank. One by one in the growing light around him the aux tanks came off the P-39s with little white puffs of fuel.

Jimmy armed his machine guns and gave first the .50s and then the .30s a burst to check function. He armed the 37-mm T9 cannon but didn't fire it. If he only had one shot he would save it for a Zero. Beside him tracers flickered past and he flinched before he remembered it was only Bellmon testing his own weapons.

The sun was a fat red ball on the horizon behind them and Lae was below them to the north. Major Wolchek led the formation into a slow turn to the right, orbiting south of the airfield. Jimmy watched above and below and around them in the morning sky with the fat puffy cumulus clouds around them.

"BANDITS! Bandits ten o'clock high!"

Zeros, Zeros above them, holy Jesus! Jimmy swiveled his head to the left, looking up and there they were, growing already, and Wolchek led the flight into a left turn and climb, throttles and manifold pressure all the way forward, accelerating as they came around. Jimmy felt as if he'd been punched in the gut, like he would vomit in his oxygen mask as the Boxcars turned into the Zeros. Then they were in range, guns and cannon winking between the Boxcars and the Zeros. A P-39 ran into a crisscross of fire from two Zeros and stumbled, tumbled, shed a wing and fell. Jimmy saw a Zero heading straight for him and he centered his gunsight above the nose of the attacking Jap fighter, holding down the trigger for the .50s and hosing out short bursts. Jimmy tried the cannon. It fired once and jammed, but there was a sparkle of bullet strikes on the Zero's engine cowling. Smoke burst from the Zero's engine as the two formations flashed past each other.

"Boxcar Red flight, follow me," said Davis over the radio. His P-39 reefed into a hard right turn and Jimmy followed him, spreading out to maintain their finger-four formation, looking over his shoulder to check on Gerry, but Gerry wasn't there.

Jimmy looked around, staying with Jack and Slim, but he couldn't see any sign of Bellmon's airplane. The sky nearby was crowded with turning airplane, shooting airplane, falling airplane, burning airplane.

"Boxcar Red Four, Boxcar Red Four, come in," Jimmy called.

Silence except for the radio calls from the Boxcar Yellows and Boxcar Whites, excited calls from the Brickbats racing away from Lae with a half-dozen Zeros on their tail three miles and more below. The Rattlers joined in the fight, causing more confusion over the radio. Jimmy glimpsed the B-26 formation turning away from Lae with flak bursting around them. Fountains of earth and smoke rose from the Lae airstrip.

The Zeros that bounced them were turning right and climbing, and there wasn't anything the Boxcars could do about it. The surprise Colonel Wagner hoped to confer had somehow been conferred upon them by the Japs, who had either guessed the plan or just been lucky. Either way, there were the Zeros, outclimbing them and positioning themselves for another attack pass where the best the P-39s could do would be to turn into the attack again. Jimmy saw a Zero diving away, heading towards Lae with a smoking engine. It might have been the one he hit. The smoke got worse as the Zero dove away. Meat on the table for someone but a formation of perfectly intact Zeros spoiling for a fight was still turning towards them.

Jimmy glanced at his airspeed, hovering around 250 mph. That was bad, because the Zero with its low wing loading maneuvered well at this speed. The P-39 did not maneuver as well, did not climb as well, the one thing it could do better than the Zero was to dive. And Major Wolchek still turned towards the Zeros, who were turning into them, turning to get on their tails and it was just like trying an intercept over Port Moresby where the Japs had all the cards of height and speed. Another half-turn and the Zeros would be coming in on their tails, but in a half-turn the P-39s would have their noses towards home. Jimmy figured Wolchek, flying as Boxcar White Leader, would order them to break off.

"Boxcar White Leader to all Boxcars, break it off, break it off, let's head for home."

Jimmy looked at his fuel state as Davis pointed his nose down. The Zeros chased them for awhile but the P-39s, riding the gravity train, left them behind as they passed 400 mph in the dive. In the escape from the Zeros Jimmy looked around, counting P-39s. The Boxcars had started out with 18 airplane and he only counted fifteen.

"Boxcar Red Four, Boxcar Red Four, this is Boxcar Red Three, come in, over," Jimmy called on the radio.

"Boxcar Red Three from Leader," Davis called. "Negative on Boxcar Red Four. Boxcar Red Leader out."

Jimmy looked ahead and to his left at Davis' airplane. Davis turned in his seat and looked back at Jimmy and slowly shook his head. Slim looked back as well, just for a moment, before resuming his scan of the sky. Jimmy went blank. He looked at the instruments, at the cockpit floor, the sky beyond his wingtips and his canopy and had a moment where he didn't know who he was or where he was or what he was doing. Then he felt his fingers on the *Gremlin's* control stick, the solid feel of the ailerons and elevator under his fingertips, the rush and flow of the air over the canopy, the high scream of the gearbox in the nose. He took a long deep breath of rubbery-tasting oxygen, then another as everything snapped back into place. He picked up his scan of the sky and the instruments. In an hour they'd be back at Seven-Mile, only Gerry and a couple of other guys wouldn't be with them.

At the debrief the intelligence officer poured Jimmy a shot of whisky. Jimmy drank it down at a single swallow.

"Now," said the intelligence officer. "What happened?"

"Pretty much according to plan except the Japs were already there and waiting for us," Jimmy said.

"How do you know they were waiting for you?"

"I guess I don't, really. But when I heard the call for bandits they were three thousand feet above us."

The intelligence officer nodded, making a few notes on his pad. "OK. So they dove on you."

"Right. The Major had enough time to turn us into the attack. We met the Zeros head-on. I saw someone in Yellow flight buy it, and somewhere in there I lost Gerry."

"Gerry?"

"Lieutenant Gerald B. Bellmon of Sioux City, Iowa," Jimmy said.

The intelligence officer looked at him and wrote that down. Jimmy sighed.

"So you lost Lieutenant Bellmon?" the intelligence officer asked.

"I mean sometime during the turn to meet the Zeros he was there, and then after the Zeros passed through our formation he wasn't. I don't know what happened to him."

"No one called any other Zeros?"

"No."

"OK. So you were turning into the attacking Zeros."

"That's right. It seems like everyone opened up at the same time. Tracers everywhere. I had a bead on a Zero, fired at him, and saw strikes on the engine cowling. He started smoking."

"Strikes on the engine cowling. Smoking. Go on."

"Well, we turned hard right, they turned hard right to stay at our six, and as soon as we were headed more or less south we headed for home in a dive. The Zeros chased us awhile and then turned for home."

The intelligence officer nodded. "Anything else?"

"I saw a Zero with a smoking engine dive away from the fight back towards Lae."

"You see him go down?"

"No."

"OK. We'll call that one a damage. Anything else?"

"No."

"Right, then. Thanks, Ardana."

The intelligence officer got up and went over to the guys from Boxcar Yellow Flight. Like the Boxcar Reds, they were short a man.

Jimmy walked out of the Ops shack. Davis and Atkins were waiting for him under the tree.

"What happened to Bellmon?" Davis asked.

Jimmy shook his head. "I don't know. He was with me when we started turning into the Zeros. Then he wasn't."

Davis nodded. "Blue Flight was behind us. Maybe one of those guys saw him."

"Maybe," said Jimmy.

"I told them I saw you get strikes on that Zero. You'll get a damage."

"Yeah."

Davis looked hard at Ardana. "Look, Jimmy, you want to know what probably happened to Bellmon? He was there on your wing, watching your ass like a good wingman. We turned into the Zeros and everyone started shooting. You were concentrating on your shooting, like a good element lead. And because there were bullets and cannon shells flying everywhere Bellmon probably took one. No radio call and he just vanished off your wing so it was probably a lucky shot that got him."

"Lucky shot?"

"Yeah. Bad luck for us, good luck for some Jap. One bullet found a chink in his armor and killed him. Like that."

"Those little yellow bastards seem to have all the luck."

"Yeah. Well, there are more of them than us, they have a damned good airplane with a lot of advantages over our airplane, and today they were fighting over their home airstrip. They don't need a hell of a lot of luck when they have all that going for them."

Someone called Captain Davis from the Ops shack. He walked off leaving Slim and Jimmy standing together under the tree.

"Didn't see a thing," Jimmy said. "How could he just be gone like that?"

Slim shook his head. "Probably like Captain Davis said. Lucky shot."

"Jesus."

"Yeah."

Jimmy started walking to Tent 7. "Guess we ought to start cleaning up his things."

"What's the drill?" Slim asked, falling in beside him.

"I don't know. Put all his stuff together on his bunk for starters. I guess we take whatever we want. The Army will ship the rest back to his folks."

While they were on the mission to Lae, someone had cleaned out Danny Evans' footlocker and duffle bag, leaving only a stripped cot, as if Danny had never been there. Now they would do the same with Gerry's stuff, and a couple of new guys would move in, and who knew how long they'd last?

Bellmon, like everyone else at Seven-Mile, lived out of his footlocker and duffle bag. They opened Bellmon's duffle bag and pulled out more or less clean uniforms and underwear.

"I think I can wear his shorts," Slim said. He looked at Jimmy when he said it.

Jimmy looked at him and shrugged. "Can't see where he'd care," he said. "And he's sure not my size."

Slim sorted through the clothes on the bunk until he came up with a loudly-striped civilian tie. There was a clip on the tie with a fraternity pin. Slim looked at it, shook his head, and tossed it in the pile that would be sent home as "personal effects".

The footlocker was next. Soap, razor blades, an almost-empty bottle of aftershave lotion was divvied up silently and without comment, as was the nearly-full box of stationery.

"Wonder who he wasn't writing to?" Slim asked, looking at the box. "Hell, there's even a nice fountain pen in here." Slim opened the cap on the fountain pen and scribbled a little with it. After a few whorls the ink started to flow. Atkins capped the pen, glanced at Jimmy, and placed the pen and stationery in his own pocket when Jimmy shook his head.

There was a small packet of letters in lavender envelopes. The last one was post-marked in April.

"Some girl," Jimmy observed. "Daphne Summers. From Ottumwa, Iowa."

"Wonder how far that is from Sioux City?"

"Who knows. Here's a couple letters from his mother."

They collected the letters and put them in separate piles. Then there was a small scrapbook with photographs. On the flyleaf was an inscription, *To my Darling Boy, To Remind Him of Home*. They flipped through it. There were two dozen small black and white photos. Mom and Dad standing on the steps in front of a house, smiling and waving. A view down the street, with cars and elm trees lining the street. A drugstore next to the Palace Theater. "I Wanted Wings" with William Holden, Ray Milland, and Veronica Lake was advertised on the theater's marquee. A school of some sort, probably the old high school Evans attended. A college campus, with students in sweaters and carrying books hurrying to class. An old woman seated in a chair, with an old man standing beside her, his hand on her shoulder. A picture of Bellmon as a teenager, in baseball uniform, standing on a field with his teammates.

They closed the scrapbook and tossed it in the pile with the letters from Bellmon's parents. About that time Captain Davis arrived.

"Going through Gerry's effects?" he asked.

"Yes, sir."

Davis sat down on Jimmy's bunk. "You guys call me Jack," he said quietly. He looked at the two small piles on Bellmon's bunk. "That all you got so far?"

Jimmy nodded. Davis knelt on the floor beside the footlocker. Jimmy wanted to ask how many times he'd done this but decided he didn't want to know.

"Corcoran from Blue flight saw Gerry wing over and dive straight down," Davis said in that same quiet tone. "He couldn't follow him all the way down but if he were coming back he'd be here before now."

"Could he have gotten out before he hit?" Atkins asked.

Davis shrugged. "Sure. Maybe. Who knows. Silly bastard might come walking in out of the jungle in a couple of months."

Jimmy thought about that. If the Blue flight guy's description was accurate it almost surely meant Gerry had been hit and hit bad. There wasn't any other reason for him to dive out like that, not straight down, anyway. And if Gerry hadn't started pulling out by the time he was at 10,000 feet in a terminal velocity dive he would either auger in or pull the wings off the airplane trying. Either way, Gerry was dead. And if he had managed to bail out he would be in Jap territory, or headhunter territory, probably hurt, maybe hurt even worse landing in his parachute.

"Not much chance then," Atkins said in that same quiet tone.

"No," Davis agreed. He straightened up. "Whatever you send to his parents be sure there aren't any condoms or dirty pictures or stuff like that in it, OK?"

"Sure thing," Jimmy replied. "But I don't think Gerry ..."

Atkins held up a small package of Australian condoms. He smiled suddenly.

Jimmy couldn't help a small grin himself. "Well, how about that," he said. "And look. It's even open. That bastard Bellmon! Maybe he didn't die a virgin after all."

Slim was still looking in the footlocker. His hand darted into the footlocker and came up with a postcard. The postcard had an extremely lurid cover, two naked voluptuous females, one blonde and Caucasian, the other black-haired and Oriental, arms about each other's waists, smiling and waving. There was a bed behind them, its coverlet turned down invitingly. The legend on the bottom of the postcard read, "Get anything you want at Madame Chiang's."

"Must have been when he and Danny Evans were in Sydney," Jimmy speculated.

"Madame Chiang's is in Brisbane. Hell, I heard about that place in Manila," Davis said. "That's one of the most famous cathouses in the Pacific. And if you children haven't figured it out yet, there are a hell of a lot of cathouses out here."

"Asian girls?" Atkins asked dubiously.

"Sure," said Davis. "Also white girls, black girls, polka-dotted girls if that's what you want. What I heard was that Madame Chiang's was a place where a man could get screwed, blued and tattooed, and by God if he was gonna die for his country he'd go out with a bang," said Davis.

"Pay for it?" Jimmy asked dubiously.

Slim hid a smile. Davis grinned.

"Well, you know, it's been paid for since the dawn of time," Davis observed.

Jimmy blushed. "I know that, it's just ..."

"Just ..." prompted Atkins with an evil leer.

"If you must know, that seems too cold to me," Jimmy observed, frowning. "Just stick it in some woman you don't know, who's had God knows how many men before you that day alone?"

"So go early," Atkins suggested. Jimmy shuddered.

"OK, OK," Davis said. He laid a hand on Jimmy's shoulder. "Do what you want with the postcard and the condoms as long as the parents don't end up with them. And don't let the chaplain see the postcard, he might have a conniption. You guys finish this up. Speaking of the chaplain, he'll be by in a bit to pick up whatever you're sending Bellmon's folks."

"OK," Jimmy said. Davis left.

Atkins rooted around in the footlocker and came up with a small copybook. "Hey, check this out." He opened it. "It's a diary," he said, flipping the pages rapidly.

"Maybe you shouldn't read that," Jimmy cautioned.

"What the hell, Bellmon is dead. He can't care if we read his private thoughts."

"You didn't even know the guy."

"OK. You read it."

"Besides, there's some kind of regulation against keeping diaries. They might fall into enemy hands."

"Well shit, listen to this, Jimmy. It's about you."

"Yeah? OK, so read it."

"Jimmy and Danny are great guys in one sense," Slim read. "I had a lot of fun in Brisbane and Cairns with Danny. Then we moved up here to Seven-Mile and all of a sudden everyone acts like they're different people. It's like, I don't know, as if they breathed something or ate something, and I just don't get it. I was right down there on the deck with those guys that first mission. OK, so I had my eyes closed and the only reason I stayed with it was because I didn't want to be left behind. I was there, wasn't I? So now Jimmy is my element leader and Danny has a half-kill and Captain Davis is an ace, and I think Jimmy might be too, some day, if we live long enough. Me? Am I even in that league?"

Atkins shut the book abruptly.

"What's wrong?" Jimmy asked.

"Man, I don't want to read any more of that shit. Let's get this over with. Better yet, we've got what we want and we've sanitized it for the folks back home. Let the chaplain handle the rest of it." Slim tossed the diary into the footlocker and closed the lid with a snap. He sat on the floor staring moodily at the footlocker.

"Why the hell did he think I'd be an ace?" Jimmy asked.

"Shut up. Don't talk about it. That's the worst sort of luck. It's tempting fate, what was it the Greeks called it?"

"You mean hubris?"

"Yeah, that's it."

"Maybe," said Jimmy quietly. "Any of this other stuff you want? He's got some uniforms. How about those shoes?"

"I can't wear that bastard's shoes. Too small."

Jimmy held the oxford shoe beside his own booted foot. "You're right. I couldn't cram my foot in there either."

Atkins got up and sat on Gerry's bunk. "You mind if I move in here?" he asked Jimmy.

Jimmy thought about it. He didn't know Atkins, but other than Captain Davis, of the only other two guys he knew, one was in the hospital and the other was missing in action. "No."

"What about this other guy? Evans?"

"Captain Davis sounded like he'd be in the hospital for at least a week."

"Yeah." Slim brooded. Then he shook his head. "OK. I'm not going to worry over it. He's gone. We're still here. We'll fly against Zeros tomorrow. What the hell. Who do you think we'll get as a replacement?"

"Some kid just like you."

Atkins barked a laugh at that. "So long as he's just like me that might not be so bad. You'll see. I'm destined for greatness myself."

"Sure you are, Slim."

"Let's go get something to eat."

"Christ. You can eat at a time like this?"

"I've had three meals in this godforsaken place so far. They were all the same, horrible, horrible and more horrible. Eating food that bad is an act of penance, pal. Damn right I can eat at a time like this."

"OK, then, you've got the lead."

"I like that. You just remember it, Jimmy me boy."

"Yeah. Don't get used to it."

They laughed and walked out of the tent.

The next morning Jimmy and Slim sat cockpit alert, which meant they were sweating in their seats, ready to start engines on the word that Japanese bombers were approaching. Two other P-39s had taken off at dawn to try and stagger to twenty thousand feet. It didn't do much good to scramble P-39s to intercept Jap bombers flying five thousand feet higher than the airplane might reasonably be expected to fly, but neither of them questioned it. You had to try and besides, they might pick up a few stragglers if the Zeros didn't collect their scalps first.

Terraine was sitting with a field telephone, which rang. The crew chief jumped and picked up the phone, held it to his ear and leaped to his feet almost at once, holding his hand and index finger up, making a circling motion with his index finger and shouting "SCRAMBLE! SCRAMBLE!" at the top of his lungs.

Jimmy cinched his seat harness down and began flicking switches. The Allison belched and ground and spat and delivered power to the propeller. Air blasted back over him and he closed the cockpit door. He pressed the TRANS button on his radio.

"Seven Mile Tower this is Boxcar Red Leader, flight of two, responding to scramble call."

"Boxcar Red Leader, cleared to taxi to the active, cleared for immediate takeoff. No friendly traffic in the pattern."

"Affirmative, Seven Mile."

They turned onto the runway. Jimmy looked back at Slim, who flashed him a thumbs-up. Jimmy pushed forward smoothly on his throttle and they accelerated down the runway until they were at 100 mph, when they lifted off, sucked up the gear and the flaps, and turned south. At once they armed and tested their guns and put their heads on a swivel. The Zeros could easily come down on the deck for a bit of fun, before or after the Betty or Nell bombers released their bomb loads. Or the Japs could have sent ahead an advance party of Zeros to suppress the field's antiaircraft defenses. A wise pilot kept his eyes open and tried to grow another pair in the back of his head.

They headed west about ten miles and climbed to seven thousand feet.

"Tallyho," Jimmy called over the radio. Four miles at least above them he could see the contrails of the Jap bombers. "Seven Mile from Boxcar Red Leader, incoming raid, I count at least twenty airplane."

"Roger, Boxcar Red Leader, understand twenty bandits inbound, thanks for the heads up."

"Hey, Jimmy."

"Yeah, Slim."

"Look out there about two o'clock level. Bogies, kind of hard to spot against the mountains. Moving towards three o'clock now."

"Okay, Two, you take the lead."

"Roger, Two has the lead, turning right now."

Jimmy swung into the wing position on Slim, picking up his scan of the tail and right hand sectors. By the time Jimmy picked up the bogies, which were probably Zeros headed for a low-level strafe of Seven-Mile or Port Moresby harbor, they might vanish. If Slim had a visual on the enemy, it made sense to switch off lead and wing positions.

In a moment Jimmy picked up a half-dozen gray and green shapes. The green was a lighter tone than the olive-drab paint scheme on their P-39s. Then the red meatballs on the fuselage jumped out at them.

Three Zeros peeled off from the formation in graceful climbing turns to the right.

"Two, they see us. You take the guy on the left, I'll take the guy in the center."

"Roger, Lead, I've got the left."

Jimmy watched the Zeros closing on them as well as the flight of three on a heading for Seven-Mile. Above them the Jap bombers turned east, which meant bombs they couldn't see yet were falling towards their targets.

"Seven-Mile from Boxcar Red Leader, engaging Zeros eight miles west of the field, repeat, engaging Zeros eight miles west of the field. Flight of three headed your way."

Seven-Mile said something but Jimmy was concentrating on the approaching Zeros.

Slim kept his attitude straight and level but both of them were at full throttle and accelerating. Jimmy knew what he would do, wait to the last moment and pull up into the Zeros diving on them. That would give them the most speed at the moment of firing. Slim pulled up into the diving Zeros, Jimmy with him almost as if it were the same hand on both sets of controls. The center Zero's wings filled Jimmy's gun sight and he and the Zero fired at the same time.

Jimmy hit the cannon switch as the roar of the .50s and the smell of burnt powder filled the cockpit. Jesus, this Zero was coming right down his throat, yellow winking flame at the cowling and the wings, and something starred his canopy at the moment one of his cannon shells hit the Zero, which promptly exploded right in front of him, so close Jimmy had to fly through the flame and debris. Something smacked into his right wing and his P-39 slewed wildly to the right and began to shudder. Then he was through the smoke and turned left, looking left for Slim and then right to see what the other Zeros were doing. Slim was already in a turn after the Zero, which was turning as well. Another Zero turned away to the north, smoking and out of the fight.

The trick with a Zero in a turn is to keep your speed up, Jimmy reminded himself, but Slim had his nose down with the P-39 reefed in tight, maybe a little too tight, holding it right on the knife-edge of an accelerated stall. The Zero abruptly rolled in the opposite direction, and that put him right in front of Jimmy, who gave him a burst as he went by. The

Zero sped off toward Seven-Mile with Jimmy and Slim in pursuit.

"Hey, pal, I saw him first," Slim called over the radio.

"Then get your ass up here," Jimmy called back. "He's headed for his friends."

The three Zeros were almost over Seven-Mile when they executed a beautiful formation turn, looking for all the world like a trained aerobatic team.

"Slim, stay with me," Jimmy radioed. "I've got the lead."

The lone Zero pulled up into an Immelmann, plainly intending to either make another run at the P-39s or get behind them to catch them between himself and the three onrushing Zeros. They could deal with that guy later, if they were lucky. Jimmy bored on towards the three incoming Zeros. He looked over his shoulder at Atkins. Slim was right with him but Jimmy saw him look back at the Zero, who was hanging on his prop as they passed underneath him.

"Spread out a bit, Two," said Jimmy. "We'll spray those bastards and hope for the best."

On the field at Seven-Mile the puffs of exploding bombs walked down the runway and the taxiways. There was a flash of a secondary explosion, then another, and then Jimmy didn't have time to worry about anything but the Zeros right in front of him.

Tracers, tracers everywhere, and his airplane still shuddering and bucking from the damn big dent in the leading edge of the left wing. His guns rumbled and barked and he walked his rudder in gentle nudges left and right, the pipper on the gunsight traveling over the two Zeros on the right as Gerry took the Zero on the left. Jimmy thought he saw pieces fly off one of the Zeros and then there was a *WHAM!* His P-39 staggered, wobbled, a Zero danced through the gunsight as he triggered his guns, and this time he was certain, the Zero was hit, hits sparked and sparkled across the cowling and front fuselage and windscreen and then *WHAM! WHAM!* as he was hit again by Jap 20-mm cannon. Then they were through the Jap formation. He looked to the left and Slim was still there. Jimmy looked behind him, pulling up a bit, but the Japs kept going. One of the Zeros on the left trailed smoke. The Zero who had pulled up into the Immelmann reefed it into a tight turn and flew after his mates.

Jimmy ran an eye over his engine instruments. Everything looked OK but the airplane was rattling and shaking and he could see a big hole in his left wing and another one on the left wingtip. The aileron on that side was shredded. The stick felt a slack in roll.

"Lead from Two, you OK, Jimmy? You got a couple of hellacious big holes in your left wing."

"She's still flying. Let's go home."

Jimmy and Slim taxied back to their revetments and shut down, breathing a sigh of relief as the propellers kicked to a stop and quiet descended. Terraine climbed up on the wing and opened Jimmy's cockpit door.

"Jesus, Jimmy," he said. "What the hell did you do to my airplane?"

"Aw, Don, it was those goddam Japs. They brought bigger rocks to throw at us today."

"No shit."

"But I got one."

Terraine's face broke into a huge grin. "You got one?"

"Blew him to bits with the cannon."

"Now that's worth the work to patch the *Gremlin* up. OK, you can play rough as long as you bring us back a scalp."

"That's a deal."

Terraine helped Jimmy out of the seat harness and the parachute. As he did Wolchek and Davis drove up in a jeep.

"Something blew the hell up out there," said Wolchek. "What happened, Ardana?"

Jimmy held his fist up and raised his index finger.

Wolchek smiled. "Good work. Hop in, we'll give you a ride to the Ops shack."

Slim got in back with Ardana and punched him on the shoulder. "Don't go getting a swelled head on me, mate, just because you're two Japs away from being an ace."

"You got bits fly off two of the bastards. It's probably the only reason they kept going. Probably saved us both."

Atkins grinned. "Hey, a half-Jap here, a couple of damages there, it all adds up."

"It adds up to you better practice your gunnery, both of you," Davis called over his shoulder as he drove. "How 'bout it, Steve? You reckon we can set up some targets somewhere for these guys to shoot at?"

"Sure, why not? You've got what, about two seconds to get enough hits to really hurt those bastards. Seconds count."

Jimmy thought about that. Two seconds. The Browning M2 .50-caliber gun in the nose of the P-39 fired about 550 rounds per minute, the .30-caliber Brownings in the wing fired at about 600. In two seconds that was twenty rounds per gun, or about 120 projectiles flying down range at a target. But you had to be in close for the .30s to make a difference.

Two seconds.

It wasn't a hell of a lot of time when someone was shooting back at you.

Jimmy thought about the hits on his wing. A little bit to one side and two seconds could be eternity.

Then they were at the Ops shack and told it all to the intelligence officer, who told them that the combat had been witnessed from all over the field. No trouble, then, confirming Jimmy's third kill.

After about an hour of talk and cigarettes and a couple of shots of Davis' horrible whisky Jimmy found himself walking down the trail towards the *Gremlin*'s revetment. Terraine and the ground crew had the panels off the left wing and were looking at the main spar, checking it for damage.

"How does it look, Don?" Jimmy asked.

"You were lucky, sir," Terraine said, running his fingers along the aluminum spar. "The Japs seem to fuse their cannon shells for impact, which tears hell out of the sheet metal and not much else. Most of this I think we can bend a few patches on and she should be flying by tomorrow morning."

"OK. Thanks, Don."

"Anytime," Terraine said, smiling. He turned back to the jagged blackened sheet metal on the leading edge of the Gremlin's wing.

Jimmy turned away and walked past the line of revetments almost to the runway. Crews were busily shoveling dirt and rocks into the bomb craters. Dodging bomb craters during the landing had been fun. In a couple of hours, though, Seven-Mile would be as good as it ever had been, which wasn't very.

The sun was going down in the west. Ardana leaned against the tree and watched the red sun throw its rays across the sky and change the colors of the towering tropical cumulus clouds.

He thought about the Jap pilot in the plane he shot down. It all happened so fast he hadn't even seen the enemy, not so much as a leather-helmeted head peering through a gunsight, only the winking machine guns in the cowling and the silver blur of the Zero's propeller. And then his cannon shell hit and there was nothing but fire and fiery bits and smoke. He was lucky the Zero's radial engine had missed him, or even the body of the pilot. Jimmy didn't think hitting a one-hundred-thirty pound Jap airman would do the *Gremlin* any good.

In the west the red sun threw out red arms and turned the cumulus clouds crimson. Somewhere an engine ran up, then another, and in the distance there was the mutter of thunder. It was going to rain soon, but it was always going to rain soon at Seven-Mile.

Two weeks ago today, he thought, Gerry Bellmon and Danny Evans and I landed at Seven-Mile Drome with Captain Davis in S-for-Sugar. Now Jack's an ace, Evans is in the hospital and Gerry is missing in action. I'm flying with some new guy, but all that means is that I'm getting to be an old sweat. I've been rained on, bombed, strafed, gotten sunburned all to hell, eaten horrible food and gotten the shits from bad water. I've even talked to some native witch doctor. And what the hell does that mean, "Yupela bilip ensel?" I've flown to Rabaul with some of the craziest bastards that ever got off the ground, and that has to include the craziest bastards that ever lived.

Jimmy shook his head. In another two months he'd be twenty-two years old. It was going to be a long couple of months.

Chapter Thirteen

"Remember"

Next afternoon Jimmy got letters from home.

The Boxcars spent the morning trying to intercept Jap air raids. First it was a bad radar sighting. The heat and humidity of the tropics did strange things to electronics and that sometimes meant seeing airplanes that weren't really there to be seen. Then just as they got refueled the air raid siren went off and they ran to their airplanes. This time it was the real thing, and some freak of atmospherics allowed detection a few minutes earlier than normal, so that the P-39s had time to stagger up to around 18,000 feet before someone called "Tallyho!" on the Japs. But the Jap bombers were at 23,000 feet and their Zero escort was already diving on the Boxcar P-39s. Then it was ten minutes of pure unadulterated fun in which the P-39s, staggering along at the limit of their performance envelope, learned once again that the one advantage they had over the Zeros was that no

Zero could catch a P-39 in a dive. The Zeros knew that too and when they had chased the P-39s down to ten thousand feet they pulled up and climbed away. Jimmy could have sworn he heard them laughing like hell while they climbed back up to altitude and followed their bombers home.

Jimmy taxied into revetment, turned around in response to the hand-signals of Sgt. Terraine, and shut the engine down. Terraine climbed up on the wing as Jimmy opened the door.

"How'd it go today, Jimmy?"

"Oh, just peachy, Don. Once again we proved that gravity is our best friend."

"Ran like hell from the Japs, huh?"

"Amen, brother."

Terraine laughed and helped Jimmy unbuckle himself from his seat harness. "I hear we got mail," he said.

"Mail? What's that?"

"Well, when I get it, it's little flimsy paper envelopes with little flimsy papers in it. With writing, you know. From people back in the real world."

"Real world, Don? Real world? This jungle isn't real enough for you?"

"Oh, it's plenty real enough. It just isn't Rome, Georgia, on a summer afternoon, sir, you know what I mean?"

"Rome, Georgia? That's where you're from?"

"Never heard of it, have you? Not surprising, even if it is the biggest little city north of Atlanta."

"Georgia? I'm a Montana boy. Anything east of the Mississippi is unknown territory to me."

"Don't worry, sir. Maybe someday we'll get you educated."

Jimmy laughed and got down from the airplane. After a few minutes of looking over the airplane he went up towards the Ops shack. The orderly on duty handed him his mail, three envelopes postmarked Choteau, Montana.

The first one he opened was from his mother.

Dearest Jimmy, he read.

He thought of the kitchen table where his mother wrote all her letters and correspondence, of his mother in her apron next to the electric stove that replaced the wood stove he remembered growing up. He kind of thought he liked the wood stove better, at least in wintertime with the snow banked up to the window sash.

Dearest Jimmy,

Your Uncle Matt was kind enough to stop by on his way out to "Somewhere In the Pacific" and said he'd keep an eye out for you. Don't know if he managed that, but he's a resourceful man and congressmen can be persuasive. He asked if I wanted to deliver you any special message but I told him I'd write you a letter. I remember when your father was in France in the last war he liked letters from home.

Jimmy, you are a man grown and you have to make your own way in the world. I know you've been crazy about airplanes since you were little and I wasn't surprised when you went into the Air Corps. I think it's the work you are supposed to do. But don't be surprised if I have a few moments where I get weak and wish you were right here where I could watch over you. I know that's wrong. It isn't that we live a safe life here. There's stampedes and loco broncs and even the occasional rustler, not to mention rattlesnakes and mountain lions. And I'll even say I'm not completely happy about your father being sheriff.

But with all of that I wish I could tell you in words the look in your father's eyes when he was talking to Matt. He was afraid for you, I could tell from the questions he asked Matt. He asked Matt if that fool kid of his had managed to stick his head in a meat grinder. Matt hesitated and that told your father almost everything. He's been a sheriff too long not to read people like a book. And I can read your father so I knew also. Matt thinks you are in terrible danger. But what he told us was that out there in the Pacific some of the bravest young men in a nation of brave young men are fighting a hard and difficult battle. He did not say the issue was in doubt. He did not say you did not have what you needed to fight. What he did say was that our boys in the Pacific were fighting as hard as they could with what they had. That told us everything important about what you and your friends are doing.

I am so proud of you and so frightened for you, but I am an American too, my son. I know there is no choice but to fight. Sometimes I see your father watching the sun set, and I know he is thinking of you from the way his eyes go bleak and hard, and the way his hand drops to his pistol belt. Your father is a fighting man, like his father before him. He understands something about what you are going through. And I know he is proud of you and afraid for you as well.

A lot of the mothers have blue stars in their windows now, and there are two who have gold stars. You remember Eddie Kambach and Joey Dahlgren? Eddie was killed in action on a destroyer in the North Atlantic and Joey was a gunner in the 22nd Bomb Group, who are Somewhere Out There with you. Maybe you could find out something about Joey. I know Mrs. Dahlgren — both of them, the wife and the mother — would appreciate it. All they got was a telegram from the War Department. Use your own best judgment about it.

This will probably be enough to write for now. All the family sends their love and best wishes. Write whenever you can.

All the best,

Mom

Jimmy folded the letter and put it into the pocket of his flight suit. He had gone to read the letter under the shade of a large tree. Now he leaned back and let himself remember home. It had been awhile since he did that, really not since that first day here, when the heat had surprised him. It still surprised him, and this was winter south of the equator. He understood from the Aussies at the weather station that yes, it was quite hot for early June, but he was to wait for December to see real heat. Some of that he put down to the habit of old hands running a job on the new boy but he wouldn't be surprised if this really was the coolest time of the year. It got hot in Montana too during the daytime but almost always at night it cooled off to the point of needing a jacket, especially if the wind kicked up.

Hot days and cool nights. Here at Seven-Mile the nights were hot and the days were hotter. Even when it rained, it was hot.

He opened the next letter. It was from his Gramma Susan.

Dear Jimmy,

Hope this finds you well. You've heard from your Ma how everyone's doing well at home so I won't bother to add anything to that.

I was down to the church a few days ago to have a talk with your grandpa. I know you young folks don't take much stock in things like that but he was in my life a powerful long time and the truth is when I sit by his headstone and just talk like he was sitting next to me I can still feel him. Sometimes I even know what he'd say back to me, and this was one of those times. I told him about you being out there in the Pacific Ocean, and how you were flying airplanes like you always wanted. That you were in a shooting war worse than the last one over there in France which was pretty damned bad, you know.

Now you remember how your grandpa would sit and listen, and when a body was done talking he'd be quiet for awhile, thinking. So there I was sitting next to his headstone and my, it was a pretty day even for Montana, nice and warm, with the flowers blooming on the graves and a car going by on the old road every now and then. And I near about jumped out of my skin when I heard your grandpa talk like he was sitting next to me.

"That boy's got good instincts," he said. "You tell him to listen to them. I always did. And I don't know much about airplanes, but gunfightin' is gunfightin'. He'll just have to figure out what it means flyin' around up there amongst the clouds instead of in a street or out in the woods somewheres."

Now if you want to say this is just your grandma's way of giving you advice, that's fine with me. I reckon I'm getting a little old myself, and maybe I'm not altogether here anymore. But it sounded like powerful fine advice to me, so I send it along for what it might be worth to you. We both know your grandpa was a gunfightin' man.

One more thing. I don't know if you remember Laura Sue Gibbons? She's a year or so younger than you. Your ma and I ran into her on the street in town yesterday and she asked about you. Said she and some girlfriends of hers were getting up a circle to write to all the local boys in the service. Your ma gave her your address, so if you get a letter from her you might want to answer back. You young men want good looks in a woman. Laura Sue may not be one of those movie stars but pretty enough, and she struck me as plenty smart and a good worker. Ten years from now this war will be over and you'll want someone like Laura Sue to come home to. Now I'm not trying to start anything, just butting in where I got no business being but you know that's a grandma's prerogative.

I love you, Jimmy, and you take care of yourself out there. I know you'll drink and smoke and go with wild fancy women because that's the way of things with young men in a war. You just do your duty and come home in one piece. We're fairly tough folks up here. We'll straighten you out. I just hope I live long enough to see you home safe.

Best as always,

Susan Baumer Ardana

Yep, thought Jimmy, that was his grandma. Always signed her full name like she was signing a deed or something.

Laura Sue Gibbons, now who the hell was she? He thought about it for a moment and vaguely remembered a tow-headed girl, kind of stocky, maybe, or maybe just not all grown up. But she did have a sweet smile and pretty green eyes. He did remember that because she had smiled at him once in a way that made him feel a little funny inside.

Jimmy put his grandmother's letter down. Laura Sue Gibbons. Now what was it about a name that could make it sound like a promise for the future? He shook his head. He was a pursuit pilot in New Guinea and the only future he could see was maybe this afternoon or tomorrow morning. If he lived through enough of those maybe his grandmother's "ten years from now the war will be over" might make sense.

He opened the third letter.

Dear Jimmy,

Hello from Choteau, Montana! I sure hope you remember me, Laura Sue Gibbons. I was a year behind you in high school.

Now don't get too stuck on yourself because some young kid from home you probably don't even remember is writing you out of the blue like this. I'm taking classes at the State college in the evenings and daytimes I'm working in the soda shop on High Street next to Mr. Swanton's hardware store. Anyway, some of my classmates dropped into the soda shop and we were talking about the war and all the boys we knew who were in the service or were already overseas, like you. In fact I saw your Uncle Kurt at the airport the other day and he told me you were somewhere in the Southwest Pacific with the Air Corps, so I told the girls about that. We decided then and there we'd find out all the boys from around Choteau or from Teton County who were in the service and write to them. Just friendly stuff, you know, the local gossip, any bits of news about friends, or changes in town, things like that so that when you get home things won't have changed without you knowing about it.

So since I remembered you I decided to make you my first serviceman to write to. I ran across your Ma and Granny Ardana downtown a few days ago and they gave me your address. Not much of an address! "Lt. James T. Ardana, FEAF Replacement Depot, APO San Francisco." How the Army figures out how to get your mail to you from that is beyond me, and maybe that's a good thing.

There are only a few boys from your class at school still in town. There's Arnold Geiser, but he can't join up because he lost a foot in that accident when he was little. Willy Holborn is still here but only because he's got orders to report to Pensacola next month for flight training in the Navy. Maybe you two can compare notes someday! Bobby Willis had TB when he was young and they wouldn't take him. The boys who turned 18 this summer mostly volunteered already and didn't wait to be drafted. They're going all over the place, some to the Marines, some to the Army and some to the Navy, even a few to the Air Corps like you.

Now a little about me. Like I wrote above I'm taking evening classes. It's an extension arrangement with the State College. We use the high school and they send instructors around. Right now I'm taking freshman courses, math and chemistry and English. I think maybe I'd like to be a doctor but I'll probably end up being a nurse. Our chemistry teacher is a funny little wisp of a guy named Schonthal and he says that the Army may start taking girls and training them to be nurses. I'm not so sure I'd like to go away from home but it might be exciting at that! Daytime I work in the soda shop which is mostly the girls and some of the younger boys. The boys who are sixteen or seventeen only talk about being old enough to join up soon. They get this funny little glow in their eyes when they talk about it.

Me, I'm not so sure. Maybe I shouldn't write you this since you're in the middle of things I can't even imagine, things you can't learn from books or listening to your folks or your grandparents talk. But I can't see fighting and killing as such a great adventure. I can understand doing your duty, and fighting to protect us here at home. You know, that's one reason we figured we'd write our boys, to let them know we understood that, and how much we appreciate it. But I don't think you're having an adventure.

What do you think?

Well, that's enough to write for now. Jimmy, we all want all of you safe and sound and back home in one piece. Write me back whenever you can and I'll write as soon as I get your letter.

With warm regards from home,

Laura Sue

Jimmy put the letter down and looked around the hut.

It was just a little two-page letter from a girl he hardly remembered except for her eyes and her smile. But somehow he could see the Montana hills and the street where she worked in the soda shop a little clearer in his mind's eye now.

How long had he been in New Guinea? Two weeks? Only two weeks but that was a lifetime. He was still alive and how many guys had he seen come and go in a matter of days or even hours?

Adventure? Jesus! Laura Sue at least sounded like she had a head on her shoulders. Flying P-39s against the Jap Zeros was exciting as hell but Jimmy was damned if he'd call it an adventure.

Captain Davis came and sat down beside Jimmy. "Get any mail?" he asked.

"Letter from my mother."

"How are things back home?"

"Oh, about the same." Jimmy would have died before revealing his mother's words of pride. Not to Jack Davis with six Jap flags painted on the side of his P-39.

Davis looked at him. "Yeah?"

"She said something about gold star mothers in town. One of them was a guy who was a gunner with the 22nd. She wondered if I could find out something about how he died."

"Sweet Jehosophat. Why do they always want to know how they died?" Davis shook his head. "Was it quick? Did he feel any pain? Was he afraid? Did he say anything about me before he died? Did his friends think he was a good man? Was he brave? How many Japs did he kill before he went down?"

"Mostly it seems to be pretty quick, at least," Jimmy said quietly. He didn't like the look in Davis' eye. It seemed to focus on something far off.

"Who knows how quick it feels to burn to death, even if it's only a minute or two in the fire?" Davis stood up. "Steve Wolchek heard from the hospital. They think Danny Evans has malaria as well as dengue, so they're sending him to Australia to recuperate. We're getting a new guy with kind of a weird name. You mind if we put him in with you and Slim?"

"Hell, no. How weird is his name?"

"Harley Holly."

"Harley? Like the motorcycle?"

"Yep."

Jimmy shrugged. "He couldn't be any worse than Danny Evans."

"The devil you know, Jimmy my boy, the devil you know."

Chapter Fourteen

"All these missions aren't that bad, are they?"

The Boxcars came down from the pass in the Owen Stanley Mountains southeast of Salamaua, hugging the treetops. To the north the Rattlers were at ten thousand feet, headed towards Lae. The Rattlers had no intention of going quite that far. They were a diversion for the Boxcars, who were going to make one pass down the new runway at Salamaua and then run like hell for home.

Boxcar Red Flight was in the lead. Harley Holly flew as Red Four on Jimmy's wing. It was Harley's first combat mission and he had only been with the squadron for two days.

"Take him up and see what he's got," Davis told Jimmy when Harley Holly reported in.

"Yes, sir," Jimmy replied and looked over at Holly somewhat dubiously.

Harley had smiled at Jimmy. He wore a painfully new flight suit with shiny new boots, even if the effect was somewhat ruined by the growing circles of sweat under his armpits. In fact Harley Holly was just too shiny and new to be quite believable.

"I was never that young," Jimmy whispered, to himself, or so he thought.

"You're right, Jimmy. You were younger," said Captain Davis, giving him a friendly punch in the shoulder. "Now go fly with the new guy."

Harley made all the new-guy mistakes, ragged on the turns, snugging in too tight when he should have been loose, but his basic flying skills were there and he made a passable takeoff and landing on the bumpy bomb-pocked airstrip. He even managed to hit some of the targets the Aussies had laid out for them on the reef off Daugo Island. And the kid even managed to be excited about it when they walked back to the Ops shack afterwards, at least until he saw that Jimmy wasn't at all excited.

Jimmy smiled to himself as Harley tried to walk down the dirt path away from the revetments with a look of bored indifference on his face, just as if he weren't jumping for joy on the inside that he was actually in *New Guinea* and actually *flying pursuits* and he was going to go into *combat soon* and all that happy crappy comic book stuff. "G-8 and his Flying Aces," Jimmy thought, the smile turning sour on his face. He turned to face Harley, to tell him this wasn't a fucking comic book, that some things that became a part of you and became precious, part of some kind of steel forged inside your mind weren't all fun and games. He looked at Harley's face and thought, what's the point? Whatever I can tell him will just be words. The first time someone tries to kill good old Harley and doesn't quit trying he'll figure it out for himself.

Right now Harley was in good formation off Jimmy's wing and Salamaua was dead ahead. The four Boxcar White P-39s were off to the left thirty seconds behind them, Boxcar Yellow to the right by about a minute. The idea was to hit from different directions in the hope of throwing off the Jap AA fire. It might even work.

"Boxcars from Boxcar Red Leader, check your panels," said Davis, who was leading the mission today.

Jimmy armed his guns and checked that his bomb release was active. Then there was the little harbor at Salamaua and the narrow isthmus to the island just offshore and the airstrip appeared over the nose. Little red balls of tracer climbed up from the AAA and there were three Zeros turning onto the field, getting ready to take off. Three more were halfway down the runway. There was a line of revetments with Zeros in them parked along the tree line with little ant figures running towards the Zeros. Then the Boxcars flashed over the trees at the perimeter of the airfield and Jimmy dropped his bomb on the runway, almost at once triggering his wing guns as a half-dozen running Japs swept across his gunsight. He looked over his shoulder at the Zeros on the runway just as their bombs exploded. One of the Zeros was tossed into the air like a paper toy by the blast but the other two sped down the strip, accelerating to flying speed.

"Boxcar White Leader, you got two Zeros lifting off Salamaua and three more in the air."

"Roger that, Red Leader."

The Zeros at the far end of the field were climbing, sucking up gear and flaps, breaking hard to the right in front of Jimmy and Holly.

"Red Four, stay with me," Jimmy called. He kicked up and over, inverted, bleeding speed in the climb with the Zeros below him still in their turn, pulling ahead of the Zeros. They were low and would only be in his gun sight for a second or two. He started firing at the Zeros, watching the tracers go out in front of the lead Jap. As they crossed his field of fire he triggered the cannon. *PUNK!PUNK!PUNK!* Three rounds and the goddamn piece of shit cannon jammed, but the lead Zero flew through the stream of tracers from Jimmy's wing and nose guns. Hits sparkled along the fuselage and canopy but the Zero kept flying. He looked over his shoulder. Davis and Slim Atkins had followed just behind Jimmy and were shooting at the Zeros too. For a moment their tracers crawled all over the Japs, who came out of their turn and went for the deck.

They ran into White Flight, who had dropped their bombs at the south end of the field. Tracers from the Zeros and the P-39s crossed each other. Smoke streamed suddenly from Boxcar White Leader, but two Zeros rolled over and exploded in the jungle east of the field. The other turned north out over the ocean with White Three and Four after him.

Jimmy pulled back on the stick and the horizon rose as he rolled upright. He looked to the right and there was Harley, in good position. Jimmy looked back and the Zero that skidded off the runway had ground-looped and ended up on its nose, tail pointed to the sky.

"Boxcar Red Leader to Red Three, let's get out of here."

"Roger, Leader."

Jack and Atkins were off to the left, pulling hard to the left to egress the target to the west as briefed. Jimmy and Holly finished their turn to the right to follow them. A stream of Jap tracer hosed up at Jimmy from the end of the airfield and he banked hard to the left, looking over his shoulder just in time to see a 50-mm cannon shell from the Jap AAA explode under Harley's right wing, flipping his P-39 over on its back. They were less than a hundred feet in the air. Harley kept rolling until he was upright and level.

"Red Four, you doing OK back there?" Jimmy called.

"The engine is good but she's a pig to handle, Three," Holly replied with the breathy nonchalance of heavy adrenaline load.

"OK. Move into the lead, Red Four, I've got your tail." Jimmy moved to cover his wingman as more 50-mm shells exploded around them. Shrapnel pinged and rattled somewhere along the *Gremlin's* fuselage. Jimmy scanned to the rear and saw the Jap Zero that got off the ground turning into the second wave of attackers, flying through his own flak to get at the P-39s.

"Red Three from Red Leader, come in, Jimmy."

"Red Three, go ahead, Lead."

"How's Four?"

"Got a hell of a hole in the right wing. Shrapnel all over the fuselage."

"OK. You guys beat it for home. Boxcar White Leader from Red Leader, how you doing, Ed?"

"Oil pressure's dropping, Red Leader. I'm going to head for that Aussie strip at Wau."

"Roger, White Leader. Red Two and I will stay over the target for a few minutes. Yellow Leader, Yellow Leader, this is Red Leader, do you copy?"

"Roger, Red Leader, we're making our run now."

"Got you, Yellow Leader."

"Red Leader, this is Red Three, Three and Four headed for the barn."

"Roger, Three, what the hell's keeping you?"

The foothills of the Owen Stanley Range leading up to the pass they had threaded their way through were only twenty miles from the coast. Jimmy looked ahead at the mountains where towering tropical clouds were building already as the sun struck the moisture-laden jungle below.

"Red Four from Three, say your fuel."

"Ahhh…Four has about 60 gallons, Three."

Jimmy thought quickly. He'd prefer to climb over the mountains but that would take a lot of fuel. In theory Harley's P-39 should be able to make it back to Seven-Mile with what he had, but that theory assumed an airplane without the parasitic drag of a cannon hole in one wing. Climbing with that amount of combat damage would consume more fuel than usual anyway, since the damaged wing didn't create the lift of a normal wing.

Jimmy looked at the mountains to the south. They'd have to climb to at least seven thousand feet to clear them here, then they'd be on the downslope with Seven-Mile to the east. One hundred sixty miles or less to get home.

At best it seemed likely that Red Four would be running on fumes when they made it to Seven-Mile. But running through the mountain passes with thunderstorms brewing all around and above them didn't seem like a good bet either. The Aussies had little strips at Wau and Kokoda where there had been gold mines before the war, but Jimmy was less sure than White Leader where they were, and the map he had showed the coast in some detail but not much of the interior. They had been warned that map locations could be off by as much as ten or fifteen miles.

All in all it looked as if the best option were to get through the pass as quickly as they could and keep rolling the dice. "Okay, Four, I'm going to form up on you but I'll do the navigation. For now, see that dark spot in between those two hills dead ahead?"

"Got the dark spot, Three."

"That's the entrance to the pass."

"Ahhh…looks kind of gloomy in there, Three."

"Yeah. What do you figure your fuel consumption will be, in a climb with that damaged wing?"

There was silence for a moment. "I guess the pass is OK with me, Boss."

They flew on in silence, passing between the hills and throttling back to best cruise speed as the clouds closed in behind and above them. Fuel consumption was now a more present danger than wandering Zero patrols.

They leveled off at seven thousand feet, setting their throttles at 2200 RPM. They were below the bottom of the clouds and above the surrounding mountains, droning on between the walls of the pass. For the next fifteen minutes they crawled along the pass as the ceiling lowered. Once lightning cracked off to their right. Turbulence rocked their airplanes, sometimes violently, and once they hit a downdraft that took them nearly to the tops of the jungle canopy below them before it let them go. Finally the ceiling lifted and their altimeters confirmed what their eyes told them, they were past the high point of the mountain range which trended down to the Coral Sea and Port Moresby to the east of them. The towering cumulus fell behind them, still building, promising vicious thunderstorms later in the day.

"OK, Four, that part is over. Turn to 100. Keep your eyes peeled for Japs."

"Affirmative, Three."

Jimmy looked around. There was a lot of cloud around, so it took him a minute to spot the now-familiar outline of Port Moresby's harbor at about ten o'clock, right where he hoped it would be. He breathed a sigh of relief. In the gloom under the clouds all that goddamn green rolling jungle looked the same to him. The sun was high overhead and began to heat his cockpit. They were nearly home, but he kept his neck on a swivel and changed his altitude and heading every so often as they approached the aerodrome. People had been shot down in the landing pattern before, after all.

"Four from Red Three, say your fuel."

"I've got 30 gallons, Three."

Jimmy nodded to himself. There was the aerodrome coming into sight over the nose, there was the patrol of P-39s just over the field and...

Shit! Those were *not* P-39s!

"Seven-Mile from Boxcar Red Three, do you have Zeros overhead, over?"

"Boxcar Red Three from Seven-Mile, that's affirmative. Six of the bastards showed up ten minutes ago. They've been beating up the field ever since."

Jimmy thought furiously. Gerry had about thirty minutes of fuel left, less if they had to fight. The Zeros could stay a lot longer than that and had been known to do so. Even as he watched something began burning and throwing up a column of smoke on the airfield. He looked at his own fuel gauge; he had about 35 gallons. Not a hell of a lot for a dogfight but he'd be right over his own field, after all, and fighting at the low end of his weight envelope.

The P-39's center of gravity envelope was one of the squirrely things about the airplane. The P-39 gave no warning whatsoever of entering a stall, and in an accelerated stall could turn inside out and even a really hot pilot like himself might find recovery difficult. Besides, dogfighting at treetop level was not the place to enter a stall of any sort. And there was Harley to consider. Damaged and low on fuel, he'd be meat on the table if the Zeros found them. Even if he managed to survive the fight by bailing out, guys had been known to go in with good chutes five miles off the end of the airstrip, which was full triple-canopy jungle, and never be found regardless of the search effort expended. If they turned towards the airfield the Zeros would spot them; if they climbed, Harley would run out of fuel that much sooner; if they stooged around out here over the jungle, waiting for the Japs to leave, Harley would run out of fuel in 30 minutes.

Jimmy sighed and keyed his mike. "Four from Three, get back on my wing but don't worry about staying too close. We're going to get you in at Seven-Mile."

"Ah, OK, Three, but those little yellow bastards might enjoy that."

"Yeah. Just follow me. We'll use the clouds for cover. When I tell you, put everything forward and run for the field. Put your ship down any way you can and when she stops moving get the hell out and run for the trees before those bastards can machine-gun you. Got it?"

"Yeah. What will you be doing?"

"That's my problem. Yours is putting the airplane down, in one piece if you can, but save your ass if you can't."

"OK, Three."

Jimmy moved into the lead and was glad to see Harley searching the sky. The kid was alert, at least. Maybe he'd see Zeros in time to yell a warning.

The Zeros were still beating up the field. One flight of three would orbit the field to one side, out of reach of the AAA fire that blackened the sky with bursting shells and ropes of tracer. The other flight of three would descend to strafe the airstrip and the airplanes parked there, their course easy enough to follow by the concentration of bursting AAA and converging tracers.

You had to hand it to the Japs, they had guts. The defenders of Seven-Mile were putting up a hell of a lot of flak and the Japs flew through it like it was a friggin' air show and they were flying a display routine. He watched them as the attacking unit flew down the airstrip and then pulled off. The other element of three peeled off from the main unit and went down to the attack. By the time they pulled off Jimmy and Harley were five miles away, heading perpendicular to the airstrip orientation, and when the Japs banked into the attack on the strip Jimmy turned hard to the right. He looked over his shoulder. Harley was falling slowly but perceptibly behind. A thin gray stream came out of his engine exhaust.

"Four, how you doing?"

"Oil pressure's dropping, Three."

"OK, just do as I said. Those guys will be pulling off, the rest will probably come for us."

Jimmy figured that the Japanese would see them any second, and ten seconds later the element peeling off for the attack on the airstrip maintained the heading that would take them towards the P-39s.

"OK, Four, showtime. See those guys coming towards us?"

"Roger, Three."

"I'm going to throttle back a little. Throw everything you've got at them, just hold the triggers down and hose the hell out of them. Once we're through them you put it on the runway like I told you. Hell, I might be right behind you."

"Roger, Three."

The Zeros grew closer. The three Zeros orbiting the field turned towards them. American AAA blossomed all around the Zeros but scored no apparent hits. Jimmy felt his mouth go dry. He started shooting short bursts at fairly long range. He tried the cannon but it was still jammed. As the range closed he steadied the ship, picked one Zero and centered the gun sight pipper on its cowling, firing all the time. Tracers streaked right by his windshield, something hit the prop which began to vibrate furiously, something else went right through the instrument panel and seared white-hot along his right ribs. The first bunch of Zeros flashed overhead and Jimmy knew without looking that they were turning tight to get on their tails if the next flight didn't finish them off. The *Gremlin*'s prop vibrated so badly Jimmy couldn't even see the instrument panel and the scream of the gearbox in the nose became a tortured howl. He throttled back and the vibration from the prop eased.

"Three, you got a lot of oil pouring out of your underside," Harley said.

"OK, then, I guess we're doing a formation landing," Jimmy replied.

Then the second set of Zeros was on them. This time Jimmy held his fire until they were close. The Gremlin was hit again. A series of ragged holes opened up in the left wing. Jimmy felt something poke his shoulder but didn't look to see what had happened. Then he was firing again, firing at one Jap while two or three others hosed him. This time he saw his tracers walk across the Jap's cowling and black smoke puffed out of the Zero's engine. Another Zero to his right puffed smoke.

"I hit him! I hit him!" Harley exulted over the radio.

The Zeros passed overhead and were past. Then there was the airstrip, just ahead, alive with the muzzle flash of AAA. Tracers from the American AAA weapons flashed past them.

"Let's put 'em down, Four," Jimmy called. He was a little fast but he brought the throttle to idle and fishtailed a couple of times, then dumped the flaps and the gear. Jimmy didn't need to see that first flight of Zeros, he could feel them with the skin and the fine hairs on the back of his neck. He rolled level out of the turn and landed hot, shut down the engine, looking over his shoulder to see Harley not fifty feet behind him, throwing up a rooster-tail of dust. With the engine shut down it was easy to hear the roar and thump of the AA guns all around the airstrip. He pushed the right brake and slewed off the runway just in time for a stream of machine-gun bullets and exploding cannon shells to streak past his wing. Then he hit a ditch, the nose gear collapsed and the *Gremlin* slewed around in a ground loop. Jimmy punched his harness release, hit the door release handle and ran across the wing towards the jungle as the second flight of Zeros roared over. Everywhere the boom and rattle of cannon and machine guns, the hiss of bullets, the flat rapping sound as bullets and shells smacked the earth, the howl of Zero engines and then he was inside the tree line. There was a bomb crater with trees collapsed over it. Jimmy dove in as the strafing continued.

Harley joined him in the crater. They kept their heads down because the air was full of shrapnel and ricochets and they did their best to dig deeper into the musty earth as the Zeros came over for another pass. Then the sound of Zero engines faded to the north. The AAA fire almost instantly began to diminish, first the machine guns, then the light cannon and then, after a few more rounds, the 75-mm guns stopped firing.

It took a minute for the silence to register. Then Jimmy looked over the edge of the crater. He could see the *Gremlin* from here, but she was a smoking wreck, as was Harley's ship.

"Jesus," Jimmy said reverently.

"Amen, brother," said Harley. "Hey, Ardana, all these missions aren't this bad, are they?"

"No," said Jimmy. "Some of them are worse."

"Did you know you were bleeding?"

Jimmy remembered being hit but it didn't seem that bad. He passed a hand over his ribs and when he did he noticed his shoulder stung.

"Just a nick," he said. "Jesus, my crew chief is going to be so pissed at me. He let me get away with messing up his baby last time because I brought back a kill. This time, hell, I don't even have a damage."

"You got that Zero on the runway at Salamaua," Harley pointed out. "And I know you got a piece of one just now. That looked like a hell of a lot of smoke to me. Bet he doesn't make it back."

Harley stood up and started brushing dirt off his uniform.

"Yep, and that's great for the war effort, but they don't count as kills. Hey, look," Jimmy said, pointing.

Overhead a flight of P-39s entered the break. It was the Boxcars by their markings, with Jack and Slim in the lead. The P-39s began to land, rolling out just past where Jimmy and Harley stood beside their smoldering airplanes.

"Come on," Jimmy said. "May as well start walking. Maybe we'll meet someone with a jeep."

Instead they were met by Terraine and a sergeant named Cobbins who was Harley's crew chief, driving a rusted old flatbed truck made from a Model A Ford with the body cut down.

"Jesus, Mr. Ardana, are you OK?" Terraine asked as he came to a halt beside them.

"I'm fine. It looks a lot worse than it is."

Terraine shook his head and smiled. "Bet my airplane is shot all to hell, then."

Jimmy hung his head and looked at Harley. "Told you he'd say that."

"Is she still on her wheels?"

"I'm afraid I put her in the ditch by the runway."

Terraine shook his head and muttered something that sounded suspiciously like "Pilots." Then he said, "Look here, Mr. Ardana, spare parts being scarce as they are ..."

"Go on, Don. Mr. Holly and I can make it up the hill."

"Thanks, sir." Terraine put the truck in gear and rushed down to the runway. Harley looked at Ardana as they started walking to the revetments and the squadron area.

"Let me get this straight," Harley said. "Stripping spare parts off a wreck is more important than taking fifteen minutes to give us a ride to the Ops shack?"

Ardana gestured, wincing a little at the twinge in his shoulder. "Look down there."

A jeep and another hybrid truck were racing Terraine and Cobbins to the wrecks. Terraine got there first. Before he skidded to a stop Cobbins had jumped out and stood on the wing of his airplane, brandishing a .45 automatic as he did. Terraine did the same thing. A hand waving, pistol-brandishing argument ensued. No shots were fired but it lasted for the three minutes it took Ardana and Holly to walk into the shade of some trees and sit down. It wasn't really any cooler in the shade but at least they were out of the sun. The Boxcars taxied past them on the way to their revetments. Davis and Atkins waved as they taxied by, until the dust from the prop wash got bad enough that they started walking again to get out of it.

Wolchek stood in the door of the Ops shack watching them. When they were in earshot he said, "Ardana, you've been hit. Are you OK?"

"Flesh wound, sir, really."

Wolchek poked his head inside the door and said something to the orderly on duty. Then he walked out to meet them.

"What the hell was that head-on pass?" he asked.

"Harley here was pretty well shot up over the target, Major, and down to about twenty minutes of fuel."

"Ah. I see. Not many choices left."

"Jesus, skipper, how crazy do you think I am?" Ardana asked.

"After that stunt with the 22nd? Pretty damned crazy."

"I'll bet," said Jimmy. "Maybe not today."

"Yeah. I sent for a medic. Looks like you got creased pretty good."

"Just a scratch, sir."

"By the way, that was pretty good flying, from what I saw on the ground. Looks like you got a piece of those bastards anyway. But you were lucky our own gunners didn't pot you. They seem to think anything with wings is a target."

"I noticed that," Ardana replied.

"Go on in and make your reports. I want to talk to Davis."

Jimmy and Harley had finished their combat reports by the time the rest of the pilots came in. In the midst of that a medic drove up in a jeep and made Jimmy unzip his flight suit to the waist so he could examine Jimmy's wounds. There were a number of wolf whistles and admiring comments at the manly physique thus exposed.

"All right, all right, you bums," Jimmy said. "Such jealousy is unbecoming to officers and gentlemen, although I use the last term loosely."

Jimmy winced as the medic swabbed out the crease wound in his shoulder and sprinkled sulfa on it before taping a bandage in place. The wound in his ribs looked a little more serious. The medic prodded the ribs above and below the wound and shook his head at Jimmy's quickly suppressed gasp of pain.

"You might have a cracked rib, there, Lieutenant," the medic said. "Can't be sure without an X-ray but since we don't have an X-ray machine any closer than Townsville that means even the Doc couldn't tell you for sure."

Wolchek said, "How long would it take to heal if it were a cracked rib?"

"Aw, Major, you played football, didn't you? Cracked ribs are the devil. A couple of weeks, maybe. And I'm no flight surgeon but if he's helling around in a P-39 pulling gees in tight turns he might crack it for sure. Right now it's maybe just tender."

"Well, we're fresh out of airplanes for the moment anyway. Light duty for a week then, Ardana. What do you think, Chelton?"

"Like I said, sir, I'm not a flight surgeon, but that should do it. He should come up and see the Doc this evening, too, just to be safe."

"OK. Thanks. Well, there you are, Ardana. A week on light duty. No flying for you and don't try to look so pitiful, my dog back home does poor-me a lot better than that."

Chapter Fifteen

"Effective immediately, you're Boxcar Red Leader."

Light duty meant that Ardana became the squadron duty officer. That meant Jimmy fielded phone calls for Major Wolchek, straightened out arguments among the crew chiefs, broke up fights and sounded the air-raid alarm. That tended to happen at least once a day. When Ardana landed on his side diving into a slit trench during an air raid he felt a stabbing pain from the rib he "might" have cracked and wondered if he had broken it for sure. He said nothing about it and was careful breathing.

The same medic came down every day to change his dressing. Wounds in the tropics could easily fester and lead to serious blood poisoning if not treated properly or sometimes even when treated properly. There were bugs and bacteria in New Guinea unknown to medical science.

"You ought to see the natives," the medic told him while strapping up his ribs. "Elephantiasis, ringworm, hookworm, scabies, cholera, Christ Almighty, sir, it's worse than the Middle Ages out there."

"How do you know all this?"

"Me and some of the other guys help out at a little clinic some Catholic missionaries run, a few miles up the road towards the mountains."

Jimmy thought of Evarra. "What do you know about the native witch doctors?"

"The sanguma men? Not much, just the name. The natives think they're the real deal, I can tell you that. They pay 'em off like one of these gangs back home."

"Gangs?"

"Yeah, you know. Well, maybe not, you aren't from New York or Jersey or anywhere like that, are you?"

"No. Montana."

"Jesus, you're that guy that carries the cowboy pistol. I've heard of you."

Ardana blinked. "Everyone carries those back home."

"No foolin'? Real Wild West stuff?"

"Well, I don't know about that. My Dad is the county sheriff. We still ride horses a lot but he gets around in a Ford pickup most places."

"How about that. I don't think I've ever even seen a horse except in the movies."

Ardana smiled. "Hell, I started riding cow ponies when I was six. I mean it's not like the stories my grandpa would tell about the old days, you know, no law west of the Pecos, that sort of thing, or these stories that Zane Grey writes."

"Who's he?"

"Zane Grey? Well, those cowboy movies you were talking about? Most of those movies are based on stories he wrote."

"No foolin'? Can you do the fast draw?"

"Fast draw? Now that really is movie stuff. My grandpa told me that once after he saw some movie with Tom Mix in it."

The medic finished taping up Ardana's ribs and helped him on with his shirt. "What did your grandpa do?"

"He sort of started the tradition of being county sheriffs, I guess. He and my grandma Susan moved up from Texas back in the 1880s. He needed a job, the town needed a marshal, then he sort of got into county politics and there you are."

"Oh. So he'd be an authority on that stuff."

"He lived through it, I guess."

The medic grinned. "Can't ask for better references than that. OK, sir, you should be good for another day."

"Hey, you hang out with these missionaries and natives. Speak any Pidgin?"

"Well, a little. It's not too hard to understand if you listen close, a lot of it is kind of what the Doc calls 'Creole.' Sort of a mishmash of different languages."

"Youpela bilip ensel?"

The medic blinked. "Do I believe in angels? Sure I do. I'm a Catholic myself, sir."

Ardana frowned. "Well, I had one of these, what do you call them, one of these sanguma men, ask me that."

"Really? What's his name?"

"Evarra. One of my ground crew knows him. He hangs around the flight line for some reason."

"These native johnnies look like a joke to us, sir, but the truth is if you got thrown out into the jungle you probably wouldn't last an hour. To those folks, though, it'sjust another day on the farm. My point would be that whatever they look like to us they probably are at least as smart as you or me. Probably this Evarra is fascinated with airplanes. I mean, who wouldn't be? A sailing ship, you know, you can understand that. They have sails on their canoes, so even one of those big two-masted trading schooners, they can see that's just a big canoe. But a steamship? Hell, that's just witchcraft to these fellows. Imagine being one of these natives and seeing a modern freighter when you've never seen one before." The medic finished replacing his implements in his bag and stood up. "Much less an airplane. See you tomorrow, lieutenant."

While Ardana was on light duty the strafing missions to Lae and Salamaua continued.

Atkins got his first confirmed kill. Harley went on loan to the Rattlers, who had a couple of pilots shot up bad enough to be sent to Australia but whose airplane were easily repairable.

The day Jimmy went back on flight status he and Jack Davis flew down to Townsville. The depot there had two brand-new P-39Ds as replacements for the airplane Jimmy and Harley had shot from under them.

They flew down in S-Sugar, the same RAAF Hudson, now patched-up and refurbished, that brought them to Seven-Mile, four weeks and an eternity ago. The crew was RAAF but none of them knew Tiny Harris or what became of him.

Jack and Jimmy slept most of the way. It was only a three hour flight at the cruising speed of a Hudson. They woke up when the pilot throttled the engines back and began his landing approach. Townsville was hot, hot as Seven-Mile, only not as humid. They got there late in the morning. No one from the USAAF was there to meet them. The RAAF ground staff had them on their manifests but it was, "Sorry, mate, all we have you down for here is transportation from Seven-Mile."

The RAAF pilot of the Hudson took pity on them. "Not much doing at the moment, chaps," he said. "You want the new airplane depot which of course is on the other side of the field. I'll see if I can lay on some transport."

"Thanks, pal," said Jack. "Maybe we'll wait on the veranda there, in the shade."

The two American pilots sat on rough wooden benches in the shade of the veranda. Fifteen percent less humidity felt almost dry after Port Moresby. There was a hot wind blowing that dried the sweat almost as soon as it formed.

"Gosh," said Jimmy. "I thought I'd never get dry again."

Davis shook his head and was soon asleep. Jimmy drowsed until he heard the sound of an auto engine. In a moment a Ford utility truck drove up outside the building and stopped. It was the Hudson pilot with another Australian driving. The man beeped his horn as Jimmy started to get up. Davis woke with a start and looked around, then got up and walked with Jimmy to the truck.

At the USAAF depot no one seemed to have heard of new P-39s or of anyone coming from Port Moresby to get them. Their informant was a particularly witless corporal who appeared to have been awakened from a sound sleep by their entry. When Davis sent the corporal for his sergeant Jimmy walked over to the window.

"Hey, Jack, look at this," Jimmy said, pointing.

Davis came over. On the apron outside, in front of a hangar where a bunch of airplane-sized crates were stacked, stood a half-dozen P-39s, brand-new, drop tanks attached, glittering in the Australian sun.

Jimmy felt his lips narrowing down but when he looked over at Davis he saw his flight leader's face turn red. Jack's lips drew back in a snarl and his fists clenched.

"Hey, Jack, take it easy," Jimmy said.

"Take it easy, hell," Davis replied. He turned and walked through the door where the lackadaisical corporal had disappeared. Jimmy followed.

They walked into a room where a half-dozen enlisted men sat playing cards. Cigars were lit and a can of beer sat in front of each man. The corporal was speaking to a large, overweight sergeant with little slits for eyes.

Jimmy walked in behind Jack. A current of relatively cool air hit him as he went through the door. Jimmy looked up and there, on the ceiling, were three paddle-bladed fans.

It was the fans that did it for Jimmy. He thought about lying in his bunk at Seven-Mile, gasping in the still, hot, saturated air between thunderstorms, trying to sleep. He looked at the beer on the table and remembered raging thirst and worrying about tainted water. His hand dropped to his Colt revolver without his brain actually willing it.

"Which one of these shitheads do you want me to shoot first, Jack?" he asked casually, slipping the thong off the hammer.

"Hey, you can't just walk in here and ..." the sergeant started. Whatever else he was about to say cut off when Jimmy drew his revolver and eared the hammer back with the slick, easy, unhesitating motion of a striking rattlesnake. Jimmy walked forward until the muzzle was a foot away from a point right between the sergeant's eyes.

"You might live longer if you don't talk," Jimmy said.

"Who's in command here?" Jack asked.

"Ah...the captain's in town," said the sergeant, who couldn't take his eyes off the muzzle of Jimmy's revolver. The rest of the men at the table were very careful to keep their hands in sight.

"In town?" Jack asked. "In town. Well, then I guess if your captain isn't here he can't object if we take a couple of P-39s back to Port Moresby, will he?"

"Ah, you can't just…"

"Sir," said Jimmy.

"Uh…what?"

"You're a sergeant. He's a captain. You say, Captain, *sir*."

"Uh, yes sir, lieutenant. Captain, sir, our captain is in Townsville, probably at the hotel if you want to talk to him. But I can't let you take anything without his say-so. We're doing inventory right now."

"I don't give a shit about talking to your captain, sergeant, and I don't give a shit about your inventory. The lieutenant and I are supposed to pick up a couple of P-39s and take them back to Port Moresby. How about those on the ramp out there?"

"Well, Captain sir, we're supposed to have some paperwork, and we haven't cataloged all the parts numbers, and …"

The sergeant was sweating now.

"Paperwork?" asked Jimmy. "Gosh. If I have to sign something I'd have to use my right hand. That means I'd have to move my trigger finger and it might slip. Do you want my trigger finger to slip, sergeant?"

"Uh, no sir, lieutenant."

"Right. Do you have something like a crew chief here? Someone who can be sure those airplanes are gassed and armed?"

"These guys are all crew chiefs," the sergeant said, indicating the other men at the poker table.

"You'd better be kidding me," said Jimmy. "These dickheads don't look bright enough to sweep a hangar floor, much less fuel an airplane."

Davis looked around while all eyes were on Jimmy and the sergeant. There were cases of beer and lubricating oil and rubber blankets and mess supplies. There were crates and cartons of other things but they were just dim bulks in the corners and reaches of the warehouse.

"What d'you have going on here, sergeant?" Davis asked casually. "I wouldn't have thought there'd be enough people up here in the Australian outback to make black marketeering profitable."

"Oh, hey, Captain sir, that's a serious accusation, I mean, we're only holding that stuff for inventory. Our colonel is really hell on inventory, sir. It has to be just right."

"Yeah, I know what you mean. Inventory. It must be hell, sergeant. But I'm quite sure these supplies are all being held here for a legitimate purpose, like resupplying our valiant troops up at the front. Right?"

"Oh, yes sir, Captain sir. Just as soon as we finish inventory."

"Inventory. Well, the lieutenant and I are taking those airplanes up to Port Moresby. That's where the fighting is. So those supplies are for us. I think we'll just do what we came here to do. Jimmy, d'you think you could supervise these so-called crew chiefs while the sergeant and I check out a couple of P-39s?"

"Absolutely, Captain." Jimmy eased the hammer forward slowly on his Colt. When it clicked softly into place in the frame the sergeant gasped and sagged back in his chair. Jimmy hadn't taken the muzzle of the pistol out of his face. Jimmy raised the pistol, opened the loading gate, put the hammer on half-cock, and rotated the cylinder to put an empty chamber under the hammer. Then he twirled the pistol and holstered it. The ease with which he handled the heavy, long-barreled pistol caused some blinking eyes among the men at the table.

"Come on, sergeant," Davis said.

"Yes, sir."

"Hey, Jimmy, I'll bet these guys wouldn't mind parting with a couple cases of beer."

"You read my mind, boss. You, and you," Jimmy said, pointing. "Let's have four cases of beer. I reckon we can fit those in the nose under the drive shaft. Maybe we'll see what else we can find that might be useful to men actually fighting a war."

Davis and the sergeant went out onto the ramp with the P-39s.

"Which one do you want me to check first, sir?" the sergeant asked.

"I don't want you checking anything, sergeant. I wouldn't trust you or any of your pals in there to find your ass with both hands. You come to attention, right the fuck now."

"Sir…"

Davis opened the flap on his .45 holster. The sergeant came to attention. The hot sun blazed down on his bare head.

Davis preflighted two of the P-39s. They were gassed and properly armed. Sometime during the preflight there was a loud booming gunshot from inside the warehouse.

"Jesus, Captain!"

"You stand there at attention and be glad it isn't you that's been shot," Davis said. He was actually amazed at how loud the old Peacemaker was. It made Davis laugh.

"Hey, Jimmy! You OK in there?" he yelled.

"I'm fine, boss. Just demonstrating the fast draw to these unbelievers."

"Thought you said the fast draw was bullshit."

"It comes in handy sometimes. You, next time you get one in the head. Now get that beer and load it in those two P-39s."

Davis beckoned to the sergeant. "Pop open the cannon access panel. Store the beer under the gun barrel."

"But, sir, what about …"

"Oh, Great Henry Jumping Jehosophat, sergeant, just put the damn beer in the damn airplane."

"Yes, sir."

"We're ready out here, Jimmy," Davis called as the sergeant opened the access panel on the first P-39.

"OK, skipper."

One of the sergeants came out with two cases of beer. Two more cases came out on the shoulder of another sergeant. Jimmy backed out the door, .45 leveled on the people inside. He was stuffing something in his flight suit.

Davis stood on the wing of his P-39. He drew his .45 automatic and held it visible on top of the airplane's canopy as the sweating sergeants stored the beer and buckled the panels back in place.

"Go ahead and start up, Jimmy," Davis said. "I'll cover you."

"Yes, sir," Jimmy replied. He got into the other P-39.

Davis told the sergeants, "Lie down on the apron, assholes."

"But, sir …"

"I might not shoot you, sergeant, but I'll sure as hell kick you bowlegged. And if you don't think I can't lick all three of you, try me. Now kiss concrete."

The sergeants got down on their hands and knees and put their noses on the concrete.

Jack climbed up onto the P-39 and got in the cockpit. He strapped on the parachute in the seat pan and ran through the start up procedure. When the engine was running strong he looked at Jimmy and made a circle with his thumb and forefinger. Jimmy nodded and held his thumb up.

Jack keyed his radio. "Townsville Tower, Townsville Tower, Army 2323 with a flight of two

P-39s at the depot, request taxi clearance to the active, over."

"Army 2323, your clearance isn't open for another hour."

"Oh, what the hell, Townsville, the airplanes are ready and so are we."

"Right-o then, Two-Three. Cleared to taxi to the active."

"Thank you, Townsville."

Davis opened his throttle a little and turned hard on the nose wheel. He and Jimmy taxied to the runway and got a green light from the tower. Then they were roaring at full throttle down the runway and lifting off.

When they climbed to six thousand feet Davis leveled out. Jimmy got on the radio. "Ah, Boss, you do know how far it is to Seven-Mile from here, right?"

"If we head north we're bound to get there sooner or later."

"If we don't go in the drink first."

Jack thought about it. Thinking gave him a nasty sinking feeling. He'd let the anger take him over and that just made him angry all over again. He was going to get these god-damned airplanes to Seven-Mile regardless of what it took, but Jimmy was right. There wasn't any point in ditching in the Coral Sea and being shark bait.

"Got any suggestions?" Jack asked.

"They had a route map tacked to the wall back there. I swiped it. Give me a couple of minutes."

Jack almost laughed aloud. Instead he concentrated on the blue sea to the right and the green and dun land of the Queensland coast on the left and the blue, blue sky above it all. He started whistling to himself, "Blue skies, smiling at me, nothing but blue skies, from now on…"

"Hey, Jack, you awake up there?"

"What you got, smart-ass?"

"There's some little place called Cooktown on the coast north of here, looks like about 280 miles. I'd say it's about four miles from the coast, in the bend of a snaky-looking river and four or five miles north of another river on the coast. Direct heading looks to be about 338 degrees."

"OK." Jack thought about it. The internal and auxiliary tanks in both P-39s were full of gas but there wasn't any point in wasting any. "Set your throttle to 2200 RPM and make your manifold pressure 32 inches. That should give us a little over 200 mph."

"Roger, throttle and manifold pressure set. We should be there in a little less than an hour and a half."

Jack looked over the side, studying the clouds below. They were drifting slowly to the west.

"Looks like we got a bit of wind from the east. Let's crab into it a bit."

There were two clicks on the microphone. Jack gave his airplane some right rudder until the angle looked right.

After that it was a pleasure cruise in the cool air at 6000 feet, flying over the Queensland coast. Jack had no real idea where they were going. The kid had the map which for the moment was fine with Jack. Let someone else do the thinking and the planning for a change.

The crab into the wind decreased their ground speed slightly. It was about an hour and a half when Jimmy called over the radio.

"Look up ahead there, Boss. Two river mouths on the coast, and you can see the bends in the one to the north. I think this is it."

Jack looked at his fuel gauge for the tenth time. He had switched over from the 75-gallon auxiliary tank to internal fuel thirty minutes ago. For now they were good on fuel.

A minute later and they were between the two rivers. To the west there was the straight-line scar of a runway about four miles inland.

"What's the name of this field?" Jack asked.

"I don't know. The name on the map is Cooktown."

"OK. Stay with me."

Jack turned west and began to circle the field at 6000 feet. There didn't appear to be any other airplanes nearby, although there was what looked like some sort of twin-engined biplane parked off the runway near a couple of huts.

"Let's land," said Jack. "There wouldn't be a contact frequency on that map, would there?"

"Nope."

"Then tuck it in tight. Let's give these guys a show."

Jack advanced his throttle and headed west, losing altitude. When he got down to 1000 feet he turned back towards the little dirt strip, still losing altitude. When they crossed the runway threshold he was just off the ground doing 330 mph, and they howled down the strip and past the buildings in less than five seconds. Jack pulled up into a right chandelle to enter the traffic pattern, leveling out as his airspeed fell to 180 mph. He looked at Jimmy, whose left wingtip was still a foot away from Jack's right wingtip. They went down the final approach like that, dropping flaps and gear on command, squeaking it down on the dirt and braking to a halt opposite the collection of shacks and huts.

They stood stretching outside their airplanes. Jack looked at the three Australians in baggy shorts and floppy hats coming towards them from the near shack.

"Well, let's see if we're under arrest," Jack muttered.

Five minutes later they were sitting in the shade of the line shack drinking cool water with the

RAAF warrant officer in charge of the ground staff of what they now knew was called Gove Airfield. A petrol bowser huffed up to their airplanes. The ground crew snaked out hoses from the bowser and began fueling.

"Nice of you chaps to give us a bit of a show," the warrant officer said.

"Our pleasure," Jack said. "Dull here, is it?"

"Oh, my dinkum word, you have no idea, Yank. Dust and flies and dingoes. It's a fair cow. Still," the warrant officer said casually, "Not as bad as New Guinea, from what I hear."

"It does get a bit warm up there," Jack said.

"Incidentally, you wouldn't know anything about airplane thieves, would you?"

"Couldn't say. Our orders were to pick up a couple of P-39s and take them back to Seven-Mile."

"Right-o." The warrant officer looked at the butt of the Colt revolver in Jimmy's shoulder holster. "Well, if anyone asks, you had the proper orders and I sent you on your way north. To Horn Island, of course."

"Of course. You wouldn't happen to know what radio frequency they use up there, would you?"

The warrant officer told him. Jack and Jimmy both wrote it down.

Two hours and 385 miles north of Cooktown they spotted Horn Island. There were a lot of little islands scattered over the narrow shallow sea between the northernmost point of Australia and the coast of New Guinea, but Horn Island was easy to find. You couldn't mistake it under the cloud of black greasy smoke billowing up from the island.

They saw the smoke from ten miles out. Immediately Jimmy moved out to give them both maneuvering room. Their necks went on the swivel and they armed their guns.

"Horn Island, Horn Island, this is Army 2323, come in, over," Jack called over the radio.

"Army 2323, we are under attack, keep clear."

"How many, Horn Island?"

"Three twin-engined bombers and six fighters. The fighters are strafing us."

"Jack, tallyho, three bombers at 11 o'clock high," Jimmy called.

The Jap bombers were a few thousand feet higher than the P-39s. They were headed west. "Dropped their bombs and headed for the barn," Jack said to himself.

He looked down at the island and saw a glint of metal in the sun for just an instant, low down, as a Zero climbed out after a strafing run. Jack looked at the shadows on his instrument panel.

"Jimmy, turn to 270," he said. "Let's get upsun of these bastards, give them a few minutes to expend fuel and ammo. Then we'll see if we can do some good."

"Turning 270," Jimmy acknowledged. "What about the drop tanks?"

They had run out of fuel in the auxiliary tanks and switched to internal fuel thirty minutes ago. They kept the drop tanks, which were valuable and not always easy to come by, for the long over-ocean flight to Seven-Mile from Horn Island.

"So maybe it'll be a little close, going home."

"Roger that."

They flew west for five minutes, climbing and looking for Zeros at altitude, clearing their tails, feeling that tightness in the belly and the sphincters, that dryness in the mouth, that knowing that you probably wouldn't see the one that got you but looking everywhere for the sonofabitch anyway.

Then they made a 180 back towards Horn Island, and two minutes later there were six Zeros in two vics of three airplanes each. The Zeros were climbing on a westerly heading, still about five thousand feet below them.

Jack was sure the Japs hadn't seen them. They just didn't act like it. Their climb was the slow, fuel-conserving kind, the formation a little too tight and sure. It was time to gamble.

So Jack let the Zeros fly past them before he kicked his P-39 into a hard left bank and dove. When he pickled his auxiliary tank Jimmy did the same, making sure he was on internal fuel.

Jimmy cleared their tails again in the dive and then spread out a little. The two formations of Zeros were one in the lead, the other off to its right. Jack was bringing them in so that they could pass through both formations. And suddenly Jimmy knew Jack would level out a little short of the near formation, blow past it and try for the fighters in the lead before breaking off and diving away, counting on speed and surprise to keep them safe.

At 400 mph they pulled out hard. G-force plastered them into their seats and there were the Japs in the near formation, fat, dumb and happy like you almost never saw the little bastards, and Jimmy waited until the Zero on the right wing of the leader filled his gunsight, filled his forward canopy, and then he squeezed the triggers. He could see the bullet strikes, the jagged holes in the fuselage and the wings, the fire suddenly spurting from the Zero's right wing root, so close yellow flame washed over him as he gave the airplane some stick and pushed down to avoid the Zero. Jimmy flew below the leader and saw Jack on his left with the left wing Zero tumbling away, left wing torn off. Ahead of them was the lead formation of Zeros and Jimmy was pulling up into the right wingman, firing, but he could tell from his tracers that he was wide. He cursed and fought the stick, trying to tighten his turn, but then he was past the Zero. There was a lick of yellow tracer over his head and then he was diving and banking to the left. He looked around and there was Jack close by.

"At your four o'clock, Lead," Jimmy radioed.

When Jimmy looked over his shoulder he could see three Zeros diving after them in a ragged formation and one Zero losing altitude with a smoking engine, still headed west. He could see Jack looking at the Zeros too, and when they had come on an easterly heading Jack rolled out, still diving away. Jimmy watched the Zeros, but they weren't getting any closer.

The Zeros chased them past Horn Island before turning away. The second the Zeros turned west, Jack turned west as well and leveled out. Jimmy looked at his fuel gauge. He had about half-tanks. They chased the Zeros for ten minutes past Horn Island before turning back and landing.

"Drop tanks for a P-39?" The RAAF flight lieutenant in charge of the smoking shambles on Horn Island shook his head at Jack's question. "Afraid not, chum. We're bloody lucky the bloody Nips didn't hit our fuel stores."

Jack sighed and looked around. The airstrip on Horn Island was pretty well torn up. He and Jimmy had made tricky landings between the bomb craters on the runway. The column of black greasy smoke was from a burning B-25 whose crew had been caught trying to start the airplane at the beginning of the raid. None of them made it out.

"How far to Seven-Mile from here?" he asked.

"Aw, look. My map says it's about 350 miles. Don't know much about your Airacobra, mate, but I hear it's got short legs. Can you make that?"

Jack looked at Jimmy, who shrugged. "Stay low, don't waste fuel climbing," he said. "The engine doesn't burn as much gas at sea level. We're over water the whole way so it's not like we could glide to the coast if an engine packs up."

Jack nodded. "Lieutenant, any idea of the weather between here and Port Moresby?

"Haven't the foggiest, I'm afraid. I'll see if we can raise the chaps at Moresby and get some idea for you."

"Thanks."

The RAAF officer nodded and started to walk off. Then he grinned and said, "You know, we got a radio about a couple of crazy Yank cowboys who stole a couple of Airacobras."

"Is that so?"

"It couldn't possibly be you chaps. A man would have to be crazy to steal an airplane and fly into a war zone." With that the RAAF officer flipped them a casual salute and went into the shack he used for an office.

Jimmy chuckled. "My dad is gonna kill me," he said.

"Oh, yeah. The sheriff."

"Well, I guess the good news is, he's in Montana and we're out here. So what do you think, Jack? We've got about four hours of daylight left. I'd hate to be looking for Seven-Mile in the dark while my fuel runs out."

"Any kind of wind from the east and we won't have to worry about looking for Seven-Mile. We'll be swimming."

"Yeah." Jimmy looked up at the Australian flag hanging from its pole. The flag hung limp and motionless.

The RAAF officer came out. "I'll have the lads start fueling your airplane," he said. "You blokes going to give it a try?"

Jack looked at Jimmy, who nodded.

"Reckon so," said Jack.

"Good-oh. By the way, we only counted three Zeros chasing you. I hope the others came to a bad end."

"Two of them did for sure," said Jack. "And I think we might reasonably hope for a third."

"Ruddy marvelous!" the flight lieutenant exclaimed. "I hate it when those little yellow buggers come over and have it all their own way. Makes a bloke feel low and out of sorts."

A sergeant came out of the shack and handed the flight lieutenant a slip of paper.

"Well, here we are," the flight lieutenant said. "Forecast for Port Moresby is afternoon thunderstorms with winds from the north, variable and gusting. What it might be between here and there I doubt anyone has any idea."

"Great. Well, as soon as you can gas us up we'll be on our way."

Jack turned to see Jimmy gazing pensively down the cratered runway to the east, out over the long blue swells of the Coral Sea.

The first hour and a half, flying at a thousand feet over the sea, were the worst. To the north lay New Guinea but they couldn't see any of it at this altitude, not even the tops of the mountains. At least the sea was calm, which meant little or no wind. Flying low over a blue, featureless ocean made time slow to a crawl, and the only thing that gave time meaning was the impossibly slow ticking of the clock, the inexorable burn of fuel, and the growing numbness of their asses on the hard parachute packs. They scanned the sky above them out of habit and cleared their tails for the same reason, but there were neither airplanes near them nor ships on the ocean below. They flew a little north of east on a heading of 77 degrees as the sun sank behind them towards the western horizon.

Jack took his first easy breath as something solid appeared on the horizon. The mountains of the Owen Stanley Range rose into view, wreathed as usual with the white clouds of afternoon thunderstorms.

"Ever land a P-39 on instruments?" Jack called over the radio. It was the first words they had spoken after taking off from Horn Island.

"I haven't landed anything on instruments since advanced flight."

"Well, let's see what the visibility is like. I'd hate to have to put these brand new airplanes in the drink."

"Yeah. What a waste of good beer."

Jack chuckled to himself but made no reply. He switched frequencies.

"Seven-Mile, Seven-Mile, this is Army 2323, leading a flight of two P-39s from Townsville."

"Army 2323, be advised we have severe thunderstorms in the area."

"Roger that, Seven-Mile, be advised we have about a half-hour of fuel remaining. What's the wind and altimeter?"

"Wind is 020 at 10, gusts to 30, altimeter two niner niner zero, visibility variable but less than two miles, ceiling about one thousand."

"Roger that, Seven-Mile." Davis bent forward to set the altimeter and then looked ahead. The whole of the coastline was shrouded in thunderstorms with tops that towered well above twenty thousand feet.

"Super," Davis growled to himself. He changed frequencies again. "Jimmy, did you copy all that?"

"Yup."

"I think we ought to go down to sea level and run below the clouds."

"Okey-doke."

"That's all? Just okey-doke?"

"Yup."

"You're a hell of a conversationalist, Jimmy. Follow me."

Jack switched on his formation and running lights. Then he trimmed the airplane for descent and eased back on the throttle. Ahead of him the ranks of the thunderstorms marching out to sea from their mountain homes rose to meet them, and then they were in the rain.

Closer to the coast the ride got bumpy. Davis looked over his shoulder and Jimmy was still there, a few feet behind him, sticking like glue, but the outline of his airplane was vague in the rain and intermittent clouds.

"Jimmy, I'm going to stay on instruments. You look ahead for the coast."

"Roger."

Two interminable minutes as the rain streamed over the canopy. Once lightning cracked nearby and blue light nearly blinded him.

Then Jimmy said, "Breakers ahead, it's a little island. That's Daugo Island, I recognize that little bit of land on the east side we use for a gunnery target."

"Roger that. We'll turn hard right when we pass over the island to about 085. How's your fuel?"

"I got about twenty minutes."

They closed on Daugo Island and Jack led them into a hard right turn just above the waves.

"Look for Bootless Inlet on the left," Jack said. "If you don't see it we'll cross the coast and reverse course. That should take us to the inlet."

"OK, got the inlet on the left about ten o'clock."

"Roger, Jimmy, turn hard left now, now, now. Change frequencies to 350."

"Changing to 350."

"Seven-Mile, Seven-Mile, this is Army 2323. We're over Bootless Inlet at 100 feet, crossing the beach at this time."

"Roger, Two-Three, the pattern is clear."

"Roger that, Seven-Mile. Jimmy, slow it up and drop flaps and gear."

Jack eased back on the throttle. The runway appeared ahead of them as he brought the nose up to maintain altitude. At 180 mph indicated he dropped flaps and gear. Their glide path steepened.

"Jimmy, you got flaps and gear?"

"Roger that, Jack, flaps down, gear down."

"OK. Stay with me."

They were at a slight angle to the runway and Davis turned a little to the right, one eye on the runway and the other on his airspeed indicator.

"Army 23, have you in sight."

"Thanks, Seven-Mile."

Davis held the nose down and the throttle slightly forward, choosing to land a little hot. They flashed over the threshold and Jack eased off the throttle, pulling his nose back, the fighter sinking down towards the muddy runway until with a squishy rumble the mains touched as Davis cut the throttle back to idle. He looked over his shoulder to see Jimmy put his airplane down right behind him.

Davis and Ardana came into the 8th Pursuit Ops shack, soaking wet, with water streaming from their hair and puddling on the wooden floor by their squishing boots. Sergeant Holmwood looked up at them with twinkling eyes in an otherwise expressionless face.

"Captain, Lieutenant, you're wanted. In the back, that is. Colonel Wagner's office."

Jack nodded. He whispered to Jimmy, "Let me do the talking."

"Roger, Lead," Jimmy whispered back.

Colonel Wagner and Major Wolchek sat in Wagner's office.

"You're at attention," Wagner said quietly. He could barely be heard over the rain.

Jack and Jimmy locked up to attention like a couple of cadets back at Kelly Field.

Wagner held up a message flimsy. "Anything you want to tell me about, Jack?"

Davis shrugged. "We brought back the P-39s. Although it wasn't easy to get those assholes in Townsville to break loose with them."

"That right? Guess who this telegram is from?"

Davis looked Wagner in the eye and decided it was no time for a smart-assed answer. "Probably the officer commanding the depot in Townsville."

"Among other things." Wagner looked from Davis to Ardana.

"Something in here about a couple of cowboys. Naturally, Lieutenant Ardana, you came to mind when I read that."

"Sir, yes sir." Ardana remained at attention, staring straight ahead at a spot on the wall behind Wagner's desk.

"A couple of cowboys," Wagner repeated softly. "OK. Make your report."

"Sir, we broke up a poker game at Townsville, took two P-39s, refueled in Cooktown, and flew to Horn Island. Upon arrival at Horn Island we found the airstrip there under attack. The Jap bombers had already left the scene on our arrival. We engauged enemy fighters and shot down two for sure with one damaged. We refueled at Horn Island and flew here."

Wagner blinked. "You shot down a couple of Zeros?"

"I got one, sir, Lieutenant Ardana here got the other one."

Wagner leaned back in his chair, which creaked alarmingly. He exchanged a look with Major Wolchek. "Can you confirm that?" Wagner asked.

"The RAAF blokes at Horn Island counted six Zeros strafing them, sir, and only three of them came chasing us after Lieutenant Ardana and I shot down two of them." Davis looked Colonel Wagner in the eye. "Otherwise, sir, you're just going to have to take our word for it."

Wagner held Jack's gaze for a moment, then nodded. "Two kills," he said, and smiled.

"That makes seven for you, Jack. And four for you, Lieutenant Ardana?"

"Yes, sir."

"OK. You guys go get some rest. Report back here at 0700 tomorrow morning."

Jack stood on the porch of the Ops shack watching the rain pour down. Jimmy sagged against the door jamb, rubbing his face. Then he yawned.

"A long damned day," Jack said.

"Yeah," Jimmy replied. "You reckon we're still in trouble?"

"Absolutely. We're at Seven-Mile Drome, Jimmy. Isn't that trouble enough?"

"I guess." Jimmy grinned. "What did your guys say when you gave them the beer?"

"Not much. But I thought I was gonna get kissed good for a second."

Jimmy laughed. "Yeah. Me too."

"Let that be a lesson to you, Jimmy. Take care of your guys, and they'll take care of you. Let's see if there's something resembling food at the mess tent."

"With you, Lead."

Jack looked at Jimmy, who looked back at him. The look went on for a long moment, a moment built of gunfire, radio calls, takeoffs, blue sky and white cloud. Then Jack punched Jimmy on the shoulder, gently, and they walked out into the rain to the mess hall for some lousy Aussie M&V.

The rain stopped during the night and the morning sun was over the horizon when Jack and Jimmy returned to the Ops Shack. Slim Atkins, blinking and yawning, was with them.

"Don't know why I'm here," Slim said when Jimmy asked. "Sergeant Holmwood just said Major Wolchek wanted to see me."

Holmwood asked Lieutenant Atkins to wait and ushered Jack and Jimmy into Wagner's office once more.

"Good morning, gentlemen," Wagner said as they entered. "I've had a busy night because of you two."

He looked up at them and smiled. "Sit down."

Jack exchanged a look with Jimmy as they sat.

"It appears that you have really, really pissed off some chair-warming colonel down in Townsville," Wagner said. "Not only did you steal two P-39s but it also appears that four cases of beer meant for the local Officer's Club made its way into your hands. And this morning I'm told by Sergeant Holmwood and Chief Halloran that your ground crews are happy and contented men. Any truth to these vicious rumors?"

"Sir, we were sent for two P-39s. We brought back two P-39s. As for the beer, well, our ground crews work pretty hard. We reckoned those assholes down in Townsville could spare it."

Wagner nodded, looking down at a small stack of message flimsies on his desk. "Of course, what really seems to have pissed this colonel off is you screwed up his inventory. Now he's going to have to start over. He wants to know what I'm going to do about it."

"Sir," Jimmy started. Then he stopped.

"Go ahead, lieutenant," Wagner said.

"Sir, that didn't look like any inventory to me. The stuff stacked in that hangar wasn't grouped in any logical order. It looked more like they were hoarding the stuff."

"Indeed, lieutenant? Do you have any other reason than what it looked like for that accusation?"

"No, sir."

Wagner nodded. "OK. Here's what we'll do." Wagner picked up the message flimsies and tossed them in his wastebasket.

"It won't be quite as simple as that, but I don't think those people down in Townsville have actually figured out this is a war and we really need the stuff they seem to be so busy inventorying. You guys didn't do things by the book and you've made trouble. I can live with that, especially since you got a couple of Zeros along the way. Besides, I have something here that will make things a little easier."

Wagner handed Davis a sheaf of papers. Jack took them.

"Your TDY is over, Captain. These are your orders back to the States."

"Orders, sir?"

Wagner nodded. "Your razor-sharp mind is as quick as ever, Jack. Seems the Air Corps wants some of us Philippines veterans back in the States. Anyway you should have just stayed in Australia, because you're going back this afternoon."

Davis sat back. He looked at the papers in his hand. "What about you, Boyd?"

"It's not official yet but I'll be going back in a month or two. Same deal." Wagner leaned back in his chair. "Your orders say to take a month's leave and then I suspect you're going to the Republic plant in Long Island for awhile."

"Republic? What the hell, aren't they building P-47s?"

"Yeah. Supposed to be a hell of an airplane but they said that about the P-39 a few years back. My guess is you'll do a little test flying on the early production models and then you'll probably get a squadron of your own. And then they'll probably ship your ass to England to fight the Krauts."

Davis shook his head slowly. "Well. That's not what I expected when I walked in here."

Wagner laughed. "I'm sure. Just remember this when you get your own squadron, Jack. Keep your guys on their toes and keep them alive. You've done fairly well with that. As well as anyone can.

Now get out of here and go pack. I want a word with Ardana."

Davis stood up. He looked at Wagner for a minute. Then he came to attention and saluted. Wagner's mouth thinned down. He stood up, came to attention, and returned Davis' salute. Then he held out his hand.

"God speed, Jack," he said.

"Thank you, Boyd. God speed to you too."

When Davis left the room Wagner looked at Jimmy Ardana. "Refresh my memory. How many missions do you have as element leader, Ardana? In addition to four Japs?"

"About twenty, sir."

Wagner nodded. "That's what I thought. Here's the deal. Steve Wolchek and I talked this over last night. You're still a little junior but I'm promoting you to first lieutenant and making you a flight commander. You've got those four Japs and a good bit of experience with ground attack."

"Yes, sir."

"Well, ground attack is going to be the P-39's role in this theater. It really isn't suited for anything else as you well know, but it does pretty well in ground attack. Sooner or later, probably much later, we'll get some of these new airplanes. Most likely the P-38, maybe this P-47, and the bomber boys will get B-25s and A-20s. We'll get all that but my guess is it's going to be six months to a year. In the meantime the P-39s and the P-40s will have to soldier on. That means you will have to soldier on. I think you have that in you, Ardana."

Jimmy nodded slowly. "Yes, sir."

"All right. Take one of those new P-39s you and Jack brought in. Paint *Gremlin II* on the side, or whatever the hell you want, but keep the number 13. I think it's good luck for you. We'll talk again later but that's all for now. Effective immediately you're Boxcar Red Leader."

"Yes, sir."

"You're not much on conversation, are you, Ardana?"

Jimmy grinned. "No, sir."

Wagner smiled. "OK. I asked Slim Atkins to come in this morning because I think he might make a good element lead for you. Anyway, he's in your flight, so that's up to you."

"Yes, sir," said Jimmy.

"Dismissed, Lieutenant."

Outside the Ops shack Jack Davis stood waiting for him with Slim Atkins. "So what did Boyd want, Jimmy?" Jack asked.

"I'm Boxcar Red Leader," Jimmy replied.

Jack nodded. "Good. That makes me feel better about leaving."

Slim stuck out his hand. "Congratulations, Jimmy."

"You say that now, but you're in my flight, Slim. I guess you're my new wingman until we get some replacements."

Jack grinned. "Speaking of which…"

He nodded towards two men standing in the corner of the shack, apparently trying to make themselves inconspicuous.

Jimmy turned to study them. Their uniforms were sweat-stained but otherwise looked new and hadn't acquired that patina of age and use even a few weeks in the tropics confer. The wings above their left pockets looked very new and very shiny. They had no other ribbons or metal devices on their uniforms. On their right collars they wore second lieutenant bars; on their left the winged propeller of the Army Air Force. Their caps still had the stiffener inside the rim.

In short, they were so new they squeaked.

"You're kidding me," Jimmy said quietly to Davis.

Davis put a hand on his shoulder. "You should have heard what I said to Wolchek when he assigned you to my flight. I wasn't too happy either, Jimmy. But you have to fight with what you have."

Jimmy nodded slowly. "I understand."

"I know you do." Davis squeezed Jimmy's shoulder and let go. "I have to attend to a few things. Drop by my tent later this afternoon."

"OK, Jack."

Jimmy exchanged looks with Slim. "Congratulations, Slim, you just got promoted to element leader."

"Oh, thanks, boss."

"You have a preference?"

Slim chuckled grimly. "Looks like there's not a lot to choose from."

"Well, hell. Let's get to work."

Jimmy and Slim walked towards the new guys, who stood up in something a little closer to attention, and whose faces took on very faint lines of strain and apprehension.

"How much time you have in P-39s?" Jimmy asked the one in front of him.

"Ah, about fifteen hours, sir."

Jimmy looked at the other one. "You?"

"Maybe twenty, sir."

"Maybe?"

"Twenty hours, sir, more or less."

"More or less. My name is Ardana. This is Atkins. You two are now in Boxcar Red flight." He looked at the man in front of him. "What's your name?"

"Forrest, sir, Nathan B."

"You're kidding me. Are you from Tennessee, too?"

"No sir, Georgia."

"Cavalrymen in your past?"

"Yes, sir!"

"Let's hope a little of that spirit got passed on. Goddam Rebel cavalry was the best in the business." Ardana turned to the other man. "You?"

"Thomas, sir, Alan S."

"Any cavalrymen in your ancestry?"

"Not that I know of, sir."

"Hm. You boys go draw parachutes and survival gear. We'll take a little familiarization flight."

"Survival gear? How far from the field will we go?" asked Thomas.

"This is Papua New Guinea, pal. That jungle five miles north of here will swallow you whole. We always fly with a full load of ammo, too, because the Japs might decide to come and play. Start getting used to it right now. Orderly!"

"Sir."

"Take Lieutenants Forrest and Thomas over to Supply."

"Yes, sir."

Slim stood with Jimmy watching them go. "Were you ever that new, Jimmy?"

"Probably newer. I didn't have any time in P-39s at all when I got here."

"God help us all."

"Amen."

An hour later Jack Davis stood on a little knoll watching a flight of four P-39s taxiing out to the battered airstrip. The fighter in the lead bore the number "13" on its nose but nothing else. Nose art would have to wait. One by one the fighters lined up on the runway and at the green light from the tower roared down its length and up into the humid air over the New Guinea jungle, wheels and flaps coming up, the wingmen a little behind and a little ragged, but that was what was to be expected of brand new wingmen.

Wagner came and stood beside him. "Saying goodbye?" he asked.

"Not goodbye exactly," Davis replied. He watched the fighters turning south towards Port Moresby. Already the wingmen were moving into a tighter formation.

"Yeah." Wagner was silent for a moment. "You did pretty good here, Jack. Don't worry about commanding a squadron when you get one. It might be rough at first but most of the kids will be like those four. And your job is simple, after all. Shoot down more of the enemy than they do of you. We managed that here, if only just."

Jack nodded. "We're here. The Japs aren't."

"And that, my friend, is the essence of victory in this time and place."

Wagner and Davis watched as the flight of P-39s dwindled with distance, still climbing for altitude, and finally became too small to see.

After Action Report

Boxcar Red Leader is the third book in the series "No Merciful War."

By the end of May 1942 the Japanese Empire was at its height; but they were repulsed at the Battle of the Coral Sea, and defeated at the Battle of Midway. Those were Navy fights, and in many ways the Pacific was a Navy war. But those two battles marked, in Winston Churchill's phrase, if not the beginning of the end, then at least the end of the beginning.

Other writers and researchers have contributed enormously to my understanding of the time in memorable works of non-fiction and history. The anonymous compilers of flight operating handbooks for the P-39, P-40, B-17 and B-26 were most likely technical writers for the respective manufacturers, Bell, Curtiss-Wright, Boeing and Martin. But they wrote a clear, simple prose that got the message across, especially, even across seven decades, to me.

Official Air Force histories are also of enormous value in the determination of times and places, as well as being interesting reading in their own right. Many of these histories were compiled in the immediate wake of the war, and document details of training programs, particular units, campaigns ("Air Action in Papua" comes to mind), tactical development, and strategic objectives. Many of these are available online for the interested party.

Two historians deserve special mention here. William H. Bartsch wrote fine accounts of the early fighting in the Philippines and Java, titled *Doomed from the Start* and *Every Day a Nightmare*. Let me recommend those books to anyone interested in the early Pacific War from the aviator's perspective.

Walter D. Edmonds' seminal *They Fought with What They Had* is an excellent, readable account of the time as well. Both Bartsch and Edmonds incorporate veteran interviews in their work, which make them all the more interesting and valuable. One might argue that Edmonds' book, being written much sooner after the fact than those of Bartsch, who interviewed veterans of the Philippines and Java in their retirement, should be considered more authoritative, but I would not argue that. My own experience with veterans of World War II – which began ten years after Bartsch published his books! – is that those who will talk to you are articulate and have a retention of detail that can be quite staggering. Sometimes, if one listens with the right frame of mind, you can almost – not quite, but almost – see through their eyes, back in time.

General George Kenney's memoir, released under at least two titles (*General Kenney Reports* and *Air War In the Pacific*) was the book that got me interested in this area of history in the first place. General Kenney commanded the 5th Air Force from 1942 through 1945, and his descriptions of conditions in the field were invaluable starting places for research.

There are other books, such as *Queens Die Proudly* by W.L. White. This account is centered around the experiences of Captain (later Major) Frank Kurtz, whose war started at Clark Field on December 8, 1941, and continued through 1943, when Kurtz brought home a war-weary B-17D named *The Swoose* (now under restoration by the Smithsonian Air & Space Museum). White's book is a valuable source of bits and pieces of personal items and individual incidents. W.L. White also wrote *They Were Expendable*, about the exploits of one of the first PT boat units in the US Navy, during the fighting in the Philippines. There was a motion picture of the same name, based on the book.

Finally, I would like to share a story about the genesis of this book. In 1996 I started kicking around an idea for several books about USAAF pilots in World War II. One of those ideas had the working title of *The Sluggers and the Palookas*, and the idea I started with, very vague, was to have two characters, one flying for a fighter squadron nicknamed "The Sluggers" and the other in an attack squadron nicknamed, you guessed it, "The Palookas." The names are obsolete boxing references (readers of my generation may remember a comic strip titled "Joe Palooka") but also referred to styles of fighting. This book went through many iterations in my mind but, aside from some inconsistent reading and research, not much else. I was more focused on a couple of police procedural novels that never went past second draft, and then returned to writing science fiction for awhile, but that was even worse; nothing went past first draft.

Then in November of 2010 I sat down to write a novel for National Novel Writers Month. I had the intention of writing a far-future fantasy titled *The Once and Future Grail*. Went pretty well for the first three days, and then the flow of ideas dried up as if my subconscious flipped a switch. I did not worry for a day or two, but to be a NaNoWriMo finalist requires that one keep to a fairly consistent schedule, averaging 1700 words a day. By day 6 I was way behind and wondering what to do, when it occurred to me to wonder if I really wanted to write *TOFG*.

Seems my subconscious was dead set on writing that novel about the guys in the SW Pacific in May and June of 1942. So that's what I did. Ultimately I decided to expand the character of Jack Davis and his brother Charlie into the first two books of this series, *Everything We Had* and *A*

Snowball's Chance. In the meanwhile, waiting for me to finish those two books, this one sat in my hard drive in first final draft form. Once I made the decision to write the other two books, I knew I couldn't finish this one until I knew what Jack and Charlie experienced.

So where do Jack and Charlie go from here?

That you can find out when I publish *Thanks for the Memories* and *The New Boys*.

Made in the USA
Las Vegas, NV
07 August 2023